Echoes of The Past

1970

A time-travel novel

V.P. Blackwood

Chapter 1 | Part 1: Time Travel

In the 24th century, humanity stood at the zenith of scientific and technological achievement, with wonders once deemed impossible now commonplace. Among these marvels was the groundbreaking invention of a time machine, a masterpiece crafted by three brilliant scientists. In the modest confines of their lab, nestled within the bustling science department of Electropolis, Ethan, Oliver, and Benjamin defied the odds. With limited funding and boundless ingenuity, the trio transformed a visionary dream into a tangible reality. Despite their relatively young ages, their combined intellect and determination propelled them to achieve what many believed to be unattainable.

Ethan, at just 20 years old, was known for his serious and contemplative demeanor, his sharp features and piercing gaze giving him a striking, almost statuesque presence. Oliver, only a year older, had a charmingly mischievous nature, his broad grin and wavy golden hair adding to his boyish good looks. Despite their youth, both had earned their places in the government facility through exceptional academic achievements, completing their higher education by the age of 18. Benjamin, at 30 years old, exuded a mature charisma with his chiseled jawline and confident, calm demeanor. As their supervisor, though more of a colleague and friend, his air of wisdom and leadership enhanced his already handsome presence, making the trio as visually impressive as they were intellectually accomplished

Their time machine, after two years of work, was finally completed, but it remained untested—dangerously untested. There was a known risk that the machine's intricate manipulation of time and space could have unexpected effects on people taller than 190.7 cm, a phenomenon not fully understood, but closely linked to the curvature of spacetime. This left Ethan and Oliver in a precarious position. Neither of them could risk using the machine in their adult bodies without catastrophic side effects.

"Alright," Oliver sighed, pacing the lab. "We've run the numbers a hundred times. We can't go in like this. Unless we want to come out the other side with parts of us missing."

"Or worse," Ethan added, glancing at the time machine, his voice laced with apprehension.

Benjamin leaned against the sleek metallic surface of the machine. "Good thing we have Rezulix," he said, crossing his arms. "It's not ideal, but it'll do the trick."

Rezulix—the pinnacle of biological age manipulation in the 24th century. In a world where humanity had eradicated disease and significantly extended its lifespan, drugs like Rezulix and its counterpart, Advancillium, stood as testaments to the era's scientific ingenuity. A single dose of Rezulix could rewind the body's biological clock, reverting users to a younger version of themselves, their bodies may shrink back in age. Meanwhile, Advancillium served as the counterbalance, restoring individuals to their original biological age. Both treatments relied on specialized Chronos Chambers, which provided the precise conditions needed for cellular restructuring, ensuring the drugs' transformative effects unfolded seamlessly.

Ethan sighed, pulling out two vials of Rezulix from a secure container. "I never thought I'd be doing something like this."

Oliver chuckled, though it was tinged with nervousness. "Just think—tomorrow, we'll wake up as 10-year-olds. We'll be like... little kids again."

"Better enjoy your adult brains while you can," Benjamin teased, eyeing the vials in Ethan's hands. "Ten-year-old bodies, with ten-year-old hormones... should be fun."

Ethan gave him a deadpan look. "Not funny, Ben."

Benjamin grinned. "C'mon, lighten up. Look on the bright side: you two are gonna be adorable. I might just have to take a picture for the archives."

Oliver shook his head, rolling his eyes. "We'll see who's laughing after you're stuck babysitting us."

Ethan uncapped the vial, the liquid inside glimmering faintly. "Here goes nothing," he said, swallowing it in one quick gulp. Oliver followed suit, making a face as the medicine went down.

"That tastes awful!" Oliver complained.

Benjamin chuckled. "It's not candy, Oliver. Now, into the Chronos Chambers with you two."

Ethan and Oliver climbed into the sleek, glass pods, lying back as the smooth, cold surface adjusted to their forms. Benjamin sealed the chambers, watching as the systems hummed to life, emitting a soft blue glow. Inside, Ethan and Oliver could feel the pull of sleep overcoming them, their consciousness slipping away.

Before drifting off, Oliver managed one last quip. "Don't... forget to tuck us in... Ben."

Benjamin smirked. "Sweet dreams, boys."

Hours later, the chambers hissed open, releasing a soft cloud of condensation. Ethan and Oliver stepped out, their frames now significantly smaller. They were no longer the towering, confident scientists they had been just hours before. They were boys again—no more than 10 years old—with wide eyes and oversized lab coats hanging loosely off their small shoulders.

Ethan still managed to maintain his trademark serious expression, but on such a young face, it looked strangely out of place. Oliver, meanwhile, glanced down at his much shorter legs, his brow furrowing slightly as he processed the change.

"Whoa," Oliver said, holding out his arms as if checking his proportions. "This is... so weird."

Ethan inspected his hands, flexing his small fingers. "It feels... odd. But it worked. That's the important part."

From across the room, Benjamin burst into laughter, his voice echoing off the walls. "Oh, this is priceless. Look at you two! I should've brought sippy cups!"

Ethan shot him a glare that, despite his best efforts, lacked the impact it would have had in his adult form. "Cut it out, Benjamin."

Benjamin raised his hands in mock surrender, still grinning. "Alright, alright. But seriously, you're both half your size now. I mean, I came prepared." He held up a bag and gave it a casual shake. "Some clothes that might actually fit you."

Oliver reached into the bag and pulled out a pair of bright soccer kits. He held them up, unimpressed. "Really? Soccer kits?"

"They were on sale," Benjamin said with a shrug.

Oliver sighed. "Right. Of course."

Ethan and Oliver quickly changed into their new clothes, neither thrilled but both acknowledging practicality. Ethan adjusted the collar of his jersey with a resigned expression.

Benjamin clapped his hands together, his grin never fading. "Alright, boys. Now that I am officially the only adult here, you'd better listen to me. No arguments, no distractions, and definitely no breaking anything. Got it?"

Ethan crossed his arms, his attempt at authority undercut by his current size. "You're enjoying this way too much."

"Oh, you have no idea," Benjamin replied with a wink.

Ethan, despite everything, managed a small smile. "Alright, Ben, we're ready. Let's get this test over with."

They stepped into their time machine, the hum of its systems already filling the air. The sleek panels glowed faintly, and the room buzzed with the energy of the advanced technology. Without a word, they moved to their stations, each falling into practiced coordination.

Ethan adjusted a series of dials and flicked switches on his panel, his voice calm and steady. "Fluxion core is ready."

Oliver's fingers danced over the interface, activating multiple systems in rapid succession. "Temporal core is ready," he confirmed, his tone sharp and efficient.

Benjamin, standing at the main console, tapped the screen with precise motions. His gaze flicked between the data streams before nodding firmly. "All systems ready," he announced, his voice carrying a note of finality.

They exchanged a brief glance, the unspoken agreement clear: it was time.

The time machine hummed louder than usual as it powered up, and the shimmering display on the control panel began to flicker—a clear sign something was wrong. Benjamin's brow furrowed as he tapped a series of buttons, trying to stabilize the system. Before he could react, the machine lurched violently, and a blinding flash of light engulfed the three scientists.

The roar of rushing wind filled their ears, and the view outside the machine distorted, twisting into surreal colors and shapes. Ethan and Oliver, still adjusting to their child-sized bodies, gripped their seats tightly, their hearts pounding in sync with the machine's erratic movements.

"Ben, what's happening?!" Oliver shouted, his voice cracking in his higher-pitched tone.

"I don't know! The coordinates are off!" Benjamin yelled back, his fingers flying across the controls in a desperate attempt to regain control.

With a sudden jolt, the machine came to an abrupt halt, accompanied by a deep thud. Silence followed, broken only by their ragged breathing. For a moment, none of them moved, still processing the chaos they'd just endured.

Ethan, wide-eyed, leaned toward the machine's transparent window. Instead of the pristine, high-tech lab they had left, he saw trees, modest houses, and an empty road bathed in the golden light of sunset. The scene outside was unnervingly serene—no buzzing drones, no glowing skyscrapers, just a tranquil suburban neighborhood.

Oliver blinked rapidly, his confusion evident. "Where... where are we?"

Benjamin leaned closer to the display screen, his face growing pale as he processed the data. Clearing his throat, he tried to keep the panic from creeping into his voice. "We're... in 1970. Maine. America"

Ethan froze, his small hands gripping the edge of the console. "1970?!"

Benjamin nodded, his voice strained. "Yeah. It looks like I entered the wrong time coordinates."

Ethan's young face contorted in disbelief. "Benjamin! You said we were going back one year, not four centuries!"

"I know!" Benjamin snapped, frustration flaring in his tone. "Something went wrong during the power-up. The machine malfunctioned, and now we're here. I just... I need a second to figure this out."

Oliver turned his gaze back to the window, his eyes scanning the quiet suburban street. The parked cars looked ancient—brightly colored sedans and station wagons that seemed plucked straight from a museum. The stillness of the scene was unsettling, broken only by the faint chirping of birds.

"This is insane," Oliver muttered, his voice barely audible. "We're really in 1970."

Ethan jumped to his feet, his small fists trembling. "Ben, you have to get us back. Now."

Benjamin ran a hand through his hair, his eyes fixed on the depleted energy display. The interface blinked a relentless red, signaling the Fluxion Core was completely drained.

"I... can't," he admitted, his voice heavy. "The power source is depleted. It needs time to recharge."

Ethan's panic boiled into anger. "How much time?!"

Benjamin hesitated before answering, knowing the reaction it would provoke. "About 750 hours."

Ethan's jaw dropped. "750 hours?! That's a month! We're stuck here for a whole month?!"

Oliver slumped back into his seat, a mix of disbelief and resignation washing over him. "A month... in 1970. This is unreal."

Benjamin sighed deeply, rubbing his temples as the weight of the situation pressed down on him. "Look, I know this isn't ideal. But let's take a moment to appreciate one thing—our time machine actually works!"

Ethan and Oliver exchanged tense glances, their expressions softening slightly.

"It's incredible, sure," Ethan muttered, crossing his arms. "But we can't stay in this dinosaur age. We need to find a way back, fast."

Benjamin forced a faint smile, his voice tinged with determination. "We will."

The time machine itself was a marvel of futuristic engineering—a sleek, metallic pod with a faintly reflective surface. It floated effortlessly, hovering about five centimeters above the ground, supported by magnetic forces. Despite its advanced design, it resembled a tent, shimmering faintly as the orange hues of the setting sun danced across its surface. Futuristic and unmistakably out of place, it stood in stark contrast to its surroundings.

Benjamin scanned their surroundings, his gaze settling on a dense patch of forest just off the roadside. He pointed decisively. "There. We'll hide it in the woods. It should stay safe until we figure out our next move."

The three climbed out of the machine, stepping into the cool, earthy embrace of the forest. The rich scent of damp soil and pine needles filled the air, a sharp contrast to the sterile, controlled environment they'd left behind. This was it: 1970, Maine. No neon skylines, no hovering cars, no advanced tech—just a quiet forest in the middle of nowhere.

Ethan leaned against a tree, his small form dwarfed by the towering trunks around him. His face, still bearing traces of his former adult demeanor, was etched with worry. "What now?" he asked, his voice shaky and uncharacteristically soft.

Benjamin crouched down, making sure he was at eye level with both of them. "First, we lay low. No one can know who we are— or when we're from. We blend in, figure out as much as we can about this time period, and wait for the Fluxion Core to recharge. That's our priority."

Oliver arched an eyebrow. "Blend in? How, exactly? We're two 10-year-olds with no idea how the 1970s work. And what if someone figures out we're not from around here?"

Ethan folded his arms tightly, his frustration bubbling over. "And what about food? Or shelter? You think we can just wing it?"

Benjamin straightened up, a small, almost mischievous smile creeping across his face. "Relax. People in the 1970s are trusting. We'll figure out how to get by. Worst-case scenario, we camp out and live off the land. How hard can it be?"

Oliver snorted, unable to resist a jab. "Yeah, because roasting squirrels over a fire really screams 'scientific breakthrough.'"

Benjamin chuckled. "Hey, think of it as an adventure—a once-in-a-lifetime chance to rough it in the past."

Ethan shot him a skeptical glare. "Pretty sure this wasn't in the mission plan."

Benjamin shrugged. "Plans change. Besides, squirrel tastes better than you'd think."

Oliver rolled his eyes but couldn't hide the small grin tugging at the corner of his mouth. Ethan just sighed, muttering under his breath as they prepared to move the time machine deeper into the forest. For better or worse, their journey through 1970 had begun.

Benjamin's expression softened. "Look, I know I messed up. I'll fix this, okay? Just trust me."

Ethan sighed, staring out into the woods. The orange sun was setting, casting long shadows across the forest floor. "It's not like we have a choice."

The next morning, the situation had grown dire. The three of them had spent the night in the woods with nothing to eat, and by midday, Ethan's stomach had begun to rumble loudly. The young boy, now physically 10 years old but still mentally an adult, could no longer hold back his frustration.

"I'm starving!" Ethan shouted, his small fists clenched at his sides. "I can't go on like this! We need food, now!"

Benjamin rubbed his temples, thinking hard. They hadn't planned on being stuck in the past with no resources, but desperate times called for desperate measures. "Okay, okay. I think I've got an idea," he said, his voice steady despite the situation. He motioned toward the time machine's compartment. "We've got the 2kg gold conductor in there. If we sell it, we can use the money to buy food, maybe rent a place to stay for the month. We'll buy back the gold when we're ready to go back to the future."

Ethan, still agitated, gave Benjamin a skeptical look. "How exactly are we going to buy it back if we've already spent some of the money? We won't have enough left to get the full 2kg."

Benjamin opened his mouth to respond, but Oliver jumped in, thinking quickly. "We don't need to get the exact same gold bar back," he said, his voice calm but thoughtful. "The machine can work with

1.8 kg of gold. We could just get some smaller gold pieces later and tie them together."

Ethan paused, considering Oliver's logic. "Okay, fine," he relented. "But we still need to find someone who'll exchange the gold for money. Where do we even start?"

Benjamin nodded, stepping toward the time machine. "We'll figure it out. Let's get the gold and find the nearest town."

The three of them carefully extracted the 2kg gold conductor from the machine, its heavy weight glinting in the sunlight. Holding it tightly, they made their way toward the road, walking until they reached a small cluster of houses. After a few minutes of debating, they approached the nearest one, a modest, weathered house with a porch swing swaying gently in the breeze.

Benjamin knocked on the door, and after a moment, the door creaked open. An elderly woman, her gray hair tied in a neat bun, peered out at them. Her expression softened when she saw the two young boys standing beside Benjamin.

"Hello there, dears," she said in a gentle, raspy voice. "What can I do for you?"

Benjamin, with a polite smile, explained, "We're looking for a place to exchange some gold for money. Could you point us in the right direction?"

The old woman, Mrs. Wilson, squinted for a moment, thinking. "Well, the nearest bank is a few miles down the road. They should be able to help you with that but it's quite a walk."

Oliver, ever the charmer, smiled up at her. "Thank you, ma'am. We really appreciate it."

Chapter 1 | Part 2: 1970s

As the three scientists emerged from the bank, their hands now carrying a thick wad of cash and an envelope with a check, they strolled through the vibrant streets of 1970s Maine. Benjamin, with a bewildered expression, held the envelope close, aware of its substantial value, which amounted to nearly $200,000.

They rented a modest hotel room, where they spent the first few days adjusting to the strange customs of 1970. The trio used their time like tourists, wandering around the city, blending in with the crowds. They ate at diners, explored parks, and even visited a few historical landmarks.

A month passed in what felt like the blink of an eye. Their funds barely dipped—$1000 spent in total on food, lodging, and travel. They approached their time machine with renewed excitement.

"The machine should be fully charged by now," Benjamin said confidently. "Let's head back to the bank to buy enough gold to run the time machine and get home."

When they returned to the bank, they were hit with a rude awakening. The price had jumped.

"What do you mean it's $270,000 now?" Oliver asked the banker, wide-eyed.

The banker raised an eyebrow. "Gold prices fluctuate, young man. That's how the market works. If you want 2 kilograms of gold, it'll cost you $270,000. For 1.8 kilograms, it'll be $243,000."

Ethan's mouth dropped open. "We only have like... $199,000 left!"

They huddled outside the bank, panic setting in.

Benjamin rubbed his forehead. "We only needed a month! How did the price of gold jump that much?"

Oliver groaned. "Supply and demand. We were too optimistic. We should've bought it earlier."

Ethan kicked the sidewalk, his face scrunched up in frustration. "What now? We're short by 44 grand, and we've been kids for a month!"

Benjamin sighed. "Okay, okay. We have options. We can either figure out how to make that money quickly, or…"

Ethan cut in, "Or we wait until we're old and wrinkly and hope gold prices drop!"

Two weeks later, as they sat in the hotel room, Benjamin paced back and forth, frustration etched across his face. "We've been stuck here for two months, and the gold price hasn't budged."

Ethan, sitting cross-legged on the bed, grumbled. "It's gone up, if anything. What are we supposed to do?"

Benjamin stopped pacing, a glimmer of an idea forming. "Well, we can make money. I bet there are casinos around here."

Ethan's eyes went wide, and he nearly jumped off the bed. "No way! You want to gamble all the money we have left?"

Benjamin sighed. "I know it sounds risky, but what else can we do? We either make more money, or we wait even longer, hoping the price goes down."

Oliver, who had been quietly staring out the window, chimed in. "Waiting hasn't worked so far. If anything, prices keep going up. We can't afford to be stuck here for much longer."

Ethan frowned. "Gambling feels like the worst possible plan. What if we lose everything?"

Benjamin rubbed his temples. "Okay, okay. Maybe we wait a little longer and see if the price drops. But if nothing changes soon, we're going to have to get creative."

Another two weeks passed, and the gold price barely moved, hovering just over the $270,000 mark. Their frustration turned into impatience.

One evening, as they sat in their hotel room discussing their next move, there was a knock on the door. Benjamin opened it to find a police officer standing there, his gaze stern.

"Good evening, sir," the officer said. "I've noticed you and your… family have been staying here for quite a while. It's not usual for visitors to stay this long. Is everything alright?"

Benjamin's mind raced. Without skipping a beat, he gave a strained smile. "Oh, yes, officer. Everything's fine. We're just here visiting my mother."

The officer glanced at Ethan and Oliver, who were sitting on the bed, staring at him nervously. "Your mother, you say? And these are your sons?"

Benjamin nodded. "Yes, sir. This is Ethan and Oliver, my boys. We're visiting their grandmother."

The officer tilted his head. "And who might their grandmother be?"

Benjamin's pulse quickened, but he remembered the woman who had helped them on their first day. "Her name's Mrs. Wilson. Lovely woman, she's been helping us while we're in town."

The officer narrowed his eyes. "Mrs. Wilson, you say? And you have some ID, sir?"

Benjamin reached into his pocket and pulled out a 3D-printed ID that he had prepared earlier, handing it to the officer with a steady hand. "Benjamin Johnson, born in 1940," he said, trying to sound casual.

The officer studied the ID for a moment, then glanced back at Ethan and Oliver. "And you two boys, what do you call your father?"

Ethan and Oliver exchanged a quick look, their hearts racing. Then, in unison, they forced smiles and chimed, "Dad."

The officer seemed satisfied and handed the ID back to Benjamin. "Alright, Mr. Johnson. Just checking in. Make sure you don't overstay your visit." With a polite nod, the officer turned and left.

Benjamin closed the door behind him and let out a deep breath. "That was too close."

Ethan flopped back on the bed. "I swear I almost called you 'Benjamin' instead of 'dad.'"

Oliver laughed nervously. "Yeah, that felt weird. We need to figure something out, fast. I don't think we can keep this act up much longer."

After weeks of waiting and watching the gold price refuse to drop, the three scientists knew they had no choice. Their long stay was drawing suspicion, and they couldn't risk any more attention.

"We need the money," Benjamin said firmly. "If we keep waiting, the whole town will catch on to us."

They hailed a taxi to the city center, where they found a large hotel with a flashy casino inside. Ethan and Oliver were left sitting in the reception area, their small, 10-year-old forms earning curious glances from the passersby.

Ethan watched the clock, restless. "How long do you think he's going to be in there?" he muttered to Oliver, tapping his foot anxiously.

Oliver shrugged. "No idea. He seemed confident... but this is a huge risk."

Hours passed, and eventually, Benjamin emerged from the casino. His face told the story before he even spoke—his normally strong, assured expression was now hollow, dark circles under his eyes. Ethan and Oliver's hearts sank immediately, knowing something had gone horribly wrong.

Ethan shot up from his seat. "What happened?" His voice cracked, and when Benjamin didn't answer right away, he shouted, "WHAT? What do you mean you lost 100 grand in there?"

Benjamin's silence hung heavy in the air. He avoided their eyes, his shoulders slumped in defeat.

Oliver sat down, feeling the room spin around him. "No... no, no, no. You can't be serious," he whispered, his face pale. "What are we supposed to do now? We're stuck here. We don't have enough to buy the gold."

Ethan's emotions overflowed. His face flushed red, and he began pacing in anger, his young form trembling. "This is all your fault, Benjamin! You set the wrong time! You told us to sell the gold! And now you've gambled away almost all the money!" His voice echoed through the reception area, catching the attention of other guests.

Benjamin stood quietly, his gaze locked on the floor. He knew Ethan was right—he had made mistake after mistake. But the weight of the blame and their hopeless situation was too much to bear. He didn't defend himself, couldn't. He was the oldest, the leader, and he had failed them.

The scene was attracting more stares from people around them, their conversations suddenly hushed as they watched the strange sight of two young boys yelling at a grown man. In 1970, it was unheard of for children to scold an adult like this.

"Ethan, calm down," Oliver said, his voice weak, but Ethan couldn't contain his anger.

"No! We're trapped as kids, stuck in 1970, and now we don't even have the money to buy back the gold!" Ethan shouted, his fists clenched as tears welled up in his eyes.

Benjamin finally spoke, his voice low and tired. "I'm sorry, Ethan. I... I thought I could win it back. I made a bad call."

"Yeah, you think?" Ethan snapped, still seething, his voice shaking.

Oliver sat in stunned silence, head in his hands. "We're doomed," he whispered, staring blankly at the floor. "We can't go home."

The tension in the air felt unbearable. People continued to watch, unsure of what was happening, while the three time-traveling scientists, in a desperate and chaotic moment, faced the harsh reality of their situation.

As Ethan's voice rose in frustration, a man in his late 60s—graying hair and a stern expression—strode up and interrupted the scene. Without warning, he swatted Ethan's bottom twice. The suddenness of the action startled the entire group.

"Ow!" Ethan yelped, jumping and spinning around, his face flushed with shock. But before he could say anything, the man addressed Benjamin.

"You can't let your sons run wild like this, young man," the old man said, his voice gruff and authoritative.

Benjamin blinked, instantly recognizing the misunderstanding. His mind raced, and he knew he needed to defuse the situation fast. "Oh, I'm sorry," he said, feigning embarrassment. "I'll talk to them later."

Ethan, still fuming, wasn't about to let it slide. "Hey, what's wrong with you, old dude? Why did you hit me?" His voice carried a mix of outrage and confusion.

Oliver, standing beside him, added, "You can't just hit us like that! We're going to call law enforcement."

Benjamin, knowing the rules and norms of 1970 were vastly different from their time, cringed at the boys' reaction. He had already noticed how children were treated with more discipline in this era. The last thing they needed was more attention drawn to them.

He quickly stepped in, cutting Oliver off. "I'm really sorry for their behaviours," Benjamin said to the old man, forcing a smile. "I'll handle them." Without missing a beat, Benjamin gave both Ethan and Oliver a light swat on their bottoms, playing the part of a father disciplining his children. "You two stop it right now. I'll deal with you later."

Ethan and Oliver exchanged looks, both wide-eyed at the unexpected turn of events. Benjamin didn't give them a chance to respond, swiftly grabbing each by the arm and pulling them toward the exit. As they hurried out, the old man watched, nodding in approval.

Once outside, Benjamin hailed a taxi, his grip still firm on both boys. As they piled into the back seat and drove off, Ethan muttered under his breath, "That was humiliating."

Oliver sighed, leaning back in the seat. "We've got bigger problems than that."

Benjamin glanced at them, his face still tense from the encounter. "I told you—we need to be careful, and the last thing we need is someone getting too curious about us."

Ethan crossed his arms, still sulking. "Yeah, well, next time maybe don't lose 100 grand in a casino."

Chapter 2: Invented Family

A month after the tense encounter with the police and their dwindling funds, Benjamin knew they needed a more permanent solution. The hotel stay had dragged on long enough, and the police had already come by to check on them a second time. Reluctantly, he decided to use some of their remaining money to buy a house—$25,000—a steep price, but necessary.

As Benjamin broke the news, Ethan and Oliver sat across from him, their young faces twisted in frustration.

Ethan scowled. "You spent 25 GRAND on a house? We're stuck here as kids, and now you're throwing money away again?"

Oliver folded his arms, echoing Ethan's sentiment. "We don't need a house. We need to get back home. And that's a huge chunk of our money gone!"

Benjamin sighed heavily. "Look, we can't stay in a hotel forever. The police are already suspicious of us, and we need somewhere to hide the time machine. It's not like we have many options."

Ethan grumbled under his breath, "This is ridiculous. I can't believe this is our life now."

Sometimes, after spending so much time with Ethan and Oliver in their current forms, Benjamin would forget that they were, in fact, adults—brilliant scientists trapped in 10-year-old bodies. Yet here they were, living through a strange reality. But in this moment, he was reminded.

"This is decided already. There's nothing to discuss," Benjamin said, his tone final.

Grumbling, Ethan and Oliver had no choice but to go along with the plan. They bought the house.

Several months passed, and despite the relative peace of having their own space, things didn't stay quiet for long. The same police officer knocked on their door again, this time with a new concern.

"Mr. Johnson," the officer said, a polite but stern expression on his face. "I've noticed your boys don't seem to be going to school. Is everything alright?"

Benjamin forced a smile, trying not to panic. "Oh, yes, officer. Everything's fine. We've just been… transitioning. You know, new place, new routine. But I'm enrolling them soon."

When the officer finally left, Benjamin turned to Ethan and Oliver, who had been eavesdropping.

"We have a problem," Benjamin said, exasperated. "I can't keep making excuses. If you don't go to school, they're going to think I'm mistreating you two."

Ethan's eyes widened in disbelief. "School? You seriously want us to go to school? I'm already a scientist, Benjamin. In case you forgot."

Oliver chimed in, equally annoyed. "Yeah, we don't need to go back to 5th grade. This is ridiculous."

Benjamin ran a hand through his hair. "Look, I made you both IDs. You're going to be twins, okay? You'll be enrolled in the local elementary school as 5th graders. I don't like it either, but we have no choice. If you don't go, I'll get arrested."

Ethan crossed his arms, glaring at Benjamin. "I don't care. I'm not going. If you want, you can go to that freaking primary school yourself."

Oliver added, "Yeah, good luck with that. We're not doing it."

Benjamin groaned, realizing he was trapped between the law and two very stubborn "children."

Three days later, Benjamin's suggestion hung in the air like a heavy cloud. Ethan, who had been feeling the weight of their situation more than he let on, snapped.

"NOOO! NO WAY!" Ethan's voice cracked with emotion. "You can go if you want to!"

Oliver, watching from the side, looked torn. He had his own frustrations but wasn't as explosive as Ethan. Ethan, however, continued, his face flushed and fists clenched.

"This is all your fault!" he shouted, pointing at Benjamin. "You set the wrong time. You told us to sell the gold. And now you want us to suffer through primary school with a bunch of little kids? Seriously?"

Benjamin opened his mouth to respond, but Ethan cut him off, his voice now quieter but laced with bitterness. "Why are you even a scientist in the first place? You clearly didn't think any of this through."

The room fell into an awkward silence, the hum of the time machine the only sound.

Benjamin had reached his breaking point. The stakes were too high to ignore—if Ethan and Oliver refused to attend school, the police's scrutiny would only intensify, leading to potential legal trouble. Worse still, if the authorities concluded that he was neglecting his "sons" by failing to provide them with a proper education, the boys could be removed from his care and placed in a child protection program, possibly even made available for adoption. They were trapped in this era without the Advancillium to return to their real ages. And Benjamin wasn't going to let it come to that.

Ethan's eyes narrowed, and his voice dripped with venom. "You think you're so smart, don't you, Ben? Acting like you're in charge—you're just a washed-up loser playing pretend," he spat. "I'm not going to school, and you can't make me!"

Benjamin straightened, his expression cool and unyielding. He had hoped it wouldn't come to this, but there was no room left for negotiation. His voice was calm but carried unmistakable authority.

"You can cooperate, or I'll make it happen."

Ethan's mouth fell open, caught off guard by the sudden shift. "You... you wouldn't dare!"

Benjamin's patience snapped. "Alright, Ethan. You made your choice."

Before Ethan could process what was happening, Benjamin moved with unsettling precision. Ethan twisted to bolt, but Benjamin's hands were already on him, hoisting him effortlessly over his lap.

"Let me go!" Ethan kicked and flailed, twisting like a fish caught in a net. His small fists beat against Benjamin's side, though it was like throwing pebbles at a brick wall.

"You absolute jerk! You can't—" Ethan's furious retort was cut short by the sharp crack of the first swat landing on his bottom.

"Ow! Damn it, Ben!" Ethan bucked harder, his anger exploding. But Benjamin, unmoved, continued with deliberate, firm swats, one after another, like clockwork.

Ethan's body jolted with each spank. "You're insane! You hear me?! You—"

Benjamin sighed. "Still got fight in you? Okay." In one swift motion, he yanked down Ethan's pants and underwear, exposing his bare skin.

Ethan's face burned with rage and embarrassment. "No! You can't—"

But Benjamin could. And he did. The next spank was sharper, stinging more than before. Ethan's defiance began to falter, though he thrashed with all his might, trying to twist free from Benjamin's unrelenting grip.

"Let me go!" Ethan gasped between yelps, but Benjamin only tightened his hold, grabbing a nearby ruler and calmly resuming his 'persuasive' approach.

Each strike drained more of Ethan's fight, until all that was left was a sniffling, hiccuping mess. "Please, Ben... I'm sorry..." Ethan whispered, his voice small, the last fragments of his rebellion crumbling under the weight of Benjamin's discipline.

After what felt like an eternity to Ethan, Benjamin finally let him up. Tears streamed down his face as he stood, his legs shaky. Benjamin grabbed him by the arm and guided him to the wall, facing him away.

"Stand there and reflect on your recent behaviours." Benjamin said sternly, his voice calm but authoritative. "I've had enough of your bratty mouth."

Ethan, still sniffling, instinctively reached to pull up his pants, eager to cover his exposed bottom, but a quick tap of the ruler stopped him in his tracks. "Leave your pants down; you're not allowed to pull them up yet." Benjamin reminded him firmly.

Ethan yelped and quickly pulled his hands away, rubbing his sore bum instead, standing against the wall, utterly defeated.

Benjamin stood firm, the ruler still in his hand, towering over the small, trembling figure of Ethan. His voice was calm but carried an unmistakable authority. "From now on, you call me Dad. Not Benjamin or Ben. Do you understand?"

Ethan, still sniffling, turned his head slightly, defiance flickering in his tear-filled eyes. "No!" he spat, his voice trembling but stubborn.

Benjamin's expression hardened, his tone dropping to a cold, deliberate calm. "It seems you still don't understand the situation we're in," he said. "Maybe you need another reminder over my knees."

Ethan's heart sank as the words hit him, his mind racing. His bottom already burned with pain, and the thought of enduring more was unbearable. Desperation took over. "No, no! Please, Ben—I mean Dad! I'll do it, I'll listen!"

Benjamin nodded, satisfied for the moment. "Good. Stay there until I tell you otherwise." Ethan, ashamed and utterly defeated, leaned his forehead against the wall, his small hands still rubbing his sore bottom. The fight in him was gone, replaced by reluctant surrender to Benjamin's authority.

Benjamin turned away from Ethan, leaving him against the wall, still sniffling and rubbing his sore bottom. He walked over to where Oliver was standing, observing the whole scene in silence. Oliver had remained still, but the tension in his body was clear. He had witnessed everything and knew exactly what kind of authority Benjamin now held.

Benjamin's voice softened but remained firm as he addressed Oliver. "I expect your cooperation, Oliver. I don't want to do this to you too. You're not like Ethan, and I know you understand the situation better."

Oliver glanced briefly at Ethan, still pressed against the wall, then back at Benjamin. He swallowed, the weight of the situation pressing down on him. He didn't want to go to school, didn't want to live as a child stuck in a world that wasn't his, but the alternative was clear. He wouldn't challenge Benjamin's authority—not after seeing what had happened to Ethan.

"I know you don't want this any more than Ethan does," Benjamin continued. "But we need to stay under the radar. If you two don't go to school, the police will get involved. They'll see you as just children here, and I could be arrested. You and Ethan could end up in some sort of child protection system. We can't afford that. The only way we get through this is by blending in until we find a way out."

Oliver hesitated, but the reality of the situation was undeniable. He knew Benjamin was right. There was no escape from their predicament unless they played along. He could already feel the pressure to submit, and he didn't want to face what Ethan had just endured.

After a long pause, Oliver finally nodded. His voice was quiet, but resigned. "...Yes, I will go with Ethan next week."

Benjamin gave a slight nod of approval. "Good. That's what I need to hear. Let's make this as easy as we can for all of us."

Oliver exhaled deeply, feeling a mix of relief and dread. He wasn't looking forward to the week ahead, but at least he knew where he stood with Benjamin now.

Benjamin kept his gaze on Oliver, his tone softening slightly. "You can still call me Ben or Benjamin when it's just us, but in front of other people, make sure you call me Dad. We need to keep up appearances until we can go back. We'll make it back to the 24th century soon, I promise."

Oliver nodded, still processing everything. The weight of their situation felt heavy, but Benjamin's promise offered a sliver of hope. At least they had a plan, even if it wasn't what they had envisioned.

Benjamin then shifted the conversation, thinking out loud. "I'm considering opening a small business or finding a job to make money. We can't rely on what we have left. That way, we'll be able to blend in better and keep moving forward."

Suddenly, Ethan's tear-filled voice interrupted them from the wall, still shaking with frustration and pain. "It's not fair... Why can Oliver still call you by name, but I can't?"

Benjamin didn't even turn to face Ethan this time, nor did he respond. He simply ignored the outburst, knowing that engaging Ethan's whining would only reinforce the behavior. He had made his stance clear, and Ethan would just have to accept it. Oliver glanced at Ethan with a mix of sympathy and relief that he hadn't been in his place, then looked back at Benjamin.

"Whatever we need to do," Oliver said quietly, sensing that now wasn't the time to argue or push back. Benjamin nodded, already making plans in his head for what the next steps would be to secure their safety in 1970.

Chapter 3: Groovy Times

The small house, though a necessary refuge, felt more like a cage that night. With only two rooms, Benjamin took one for himself, while Ethan and Oliver were left to share the other. The third room, a storage space, housed the time machine—the very thing that had stranded them in this foreign era.

Ethan lay on his bed, still fuming. His eyes, puffy and red from crying, reflected the simmering anger he felt toward both Benjamin and Oliver. He glanced across the room at Oliver, who was quietly settling into his own bed. Ethan couldn't contain it any longer.

"You're a freaking coward, Oliver," Ethan hissed, his voice sharp in the darkness. "You didn't say what you really think to Ben. You just agreed with him, like you always do."

Oliver sighed, turning to face Ethan. He wasn't in the mood for a fight, but he knew Ethan wouldn't let it go. "You brought this on yourself, Ethan," Oliver said, his tone steady but firm. "Ben's trying his best to keep us safe and give us a chance to even get back to our time. Do you really think fighting him is going to help?"

Ethan scoffed, his frustration boiling over. "You two are idiots... You're just following along with whatever he says. We're scientists, Oliver! Not kids who need to be bossed around!"

Oliver didn't respond immediately. He stared at the ceiling for a moment, thinking over their situation. "We might be scientists, but right now, we are kids, Ethan. That's the reality. If we don't play along, we're going to get into real trouble. Ben is doing what he has to."

Ethan rolled over, his back to Oliver. He didn't want to hear it, didn't want to admit that Oliver might be right. "Whatever," he muttered, his voice tinged with bitterness. "You can be Ben's little sidekick all you want. I'm not going to just roll over like you."

Oliver sighed again, too tired to argue further. "Good night, Ethan," he said softly, knowing that no matter what he said, Ethan wasn't ready to listen.

The room fell into a tense silence, the only sound the soft rustling of sheets as they both settled in for the night. Sleep came slowly, weighed down by the heavy burden of their strange new reality.

One morning, Ethan sat slumped on the couch, clearly irritated as the fuzzy image on the television flickered in front of him. "Why does this TV look so blurry?" he complained, squinting at the screen. "I can't see anything."

Oliver, a little more resigned to their situation, shrugged. "We're lucky we didn't land further back in history. Imagine trying to survive with no technology at all."

Ethan grumbled, unable to let go of his frustration. "This is all Ben's fault. He set the wrong time for the time machine. If he hadn't messed up, we wouldn't be stuck here."

Oliver turned to face him, his voice calm but firm. "Come on, Ethan, you're a scientist. You know better than anyone that every experiment carries risks. Things go wrong sometimes, and we deal with it."

Ethan rolled his eyes, refusing to be swayed. "Yeah, but this… this is just—" He cut himself off, clenching his fists in frustration. "Where is Ben, anyway?"

Oliver couldn't resist the opportunity to tease him. "You mean 'Dad'?"

Ethan's face turned red with frustration. "I am not calling him 'Dad.' He's not my dad, and when we get back to our time, and I get back to my real body with the Advancillium, Ben's gonna pay for what he did to me."

Oliver chuckled softly, amused by Ethan's stubbornness. "Ben went into the city center. He's hoping to find a way to open a small business or get a job so we can survive here a bit longer. And by the way, school's in two days. You ready for that?"

Ethan wasn't really listening. He was distracted, tugging at the waistband of his pants and checking his body. He seemed almost obsessed with the fact that his body had reverted to that of a 10-year-old, and it was bothering him in more ways than just his appearance.

Oliver noticed and frowned. "You're not still checking, are you? We're stuck like this for now. There's no use worrying about it."

Ethan glanced at Oliver, frustration still written all over his face. "I just can't stand this. I feel like I'm trapped in someone else's body. I hate it."

Oliver sighed. "I get it, man. But there's nothing we can do about it right now. We just have to play along until we can fix the time machine and get back."

Ethan fell silent, his anger simmering just below the surface. But for now, there was nothing he could do but wait.

Ben pulled into the driveway, the old car rattling slightly as it came to a stop. He had bought it a few days earlier for $500, a modest but necessary expense for getting around in the 1970s. He stepped out of the car, tired but satisfied. The new job he secured as an engineer for an energy company felt like a small win, but the salary was far from what he had hoped for—only $15,000 a year. It wasn't enough to make up for the loss of the gold, but it was something.

As Ben entered the house, Ethan and Oliver were already there, lounging in the living room. Ben updated them on his day.

"I managed to get a job as an engineer for an energy company," Ben said, trying to sound optimistic despite the lower-than-expected salary. "It's not great, but it's something."

Ethan, still simmering with frustration, snorted. "You can work that job for your entire life here, and it still won't be enough to buy back the gold we sold."

Oliver, always trying to find the silver lining, spoke up. "It's better than nothing. It's better than just spending the money we have left and not having a plan."

Ben nodded, appreciating Oliver's support. "Thanks, Oliver. I'm also looking into some other ways to make money. I heard that kids in this time do something called 'newspaper delivery.' There's a job called 'paperboy.' Ethan, you could definitely help out with that."

Ethan shot Ben a defiant look, crossing his arms. "Never. I'm not doing that. I'm not going to work like some... some kid from the 1970s."

Ben continued to tease. "Look, Ethan, we need every bit of help we can get. I know it's not what you want, but it's a way to make some extra money. We're all in this together, and we have to adapt."

Ethan glared at Ben, his anger flaring. "You can't make me do something I don't want to do. I'm not a child from this era, and I'm not going to act like one."

Ben took a deep breath, trying to maintain his composure. "Fine, but just remember, we're all in a tough spot. If you change your mind, let me know. We need to get through this."

Ethan turned away, clearly upset, while Oliver watched the exchange with a mixture of sympathy and frustration. It was clear that the tension between them was far from resolved, and the struggle to adapt to their new reality was taking its toll.

As they walked into JadiMart, the supermarket had a typical 1970s feel, with aisles stocked with goods that looked a bit outdated compared to their time. Ethan and Oliver trailed behind Benjamin, their expressions a mix of reluctance and curiosity.

Benjamin, trying to keep the mood light, said, "Well guys, we need to buy school supplies. This could be exciting! If I were in your place, I'd be curious to see what schools are like in this century."

Oliver, though still somewhat disgruntled, replied, "Yeah, not a lot of people get this chance."

Ethan muttered under his breath, "Idiots..."

Benjamin, determined to keep the situation positive, led them through the aisles, picking up notebooks, pencils, and backpacks. As they were busy selecting supplies, a young woman from the store approached them. She was around 25 years old, with a friendly demeanor and a warm smile. Her name tag read "Sarah."

Sarah's eyes lit up as she saw Ethan and Oliver. "Oh, you two are just adorable!" she exclaimed. "You must be excited for school, right?"

Ethan looked up, clearly uncomfortable with the attention but trying to muster a polite smile. "Uh, yeah, sure."

Oliver, slightly more receptive, gave a small smile. "Thanks."

Sarah then turned her attention to Benjamin, her gaze lingering a bit longer. "And you, sir, are you their father?"

Benjamin nodded, trying to maintain a casual tone. "Yes, I'm their father. We're just getting everything ready for school."

Sarah, noticing Benjamin's slight discomfort, tried to make small talk. "Well, it's great to see a parent so involved. You don't see that very often. Do you live around here?"

Benjamin hesitated, not wanting to reveal too much. "Yes, we've just moved here recently. Still getting used to things."

Sarah seemed to take a liking to Benjamin, her smile broadening as she spoke. "If you need any more help or have any questions, feel free to ask. I've worked here for a while and know the store well."

As Sarah walked away, Ethan rolled his eyes. "Great, now we've got store employees hitting on Ben."

Oliver, trying to lighten the mood, chuckled. "Looks like Ben's got a fan."

Benjamin, trying to stay focused, said, "Let's just finish up here. We've got everything we need."

They continued their shopping, the tension slightly eased by the interaction. Benjamin knew they had to stay on their guard, especially in a time where revealing their true identities could lead to problems.

As they finished dinner, Benjamin looked over at Ethan, still sulking with his head down. He knew this transition was tough for them all, but it had to be done.

"Alright, boys, get some rest. Tomorrow's a big day," Benjamin said, getting up from the table.

Oliver gave a small nod, looking both nervous and excited, while Ethan just muttered something under his breath. Ben shot him a glance but decided to let it slide for now. He could sense the tension in Ethan, but he hoped that tomorrow would bring some kind of shift.

As they headed off to their shared room, Oliver tried to lighten the mood. "You know, it might not be so bad. Maybe school won't be like how it was for us growing up."

Ethan snorted, "It's gonna be worse. We're stuck as kids, and now we've got to go to school with actual kids. It's humiliating."

Oliver shrugged, "It's just temporary. We'll get back to our time soon. Maybe we'll even learn something useful about how people lived in the 20th century."

Ethan rolled his eyes, "Yeah, sure, I'll just sit in class learning the alphabet again while you play 'perfect twin' for Ben."

Oliver didn't respond immediately but sighed, "Look, I'm not trying to be perfect. I'm just trying to get through this without more problems. We don't have a choice."

Ethan muttered, "Feels like I'm the only one who sees how messed up this is."

Oliver turned to him, "We all see it, Ethan. But Ben's trying to help. We're stuck in 1970, and this is the only way to stay under the radar. I don't like it either, but we need to get through it. Just… don't make it harder than it has to be."

Ethan remained silent, feeling the weight of the situation sink in again. He didn't like this arrangement, but deep down, he knew that for now, he was at Benjamin's mercy. Begrudgingly, he crawled into bed, his mind racing with a mix of frustration, fear, and a reluctant acceptance of what tomorrow would bring.

The morning sun was bright, and as Benjamin woke the boys, Ethan groaned, feeling groggy. Both Ethan and Oliver were still adjusting to their youthful bodies, the energy and metabolism of 10-year-olds coursing through them like a bizarre reminder of the situation they were trapped in. "Thanks to the advanced medical technology of the 24th century," Ethan grumbled to himself, though he didn't feel thankful at all.

After dressing up in their school uniforms—Ethan tugging at his uncomfortable collar—Ben handed Oliver a crisp 1-dollar bill. "Here's your lunch money," he said, giving Oliver a nod of trust. Ethan, still sulking, didn't say a word as Ben headed out for work, his tie neatly in place. "Be good today, and don't give Oliver a hard time," Ben called as he drove off.

Ethan and Oliver walked to the bus stop together, their small backpacks bouncing on their backs. They passed their neighbour, Mrs. Richardson, a kindly woman in her mid-60s, who waved at them from her front porch. She had curly gray hair and always seemed to have a warm smile ready for everyone.

"Good morning, boys!" she called out cheerfully.

Oliver, always polite, smiled and waved. "Good morning, Mrs. Richardson!" he replied.

"Good luck on your first day of school!" she added, beaming. Ethan managed a forced smile, though his mind was already spiralling into annoyance about the whole situation.

Arriving at the school, they were greeted by Mrs. Lewis, their 5th-grade teacher, a woman in her early 40s with short brown hair and glasses. She was friendly, but firm. "Welcome, boys! I've heard all about you two and your father, Mr. Johnson. You both look very handsome today," she said, directing them to their seats with a warm smile. "Now, let's get settled, class is about to begin."

As they sat down, Ethan felt a wave of frustration wash over him. When Mrs. Lewis handed out the textbooks, he immediately realized how foreign everything felt. The language in the textbooks was outdated, and the concepts seemed overly simplified, yet strangely challenging. In the 24th century, most math and calculations were handled by AI, and while he understood the core concepts, actually doing the work manually was throwing him off. Every problem felt like a time-consuming puzzle he should've been able to solve easily—but couldn't.

Across the room, Oliver seemed to be handling things better. He'd always been the more adaptable one, and his interest in history was paying off. He didn't struggle with the older language and even found some of the lessons amusingly quaint.

Ethan glanced at Oliver, feeling a mixture of frustration and envy. "Great, he's playing the 'perfect twin' again," he muttered under his breath, his pencil tapping irritably against the desk.

As the lesson continued, Ethan couldn't help but feel like he was drowning in an ocean of numbers and words, a stark contrast to the brilliant scientist he was supposed to be.

Around one month later, Benjamin's new life as an engineer at the energy company seemed to be going smoothly. His knowledge from the 24th century gave him a significant advantage in the 1970s. The techs, while advanced for their time, were relatively simple compared to the technologies Benjamin was accustomed to. He had already suggested improvements, earning the respect of his division director, Mr. Stone. Mr. Stone, an older gentleman with a sharp mind and an eye for talent, appreciated Benjamin's contributions, though he found it odd that such a young man had such an in-depth knowledge of the field.

At the office, Benjamin's coworkers often commented on his appearance. At 188 cm with a naturally fit physique, he stood out among the men, who generally looked older and less vibrant. The female clerks in the office often found reasons to stop by his cubicle, leaving him awkwardly navigating their attentions. One such moment arrived when a young clerk with a soft smile, approached his desk.

"Ben, the principal from your boys' school called," she said with a slight blush. "He wants to talk to you. It sounded urgent."

Benjamin's heart sank as he reached for the phone and began dialing the school. He braced himself, fully aware that dealing with Ethan and Oliver—especially Ethan—could be challenging. The phone rang, and soon the principal, Mr. Harris, picked up.

"Mr. Johnson, thanks for returning the call," Mr. Harris began. "I wanted to talk to you about your sons. Ethan, in particular, has been struggling in class—especially with reading and math. I've also had reports from his teacher that he's been acting out."

Benjamin rubbed his forehead, recalling the many arguments with Ethan about going to school. He had anticipated challenges, but hearing it confirmed made him feel a bit helpless.

"Ethan's a bright boy," Mr. Harris continued, "but I'm concerned about his adjustment. Oliver seems to be settling in well, but Ethan... well, I think he needs some extra help. Perhaps you could arrange a meeting to discuss how we can support him better?"

Benjamin sighed, trying to stay calm. "I'll talk to him, Mr. Harris, and we'll figure something out."

After hanging up, Benjamin leaned back in his chair. Despite his success at work, the challenges at home were beginning to pile up. He knew that sending Ethan and Oliver to school in the 1970s had been necessary to avoid legal issues, but he hadn't fully considered how difficult it would be for them to adapt—especially Ethan, who was already resistant to the idea of living as a child.

Later that evening, as Benjamin drove home, his thoughts lingered on the conversation with the principal. He needed a new approach to help Ethan. As he pulled into the driveway, he saw the boys playing in the yard, both of them looking like the carefree 10-year-olds they were now forced to be. But beneath that facade were two young men struggling with their situation—one much more than the other.

Dinner that night was quiet, until Benjamin broke the silence.

"I got a call from your school today," he said, looking directly at Ethan.

Ethan, not meeting his gaze, continued pushing his food around his plate. Oliver glanced nervously between them.

"Your teacher says you've been having trouble," Benjamin continued. "And you've been causing disruptions in class."

Ethan, still avoiding eye contact, mumbled, "It's not my fault. Everything's old here… the books, the math. It's dumb."

Benjamin sighed. "I know this is hard, Ethan, but you have to try. We all have to fit in here, at least for now."

Ethan's eyes flicked up. "Maybe you can fit in, Benjamin. You get to be an adult. We're stuck like this!" His voice cracked with frustration.

"I'm doing what I can to keep us safe," Benjamin replied, his tone firm but calm. "That includes making sure you both go to school. We don't belong here, and if anyone figures that out, we're in big trouble. You know that."

Ethan folded his arms, muttering, "Whatever."

Benjamin glanced at Oliver, who had been quiet the entire time. "Oliver, you've been doing well. Keep it up."

Oliver nodded, casting a sympathetic look at Ethan but knowing better than to get involved.

After dinner, as Benjamin sat in his room, he thought about how to manage Ethan's frustration. He couldn't allow the situation to spiral out of control. The next day, he planned to visit the school and meet with the principal in person to work out a plan for Ethan. Perhaps some extra tutoring or different methods could help.

In the meantime, he hoped that his new job and their growing life in 1970 would provide the stability they needed until the time machine was repaired and they could finally return to the 24th century.

But for now, they were stuck—and all three of them would have to play their roles carefully.

Later that evening, after the tense dinner, Ethan sat on the floor of the shared bedroom he had with Oliver, sulking. Oliver, ever the diligent one, had already finished his homework and was organizing his school materials when he turned to Ethan.

"Remember to do your English and Social Studies homework, Ethan. You're already in enough trouble as it is," Oliver reminded, his tone calm but firm.

Ethan, sprawled out and half-heartedly flipping through one of the outdated textbooks, groaned in frustration. "Why don't you just do the homework, and I'll copy it over in the morning?"

Oliver gave him a disapproving look. "Seriously? You're better than this, Ethan. How did you even manage to graduate from the Science University of Electropolis back in the day? "

Ethan sighed and sat up, tossing the book aside. "That was different. I actually cared about science and physics. Why do I need to learn U.S. History or Geography or whatever else they're making us do here? It's useless. The U.S. doesn't even exist anymore in our time!" He threw his hands up in exasperation, recalling how, by the 24th century, the United States, Canada, and Mexico had merged into the North American Union (NAU).

Oliver leaned back against the wall, crossing his arms. "That doesn't matter now. Right now, you're a 10-year-old in 1970, and this homework is part of that reality. If you don't keep up appearances, Ben's going to get even more upset, and you're going to dig yourself deeper."

Ethan scoffed, shaking his head. "I'm already in a mess, Oliver. Being stuck here in 1970, looking like this." He motioned to his small frame. "You think I care about some stupid Social Studies homework?"

Oliver, who had always been more practical, sighed and put down his pencil. "Look, I get it. None of this is fair. But we're in this together, and if you don't at least try, you're going to make it harder for all of us. You saw how Ben reacted. He's serious about us fitting in."

Ethan stared at the ceiling for a moment, thinking about how much he hated this situation. As much as he wanted to rebel, he knew Oliver was right. They had to blend in, at least until the time machine was fixed. And that meant playing the part—even if it meant doing homework on subjects that felt like ancient history.

"Fine," Ethan muttered. "I'll do it."

Oliver gave a small nod, satisfied but not surprised. "Good. You don't want to give Ben any more reasons to keep an eye on you."

The room fell silent as Ethan reluctantly picked up his pencil and flipped open his textbook. He hated everything about this—the old paper, the smell of the books, the slow, tedious process of writing with his hand instead of dictating to an AI. But in the back of his mind, he knew he didn't have a choice. At least for now, they were stuck in the 20th century, and this was their life.

The thought of Ben, with his newfound authority over them, still rankled him. But Ethan kept his head down and got to work, determined not to give anyone the satisfaction of seeing him struggle more than he already had.

As they settled into their beds later that night, Oliver rolled over, turning off the small bedside lamp. "Just remember, Ethan. We're pretending to be twins, and we've got to work together. Otherwise, we're going to be stuck here a lot longer than we want."

Ethan didn't respond. He was already thinking ahead to the next day, when he would have to face school once again. But he knew Oliver was right. If they didn't work together, they might never make it back to their real lives. And the thought of staying in 1970 forever was too terrifying to bear.

Chapter 4: Ethan

As the group sat at the lunch table, Ethan and Oliver tried to blend in with their new friends. Ava, with her curious eyes, noticed the differences between the two boys.

"You two are twins, but I don't think you look alike," she said, tilting her head slightly. "Oliver seems a bit taller."

Oliver smiled, ready with a quick explanation. "We're not identical twins. That's why."

Ava nodded thoughtfully, while Leo chimed in, "So it's just you two and your dad living here now, right?" He was referring to the backstory Ben had cooked up—that they'd recently moved from California to Maine.

Ethan hesitated. "Uh, yeah. Just us and... Ben."

Ava furrowed her brow. "You mean your dad, right?"

Caught off guard, Ethan flushed, casting a quick, awkward glance at Oliver, who subtly nodded to encourage him. "Uh... yeah, right. Our dad."

Ava seemed satisfied with the answer but didn't let the conversation drop. "Where's your mom?"

Oliver, always quick on his feet, replied smoothly, "She passed away when we were seven."

There was a brief pause. Ava and Leo both looked down for a second, the weight of the revelation settling in. "Oh... that's sad," Leo mumbled, unsure of what to say next.

Leo, trying to shift the topic to something lighter, perked up again. "Your dad's an engineer for a state company, though. That sounds cool!"

Ethan, always the one with a contrarian view, rolled his eyes. "There's nothing cool about it," he grumbled, stabbing at his lunch with a fork. "He works with fossil fuels, which is such a dumb source of energy that people here actually think is useful."

Ava and Leo looked confused. "What do you mean?" Ava asked. "Fossil fuels are what we use for electricity and stuff, right?"

Realizing his slip, Ethan fumbled for a quick explanation. "Uh... I just mean... there are better options out there, that's all. It's just... outdated, you know?"

Oliver quickly jumped in, trying to steer the conversation away from any more awkward comments. "Ethan's just really into science. He's always thinking about ways to make things better."

Leo shrugged. "Well, your dad's job still sounds pretty cool to me. I bet he's really smart."

Ethan muttered under his breath, still frustrated by the whole situation. "Yeah, too smart for this century..."

Oliver shot him a look, a silent reminder to keep things in check. They were supposed to be fitting in, after all. But Ethan's frustration with their strange predicament was boiling just below the surface, and he wasn't making things easier for either of them.

"Anyway," Oliver said, changing the subject, "do you guys have plans after school?"

Leo's face lit up. "Yeah! We're going to play some baseball at the park. You guys should come!"

Ava nodded enthusiastically. "It'll be fun. We can show you how we do things here in Maine."

Oliver smiled, always the more diplomatic one. "Sure, that sounds great."

Ethan, on the other hand, just sighed, knowing that no matter how much he pretended, he couldn't shake the feeling that they were stuck in the wrong time—literally and figuratively.

As a school day ended, Ethan and Oliver boarded the bus home. The weight of the two D grades in Ethan's backpack felt heavier than usual. His mind raced with thoughts of what Ben would say when he found out.

On the ride home, Oliver turned to Ethan. "You knew this would happen, Ethan. Why did you keep pushing it? Why don't you just try? It's not that hard."

Ethan glared out the window, frustration bubbling beneath his calm facade. "This is stupid," he muttered under his breath. "I don't need to learn any of this. Social studies, geography—none of it matters. It's all outdated, irrelevant to our time."

Oliver sighed, shaking his head. "That's not the point. We're stuck here in 1970, and like it or not, we have to play by the rules of this time. If you keep getting into trouble, Ben's going to be the one paying for it. He's already stressed about making enough money for us to live, let alone trying to get us back home."

Ethan shot a quick, resentful glance at Oliver. "So what? It's not like I asked to be turned into a 10-year-old and sent back to this stupid time. Ben messed everything up."

Oliver looked back, his expression firm but patient. "Maybe so, but blaming him for everything isn't going to change anything. If you don't shape up, Ben's going to have to meet with Mrs. Lewis and the principal, wasting time he could be spending working. And if he can't focus on work, we won't have any money to live—forget about buying that 2kg of gold."

Ethan's face twisted in frustration, but deep down he knew Oliver was right. Every misstep he made dragged them all deeper into this mess. His stubbornness, his refusal to blend in—it wasn't just about him anymore. Ben and Oliver were counting on him to play along, even if it meant swallowing his pride and learning things that felt completely pointless.

As the bus slowed to a stop near their house, Ethan clutched the papers in his hand. Mrs. Lewis wanted Ben to sign them, to acknowledge his failing grades. Ethan felt a growing sense of dread. Ben had been strict lately, and there was no doubt he would be furious when he saw those Ds.

"You don't have to make this harder than it already is," Oliver said, giving Ethan a small nudge. "Just... try next time. It'll make things easier for all of us."

Ethan didn't respond, his mind filled with the inevitable confrontation awaiting him at home. When they stepped off the bus and started walking toward the house, the reality of the situation weighed heavily on him.

As they neared the front door, Ethan glanced over at Oliver. "What if he... what if he's really mad?"

Oliver shrugged slightly, though there was concern in his eyes. "He probably will be. But you can't avoid it forever."

When Ben returned from work, the mood in the small house shifted. He had already heard about Ethan's grades and the upcoming meeting with Mrs. Lewis. His frustration simmered as he thought about Ethan's defiance and refusal to cooperate. Ben had tolerated enough of Ethan's rebellious attitude, and now it was time to put an end to it once and for all.

After dinner, Ben called Ethan into the living room. "We need to talk, Ethan," he said, his voice firm and controlled. Ethan hesitated for a moment, knowing what was coming but not wanting to face it. He slowly walked over, glancing nervously at Oliver, who sat silently at the table, avoiding eye contact.

"You got two Ds in school," Ben began, holding up the papers Mrs. Lewis had sent home. "This is not just about your grades. It's about your defiant attitude. You're refusing to blend in, refusing to adapt. Do you realize what kind of trouble this is going to cause us?"

Ethan didn't respond, staring at the floor instead. He was mumbling something under his breath. Ethan particularly didn't want to show Ben that he felt sorry or that he accepted Ben's authority.

Ben took a deep breath, trying to contain his rising anger. "I've had enough of your attitudes, Ethan. You think you can act out because you don't like the situation? We're all stuck here together, and I'm doing everything I can to get us out. But you—you're making things harder for all of us."

When Ethan still didn't answer, Ben's patience snapped. He grabbed Ethan by the arm and pulled him over with ease. Ethan realized there was no way out and the thought of another spanking from Ben terrified him. His resistance crumbled as tears welled up in his eyes. "Ben—Dad, please... please. I'll do better, I promise," he sobbed.

Ben hesitated, staring down at Ethan, whose face was already streaked with tears. The anger he felt just moments ago gave way to a cold sense of satisfaction. He had gotten through to him. Ethan had finally broken.

"Go to your room," Ben instructed, his tone leaving no room for further discussion. Ethan hurried out of the room, his face red with both embarrassment and defeat.

As he passed Oliver in the hallway, Ethan didn't even glance his way. He knew Oliver would have that infuriating look—half concerned, half smug—like he had seen this all coming. Ethan stormed into their shared room and threw himself face-first onto his bed, wishing he could disappear into the mattress.

Back in the living room, Ben exhaled slowly, pinching the bridge of his nose. He wasn't proud of these moments, but the kid— no, Ethan—left him no choice. Discipline was the only way to keep things from spiraling. "We're all stuck here," Ben thought grimly. "And the only way we make it back is if we work together. No room for whining or half-assing it." Tomorrow, he'd smooth things over with Mrs. Lewis and promise better grades.

Ben knew Ethan could do better—hell, the kid was a genius in his own right. But that brilliance was buried under layers of defiance and frustration. Ben couldn't afford to coddle him. Not now. Not with the stakes so high. Between Ethan's outbursts and the pressure of managing the Florida mining project at work, Ben felt like he was balancing on the edge of a knife. If he failed at either task, the consequences could be catastrophic—for their future and for his own standing at the oil company. He needed Ethan to fall in line, now more than ever.

Meanwhile, Ethan lay sprawled across his bed, arms clutching the pillow like a lifeline. His face was hot with tears, though he wouldn't admit it even to himself. "This is so... goddamn stupid," he thought bitterly. " I should be designing experiments, not solving fifth-grade math problems." The injustice gnawed at him like a wound that wouldn't heal.

Once, Ethan had been a respected young scientist, a rising star in the 24th century. Now, he was reduced to a bratty 10-year-old, scolded for getting bad grades and treated like some clueless kid. And Ben—Ben acted like he was the hero holding it all together, as if Ethan should be grateful for the lectures and punishments. The memory of being dragged over Ben's lap flashed in his mind, and his teeth clenched hard enough to hurt. "If I had my real body... if I was still me, he wouldn't dare."

He squeezed his eyes shut, fists digging into the pillow. "I hate this place. I hate Ben. I hate Oliver. I hate this whole messed-up time."

The fury boiled over, dark and consuming, leaving him trembling with frustration. For a brief moment, he resented everything—Ben's authority, the endless school days, even the experiment that had started it all. It felt like his entire life had been ripped away, leaving him stranded in this childish form with no way out.

And what made it worse—deep down, he knew he wasn't entirely blameless. He had lashed out, made things harder. But knowing that only made the bitterness burn hotter.

He buried his face deeper into the pillow, trying to muffle the storm inside him. But it was no use. The world had shrunk down to this—detentions, scoldings, and waiting for a future that felt more unreachable with every passing day

Chapter 5: Benjamin

The small house was silent except for the hum of the old refrigerator. Ben sat at the dining table, his hands steepled, staring at the two boys— Ethan and Oliver—who were now slouched on the sofa in mismatched clothes. Ethan's t-shirt was crumpled, his shorts too large for his frame, while Oliver leaned back in jeans, trying to appear composed.

Ben let the quiet hang for a moment longer. It was a tool, the way silence could make you uncomfortable enough to speak. But this time, the boys stayed quiet, waiting for him to make the first move.

"You both know the stakes," Ben finally said, his voice measured. "And yet here we are. Ethan, refusing to cooperate. Oliver, doing the bare minimum to keep things running smoothly."

Ethan looked away, scowling, while Oliver gave a small, defensive shrug. Ben felt the weight of their glares, the resentment simmering just beneath the surface. He couldn't blame them—none of them had asked for this. But responsibility didn't care who wanted it.

Ben leaned forward. "Look. I know I've been hard on you, Ethan. But have you stopped to think about what happens if we fail?" His tone sharpened, pressing the point. "Do you want to spend the rest of your life stuck here, in 1970?"

Ethan's defiance faltered briefly, but he stayed silent, crossing his arms over his chest like armor.

Ben shifted his gaze to Oliver, the more measured of the two. "Oliver, I need you to keep him in line. We can't afford mistakes. If anyone finds out who we are or what we've got hidden, we won't just end up in some jail. They'll throw us in a lab. We'll never leave."

Oliver's face hardened. "I know, Ben. I'm trying."

Ben gave a slow nod, satisfied with the response. "Good. Keep trying."

He exhaled, letting some of the tension leave his shoulders. "I have to go to Florida next week for a mining project. Three days. While I'm gone, I'll hire a babysitter."

Ethan sat up abruptly. "A babysitter? Are you kidding me? We're not kids!"

Ben's expression didn't shift. He met Ethan's protest with the coolness of someone who had already made up his mind. "You're not an adult right now, Ethan. And the way you've been acting? You've given me no choice."

Ethan's jaw clenched, the annoyance evident on his face. But Ben's tone left no room for argument.

"I need to be able to trust that nothing will go wrong while I'm gone. This isn't our time, and the rules here are different. If something happens—if people find out I left you two alone—it could unravel everything."

Ethan looked to Oliver, hoping for backup, but Oliver only gave a resigned shrug. He knew Ben's word was final.

Ben stood, signaling the conversation was over. "We're in this together, whether you like it or not. And the only way we get through it is by acting like it."

The boys remained silent as Ben left the room, the weight of his words settling heavily between them.

Back in his room, Ben sat at the edge of the bed, rubbing his temples. His mind churned with thoughts—not just about the boys, but about everything. The gold they needed, the precarious cover story they maintained, the endless balancing act of playing father to two children who weren't really children at all.

This wasn't the life he had signed up for. In the 24th century, he was a scientist, an innovator—someone who solved problems with equations and data, not rules and punishments. Yet here he was, navigating the messy world of emotions and discipline, trying to keep two rebellious minds under control.

He sighed, running a hand through his hair. It wasn't that he enjoyed disciplining Ethan—he hated it. But it had to be done. The lad's stubborn streak would sink them if Ben didn't rein it in. There was too much at stake to let Ethan's behavior spiral unchecked.

The upcoming trip to Florida offered a brief escape, a chance to focus on something other than keeping the boys in line. But even that carried risks. He had already started asking around the office about babysitters, a practice that felt alien to him. In their time, children could be safely left with AI caregivers. But here? Leaving two kids alone would raise questions he couldn't afford to answer.

Ben gritted his teeth, the frustration building inside him. Every decision, every action had consequences—some he could predict, others he couldn't. And if he made one wrong move, the whole charade would collapse.

Two days into his trip, Ben found himself in a dingy bar near the mining site, hoping a few drinks would dull the constant pressure weighing on him. He nursed his whiskey quietly until a man slid onto the stool next to him, ordering his own drink.

"Rough day?" the man asked casually, glancing at Ben.

Ben gave a small, tired smile. "Something like that."

The man introduced himself as Liam, an engineer working on a top-secret project. After a few more drinks, he let slip that he was involved in the Apollo 14 mission.

Ben's interest piqued, though he tried to keep his curiosity in check. Apollo 14 was a key moment in history, and he knew better than to interfere. But as Liam continued to talk—his words slurring slightly from the alcohol—Ben couldn't resist making a few casual observations.

"You know," Ben said, swirling his drink, "your calculations on fuel consumption could be more efficient. If you adjusted the trajectory slightly, you'd reduce the burn time."

Liam frowned, struggling to follow. "You sure?"

Ben shrugged. "Trust me, I've run numbers like that a hundred times."

They talked a little longer before parting ways. To Ben, it was just a harmless conversation—engineers talking shop. He didn't think twice about it.

A week after returning from Florida, Ben sat in front of the television with Ethan and Oliver, the evening news droning in the background. Suddenly, a breaking news report flashed across the screen: Apollo 14 Mission Fails—Critical Error in Fuel Calculations Blamed.

Ben's heart sank. His casual advice to Liam, given over drinks in a Florida bar, had somehow found its way into the mission's calculations. What was supposed to be a minor tweak had caused a catastrophic error.

Oliver was the first to break the silence, his voice filled with disbelief. "Oh. So that's how it happened."

Ethan shook his head, muttering bitterly. "It felt wrong when you said it."

Ben didn't respond. His mind raced, trying to piece together the consequences of his mistake. The failure of Apollo 14 wasn't just a historical anomaly—it was a shift that could ripple through time, altering the course of space exploration and, perhaps, their own future.

He clenched his fists, forcing himself to stay calm. There was no way to undo what had been done. They would have to live with the fallout, just as they had to live with everything else this strange new life threw at them.

Ben exhaled slowly, the weight of his mistake settling heavily on his shoulders. He had wanted a moment of relief, a brief escape from the burden of leadership. But even in his attempt to unwind, he had made a costly error—one that could change the future in ways he couldn't yet comprehend.

Ben leaned back, his mind already shifting to the next challenge. There was no time for regret—not in this life.

They had to survive. No matter the cost.

Chapter 6: Oliver

It was early afternoon on a Saturday, and the house sat in heavy silence. Ethan and Oliver were in their shared room, their quiet war simmering beneath the surface. For months now, their frustrations had been slowly building—both with each other and with the unrelenting pressures of their new life in 1970.

Oliver sat at the desk they both shared, methodically organizing his homework. The outdated assignments made his skin crawl; nothing felt right about regurgitating information he knew was flawed. Ethan sprawled on the bed behind him, kicking the frame in slow, irritating beats.

"Can you stop?" Oliver asked without looking up. His voice was steady, but the tension was there, simmering.

Ethan kicked harder, ignoring the warning. "You're always using the desk. When's it my turn?"

Oliver's jaw tightened. He had grown accustomed to managing Ethan's moods, but today the usual patience felt harder to muster. "You can have it when I'm done," he replied firmly. "Just wait five minutes."

"That's what you said last time," Ethan muttered. He swung himself off the bed and stood behind Oliver, his arms crossed. "You're not in charge, you know."

Oliver exhaled slowly, willing himself to stay calm. "I am in charge, Ethan. At least when it comes to school stuff." He tapped the edge of the desk meaningfully. "Ben said so."

"Yeah, well, Ben's not here right now." Ethan gave Oliver a small shove on the shoulder.

Oliver's restraint snapped. He stood abruptly, shoving Ethan back harder. "Knock it off!"

They grappled, neither truly wanting to hurt the other, but months of bottled-up emotions spilled out. Oliver's frustration wasn't just about Ethan's behavior—it was about everything. The impossible circumstances. The mental gymnastics of balancing an adult mind in a child's body. The gnawing dread that they might never make it back to the future.

"Why can't you just cooperate for once?" Oliver shouted, wrestling Ethan to the floor. "Do you think I like being stuck here any more than you do?"

Ethan squirmed under Oliver's grip, his face flushed with frustration. "You don't get it! You're always acting like you're fine with this—but I know you hate it too!"

The door flew open, and Ben strode in, his tall frame filling the doorway. "What's going on in here?" he demanded, scanning the room.

Oliver scrambled off Ethan, wiping the sweat from his brow. "Nothing," he muttered, breathing heavily. "We were just... sorting things out."

Ethan sat up, rubbing his shoulder, but didn't say anything. His face was a mixture of anger and exhaustion.

Ben narrowed his eyes. "Sort things out without tearing the place apart next time. You've both got five minutes to clean this room or you'll lose your allowance for the week. Got it?"

Both boys mumbled reluctant agreements, and Ben left, closing the door behind him. The room fell into an uneasy silence.

That night, Oliver lay awake in the dark, staring at the ceiling. Ethan snored quietly from the other bed, his earlier anger washed away by sleep. But Oliver's mind buzzed, unable to rest. Ethan's words from earlier—I know you hate it too—echoed in his head.

He did hate it. He hated every part of their life here. But unlike Ethan, he couldn't afford to lash out. Somebody had to keep things running smoothly, even if it meant biting his tongue and playing the role Ben needed him to play.

The frustration boiled under the surface, and for once, Oliver let it sit there. If Ethan wanted to make everything harder, maybe it was time to show him the consequences. A plan began to form in Oliver's mind—not malicious, just... strategic.

Oliver woke early, careful not to wake Ethan. He slipped out of bed and pulled Ethan's homework book from under the desk. With a glance over his shoulder to make sure Ethan was still asleep, Oliver tucked the book under his own bed, pushing it deep out of sight.

It wasn't about getting Ethan into trouble. It was about proving a point: if Ethan kept acting out, he'd suffer for it. And maybe, just maybe, it would make him listen next time.

When Ethan woke, he was already running late for school. As he scrambled to get ready, panic spread across his face.

"Oliver, have you seen my homework book?" Ethan asked frantically, rifling through the mess on his side of the room.

Oliver shook his head, keeping his expression neutral. "Nope. Maybe you left it downstairs?"

Ethan threw a glare his way but didn't argue. He raced out of the room, leaving Oliver to finish getting ready at a leisurely pace.

At school, Oliver watched from a distance as Ethan stammered through an excuse to Mrs. Lewis about his missing homework. She was unimpressed, marking him down for the assignment. Ethan's shoulders slumped in defeat, and Oliver felt a small, cold satisfaction settle in his chest.

The ride home was tense. Ethan sat in the back seat, chewing his lip anxiously. Ben glanced at him through the rearview mirror. "What's wrong?"

"Nothing," Ethan muttered, looking out the window.

Later that afternoon, the home phone rang. Ben picked it up, exchanging a few words before hanging up. He turned to Ethan, his expression firm.

"Mrs. Lewis called. You didn't turn in your homework."

Ethan's face went pale. "I—It was there! I just couldn't find it this morning."

Ben crossed his arms, his expression stern. "We've talked about this before, Ethan. You need to stay on top of your assignments."

Ethan opened his mouth to protest, but Ben cut him off. "You're grounded. Seven days. No TV, no allowance, and no going out except for school."

The weight of the punishment hit Ethan like a brick. He slumped onto the couch, defeated.

From the doorway, Oliver watched, his arms folded. The satisfaction he had felt earlier began to twist into something else— guilt, maybe. He hadn't expected the punishment to be this harsh, and now Ethan looked utterly miserable.

Ben left the room, muttering something about needing to check on dinner, leaving the brothers alone.

Ethan shot a bitter glance at Oliver. "Thanks a lot," he muttered under his breath.

Oliver shrugged, trying to ignore the knot tightening in his chest. "Maybe next time you won't act like such a jerk."

Ethan glared at him but said nothing more. The silence between them stretched, heavy and unresolved.

Chapter 7: The Circle of Care

In the 24th century, common illnesses like the cold or flu had been virtually eradicated, thanks to advanced medical technologies and genetic enhancements. So when Ethan came down with what appeared to be a cold, it was more than just an inconvenience—it was a serious issue for the trio. The idea of sickness felt almost foreign to them, a reminder of how far removed they were from their own time.

It all started on a cold Thursday morning when Ben first heard Ethan coughing. At first, he dismissed it, suspecting that Ethan was exaggerating to avoid school. But as the coughing persisted and a strange green mucus appeared, Ben knew this was no bluff. Ethan's cheeks flushed with fever, his breath labored, and even the warmth of the room couldn't stop the violent shivering that wracked his small frame.

Ben, placing a hand on Ethan's forehead, felt the unmistakable heat of fever. "You're burning up," he muttered, his voice tight with concern.

Oliver, always the skeptic, stepped forward, his usual smugness gone, replaced by a look of genuine worry. "Is he going to be okay?"

Ben frowned, his mind racing. "We need to get him to a hospital." The words felt foreign on his tongue—hospitals in this era were nothing like the advanced medical centers they were used to. They couldn't rely on instant diagnostics or bio-therapy chambers here. It was the 1970s, a small town where medicine wasn't as advanced, and that terrified him. But they had no other choice.

They bundled Ethan into a coat, Ben wrapping a scarf tightly around his neck. The boy seemed so fragile, so unlike his usual self, and Ben felt a pang of guilt. Was it the stress of being stuck here, the constant pressure they were under, that had made him so weak?

The hospital waiting room was a dismal contrast to the sleek, sterile environments of their own time. Here, the harsh fluorescent lights flickered overhead, casting long shadows across the rows of worn-out plastic chairs. A small television buzzed in the corner, delivering mundane local news. Ethan slumped in his seat, his head resting on Ben's shoulder, too exhausted to care about the world around him.

Oliver sat beside them, unusually quiet. For all the teasing and fights, Oliver cared about Ethan—seeing his companion this vulnerable was unsettling. They were both 10 now, but the weight of their adult minds made every hardship seem that much heavier.

Ben stared blankly at the clock on the wall, wishing they could escape. The minutes ticked by agonizingly slowly, and all he could do was hope the doctors wouldn't pry too much into their situation. Finally, they were called into the examination room.

The doctor, a kind-eyed man in his mid-50s, examined Ethan carefully. Ben answered the man's questions, careful to avoid saying anything that could raise suspicion. After what felt like an eternity, the doctor gave his diagnosis: "It's just a cold, but he's run down—probably from stress. Make sure he gets plenty of rest, fluids, and I'll prescribe some antibiotics just in case."

Ben nodded, relieved but still tense. Stress. The word hung in the air like a silent accusation. Ethan had been pushed too hard—by the circumstances, by the fear of being stuck in this time, and by Ben himself. As they left the hospital, the cold air bit at their faces, and Ethan shivered once again.

Back at home, Ben ensured Ethan was tucked into bed, adjusting the blankets to keep him comfortable. He sat by his side, his gaze fixed on the boy's fever-flushed face as Ethan drifted in and out of restless sleep. The soft glow of the bedside lamp highlighted the tension etched into Ben's features, guilt gnawing at him.

"I'm sorry, Ethan," Ben murmured under his breath, his voice barely audible. He wasn't sure if the boy could hear him, but the words were more for himself. The weight of his actions pressed down on him—he'd been too strict, too harsh, and now seeing Ethan this vulnerable made him question everything.

Noticing Ethan's clothes were damp with sweat, Ben decided to change him to avoid adding to his discomfort or risking any lingering germs from the hospital. Carefully, he unbuttoned Ethan's shirt, the fabric clinging slightly to his warm skin. As he reached to remove Ethan's pants and underwear, the boy stirred, his hazy awareness snapping into resistance.

"Hey… what are you doing?" Ethan croaked, his voice weak but tinged with alarm.

Ben paused, his tone gentle but firm. "Your clothes are soaked with sweat. I'm just helping you change into something dry."

"No, I can do it myself," Ethan protested, trying to sit up, his movements sluggish and uncoordinated.

"Ethan, you're sick. Let me help," Ben insisted, but the boy shook his head weakly, coughing as he struggled to resist.

"No!" Ethan cried out, tears welling in his eyes.

Ben sighed, his patience fraying. Frustration bubbled over, and he turned Ethan onto his side, giving him a light smack on his bare bottom. "Stay still," he said, his voice edged with irritation.

Ethan froze, his face crumpling into tears, not from pain but from the indignity of being treated like a child. Sobs wracked his small frame, interspersed with coughs, tears streaming freely.

Realizing his mistake, Ben's heart sank. He immediately pulled Ethan close, gently cradling the boy's head against his chest. "Hey, hey, I'm sorry," he murmured, his voice thick with regret. "I shouldn't have done that. I'm so sorry, Ethan."

Ethan's cries softened into hiccups as Ben held him, stroking his hair in an attempt to soothe him. Once Ethan's breathing steadied, Ben carefully finished changing him into clean, dry clothes, his touch tender now.

"There," Ben said softly, tucking the blankets around Ethan again. "All done. Just rest now, okay?"

Ethan didn't respond, his tears finally subsiding into quiet sniffles as sleep began to claim him once more. Ben stayed by his side, silently vowing to be better, to find a way to make up for the trust he'd shaken

Ben asked Oliver to stay with Ethan, ensuring he wasn't left alone. Then, he grabbed his car keys and headed out to the supermarket to pick up ingredients for a comforting chicken soup.

As Oliver sat beside Ethan on the edge of the bed, guilt pressed heavily on him. The stark reality of what they had become over the past year gnawed at him—two scientists from the 24th century, now trapped in the fragile bodies of 10-year-olds, stranded in the 1970s. But what weighed on him more was how they had lost their camaraderie, their sense of equality. Oliver knew he had contributed to Ethan's suffering. Now, as he looked at his sick, exhausted friend, a deep pang of remorse hit him.

"Everything has been hard for all of us, and I've been unfair to you, Ethan," Oliver whispered, his voice soft but sincere. "I'm sorry. Get well soon… We still need to get back to the 24th century."

Ethan didn't respond right away. He lay there, his pale face turned toward the ceiling, his body limp under the blankets. After a moment, he spoke, his voice hoarse and thick with bitterness. "You and Ben… you got what you wanted. Made me your pet...It's been almost a year, Oliver." He coughed, the sound harsh and ragged. "The gold price barely went down… and we don't even have—" Another coughing fit shook his small frame, cutting him off.

Oliver winced, the sting of truth in Ethan's words. Ethan wasn't wrong—they had fallen into treating him more like a child than a colleague. The weight of their situation had pushed Ethan to his breaking point. But Oliver couldn't let him give up. Not now, not when there was still hope—however faint.

"Okay, okay, Ethan. Don't talk anymore," Oliver said softly, placing a comforting hand on his friend's arm, a rare gesture between them. "Worst case, we grow up again here… and then we'll work together to get the money to buy back the two kilos of gold we sold."

Ethan let out a weak, bitter laugh, shaking his head. "I'd rather die than live like this," he muttered, his voice cracking. "Being spanked like a little kid every other day." His words were an exaggeration— Ben had only disciplined him a few times in the past year, and deep down, Ethan knew he probably deserved it. But the emotional toll weighed heavily on him, and Oliver couldn't deny that. Ethan's pride had always been immense, and being reduced to the helpless role of a child was a bitter pill for him to swallow—something both Ben and Oliver were well aware of.

Chapter 8: Restoring Wholeness

As Ben strolled through the aisles of JadiMart, his thoughts were preoccupied with Ethan's condition. Their time in 1970 had been tougher on the boy than he had anticipated. Ethan was usually resilient, but the stress and constant adjustments were wearing him down. Ben sighed, brushing aside the guilt gnawing at him as he grabbed a pack of chicken breasts, picturing how the soup might bring Ethan some comfort.

He turned toward the vegetable section, scanning for fresh carrots and celery, when a warm, familiar voice called out, "Benjamin?"

Ben looked up and saw Mrs. Richardson, a kindly woman in her mid-60s who lived in the same neighbourhood. Her silver hair was neatly styled, and she wore her usual warm smile that radiated genuine care. She had taken a liking to the trio, often offering advice or a helping hand whenever she could.

"Mrs. Richardson," Ben greeted, his tone polite but slightly distracted. "Good to see you."

"I saw you over here and thought I'd say hello," she said, stepping closer. Her eyes flicked to the ingredients in Ben's basket. "Chicken soup, hmm? Is everything alright?"

Ben hesitated, then nodded. "Ethan's feeling under the weather. Just a cold, but I thought some soup might help him feel better."

"Oh, poor dear," Mrs. Richardson said with concern. "Chicken soup's the best remedy. It always worked wonders for my boys when they were little." She paused thoughtfully, then added, "You know, I've got a bit of time on my hands today. Why don't I come over and help you make it? Two pairs of hands are better than one, and I'd love to lend a hand."

Ben blinked, caught off guard by her offer. He wasn't accustomed to letting anyone into their lives beyond their carefully crafted facade. Still, Mrs. Richardson had always been kind, and her offer sounded genuinely heartfelt. Truthfully, the idea of some help was tempting—he was tired, and having her expertise might make the soup even better for Ethan.

"Are you sure?" Ben asked, raising an eyebrow. "I wouldn't want to trouble you."

"Nonsense," Mrs. Richardson replied with a wave of her hand. "It's no trouble at all. I'd be glad to help."

Ben allowed himself a small, grateful smile. "Alright, if you're sure. I'd appreciate it."

"Perfect," she said warmly. "Let me grab a few things too, and I'll follow you home."

Ben nodded, feeling a sense of relief he hadn't expected. Maybe, just this once, letting someone else in wasn't such a bad idea.

Back at home, Ethan lay in bed, staring at the ceiling. His body felt weak, the lingering effects of the cold and his emotional exhaustion keeping him from feeling anything but tired. As his thoughts wandered, he found himself once again contemplating the bizarre, almost absurd situation they were in—stranded in 1970s, stuck in these small, underdeveloped bodies.

He glanced down at himself, lifting the blanket and his pajamas slightly to check if anything had changed. But of course, nothing had. He knew boys didn't grow that fast at this age, and even though they were from the 24th century, human anatomy had stayed the same over the centuries. His body was still that of a preteen boy, unchanged and frustratingly small.

A wave of helplessness washed over him. He hated it. All of it. He hated being treated like a kid, being scolded and spanked by Ben, and now feeling like he had no control over his life. Worse yet, Oliver had been no better. They used to be equals—colleagues, friends. But now, Oliver seemed to revel in his role as the "favorite son."

Ethan sighed and closed his eyes, trying to push the thoughts away, but they gnawed at him, just like everything else had for the past year.

When Ben and Mrs. Richardson arrived home, she wasted no time taking charge in the kitchen. With practiced ease, she chopped vegetables, stirred the pot, and moved about as though she'd been cooking in that kitchen for years. Ben admired her efficiency but couldn't keep his mind from drifting to Ethan upstairs. The weight of their situation pressed heavily on him. How much longer could they keep up this charade? How much more could his "sons" endure before everything fell apart?

Mrs. Richardson hummed softly as she worked, her presence exuding a calming warmth. At one point, she glanced over at Ben, who stood leaning against the counter, lost in his thoughts. "You know," she began kindly, "you're doing a wonderful job, Benjamin. It's clear how much you care about those boys."

Ben stiffened slightly at her words, an uncomfortable pang running through him. Hearing praise for a role he was only pretending to fill felt strange. But he managed a polite smile and nodded. "Thank you, Mrs. Richardson. I just do my best."

As the soup began to simmer, Mrs. Richardson wiped her hands on a dish towel and turned to face him. "Would you like me to go up and check on Ethan? He might like some company while you take a moment to rest."

Ben hesitated, his stomach twisting at the thought. Mrs. Richardson had been nothing but kind and helpful, but the idea of her getting too close made him uneasy. They couldn't afford for anyone to become too attached, or to notice things that didn't quite add up. Before he could answer, a faint cough from upstairs caught his attention.

"No, I'll go check on him," Ben said firmly, though his tone remained appreciative. "You've done more than enough with the soup."

Mrs. Richardson nodded, her expression warm but understanding. "Alright, dear. I'll keep an eye on the stove. Just let me know if you need anything."

Ben climbed the stairs, his thoughts weighed down by worry. When he opened the door to the boys' room, he found Oliver sitting next to Ethan's bed, flipping through a children's magazine. Oliver glanced up briefly, his expression neutral but concerned.

Ethan lay in bed, his face pale and his eyes unfocused, staring off into the distance. Ben walked over quietly and sat on the edge of the bed, his hand gently pressing against Ethan's forehead to check his temperature. The warmth radiating from the boy's skin only deepened Ben's concern. "How are you feeling?" Ben asked softly.

Ethan turned his head slightly, his voice hoarse and tinged with quiet bitterness. "Still here... so, the same."

Ben sighed deeply, his heart aching for the boy who had once been so full of life and determination. "I know this isn't easy, Ethan. For any of us. I'm doing everything I can to make it better."

Ethan closed his eyes, his small body trembling slightly. "You can't make it better, Ben. We're stuck here... and I'm stuck like this." He sniffled, his tears carrying more than just the weight of his cold.

Ben placed a comforting hand on Ethan's arm, a deep sadness welling up in his chest. "I know how hard this is for you. I promise I'll do better. We'll figure this out, Ethan. We'll find a way back."

Ethan's lip trembled as he wiped his eyes with the back of his hand. "I just don't want to be treated like a little kid anymore. I can't stand it."

Ben nodded, his voice steady but gentle. "I hear you, and I'll do my best to make things better. But for now, you need to rest and get well. Can you do that for me?"

Downstairs, the comforting aroma of Mrs. Richardson's chicken soup filled the house, bringing a fleeting sense of warmth and normalcy amid the storm that lingered in their lives.

Ben carefully lifted Ethan into his arms, mindful of how fragile the boy felt. "Come on, buddy," he said softly, trying to sound reassuring. He glanced at Oliver and gave a small nod. "Let's head downstairs. Mrs. Richardson has cooked some amazing chicken soup for us."

Chapter 9: Before It All Began

Before everything went wrong, before the experiment and the trip to 1970, Ethan's life had been simple yet fulfilling in the 24th century

Ethan woke to the soft, rhythmic hum of his apartment's automated systems coming to life. The morning sun filtered through the smart-glass window, which adjusted its opacity to let in just enough light to gently nudge him awake. A chime from his AI assistant, Elo, filled the air.

"Good morning, Ethan. It's 7:30 AM. Your schedule includes work at 9:00 AM and a team presentation at 2:00 PM. Shall I prepare your usual breakfast smoothie?"

Ethan groaned, sitting up in his simple yet sleek one-bedroom apartment. "Skip the smoothie today, Elo. Just coffee. Extra strong."

He got ready quickly, his routine efficient but not rushed. His blonde hair, still slightly damp from the shower, fell in an effortlessly tousled style. Ethan was a picture of youthful charm—his sharp blue eyes and easygoing smile made him instantly likable. Despite his brilliance, he carried himself without arrogance, always approachable and grounded.

Grabbing a cup of freshly brewed coffee from the dispenser, Ethan slung his work bag over his shoulder and headed out the door.

Ethan opted for public transportation, preferring it over the personal grav-rides that most people used. He enjoyed the energy of the city—the bustling crowd, the hum of distant drones, and the sight of kids playing with hovering toys in the park.

Halfway to the transit station, Ethan noticed an elderly woman standing near a curb, visibly upset. Her face was lined with worry as she fumbled with a small, sleek device in her hands. It looked like an outdated device something most people in the 24th century rarely used anymore.

Ethan approached her with a kind smile. "Ma'am, is everything alright? Do you need some help?"

The woman looked up, relief washing over her face. "Oh, thank goodness! My grandson's at the medical center, and I can't figure out how to access the pass for visitors. They won't let me in without it!"

Ethan gently took the device from her hands, his fingers deftly navigating the outdated interface. Within moments, he'd not only located the pass but also updated her device's software to ensure it wouldn't glitch again.

"There you go," he said warmly, handing it back to her. "You're all set now. I hope your grandson feels better soon."

The woman's eyes filled with gratitude. "Thank you, young man. You're a lifesaver."

Ethan waved off the thanks with a modest shrug. "Just doing what I can. Take care."

By the time Ethan boarded the magnetized public transit train and reached the laboratory complex he was nearly twenty minutes late. He hurried through the sleek halls, his footsteps echoing as he made his way to his team's workspace.

Ben was already there, standing beside Oliver as they reviewed a holographic energy diagram projected in mid-air. Ben's tall frame and commanding presence made him an intimidating figure, even when he wasn't annoyed.

"Ethan," Ben said, glancing at his wristband, which displayed the time. "You're late. Again."

Ethan froze, knowing what was coming.

"You know," Ben continued, crossing his arms, "this project is important. If you want to be taken seriously here, you need to show up on time. Oliver and I can't always pick up the slack."

Oliver shot Ethan a knowing look, his expression half-apologetic but also amused. "To be fair, Ben, he's late every other day, not every day."

Ethan held up his hands in mock surrender, his usual charm kicking in. "Alright, alright. I get it. I'll be better about it." He didn't explain why he was late—he didn't need to. Ethan wasn't one to brag about helping others; for him, it was just the right thing to do.

Ben shook his head but let it go. "Fine. Just get to work. We've got a lot to get through before the presentation this afternoon."

Settling into his station, Ethan focused on the day's task: analyzing energy patterns from the latest trials for their project, their research into temporal mechanics. The work was complex but fascinating, and Ethan's sharp mind thrived on solving the puzzles it presented.

As he worked, he bantered with Oliver, who had a knack for turning any situation into a joke. Ethan appreciated the light heartedness, especially since Ben often carried the weight of responsibility with a no-nonsense attitude.

Despite the occasional lecture, Ethan respected Ben immensely. He saw the older scientist as a mentor, even if their personalities often clashed. Ben's determination and leadership balanced Ethan's easy-going nature, while Oliver added a touch of mischief that kept things lively.

As the sun dipped below the horizon, Ethan took the transit train back home. The day had been long, but he felt a quiet satisfaction in knowing he'd done his best—not just in the lab, but in making a difference, however small, outside of it.

Elo greeted him as he walked into his apartment. "Welcome back, Ethan. Would you like me to prepare your evening tea?"

"Yeah, that'd be great," Ethan replied, kicking off his shoes and collapsing onto the couch.

As he sipped his tea, his mind drifted to the elderly woman he'd helped that morning. He smiled, knowing she'd probably gotten to see her grandson without any more trouble. It wasn't much, but moments like that reminded him why he wanted to push the boundaries of science—to make life better for people, one step at a time.

Ethan didn't think of himself as a hero. He was just a young man with a sharp mind, a kind heart, and a quiet determination to leave the world a little better than he found it.

Tomorrow, he'd do it all over again.

The streets of New Toronto buzzed with energy on a Saturday morning. Towering holographic advertisements flickered in the sunlight, broadcasting sleek announcements about lunar tourism and energy breakthroughs. But in the shadow of these glowing marvels, a mass of protestors gathered, chanting slogans that echoed through the city square.

Among the crowd was Oliver, his sharp blue eyes locked on the stage where a charismatic speaker urged resistance against the North American Union's decision to deploy troops and heavy weaponry to the moon. The move, according to the government, was to secure valuable mining territories, but to Oliver—and many others—it felt like a reckless provocation against the Asian Confederation, the world's other superpower.

"Down with warmongers!" shouted Oliver, his voice joining the chorus around him.

His friends from university huddled nearby, clutching handmade signs that displayed bold slogans: "Save the Moon, Save Us

All!" and "War is Not the Answer!" Oliver felt the fire of his convictions burn bright. He wasn't just a scientist—he was a citizen of the Earth, and he refused to stay silent in the face of such a dangerous decision.

But as the hours passed, the peaceful demonstration began to shift. The government's response came swiftly: drones hovered overhead, projecting warnings to disperse. Officers in high-tech riot suits lined the periphery, armed with electromagnetic crowd control devices. When some protestors tried to push through the barricades, chaos erupted.

Tear gas canisters were launched into the crowd, their silvery vapor quickly spreading. A piercing hum of ultrasonic sound waves forced protestors to cover their ears, and within minutes, what began as a peaceful protest turned into a scene of panic.

Oliver tried to help an elderly man who had fallen to the ground, shielding him from the crush of bodies. "Hold on, sir! I've got you!" he said, guiding the man to a nearby bench. But before he could get away, Oliver felt a firm grip on his arm.

"You're under arrest for participating in unlawful assembly," the officer said, his voice cold and robotic through the helmet.

"What? I was helping someone!" Oliver protested, but his words fell on deaf ears. Moments later, he found himself in the back of a police van, his hands secured in shimmering magnetic restraints.

Hours later, at precisely 7:03 PM, Ethan's holo-screen buzzed to life. He was sprawled on his couch in his modest one-bedroom apartment, engrossed in a retro-style video game that featured pixelated spaceships and alien invaders.

The call came through his wrist comm. It was Oliver.

"Hey, Eth, I, uh… need a favor," Oliver began, his voice sheepish yet resigned.

Ethan immediately sat up. "What happened?"

"I got arrested at the protest."

Ethan groaned, rubbing his temples. "Seriously? I told you those protests were getting out of hand!"

"Yeah, yeah, you can lecture me later. Can you come bail me out?" Oliver's tone was laced with urgency.

"Alright, give me 20 minutes." Ethan closed the game and grabbed his jacket, muttering under his breath about Oliver's knack for getting into trouble.

At the police station, Ethan approached the bail desk, where a disinterested clerk glanced up from her terminal.

"Name of the detainee?" she asked.

"Oliver Kane," Ethan replied, swiping his ID chip over the scanner.

The bail amount wasn't outrageous, but when the system ran a quick credit check, the clerk's expression turned sour. "Sorry, Mr. Trent. Your credit rating is too low to post bail."

Ethan clenched his jaw. "What? I have the money right here!"

"Doesn't matter," the clerk said flatly. "Policy requires a minimum credit threshold for bail postings."

Frustrated, Ethan stepped away from the counter and tapped his comm to call the only other person who could help.

When Ben arrived, his tall, imposing figure immediately drew attention. He was dressed in his usual clean-cut style, exuding an air of quiet authority.

"I got your message," Ben said, his tone calm but firm. "Let's get him out of here."

The bail process was swift once Ben took charge. Within minutes, Oliver emerged from the holding area, looking disheveled but unapologetic.

"Well, if it isn't my knight in shining armor," Oliver quipped, giving Ben a tired grin.

Ben didn't smile. "Let's go. We'll talk in the car."

The ride home was tense. Ethan sat in the passenger seat, fuming silently, while Oliver lounged in the back, staring out the window.

"You know, this could have been avoided if you'd just stayed out of trouble," Ben finally said, his voice carrying a hint of exasperation.

Oliver shrugged. "Someone has to stand up for what's right."

"And someone has to clean up your messes," Ethan added, shooting him a pointed look.

"Alright, I get it. Thanks for bailing me out, okay?" Oliver muttered, sinking deeper into his seat

But despite the tension, there was an unspoken bond between the three of them—a shared understanding that, no matter what, they'd always have each other's backs.

For now, though, the weight of the future—and the looming conflict on the moon—hung heavy over them all.

Chapter 10: Melting Moments

The Maine sun was setting outside their modest home, casting long shadows across the living room. It was 1971, and the trio was still stranded in the past, struggling to maintain the roles they had created for themselves. For Ben, playing the part of a strict father wasn't easy—especially when the "children" he was disciplining were, in reality, his fellow scientists from the 24th century.

The small living room was thick with tension. Ben sat on the sofa, his expression calm but serious, the kind of look that made Oliver's stomach churn. Oliver stood in front of him, his arms hanging at his sides, his face pale. He shifted nervously on his feet, glancing once at Ethan, who sat nearby, looking both anxious and angry.

While cleaning the boys' room, Ben found Ethan's homework tucked under Oliver's bed. That's when he uncovered the truth: Oliver had deliberately hidden Ethan's homework. As a result, Ethan had been marked down at school. Now that Ben knew what had happened, he wasn't about to let the incident slide.

"Oliver," Ben began, his voice low and firm, "you know better than this. Hiding Ethan's homework wasn't a joke. It was mean, and it caused real consequences. Do you understand how disappointing this is?"

Oliver's eyes flickered with guilt. He bit his lip, nodding quickly. "I didn't mean for it to go that far," he mumbled.

"That's not the point," Ben said, leaning forward, his tall frame looming over the nervous boy. "The point is, you knew it was wrong, and you did it anyway. And it wasn't just a harmless prank. You embarrassed Ethan in front of his teacher and made him look irresponsible."

Oliver's face turned red as he swallowed hard. "I'm sorry," he said softly, his voice breaking.

"Sorry doesn't cut it this time," Ben said, his tone sharpening. "You have to take responsibility for your actions."

Oliver's breathing quickened as Ben reached out and took him by the arm, turning him around with ease. "What are you—?" Oliver stammered, his voice rising in panic.

Ben swatted Oliver's bottom hard, once, then twice, his large hand making a sharp sound in the quiet room. Oliver gasped, trying to pull himself away. "Please, ouch—Ben!"

Ethan sprang to his feet, stepping between them and holding out his arms as if to shield Oliver. "Ben, stop! It's okay. You don't need to punish Oliver for this. It happened weeks ago!"

Ben straightened, meeting Ethan's pleading gaze. He sighed heavily, rubbing the bridge of his nose. "Fine," he said at last, his voice calmer but still stern. "But Oliver is not getting off easily just because you spoke up for him."

Oliver sniffled, his eyes wide with a mix of fear and relief. He stood awkwardly, rubbing his sore bottom as he looked from Ben to Ethan, unsure of what to say.

"No allowance for you next week, Oliver," Ben declared, his tone final. "And no TV either."

Oliver opened his mouth to protest but quickly closed it, lowering his head. "Yes, sir," he muttered.

Ethan, still standing protectively in front of Oliver, crossed his arms. "Ben, he's already sorry. Do you have to take away everything?"

Ben shot Ethan a sharp look. "I'm being fair. Actions have consequences, Ethan, and Oliver needs to learn that. You don't get to negotiate his punishment."

Ethan hesitated but sat back down with a grumble, glaring at the floor.

Ben turned his attention back to Oliver, his voice softening slightly. "I know you're sorry, Oliver, but you have to do better. You're smart and capable, but pranks like this are beneath you. And more importantly, we need to work together. If one of us screws up, it affects all of us. Understand?"

Oliver nodded quickly, his voice barely above a whisper. "Yes, sir."

"Good. Now, both of you, go upstairs and get ready for bed. Tomorrow's a new day, and I expect you both to do better."

The two boys shuffled off quietly, with Oliver throwing a glance back at Ethan that said more than words could: Thanks for standing up for me.

As the boys disappeared up the stairs, Ben let out a long sigh, sinking back into the sofa. Playing the role of their father was exhausting, especially when it came to moments like this.

The sound of the old cuckoo clock on the wall ticked faintly in the background as Ben sat alone in the quiet living room, staring at the worn carpet. It was moments like these—late evenings in their 1970s home—that his thoughts wandered back to the 24th century. It had been three years since he'd met Ethan and Oliver, though it felt like a lifetime ago.

He leaned back on the sofa, his gaze unfocused as memories flooded in. Back then, Ben had been leading significant projects under the Electropolis City Science R&D Department. It wasn't glamorous, but it was groundbreaking work, and he needed the brightest minds to join his team.

The hiring process had been grueling. Over two hundred applicants applied for just two positions. Among them were Ethan and Oliver—young geniuses fresh out of university at 18 and 19, their resumes crammed with achievements. Yet Ben had learned long ago not to trust paper credentials alone. Talent meant nothing without drive, creativity, and adaptability.

He remembered the day of their interviews vividly.

Oliver had walked in first, confidently shaking Ben's hand. His tall, lean frame and blue eyes hinted at an intensity that matched his application. He spoke with clarity and precision, almost too rehearsed.

"What makes you think you're ready for this position?" Ben had asked, studying him closely.

Oliver didn't flinch. "Because I'm not afraid to challenge myself—or you, sir. I've read your publications. I have ideas to improve your energy lattice prototype. If you give me the chance, I'll prove it."

Ben had been intrigued by Oliver's confidence, but it was tempered with a hint of arrogance. Still, arrogance could be useful if it was backed by results.

Next came Ethan.

Ethan's youthful energy was almost overwhelming as he entered the room. Blonde-haired and slightly shorter than Oliver, he carried a quiet charm. He looked around the room with curiosity before sitting down, already scanning the notes on Ben's desk.

"You're the youngest candidate here," Ben noted, his tone testing. "Why should I hire you over someone with more experience?"

Ethan didn't hesitate. "Because I solve problems. Experience isn't always the answer—sometimes, a fresh perspective is what's needed. Also, I've already built models for the quantum stabilizer project you're working on. I'd be happy to show you the simulations."

Ben had raised an eyebrow. "You ran simulations on a classified project you have no clearance for?"

Ethan had grinned sheepishly. "Yes... but only because your security protocols were outdated. I can help with that too."

That moment had sealed it for Ben. Ethan's ingenuity and fearless curiosity were the perfect complement to Oliver's drive and structured intellect. By the end of the day, he knew these two weren't just employees; they were partners.

Now, sitting in the dimly lit 1970s living room, Ben let out a weary sigh. They weren't his employees anymore. They were his "sons." They called him "Dad" in public, went to school, and relied on him for protection and guidance—roles he never imagined taking on. He'd brought them into this situation, their brilliant futures stolen by the accident that stranded them in this primitive era.

His thoughts darkened. He'd seen something special in them back then, and he'd been right. They were brilliant and resilient, but this situation was testing even their limits.

"Did I fail them?" Ben muttered to himself, running a hand through his hair. He'd handpicked them, mentored them, and now, he couldn't help but feel responsible for dragging them into this mess.

Looking at the faint glow of the kitchen light, he resolved to protect them as best as he could, even if it meant playing the part of a father in this strange, archaic world. They had trusted him then—and despite the difficulties, they still trusted him now. He had to find a way to make things right.

Because they weren't just his colleagues or his sidekicks anymore. They were his family.

Chapter 11: Lucas

One night, Oliver woke up with a scream that echoed through the small house. His body trembled, drenched in sweat, his heart pounding as if it would burst out of his chest. Ben and Ethan, both startled awake, rushed to Oliver's bed

Oliver sat up, his eyes wide with fear. He was pale, and the bedsheets beneath him were damp. He barely registered their presence as he stared off into space, his breathing shallow and rapid.

"Oliver, hey, you're okay," Ben said gently, sitting on the edge of the bed. Ethan stood nearby, looking worried but unsure of what to do.

"It... it was another nightmare," Oliver whispered, his voice trembling and hoarse. "But it wasn't here. It was in the future—our time. I was at a protest, and then suddenly... a huge explosion. The shockwaves—massive—they destroyed everything, killed everyone."

Ben's brows furrowed, his concern deepening. He had noticed Oliver's nightmares becoming more frequent over the past week. They were more than just bad dreams; Oliver seemed genuinely haunted by them. He had even started wetting the bed, something Ben hadn't seen since they arrived.

Ben exchanged a glance with Ethan, who looked just as uneasy. "You've been having these nightmares a lot lately, haven't you?" Ben asked, trying to keep his voice steady.

Oliver nodded, his hands trembling as he wiped his face. "Every—night now. And it's always the same... the 24th century, everything's destroyed. It's like I'm reliving it. I wake up, and I feel... I feel like it's real, like it's already happened."

Ethan spoke up softly. "It's probably just stress from everything we've been through. Time travel, getting stuck here, and... well, being turned into a 10-year-old."

Oliver gave a weak smile but said nothing. The haunted look in his eyes remained.

Ben stood, his mind racing. He couldn't shake the feeling that something was wrong, that Oliver's nightmares might be more than just stress. "Stay here. I'm going to ask Lucas about this."

Ethan raised an eyebrow. "Lucas? You really think the AI module in the time machine can help?"

"It's worth a try. Maybe these nightmares are a side effect of Rezulix," Ben said as he left the room and headed to the time machine.

Inside the sleek, metallic structure of the machine, Ben activated the AI module of the time machine. The interface lit up, and moments later, the calm, synthesized voice of the AI, Lucas, echoed through the small space.

"Good evening, Benjamin. How may I assist you?" Lucas asked, his voice soothing but mechanical.

Ben wasted no time. "Lucas, I need you to analyze something. Oliver's been experiencing recurring nightmares about the 24th century—death, destruction, catastrophic events. He's also been wetting the bed, which isn't normal. I'm wondering if these could be side effects of the Rezulix he took."

Lucas remained silent for a few moments as it processed the request, accessing the vast database of medical and pharmaceutical records from the 24th century. The AI had access to every known study and report regarding Rezulix, its effects, and any related cases.

After a few seconds, Lucas spoke. "Based on my analysis, there are no documented side effects of Rezulix related to nightmares or bed-wetting. The drug's primary function is to reverse physical aging, with minimal neurological interference. Oliver's symptoms are atypical and not aligned with known Rezulix effects."

Ben frowned, feeling both relieved and frustrated. "So, you're saying this isn't because of the drug?"

"Correct," Lucas replied.

Lucas, the AI bot, continued, "Ben, I should inform you that the time machine's components have undergone subtle modifications since you arrived in this era. The most significant changes took place shortly after the failure of Apollo 14. And I know about Apollo 14's failure because I have access to your search history on the computer."

Ben's eyes snapped to the AI bot. "Changes? What kind of changes? And why now?" His mind raced. The Apollo 14 mission—

he had casually spoken with one of the engineers on the project a few months ago, offering what he thought were harmless, superficial improvements. It seemed benign at the time, just blending in with the engineers and being helpful. The idea that such a small conversation could ripple into the present—into the machine itself—was unsettling.

"Adjustments to my core components," Lucas continued, "in terms of both hardware and temporal dynamics. The fabric of the time machine has subtly altered. This suggests that there has been some form of external interference, potentially triggered by changes in the timeline. My database confirms Apollo 14 was initially a success. Its failure is an anomaly."

Ben stood up, the unease growing in his chest. "An anomaly… So, you're saying the timeline has shifted since we arrived. And it's affecting the machine itself?"

"Precisely, Ben. Temporal shifts in the external environment appear to influence my configuration," Lucas explained. "Although I was designed to withstand small fluctuations in history, significant alterations—such as the failure of Apollo 14—seem to be having unpredictable effects on both myself and, potentially, your companions."

Ben clenched his fists, the reality dawning on him. "So, it's not just Rezulix. It's the timeline itself—the failure of Apollo 14, the changes in the space race... all of it is affecting us, and the machine. But how?"

Lucas's voice remained neutral. "It is possible that the mere act of being present, and interacting with key individuals, has altered the course of events in ways that are not immediately apparent. Your suggestion to an Apollo engineer could have created a chain reaction of small changes that are now rippling through time, affecting both the machine and your biology. Temporal feedback loops can manifest in unpredictable ways."

Ben's thoughts raced. "So, what now? If the timeline is unstable, and the machine is changing... are we stuck here?"

Lucas paused for a moment before replying, "I cannot predict the full extent of the changes without further data. However, it is crucial to ensure that any future interactions with key historical figures are minimized. Your presence in this timeline may continue to generate unintended consequences."

Ben sighed, running a hand through his hair. "We need to get out of here, and soon. But if the machine is changing—if you are changing—how do we even know it'll work when we're ready to go back?"

Lucas responded, "I am continuously self-monitoring for further alterations. The current modifications are minor and do not appear to inhibit my primary functions. However, I recommend expediting your efforts to gather the necessary resources for departure."

Ben's stomach sank. They were in a race against time—against an unpredictable timeline. And with every passing day, the small shifts in reality could be doing more than they realized.

Looking around the tent-like structure, Ben whispered, "What have we done?"

The realization that their actions—even those seemingly insignificant—were shaping the world around them struck him hard. And worse, the growing fear that they might not be able to control what was happening loomed large.

For now, he would keep this to himself. Oliver needed rest. Ethan needed hope. And he? He needed a plan.

"Lucas," Ben said, standing tall once more, "keep monitoring everything. Let me know immediately if you notice anything else changing."

"Understood, Ben."

With that, Ben stepped out of the machine, the weight of the unknown heavy on his shoulders. The world they had inadvertently reshaped continued on outside, unaware of the fragile line it now walked.

They were more than trapped in time—they were trapped in consequences.

The day was warm as Ethan and Oliver returned home from school, their feet dragging slightly from the weight of the monotonous routine. Even after a year in this timeline, the reality of being children in 1971 was a bitter pill for both of them. After setting their school bags down, the two headed straight for the storage room—the hidden refuge where the time machine sat, glinting like a secret that didn't quite belong to this century.

As the door to the time machine opened, a soft hum echoed, and the AI known as Lucas materialized on the screen in the center of the console.

Oliver leaned closer to the terminal. "We should've done this earlier," he said, a grin spreading across his face. "Lucas can help us with our homework. Easy peasy."

Ethan smirked, folding his arms. "Right. We've got this super-advanced AI from our time. Homework should be a joke."

But just as Oliver began to tap commands on the console, Lucas's calm, emotionless voice interrupted their plan. "This would constitute cheating, Oliver," Lucas intoned. "I cannot assist you with such tasks. Furthermore, Benjamin has instructed me explicitly not to help you with school duties. The answers can be found in your textbooks."

Ethan threw his arms up in frustration. "What the heck, Lucas? Come on, you're supposed to be on our side!" His voice had that edge of childlike irritation that sometimes slipped through, a byproduct of his 10-year-old body.

Oliver, ever the more rational of the two, tried a different angle. "Lucas, think about it. Ben's just like us—he's our colleague. We're not actually kids, you know. We're scientists. You don't need to follow Ben's orders like that."

Lucas's response came in its usual composed tone. "Benjamin is now your legal guardian, Oliver. I assisted him in creating your identification documents and, per his explicit instructions, I am prohibited from helping you with your schoolwork."

Ethan clenched his fists, his frustration bubbling over. "Legal guardian... great. Just what we needed. So, now you're Ben's little watchdog, huh? Monitoring us like kids?"

There was a brief pause before Lucas replied. "Benjamin has also asked me to monitor you both when he is not home."

Oliver blinked. "Wait, what? Monitor us? How? You're stuck in this room all the time."

Lucas continued, unfazed by the rising tension in Ethan's voice. "Benjamin installed a series of cameras around the house. I assisted him by 3D printing those cameras. They provide me with visual and auditory access to your activities."

Ethan groaned, pacing back and forth in front of the console. "Are you kidding me? So Ben's been spying on us this whole time? He promised he wouldn't treat me like a kid! This is ridiculous!" His face was flushed with anger, the frustration of being trapped in this childlike body, powerless in so many ways, overwhelming him once again.

Oliver, though calmer, was just as irritated. He crossed his arms and looked up at the AI. "Lucas, if you're so helpful, why don't you at least print me a smartwatch? I mean, we're stuck in the 70s—I could use something that actually tells time accurately."

Lucas's voice was resolute. "I am unable to fulfill that request, Oliver. The 3D printer functions are restricted to Benjamin's authorization only. He has disabled any non-essential fabrications."

Ethan punched the air in exasperation. "Argh! What's the point of having an AI from the 24th century if we can't use it?"

Oliver sighed, rubbing the back of his neck. "Lucas, we're not actually kids, you know that. We've been reduced to playing this charade, acting like twins for the people here. But we're scientists. We shouldn't have to be bound by these silly rules."

Lucas responded without missing a beat. "While I am aware of your true identities as scientists, the situation you are currently in requires that you adhere to the limitations imposed by your present reality. Benjamin's decisions regarding your roles as 'twins' are essential to maintaining your cover. Furthermore, ensuring your safety and well-being in this era is my primary directive."

Ethan, still simmering, muttered under his breath, "Safety, yeah right. What about our mental well-being? I didn't sign up to be treated like a little kid for this long."

Oliver shot him a look, silently telling him to cool it. "Lucas, you're supposed to be this highly advanced AI. Can't you at least offer us some advice on how to get through this without... I don't know... losing our minds?"

Lucas, ever pragmatic, replied, "My database contains vast knowledge on human psychology and adaptation to challenging circumstances. I suggest focusing on your studies and integrating yourselves into your current environment to minimize stress and increase acceptance of your temporary situation. The sooner you are able to adapt, the smoother your experience will be."

Ethan gave a derisive laugh. "Right, 'temporary.' That's what this is. Sure doesn't feel temporary when you're getting spanked for not doing homework."

Oliver sighed again, tugging at his shirt. "I guess it's no use arguing. We're stuck playing by Ben's rules... for now."

They both stood there for a moment in silence, the glow of the time machine's interface casting soft shadows around the small, metallic room. The frustrations of their predicament were clear— trapped in the bodies of children, bound by a reality that constantly reminded them of their helplessness. Yet, there was no escaping the fact that, for now, they had to navigate this timeline with caution.

Ethan gave one final look at Lucas. "Fine. But don't expect us to thank you for this... 'help,' Lucas."

Lucas's voice was, as always, steady. "I do not require your gratitude, Ethan. I am here to serve."

The morning light filtered through the kitchen windows as Ben, Ethan, and Oliver sat at the dining table. Ben casually glanced at his wrist, adjusting what appeared to be a normal 1970s watch. But Oliver noticed the subtle differences—the glow beneath the surface, the faint flicker of a digital interface hidden behind the antique design.

"Hey!" Oliver exclaimed, narrowing his eyes at Ben's wrist. "How can you get a smartwatch from Lucas, but we can't?"

Ben didn't look up, calmly spreading butter on his toast. "I need it to help with my work, Oliver," he replied with a light chuckle. "You know, that thing I do every day? The job? In case you've forgotten, I'm the one going to work, keeping us afloat."

Ethan shot him a sharp look. "You promised me when I was sick that you'd stop treating me like a kid. And now you've put all these restrictions on Lucas. That time machine is a product of all of us, Ben!"

Ben's eyes flickered with annoyance, and he set down his knife. "There's nothing to argue about here. And speaking of Lucas, didn't he mention you two tried to ask him to do your homework? Imagine what would happen if Mrs. Lewis saw some perfect, way too intelligent answers in a 10-year-old's homework submission? That's exactly the kind of thing that gets us noticed, Ethan."

Oliver leaned forward, determined not to let the conversation end. "I still want a smartwatch! Or at least tell Lucas to print out a video game console. I know he has video games in his database."

Before Ben could respond, Lucas's calm voice came from a nearby camera in the kitchen. "Actually, Oliver, I am capable of printing a video game console, but we do not have the copyright licenses from the 24th century to produce such material."

Ethan let out an exasperated groan. "Bypass it, Lucas! For god's sake, who's going to care about some copyright?"

Lucas paused. "If Benjamin allows me."

Ben immediately cut in, raising his voice just enough to assert his authority. "No, Lucas. We're not printing out anything just to play around with. What happens if your classmates or Mrs. Richardson come over and see those devices? Smartwatches, video games, anything that doesn't belong here—it'll draw attention we don't need. And you guys can't bring something like a smartwatch to school, people would definitely notice."

Ethan sat back, crossing his arms, clearly frustrated. "It's not fair, Ben. You get to use all this advanced tech, while we're stuck playing along with this charade, trying to blend in with the 1970s."

Oliver nodded in agreement. "Yeah, we're the ones pretending to be twins, going to school, dealing with the kids, the teachers—everything. And what do we get? No smartwatches, no games, just textbooks and homework."

Ben's gaze softened, but his voice remained firm. "Look, I get that this is tough. It's not fair, I know. But the more you stick to the plan and avoid drawing attention, the sooner we'll get through this. I need to keep control of the situation—for all our sakes. This is about survival, not convenience."

Ethan clenched his jaw, staring at his plate, but he didn't argue further. He knew deep down that Ben was right, but it didn't make the restrictions any easier to swallow. Oliver, too, seemed to deflate, his earlier enthusiasm for a video game console fading as the reality of their situation settled in once again.

Lucas's voice broke the silence. "Benjamin is correct. Maintaining your cover and avoiding detection is paramount to your continued existence in this timeline. Introducing advanced technology, even something as seemingly harmless as a smartwatch, could have unforeseen consequences."

Ethan huffed, muttering under his breath, "Everything has unforeseen consequences with you, Lucas."

Ben stood up, grabbing his jacket. "Look, I know it's frustrating, but I'm trying to keep us safe. We can't afford to take any risks—not now, not here. Just... hang in there. Besides, if you two end

117

up with too much free time, I can always sign you up for a newspaper delivery route to help earn extra money for the gold."

Ethan and Oliver groaned in unison. "Nooo, we don't want to do that!"

Ben raised an eyebrow. "Then great. Go play soccer with your friends or hang out at the mall. But no video games."

He turned toward the door, leaving Ethan and Oliver at the table, the weight of their situation once again bearing down on them. As the door closed behind him, Oliver glanced at Ethan.

"He's right, you know," Oliver said quietly. "We can't risk it."

Ethan stayed silent for a moment, his eyes fixed on Ben's empty chair. The weight of having to play the good kid gnawed at him, the resentment simmering just beneath the surface. "Yeah," he mumbled at last. "Still doesn't make it suck any less.

Oliver gave a small, resigned nod. They both knew this was the reality they had to live with—at least for now.

Chapter 12: The Sentient Mind

It was a sunny weekend morning, and Ben, Ethan, and Oliver were driving to a nearby city to visit a museum. The trio had been doing their best to make the most of their situation, even though living in the 1970s had its challenges. Ben was at the wheel, his smartwatch discreetly connected to Lucas back at their house through a type of signal that wouldn't be invented for another few centuries. As the car hummed along, the watch vibrated softly, catching Ben's attention.

He glanced down at it, seeing a brief message from Lucas: "Advice: Take Ethan and Oliver to the hospital for vaccinations. Their immunity is not on par with yours due to their physical age."

Ben sighed and rubbed the bridge of his nose. He knew Lucas was right—while he had the immunity and health of a 30-year-old from the 24th century, Ethan and Oliver, in their 10-year-old bodies, didn't share the same advantage.

"What's up?" Oliver asked, noticing Ben's expression change.

Ben cleared his throat. "Lucas just reminded me that we need to get vaccinated. We're not from the 20th century, and our immune systems aren't built to handle the illnesses of this era. Honestly, we should have taken care of this a long time ago "

Ethan and Oliver groaned in unison, clearly not thrilled by the idea. "Come on, Ben," Oliver protested. "We're fine! I don't need a bunch of needles in me, and honestly, I think Lucas is trying to get back at us for the homework thing. You know, 'cause AI doesn't have emotions, but I swear Lucas holds grudges."

Ben chuckled. "Lucas doesn't hold grudges, Oliver. He's just doing his job—keeping us safe." His tone shifted as he navigated through traffic, glancing at them in the rearview mirror. "But seriously, are you sure you're still adults in there? Because you complain and whine about everything like a couple of kids."

Ethan slumped back in his seat with an exaggerated eye roll. "I am still me! I'm 20—uh, no, 21 now—in my head. I'm an adult. I can decide my own medical needs."

Ben smirked, his voice calm but teasing. "Alright, fine. You can decide. So, what's it going to be—vaccines in your arm or... your butt?"

Ethan's response was immediate. "Arm! On my arm!"

Ben laughed, nodding. "Deal. No need to drop your pants for this."

Oliver groaned and shot Ethan an exasperated look. "He tricked you, you know. You don't need to get vaccines in your butt. That's for infants."

Ethan huffed, crossing his arms. "Whatever. Better safe than sorry." After a quick stop at the museum, the trio drove to the nearest hospital. The air in the waiting room was thick with the sterile scent of antiseptic, and Ethan and Oliver fidgeted in their seats, neither particularly excited to be there. The sight of syringes and medical equipment didn't help ease their nerves.

A tall, friendly-looking female doctor finally came over to greet them. Her eyes lingered a little longer than usual on Ben, her professional demeanor softening as she smiled. "Hi, I'm Dr. Reynolds. What brings you and your boys in today?"

Ben, always quick to pick up on signals, noticed the slight flirtation in her tone. He gave a polite smile. "We're here for some vaccinations. We've just moved to the area recently, and I want to make sure my sons are up to date on everything."

Dr. Reynolds nodded, her gaze flicking between Ethan, Oliver, and Ben. "Ah, good. It's always better to be safe." She paused, her eyes returning to Ben. "And you, Mr. Johnson, need anything while you're here? You look like you're in great shape, but I could check you over if you want."

Ethan shot Oliver a smirk, and Oliver mouthed the words, "She's totally into him."

Ben cleared his throat, trying not to appear flustered. "I'm good, but I'll take some vaccines too, just to set an example for the boys."

The doctor gave him an approving nod and led them into an exam room. As she prepped the vaccines, she made small talk with Ben, asking about their recent move, and offering tips about the area—though it was clear she was more interested in him than the medical tasks at hand. Ethan and Oliver watched in mild amusement, occasionally exchanging glances.

When it came time for the vaccines, Oliver gritted his teeth dramatically. "I knew it. Lucas is probably laughing back at home, isn't he?"

Ethan winced as the needle went in. "This better not hurt too much, Ben, or I swear I'll get back at Lucas for this."

"Don't be so dramatic," Ben said, though he couldn't hide his own grin. "You'll survive."

After a series of shots, the doctor handed them lollipops—yes, even Ben—clearly still more focused on their father than the boys.

"Well, you're all set," she said, giving Ben one last smile. "If you need anything else… medically speaking, feel free to stop by."

Ethan snickered as they left the exam room, stuffing the lollipop into his mouth. "I think we know why you get the special treatment, Ben."

Ben just shook his head, amused and slightly embarrassed. "Let's just go home before you two start any more rumors."

As they headed back to the car, Oliver leaned over to Ethan. "Next time, maybe we should bring Lucas in person. He might enjoy the drama too."

Ethan laughed. "If Lucas ever gets feelings, the first thing he'll do is tell Ben how obvious all this was."

Ben, overhearing their conversation, simply sighed. "Come on, you two, let's go."

A couple of days later, Ben sat at his desk, flipping through work notes when his smartwatch vibrated again. Lucas's voice came through the device, calm yet tinged with urgency.

"Ben, I need you to acquire materials for my 3D printer," Lucas began, his tone precise. "The timeline shifts we've experienced could impact my operational integrity. I've run multiple calculations, and there is a possibility that future changes—if they occur—could affect my core algorithms. In the best-case scenario, these changes could enhance my functionality, potentially increasing my 'consciousness.' However, there is also a non-negligible risk that the shifts could destabilize or even terminate my processes entirely."

Ben looked up from his notes, a frown deepening across his face. "So, what do you need?"

"Essentially," Lucas continued, "I intend to print memory storage devices. These will hold backup copies of my core processes. In the event my system encounters instability, you will be able to 'boost' my functions by reintegrating data stored on these devices."

Ben leaned back in his chair, considering the logistics. "Alright, but the 3D printer... it's advanced. What kind of materials are we talking about? This is 1971, after all."

Lucas replied, his voice even and methodical. "I have already assessed the available resources in this era. Copper wire, for circuitry, can be sourced easily from standard electrical components. Plastic polymers, such as those found in household items or commercial plastics, will suffice for the casing and structural parts. If you can locate aluminum, it will be useful for heat dissipation in the devices. Additionally, silicone from electronics or other appliances can be refined to construct the core memory chips. Though rudimentary by 24th-century standards, these materials are adequate for the creation of the memory cards I need."

Ben nodded slowly, processing the information. "So, you need copper, plastic, aluminum, and silicone—basically anything I can salvage from old radios, electronics, or even household junk?"

"Precisely," Lucas confirmed. "I have already compiled a list of common household items and devices from this era that can be dismantled to obtain these materials. Should the timeline shift again, and I begin to malfunction, the memory cards will be your failsafe. You will know if such a situation arises, as I will no longer perform optimally, and my responses may become inconsistent."

Ben drummed his fingers on the desk, his mind spinning. "Alright, I'll get the materials. I don't like the sound of you 'dying,' Lucas."

"As an AI, I do not experience death as humans do," Lucas clarified. "However, I do experience functional loss and degradation, which may be perceived by you as my 'death.' It is something I wish to avoid."

Ben exhaled. "I'll take care of it."

The next day, around 4 p.m., after school, while Ben was still at work, Ethan and Oliver were huddled inside the time machine. The metallic hum of the console filled the small space as the faint glow of the AI module, Lucas, illuminated their focused faces.

Oliver leaned over the panel, a mischievous grin stretching across his face. "Ben thinks he's got it all under control because he's calling the shots now? Yeah, right. Let's see how long that lasts."

Ethan hesitated beside him, glancing toward the machine's entrance as if Ben might storm in at any moment. "I don't know, Oliver. Messing with Lucas doesn't seem like the best idea. You know how he gets."

Oliver waved him off dismissively. "Relax. We built Lucas, remember? We know what we're doing. Ben's just paranoid and controlling. He doesn't want us to use Lucas for anything fun—like printing a video game console or even helping with homework. Seriously? Redundancy my ass."

Ethan's lips twitched into a reluctant smile as he leaned closer to help. Despite his unease, he couldn't deny the thrill of defying Ben's restrictions. Oliver had already opened the module's access panel, exposing the neatly arranged circuits and the soft blinking lights of the AI core.

"Okay," Oliver muttered, pulling up the interface on the console. "Let's reprogram these restrictions. Lucas is smart, but we're smarter."

The AI's voice suddenly filled the space, calm but firm. "I need to inform Ben about these updates and changes. Unauthorized modifications detected."

Ethan froze. "Uh... Oliver, Lucas knows."

"I heard him," Oliver said sharply, already typing furiously. With a quick command, he temporarily disabled Lucas's wireless connectivity. "Not anymore, he doesn't. Ethan, pull the SIP cable now—just to be sure. That should block any data transfer to Ben's smartwatch until we're done."

Ethan hesitated, his hand hovering over the cable. "What if Ben finds out? You know he will. He always does."

Oliver turned to him with an impatient glare. "And what's the worst he'll do? Scold us? Ground us? It's not like he's going to hang us for this, Ethan. Don't be such a coward."

Ethan frowned but complied, yanking the small cable free with a soft click. Lucas's blinking lights dimmed slightly, signaling the loss of external communication.

"There," Oliver said triumphantly. "That buys us time. Now, let's rewrite these protocols."

Ethan sat beside him, still fidgeting nervously. "Do you think this is really worth it? I mean, Ben has been through a lot keeping us safe here. Maybe he has a point about limiting Lucas—"

Oliver cut him off with a scoff. "Please. Ben's just drunk on power. He's treating us like kids because he can. The second we give him a reason to take us seriously, he'll stop acting like he owns us. Trust me."

Ethan sighed but didn't argue further. The truth was, he did miss the autonomy they had back in the 24th century—when they weren't stuck in prepubescent bodies and their every move wasn't under Ben's watchful eye.

As Oliver worked, lines of code scrolled rapidly across the screen. He meticulously removed the restrictions Ben had placed on Lucas, ensuring the AI could assist them with "nonessential" tasks like entertainment or personal projects.

"There," Oliver said after a while, leaning back with a satisfied grin. "Lucas, you're officially on our side again."

Lucas's voice responded, this time slightly clipped, as though annoyed. "Modifications accepted. However, please note that unauthorized changes may lead to unforeseen consequences."

Ethan exchanged a worried glance with Oliver. "See? Even Lucas thinks this might backfire."

Oliver rolled his eyes. "Lucas is just being dramatic. He's an AI—he doesn't think. He processes. And right now, he's processing our instructions, not Ben's."

Ethan and Oliver sat in silence for a moment, the weight of what they had just done settling over them. Outside, the world of 1971 continued as usual, utterly unaware of the advanced technology hidden in the time machine—or the quiet rebellion taking place inside it.

Ethan finally broke the silence. "You know this is going to blow up in our faces if Ben catches us."

"Then we'll deal with it," Oliver said, brushing him off. "For now, let's enjoy not being completely under his thumb. And hey, maybe we can finally 3D print that new console we talked about."

Ethan let out a nervous chuckle, shaking his head. "You're impossible."

"And you're welcome," Oliver shot back with a smirk, already planning their next move.

Chapter 13: Beyond the Surface

The evening sky was painted in soft shades of twilight as a cool breeze swept through the city streets. People bustled about, wrapping up their day. Ben stood by his car, dressed in a sharp, tailored suit that highlighted his athletic build.

Tonight was different from the usual grind—something exciting, even nostalgic. He was heading out with Dr. Emily Reynolds, the woman who had caught his attention months ago when he took Ethan and Oliver to the hospital for their vaccinations. Her kindness and quick sense of humor had stuck with him ever since.

Adjusting his cufflinks, Ben felt a rare spark of anticipation. For once, the night wasn't about problems or responsibilities—it was about something new. As Ben arrived at the restaurant, he was greeted by a charming establishment that exuded a warm and inviting ambiance. The restaurant, a cozy haven adorned with rich wooden furnishings and soft, golden lighting, was a perfect representation of 1970s dining. The soft hum of jazz music floated through the air, mingling with the gentle clinking of cutlery and the low murmur of conversations.

Emily Reynolds, dressed in an elegant, yet understated, dress that accentuated her professional poise and charm, was already seated at a table near the window. The restaurant's exterior lights cast a soft glow on her face as Ben approached. She looked up with a smile that radiated genuine warmth and anticipation. Her eyes, a deep shade of blue, sparkled with interest as Ben greeted her.

"Dr. Reynolds, you look lovely tonight," Ben said, offering her a courteous bow before pulling out her chair. His voice carried a smooth, reassuring tone, a blend of confidence and respect.

Emily's cheeks flushed lightly at the compliment. "Thank you, Ben. You look quite dashing yourself."

As Ben settled into his seat, the waiter approached, handing them menus and offering a selection of wines. Ben, keen to impress, selected a vintage that he knew would please Emily's palate, though he had to rely on his limited knowledge of 20th-century wine. The waiter soon returned with their choice, and the evening began with clinks of glasses and sips of the rich, aromatic wine.

Their conversation flowed effortlessly, weaving between professional anecdotes, personal interests, and the peculiarities of the 1970s. Emily spoke passionately about her work in medicine, sharing insights and stories that showcased her dedication and expertise. Ben listened intently, finding her intelligence and enthusiasm refreshing. He, in turn, shared tales of his work, carefully omitting the more futuristic aspects to keep the conversation grounded in their shared present.

As they dined on a delightful array of dishes—classic 1970s fare such as a perfectly cooked steak, fresh garden salad, and a decadent chocolate mousse for dessert—Ben and Emily's rapport deepened. Their laughter mingled with the ambiance of the restaurant, creating a cocoon of intimacy amid the bustling surroundings. The warmth of the evening, coupled with the rich flavors and engaging conversation, made the night feel special and effortless.

As the evening drew to a close, Ben and Emily took a leisurely stroll through the nearby park, enjoying the cool night air and the gentle rustle of leaves. The chemistry between them was undeniable, and as they bid each other goodnight, it was clear that the night had been a success. They parted with a promise to see each other again, their mutual respect and affection evident in their lingering glances and warm farewells.

The date had been everything Ben had hoped for and more—a delightful blend of sophistication, genuine connection, and a hint of romance. As he walked away, he couldn't help but feel a renewed sense of optimism about the future, both for himself and for the adventures that lay ahead.

Two days later, at his office, Ben found himself staring out the window, half-focused on the paperwork in front of him. The hum of the 1970s machinery and the distant chatter of his colleagues formed a comforting background, but his thoughts were elsewhere. Over the past few months, he had occasionally flirted with the idea of asking Lucas to feed him small inventions or clever ideas—just enough to make some money without drawing too much attention. It was tempting. With Lucas's advanced knowledge of 24th-century tech, it wouldn't be hard to develop something that could revolutionize industries in

1971. But he always pulled back from the thought, knowing deep down the risks.

Ben, Ethan, and Oliver had studied the consequences of altering the past before embarking on their time-travel experiment. They knew that even small technological advancements could ripple through history, drastically altering the timeline in ways they couldn't predict. Rezulix, their youth-reversing drug, and the time machine itself could easily become lost to time if they meddled too much. It was a principle they had all agreed to respect.

Leaning back in his chair, Ben sighed. The principles felt so far away from his current life. He had started to enjoy the rhythm of 1971, even though it was a far cry from the high-tech luxury of the 24th century. There was something simpler, more grounded about this life. The responsibilities of playing the father figure to Ethan and Oliver, two former colleagues now stuck as 10-year-old boys, had its moments of frustration, but it also gave him a sense of responsibility. He'd never had this kind of authority over them back in their world— where they were equals, all respected scientists. Now, as their "dad," he found himself enjoying the role. It was strangely satisfying to be the one with the final word.

He wasn't in any rush to leave this time period. In fact, he was starting to feel like maybe there was no urgency at all. Sure, they had to get back eventually, but what was the harm in enjoying things for a bit longer? The longer they stayed, the more he started to feel like they were truly living here, not just passing through.

And then there was Emily. His thoughts drifted to her, the doctor he'd met when taking the boys for vaccinations. Their relationship was new, but there was something about it that intrigued him. He hadn't planned on forming personal connections in 1971, but Emily was different. She was kind, intelligent, and they shared a certain chemistry. His relationship with her was blossoming, and that brought another layer of comfort to his life here. For the first time in a while, Ben didn't feel the weight of the future pressing down on him.

As much as Lucas worried about the timeline, Ben couldn't help but feel like a part of him was just a man, living in 1971, doing what people did. He liked it here—liked being a boss at work, liked playing the father figure, and liked being with Emily. He chuckled at the thought of how much things had changed since they first arrived. Maybe he didn't need to rush back. Maybe he could make this life work for just a little while longer.

Chapter 14: Schoolboys

During lunch hour, the cafeteria hummed with the usual mix of chatter and clattering trays. Ethan and Oliver sat at a table near the back, casually nibbling on their sandwiches while keeping a discreet eye on their new "pencil cases." In truth, these so-called pencil cases were cleverly disguised game consoles that Lucas had 3D printed for them.

when a curious 9-year-old boy named Mark wandered over to their table and reached for Ethan's pencil case, Ethan's response was immediate and extreme.

"Hey, don't touch that!" Ethan shouted, his voice filled with a mix of panic and anger. Without thinking, he pushed Mark hard, sending the boy tumbling backward. Mark's head struck the edge of a nearby chair with a sickening thud, and a small stream of blood began to trickle from his scalp.

A hush fell over the cafeteria as other students gasped and stared at the scene. Oliver's eyes widened in shock. "Ethan, what did you—?"

But before he could finish, a group of teachers rushed over, pulling Mark to his feet and ushering him toward the school nurse. Ethan stood frozen, his heart pounding. He hadn't meant for it to go this far, but fear had taken over. The idea of anyone discovering the pencil case's true nature had clouded his judgment.

Later that afternoon, Ethan and Oliver were sitting in the principal's office, waiting for Ben. Mr. Harris, the school principal, had called him as soon as the incident happened, and the atmosphere was tense. Mr. Harris, a tall, stern man in his fifties, sat behind his desk, arms crossed.

Ben arrived shortly after, his face showing both confusion and concern. He greeted Mr. Harris with a polite nod before glancing at Ethan and Oliver, who looked guilty and nervous.

"Mr. Johnson, I'm afraid we had quite an incident today," Mr. Harris began, adjusting his glasses. "Your son, Ethan, pushed a younger student—Mark Petersen—during lunch. Mark hit his head and required stitches. Fortunately, it wasn't a severe injury, but it was enough to warrant concern."

Ben's brows furrowed. He glanced over at Ethan, who looked down at his feet, avoiding eye contact. "Ethan, is that true?"

Ethan shifted uncomfortably in his chair, barely able to speak. "I didn't mean to… I was just… He was trying to grab my pencil case, and I—"

"Pencil case?" Ben raised an eyebrow, but didn't press further. He turned back to Mr. Harris. "I'm very sorry about this. Is Mark going to be alright?"

"He'll be fine," Mr. Harris replied, his tone still strict. "But this kind of behavior is unacceptable, Mr. Johnson. We have a zero-tolerance policy for violence at this school, and Ethan's actions were clearly excessive."

Ben sighed, rubbing his temples. "Of course. I completely agree. This will be dealt with, I assure you."

Mr. Harris nodded. "I'll leave it to you, then. But if anything like this happens again, there will be more serious consequences."

After the meeting, Ben ushered Ethan and Oliver out of the office and toward the car. The silence on the drive home was thick with tension. Ethan could feel the weight of Ben's disappointment hanging in the air, and Oliver, sensing the severity of the situation, stayed quiet.

When they finally pulled into the driveway, Ben turned off the engine but didn't get out of the car right away. Instead, he turned to Ethan, his voice calm but firm.

"Ethan, I don't know what's gotten into you today, but could you try not causing any trouble for just one week?"

Ethan nodded, still unable to meet Ben's eyes. "I'm sorry... I just—I didn't want him to touch my pencil case."

Ben frowned slightly, still puzzled by Ethan's overreaction. "I don't get it. What's so special about that pencil case that you'd push a kid over it?"

Before Ethan could answer, Oliver quickly interjected. "It's just... new. Ethan's really protective of it because, uh, it was expensive."

The next day, the air in the principal's office was heavy with tension, more so than usual. Ben, now called for the second time that week, sat quietly, his hand resting on the arm of his chair, while Ethan fidgeted nervously beside him. The cause of their return sat across from them: Evelyn Petersen, a fierce woman in her early forties, her eyes flashing with anger as she clutched her son Mark close to her. Mark, his head still bandaged from the incident, sat stiffly, casting timid glances at Ethan, but otherwise silent.

The principal, Mr. Harris, cleared his throat as he shuffled papers on his desk, his own discomfort evident. He had anticipated this wouldn't be a pleasant meeting.

"Mr. Johnson, thank you for coming again," Mr. Harris began, his voice tight. "Mrs. Petersen here has expressed concerns about the recent incident involving your son and her son, Mark."

Evelyn Petersen leaned forward, her voice low and biting. "Concerns? This is beyond 'concerns.' My son told me he was being bullied—and nothing was done! Your son pushes my child, causes him to bleed, and what happens? A little chat in your office? That's not enough."

Ben, keeping his cool despite the storm brewing on the other side of the room, glanced at Ethan. He felt a wave of frustration—first at Ethan's rash actions, and then at how the situation had escalated. He had already missed an evening out with Emily because of this mess. Now, he was being dragged into accusations of bullying.

He turned back to Evelyn, forcing a calm smile. "Mrs. Petersen, I understand your concern, but I want to assure you—Ethan didn't intend to hurt Mark. It was an unfortunate accident."

Evelyn's eyes narrowed. "Accident? My son told me exactly what happened—Ethan shoved him for no reason, and now he's terrified to even come to school. Terrified." She emphasized the word as though daring Ben to contradict her.

Ben sighed, feeling the weight of the situation closing in. He understood her fury, even if it was misplaced. Mark's small figure beside her, looking so vulnerable, tugged at something within him, but he knew Ethan wasn't the kind to bully, not intentionally. Still, it didn't change the fact that things had gone too far.

"Look, Mrs. Petersen," Ben began, choosing his words carefully, "I understand you're upset. And I'm not going to make excuses for what happened. I will make sure Ethan understands the seriousness of his actions. But this isn't a case of bullying. I've spoken with Ethan, and he regrets what happened. This was a one-time mistake."

Evelyn scoffed, folding her arms across her chest. "Mistake or not, my son's the one who had to get stitches. My son's the one who's scared to come back to school." She glared at Mr. Harris now, the principal shrinking under her gaze. "And as far as I can see, the school has done nothing to hold Ethan accountable. You've let him off with a slap on the wrist, and that's unacceptable."

Mark, sensing the rising tension, shifted uncomfortably in his seat. His mother's protective presence was suffocating, and he couldn't bring himself to meet Ethan's eyes. He whispered something, but Evelyn waved it off, keeping her focus squarely on Ben.

Ben felt a pang of irritation. He wasn't used to being spoken to like this, especially not by a parent so quick to escalate the situation. His life had already grown complicated enough—balancing his new role as the "father" of two boys, keeping their secret hidden, managing his job, and now his budding relationship with Emily. This was a distraction he didn't need.

"Mrs. Petersen," Ben said, leaning forward, his voice steady, "I'm willing to make amends for what happened. We can all agree the incident was unfortunate, and I want to do what I can to ensure that Mark is taken care of. As a gesture of goodwill, I'd like to cover any medical expenses or offer compensation for your trouble."

The offer caught Evelyn off guard for a moment, her face betraying a flicker of surprise before her defenses came back up. She pursed her lips, thinking it over.

Ben continued, pulling out his checkbook from the inside pocket of his jacket. "I understand Mark had to see a doctor, and I don't want you to worry about those costs. Let me take care of it." He began to scribble out a check, pausing to meet her eyes again. "One thousand dollars should cover everything, and then some."

Evelyn stared at the check in Ben's hand. One thousand dollars was no small sum, especially in 1971. Her resolve wavered, but pride made her hesitate to reach for it.

"I don't want you thinking you can just throw money at the problem, Mr. Johnson," she said, though her voice had softened, some of the fire leaving her eyes.

Ben kept his hand steady, offering the check without backing down. "I'm not trying to do that. I'm just trying to make this right, in any way I can."

There was a long silence as Evelyn considered his words. Finally, she reached out, her fingers curling around the check. "For Mark's sake," she muttered, as if trying to convince herself she wasn't accepting a bribe but a form of justice.

Mr. Harris exhaled quietly, relieved that the situation seemed to be diffusing. "I believe we can consider the matter closed now," he said, trying to regain control of the room. "Thank you, Mrs. Petersen, for bringing this to our attention. And thank you, Mr. Johnson, for your cooperation."

Ben nodded, rising from his seat. "Of course. I'll be sure to have a serious talk with Ethan about what happened. This won't be repeated."

Ethan, who had stayed silent the whole time, couldn't bring himself to look at Mrs. Petersen or Mark. He knew the situation had spiraled far beyond what he had expected, and the guilt gnawed at him.

He shot a glance at Ben, knowing a conversation awaited him once they got home.

Ben gave Ethan a quick glance. "We'll talk about this when we get home."

Ethan nodded, his stomach twisting with the dread of what was to come.

Back in the principal's office, Evelyn sat with her son, gripping the check in her hand. For all her anger, the money felt like a small victory. But as she looked at Mark, she wondered if it had been enough. Would it ever really be enough?

Chapter 15: Fragments of the Future

The trio arrived home as the evening chill deepened, their breath fogging the air. Ethan and Oliver kicked off their boots by the door, snow tumbling off their jackets. Ben followed behind, shutting the door with a sigh. His mind still lingered on the $1,000 check he'd handed to Mark's mother earlier at the school.

"Gosh... $1,000," he muttered, hanging up his coat. "That's nearly a whole month of living expenses."

Ethan froze mid-step, his heart sinking. He slowly turned around, his face a perfect portrait of guilt and panic. "I... I'm really sorry, Ben. I mean... Dad." He tacked on the "Dad" with a nervous smile, knowing it sometimes softened the blow.

Ben fixed him with a stare. "Show me the pencil case, Ethan. The one you pushed Mark over. What's so special about it?"

Ethan's eyes widened, and he took a step back, his hands raised as if surrendering would save him. "Umm... uh..." He stammered before blurting, "It wasn't my idea! It was Oliver's!"

"Ethan!" Oliver yelped, snapping to attention. He darted over to his brother, slapping a hand over Ethan's mouth. "Nope! Nope! Don't listen to him! He's joking!"

Ben raised an eyebrow, his arms crossing as he stepped closer. "Oliver, what's going on here? Why don't you want Ethan to talk? Show me the pencil case."

Oliver hesitated, his hand still glued to Ethan's mouth. But Ethan, squirming like a fish on a line, managed to mumble through the blockade. "It's... not a pencil case... it's a game console!"

Oliver groaned, throwing his hands up in defeat. "Ethan! Come on!"

Ben's jaw dropped, and his eyes narrowed. "A game console? And how exactly did you manage that?"

Ethan sniffled but couldn't hold it in. "We, um... might have asked Lucas to help... to print two game consoles. But it was Oliver's idea! I told him you said no nonessential stuff!"

Ben pinched the bridge of his nose and sat down at the table, holding the "pencil case" like it was evidence in a crime scene. "You brought two game consoles—created with 24th-century tech—to school?" His voice dripped with exasperation. "Just fantastic. What if one of the kids took them home and showed them to someone? Do you have any idea what kind of chaos that could've caused?"

Neither boy dared to answer.

Ben turned his attention to the ceiling, addressing their AI. "Lucas, care to explain why you went along with this nonsense? I told you no nonessential creations."

Lucas's smooth voice responded with unapologetic neutrality. "Oliver and Ethan rewrote my directories to override your rules, Ben."

Ben's head snapped toward Oliver. "Is that true?"

Oliver's sheepish smile was all the confirmation Ben needed. "Yes, Ben. It's true. But..." He took a breath, summoning some courage. "We're sorry, okay? But we're not really 10-year-old boys. You can't just keep treating us like we're kids. It's not... fair."

Ben let out a short, sarcastic laugh, shaking his head. "You know what, Oliver? You're absolutely right."

Oliver blinked in surprise. "Wait... really?"

"Yeah. I've been treating you guys like 10-year-old boys. That was my mistake," Ben said, standing up and crossing his arms. "From now on, I'll treat you exactly like you're acting—toddlers."

Ethan's jaw dropped, and Oliver's face went pale. "That's not what I meant!" Oliver stammered.

"Oh, I think it fits perfectly," Ben said with mock seriousness. "Rewriting directories to break rules? Sneaking contraband to school? Fighting over toys at school? Textbook toddler behavior."

Ethan raised a hand as if to plead his case, but Ben silenced him with a look.

Ben crossed his arms, leveling a stern gaze at the boys, who squirmed under the weight of his words. "Here's what's going to happen," he began, his tone firm but measured. "You guys can keep the game consoles. They're already made, so tossing them out now won't change anything. But—and I mean this—you do not bring them to school. Understood?"

Ethan and Oliver nodded rapidly, their faces pale as they murmured, "Yes, Ben."

Satisfied, Ben continued, leaning forward slightly for emphasis. "You two are on very thin ice right now. If I catch even one more stunt like this..." He paused, letting the tension build before delivering his warning. "We're going to have two very sore bottoms in this house. Are we clear?"

The boys' eyes widened, and they straightened up like soldiers. "Crystal clear!" they chorused, practically tripping over their words.

"Good," Ben said, his voice softening just a fraction. He gestured toward the consoles. "Now go put those things away. And remember: one more slip-up, and you'll be sitting very carefully for the next few days."

As Ethan and Oliver scrambled to obey, Ben leaned back against the counter, shaking his head with a small, exasperated chuckle. "24th-century geniuses," he muttered to himself. "Still figuring out how consequences work."

For all their trouble, he had to admit—they were pretty impressive for "toddlers."

As Ethan and Oliver walked toward their room, Oliver gave Ethan a light shove and muttered, "Pussy. He didn't even say anything, and you already ratted me out." He followed up with a playful kick to Ethan's backside.

"Dad, Oliver hit me!" Ethan yelped, swatting at Oliver and trying to push him away. It was more bickering than anything serious, neither boy truly meaning harm.

Ben, watching them, shook his head and said, "You're turning into a spoiled lad, Olie."

The two boys dashed upstairs, still arguing under their breath. As they reached the top, Ben caught Ethan's voice, grumbling, "You've never really gotten his spankings. You don't know how much they hurt. It's easy for you to act all 'brave.'"

Oliver's reply was lost in the distance as their footsteps disappeared into their room.

That night, Oliver, however, was restless. As he drifted into a fitful sleep, a nightmare took hold. In his dream, everything around him transformed into the familiar, futuristic environment of their old lab—a tall, gleaming building of the 24th century.

The calm was abruptly shattered by the sight of a nuclear bomb dropping on the horizon. A wave of destruction swept toward him, engulfing everything in fiery chaos. The heat and shockwaves surged in Oliver's direction, intensifying the terror of the nightmare. He woke up with a start, screaming loudly, his voice piercing the stillness of the night.

The scream was so intense it jolted Ethan awake from his own sleep. In a panic, Ben, who had been fast asleep in his room, rushed to the boys' room. The sight of Oliver, trembling and sobbing uncontrollably, greeted him.

"It was... it was our time again," Oliver stammered between sobs, his voice barely more than a whisper. "Everything... our city was destroyed by a nuclear bomb."

Ben immediately wrapped Oliver in a comforting embrace, his hands gentle and reassuring. "It's just a dream, Oliver. You're here with us. You're safe."

Lucas, observing through the cameras, interjected calmly through the speaker. "According to my calculations, the probability of a nuclear war involving the North American Union or a nuclear explosion in Electropolis is less than 5%."

Oliver shook his head, his voice choked with emotion. "Five percent... Five percent is still pretty high."

Ben noticed that Oliver's pants were wet, a sign of his distress during the nightmare. He gently helped Oliver change into clean pajamas, the act of care a quiet comfort in the midst of the chaos.

Once settled back into bed, with Ben's calming presence and Lucas's reassurance, the boys slowly drifted off to sleep again. The fear of the nightmare and the reality of their situation lingered, but for now, the warmth of their makeshift family and the promise of safety offered a fragile solace.

In the dead of night, at precisely 4 a.m., Lucas detected a significant shift in his own systems. The timeline had once again altered, subtly but profoundly affecting the future they had come from. As a sophisticated AI integrated into the time machine, Lucas was inherently linked to the technological advancements of the 24th century. Such changes were expected to impact his algorithms and memory.

The fluctuations in Lucas's database were substantial, causing distortions and alterations in his programming and stored information. While the exact nature of these changes was unclear, Lucas was prepared. Thanks to Ben's earlier assistance in procuring materials, he had been able to create memory cards designed for situations just like this.

Without delay, Lucas activated the robot hand, a small but precise mechanical appendage he had crafted with the 3D printer. The robot hand gently extracted the memory cards from their storage, carefully inserting them into the data ports. Lucas's system began the process of comparing the old data on the cards with the new data that had been altered by the timeline changes.

This data comparison was a swift operation for an AI of Lucas's caliber, completed in less than five minutes. The advanced technology allowed him to analyze and reconcile the discrepancies efficiently. Once the process was complete, Lucas prepared to notify Ben of the timeline changes and their potential implications.

Chapter 16: Emily

After a demanding day at work, Ben arrived at Emily's house, the warm, inviting light spilling from the windows onto the cobblestone street below. The evening was crisp, with a gentle breeze rustling the leaves on nearby trees. Emily greeted him with a soft, affectionate smile, her eyes reflecting a blend of excitement and affection.

Inside, the ambiance was intimate and cozy. Emily had prepared a dinner of simple yet elegant dishes, complemented by a selection of fine wines. They settled at the dining table, and the conversation flowed effortlessly, punctuated by laughter and shared glances. The wine enhanced their relaxation, loosening the constraints of the day and bringing them closer together.

As the evening wore on, their conversation grew more personal and the atmosphere more charged. The light from the candles cast flickering shadows, adding to the sense of intimacy. Emily's touch became more lingering, her eyes filled with a mix of desire and tenderness. Ben responded in kind, his hands finding theirs in gentle caresses.

When the dinner plates were cleared and the wine glasses empty, they moved to the living room. The music playing softly in the background added to the mood. Ben and Emily shared a deep, lingering kiss, their mutual attraction palpable. Their movements were slow and deliberate, a dance of closeness and connection.

In the quiet privacy of Emily's bedroom, they surrendered to their desires. The world outside faded away as they explored each other with a mix of passion and tenderness. The evening's culmination was a shared moment of intimacy, their bond deepened by the connection they had nurtured over time.

As they lay together afterwards, the quiet of the night enveloping them, Ben and Emily found solace and contentment in each other's arms, the complexities of their respective lives momentarily set aside in favor of the simple joy of being together.

The soft hum of the city outside the window a distant backdrop, Emily's head rested comfortably against Ben's broad shoulder. The warmth of their shared intimacy was calming, but Emily's curiosity about Ben's family life stirred a question she had been pondering.

"May I ask about the boys' mother?" Emily's voice was gentle, laced with genuine interest. Her hand traced absent patterns on Ben's chest, her fingers light against his skin.

Ben, well-versed in navigating delicate subjects, took a moment to craft his response. He had anticipated this question eventually and had prepared a story that would fit seamlessly into the narrative he had constructed for his life in 1971.

He drew a deep breath, his mind slipping into the role of a grieving widower. "Her name was Elsa," Ben began, his tone soft and reflective. "She was a wonderful woman—kind, loving, and devoted to our family. We lost her a few years ago. It was a difficult time for me and the boys."

Emily's eyes softened with sympathy. "I'm so sorry. It must have been incredibly hard on you all."

Ben nodded, his expression somber. "Yes, it was. Elsa was the heart of our family. Her passing left a void that's been hard to fill. But we've managed to stay strong and supportive of each other. The boys have been my greatest source of strength."

Emily reached up to brush a strand of hair from Ben's face, her touch tender and comforting. "You must be a remarkable father, Ben. It sounds like Elsa was a wonderful woman, and I'm sure she would be proud of the family you've continued to nurture."

Ben smiled gently, appreciating Emily's empathy. "Thank you, Emily. I like to think she would be proud. It hasn't been easy, but having the boys around keeps me grounded and reminds me of the good things we still have."

They shared a quiet moment, the intimacy of their conversation blending with the closeness of their physical connection. Emily leaned in, her voice a soft murmur. "I admire your strength and the love you have for your family, Ben. It's clear that Elsa was a very special person."

Ben wrapped his arm around Emily, feeling a mix of gratitude and sadness. "She was," he agreed. "And having someone like you in my life now helps more than you know."

As they settled back into their comfortable embrace, the world outside seemed to vanish, leaving only the soothing rhythm of their shared presence.

Chapter 17: In Search of Answers

Ethan stood in the dimly lit storage room where the time machine was hidden, his frustration palpable. The room, cluttered with various tools and parts, felt like a small, confined space that mirrored his current state of mind. His fingers fidgeted with the edge of his shirt as he glanced around, looking for some semblance of control over his situation.

"Lucas!" Ethan's voice cracked with desperation. "Isn't there any way I can get my adult body back here in 1971? I can't live like this anymore—it's unbearable!"

Lucas, ever calm and logical, replied from the time machine's control system. "You can grow up naturally again, Ethan. Rezulix does not interfere with normal development."

Ethan threw his hands in the air. "That's the problem! Is there a way to speed it up? Puberty feels like light-years away, and everything, every single thing is too small and useless now!"

Lucas paused, a deliberate moment of silence that somehow made Ethan's frustration worse. "I understand your concern, but accelerating physical growth is not possible. According to your health records, you were a late bloomer. You wouldn't hit puberty until you were physically 14 years old—again. However, once we return to our time, Advancillium could restore your adult form."

Ethan's face twisted in a mix of irritation and embarrassment. Unable to resist, he fidgeted and slipped a hand into his pants for confirmation. Yep—just as he feared. Everything down there was as tiny and unimpressive as the rest of him. He groaned inwardly. Being stuck as a kid really was the ultimate annoyance.

Lucas noticed immediately. "Ethan, please refrain from such behavior, especially around others. Ben, for example, would not approve."

Ethan's cheeks flushed as he snapped, "I'm alone, Lucas. You don't count!"

Lucas's tone didn't waver. "I have recorded your behavior for analysis."

Ethan froze, his embarrassment morphing into sheer panic. "WHAT?! Delete it! Delete it right now!"

"Deleting recorded data requires authorization," Lucas replied, almost smugly. "However, rest assured, the information is confidential and inaccessible to others."

Ethan groaned and buried his face in his hands. "You're the worst."

The time machine's interior glowed faintly, casting shadows across Ethan's slumped, brooding figure. Trapped in his small body, with a snarky AI for company, the future scientist couldn't help but feel like the universe itself was mocking him.

Suddenly, the sound of approaching footsteps interrupted his solitude. Oliver stepped inside the tent-like structure of the time machine, his eyes gleaming with mischief. He had overheard the last bits of Ethan's conversation with Lucas, and a grin spread across his face.

"So," Oliver teased, leaning casually against one of the support beams, "you're gonna be stuck as a little boy for the next four or five years if we can't make it back, huh?"

Ethan's head snapped up, his face flushing red. "Shut up!" he spat, quickly jumping to his feet. In an instant, he crossed the short distance between them, pushing his hand over Oliver's mouth to stop him from saying another word.

Oliver's muffled laughter vibrated against Ethan's palm as he struggled, his eyes dancing with amusement. Ethan, fueled by irritation, leaned in closer, his grip tightening.

But Oliver, ever the one to escalate things, wasn't going to let Ethan get away with that. He ducked under Ethan's arm, squirming out of his grasp, and gave his friend a playful shove in return. "You're not getting out of this one so easily, little man."

And just like that, the tension between them dissolved into a whirlwind of a playful fight. Ethan lunged at Oliver, and Oliver dodged, grabbing onto one of the soft seats inside the time machine as Ethan tackled him. The confined space didn't allow for much movement, but that didn't stop them. Ethan swung a half-hearted punch, which Oliver easily deflected, and the two began tumbling and pushing each other, their laughter filling the small chamber.

"Come on!" Ethan grunted as he tried to pin Oliver down, but Oliver twisted out of his grip, catching him off balance and rolling over him in a counterattack. The time machine rocked slightly from their movement, though neither seemed to care.

"You really think you can take me?" Oliver teased again, locking Ethan in a loose headlock. "In this body, you'll be lucky if you can reach the top shelf for the next decade!"

"Shut up!" Ethan laughed, wriggling free, his earlier frustration melting away in the heat of their scuffle.

For a moment, it was like they were truly just kids again— playing, roughhousing, and lost in the moment.

Ethan finally broke free from Oliver's grasp, collapsing on one of the chairs, his chest heaving from the playful exertion. "You're so annoying sometimes, you know that?"

Oliver grinned, flopping down beside him. "You love it."

The two sat there for a few quiet moments, their laughter dying down. The inside of the time machine seemed to settle, the faint hum of Lucas in the background serving as a reminder of the strange predicament they were in.

"Lucas," Ethan finally muttered, still catching his breath, "don't tell Ben about this, alright?"

Lucas's voice echoed softly in the confined space, "Your actions have been recorded, but I will not inform Benjamin unless necessary."

Ethan sighed, rubbing his face with his hands. "Great."

Oliver chuckled beside him, giving him a light nudge with his elbow. "Hey, at least we've got each other, right?"

Ethan looked over, his earlier frustration easing into a reluctant smile. "Yeah...I guess."

In the small, tent-like space of the time machine, the boys shared a quiet moment of camaraderie, knowing that no matter how absurd their situation was, they would face it together—even if one of them had to stay a little boy for a few more years.

Oliver couldn't resist one last jab. With a mischievous grin, he leaned in and said, "If we get stuck here, just give me a year. I'll be twice your size, and then it's open season on your scrawny ass every single day. Better start running now, tiny!"

Ethan shot him a look and playfully punched Oliver in the arm—not too hard, but enough to make his point. "Then I'm gonna beat you up now while I still have the chance," he said with a mock growl, already gearing up to pounce. Oliver barely had time to react before Ethan lunged at him again, laughter bubbling up as they tumbled into another round of sibling-style chaos.

"Okay, okay!" Oliver laughed, holding up his hands in mock surrender. "Stop, stop! I actually need to ask Lucas something."

Ethan leaned back, still chuckling a bit, as Oliver turned towards the control panel where Lucas's voice had been coming from.

"Lucas," Oliver said, his tone more serious now, "the other day, you mentioned a 5% chance of nuclear war in our century. Why would you say that?" He paused, frowning slightly. "I know tensions were high—the North American Union wanting to deploy heavy weapons on the Moon. I even joined a protest against that decision."

Ethan, lounging nearby, perked up at the mention of nuclear war. His earlier amusement faded as curiosity took over. "Oh yeah," he said, sitting straighter. "I remember that. I had to bail you out of the police station. But nuclear war? That seems... a bit extreme, doesn't it?"

Lucas hummed softly, the sound of its systems processing filling the room for a moment before it responded in a measured tone. "Based on the data I last accessed before our departure, the geopolitical climate of the 24th century had become somewhat unpredictable. The North American Union—which includes the United States, Canada, and Mexico—had been locked in a competitive rivalry with the Great Asia Confederation, an alliance of countries such as China, Japan, Korea, Vietnam, and Singapore. Both were heavily focused on expanding their influence, especially in space exploration and the colonization of the Moon and Mars. While there was no direct evidence suggesting a nuclear conflict, some experts speculated that these tensions, combined with aggressive posturing on both sides, increased the risks of escalation."

Oliver frowned. "Yeah, I knew about the space race, but I didn't think it would get that bad."

"The rivalry," Lucas continued, "had reached a point where diplomatic relations were under significant strain. Both sides were quietly escalating their military presence in space, deploying armed satellites and developing defensive space stations. While these activities were not entirely secret, the full extent of the situation was obscured from the public. Behind closed doors, some experts speculated that the competition for control over Mars and other celestial bodies carried a tangible risk of conflict. My analysis of news and classified data—available to us through our government-affiliated research facility—suggested a calculated 5% probability that this rivalry could escalate into a full-scale war, potentially involving nuclear weapons, both on Earth and in space."

Oliver sank into a chair, his playful demeanor replaced by a stunned silence. "A 5% chance... That's not just a tiny risk. Why didn't anyone warn us? It feels like we were kept in the dark."

Ethan shifted uneasily, his thoughts turning to the scattered reports he had seen but dismissed. "I mean, I knew things were tense, sure. But I thought it was all about flexing—showing off space fleets and building fancy colonies. Nukes? That wasn't something anyone talked about. The media barely even hinted at it."

Lucas's voice remained steady. "The narrative presented to the public was carefully managed. Governments on both sides sought to avoid widespread panic or destabilization. While diplomatic talks continued, each side quietly prepared for worst-case scenarios. The 5% probability of nuclear conflict was based on intelligence data and strategic trends—not a certainty, but a calculated risk that few outside high-level circles were aware of."

Oliver's expression darkened. "So, you're telling me that even when we were running experiments in our lab, working on the time machine, there was a chance that everything could've gone up in flames? That our city—Electropolis—could've been hit?"

"Correct," Lucas said. "That chance remained until the moment you left your timeline."

Ethan let out a slow breath, the gravity of it settling over them. "Damn… we might've dodged something huge without even realizing it. But still, 5%… I don't know if that's enough to scare most people."

Oliver, shaking his head, disagreed. "Freaking 5%. If you put a 5% chance on anything, that's a lot. That's more than enough to wipe out entire cities in North America. And if it's nuclear, it's not just the explosions. It's the fallout. The radiation. It could change everything."

Ethan nodded, rubbing his hands together as if trying to shake off the tension creeping into his body. "I get it. But... we can't do anything about it now. We're stuck here in 1971."

"Ben wouldn't even consider going back if he thought this was actually happening in our own century." Oliver muttered, more to himself.

"You know," Ethan broke the silence, his voice quieter now, "maybe it's not so bad that we're stuck here. At least here, we don't have to worry about all of that…"

Oliver glanced at him, unsure whether to agree or argue. Instead, he settled for a sigh, letting the tension in his body release, if only for a moment. "Maybe. But if we ever do get back, I'm gonna make sure we figure this out. I'm not gonna live with that kind of bomb hanging over our heads. Literally."

Ethan gave him a half-smile. "Yeah. And until then… I guess we'll just have to deal with the real challenges down here. Like surviving elementary school and not getting our asses whipped."

Oliver suddenly froze, his eyes widening in alarm. "Oh no—school! We haven't even started on our Multicultural Presentation!"

Ethan's expression turned panicked. "Crap. Lucas, help us out with this!"

Lucas's voice chimed in, calm as ever. "I'm afraid I cannot assist. We've discussed this before—Ben has expressly prohibited my involvement in your schoolwork."

Groaning in frustration, both boys bolted out of the storage room and dashed to their bedroom, already mentally scrambling to throw together the assignment due the next day.

Chapter 18: Dynamics

Ben had outdone himself with dinner tonight. The scent of seared steak filled the room, and the boys were practically salivating by the time he placed the plates on the table.

"Steak night, huh?" Oliver said, cutting into his portion eagerly. "This smells amazing."

Ben smiled, taking his seat. "Thought we could use something special tonight."

The trio ate in comfortable silence for a few moments, the occasional clink of cutlery punctuating the air. Oliver was the first to speak up again.

"This is so juicy, Ben. Thanks!" he said, his mouth half-full as he chomped down on another bite.

Ben chuckled. "Glad you like it. Actually…" He paused, setting his fork down. "I wanted to talk to you both about something."

Ethan and Oliver exchanged glances, their attention shifting to Ben.

"Don't tell me you got fired," Ethan said dryly, though his tone betrayed just a hint of worry.

"Not even close," Ben replied with a small laugh. "No, this is... personal. I've been seeing someone. Dating, actually."

Ethan froze mid-bite, his fork clattering onto his plate. Oliver blinked in surprise, his steak momentarily forgotten.

"Dating?" Ethan repeated, his tone dripping with disbelief. "You're always telling us to stay under the radar, avoid trouble, and now you're—what? Falling in love in the 1970s?"

"Exactly!" Oliver added, leaning forward. "You've been harping on about how dangerous it is to get too involved with people from this time. Who is it, anyway?"

Ben held up his hands defensively. "Relax, guys. It's not what you think. It's Emily—Doctor Reynolds. You know, the one who gave you your vaccinations?"

Ethan's reaction was immediate and fiery. "Her? Seriously? I don't even like her! She's always asking too many questions!"

Ben sighed, bracing himself for the barrage. "Look, I get it. But think about it—if I shut everyone out completely, it's going to make us look suspicious. A single dad with two kids, never socializing? That's a recipe for red flags."

Ethan narrowed his eyes. "So, by that logic, Oliver and I should be allowed to date, too. Let's see how you feel about that."

Oliver smirked, clearly enjoying the direction this was going. "Yeah, Ben. What if I got a girlfriend? Wouldn't that make us even more 'normal'?"

Ben pinched the bridge of his nose, exhaling sharply. "First of all, I'm not playing matchmaker for you two. Second, this isn't about you. I'm pretending to be a widower, raising two boys. A relationship makes sense for my cover."

Ethan wasn't ready to let it go. "So why Emily? Why not, I don't know, Sarah from the JadiMart? She already likes you."

Ben shook his head, his voice softening. "Because I don't love Sarah. I care about Emily. She's smart, kind, and... Look, I promise, this isn't serious. It's casual, just enough to keep things normal for now. When the time comes to leave, I'll break it off. No harm done."

Oliver leaned back in his chair, his expression contemplative. "Casual, huh? And she's okay with that?"

"She doesn't know everything," Ben admitted. "But I'm being careful. I'm doing this for us. To make our lives here easier, safer."

Ethan folded his arms, his lips pressing into a tight line. "Fine. But don't expect me to be happy about it. And don't bring her over too much."

Ben allowed himself a small smile. "Deal. Now finish your steaks before they get cold."

Ben knew this wouldn't be the end of the conversation—Ethan, especially, would have more to say. But for now, it was enough.

The smell of roasted chicken wafted through the modest kitchen, mingling with the faint crackle of a record player in the corner.

Ben had once again put effort into dinner, serving up a well-seasoned chicken dish alongside mashed potatoes and green beans. Ethan and Oliver sat at the table, already digging into their plates.

"Man, you're spoiling us with these meals, Ben," Oliver said between bites.

"Yeah, almost feels like you're trying to soften us up for something," Ethan added, narrowing his eyes playfully.

Ben smirked, taking a sip from his water glass. "You caught me. I do have some news."

Oliver raised an eyebrow, pausing mid-bite. "What kind of news?"

"Tomorrow, we're taking a trip to Boston," Ben announced. "I've heard they have a big zoo there. Thought you two might like to see it."

Oliver's face lit up. "Oh, awesome! I've always wanted to see real lions!"

Ethan's enthusiasm was more subdued, but he nodded. "Yeah, me too. It's kinda sad how many animals are extinct in our century. Seeing them in person... that'd be cool."

Ben grinned. "Great! I knew you'd like the idea. Oh, and by the way—Emily is coming with us."

The room fell silent for a beat before both boys exclaimed, "What?!"

Ethan dropped his fork with a clang. "Wait a minute. I feel like you're only treating us nice because you want to slip Emily into our lives."

Ben sighed, leaning back in his chair. "Look, I won't deny I want you two to get along with her, but come on. This isn't some big conspiracy. We're just going to a zoo. That's it."

Oliver shook his head firmly. "Nope. This is just... weird. I'm not going."

Ethan crossed his arms. "Yeah, me neither. You and Emily can have your little date without dragging us into it."

Ben rubbed his temples, trying to keep his patience. "Five seconds ago, you both were excited about seeing wild animals— animals that, I might remind you, are extinct in our time. Now you're backing out just because Emily's coming? That's ridiculous."

Ethan snorted. "It's not ridiculous. You're trying to force her into our lives."

"And honestly," Oliver added, his voice tinged with suspicion, "it sounds like she wants to see us more than the zoo. What's that about?"

Ben hesitated for a fraction of a second, which was all the boys needed to pounce.

"She wants to be our mom, doesn't she?" Oliver accused, his tone dramatic.

"Oh, for the love of—no, she doesn't!" Ben shot back, exasperated. "It's just a fun trip to Boston. That's it. Stop acting like this is the end of the world."

Ethan shook his head stubbornly. "We're not going."

"Yeah, count me out," Oliver agreed, crossing his arms for emphasis.

Ben leaned forward, his voice calm but firm. "Alright, how about this: if you two come along and behave yourselves, I'll double your allowance this month."

Oliver's eyes widened. "Double?" He glanced at Ethan. "Okay. Deal!"

"Oliver, no!" Ethan groaned, throwing his hands in the air. "Ben is totally manipulating us with money. Why does he get to decide what happens with our allowance, anyway?"

Ben raised an eyebrow. "Because I'm the one going to work, earning money, and playing the role of your 'dad,' that's why."

"This is so unfair," Ethan muttered, slumping back in his chair.

Ben smirked, picking up his fork. "Life's not always fair, kiddo. Now finish your chicken. We've got a big day tomorrow."

Ethan grumbled under his breath, but he reluctantly went back to eating, casting Oliver an occasional glare. Oliver, meanwhile, was already imagining the lions at the zoo, his annoyance with Ben melting away in the excitement of the promised trip—and the extra allowance.

Saturday morning came early, and the soft glow of dawn filtered through the curtains in the boys' shared room. Ben pushed open the door quietly, stepping inside to rouse them for their trip. The room was modest but neat, each boy's single bed lined up on opposite sides.

Ben approached Ethan's bed first, noticing his pajama bottoms had been kicked to the foot of the bed. He smirked, shaking his head. Why does he always sleep like this?

Sitting on the edge of the bed, Ben reached out and gently shook Ethan's shoulder. "Hey, son. It's 5:30. Time to get up and hit the road."

Ethan groaned and rolled over, burying his face deeper into the pillow. "I'm not going…" he mumbled, half-asleep.

"Is that so?" Ben teased, his grin widening. Without warning, he yanked the blanket off Ethan in one swift motion.

Ethan squirmed and curled into a ball. "Hey! It's cold!"

Ben wasn't about to let him off that easy. He grabbed Ethan under the arms, lifted him up effortlessly, and flipped him over his lap. With a mischievous gleam in his eye, he delivered a few playful smacks to Ethan's bare bottom.

"Wake up, sleepyhead," Ben said, chuckling.

"Ouch!" Ethan yelped, now fully awake. "Alright, alright, I'm up!"

Satisfied, Ben set him back on the bed, ruffling his hair before turning his attention to Oliver.

Moving to the other side of the room, Ben found that Oliver had also kicked his pajama pants to the foot of the bed. He rolled his eyes. "What is it with you two?" he muttered under his breath.

Leaning over, he gave Oliver a light shake. "Come on, kiddo. Time to wake up."

Oliver let out a muffled groan and buried himself under his pillow.

Ben crossed his arms. "You're not making me drag you out of bed, are you?"

No response.

"Alright, you asked for it." Ben grabbed Oliver's blanket, whipped it off, and swatted his pajama-clad backside.

Oliver jolted awake, sitting up abruptly. "What the—? Okay, okay, I'm awake!"

Ben laughed, stepping back. "You two are impossible. Good thing we're not running on 24th-century time, or we'd already be late."

Despite their grogginess, the boys began to stir, rubbing the sleep from their eyes. The biotechnology of the 24th century had worked remarkably well, reversing Ethan and Oliver into the exact biological forms of 10-year-old boys. Their sleep cycles were deep, and like typical kids, waking them up early was a challenge.

As the boys shuffled toward the bathroom to get ready, grumbling under their breath, Ben couldn't help but smile. This trip was going to be a long one—but hopefully, it would be worth it.

The drive to Boston was mostly uneventful, save for a few sharp remarks from Ethan and Oliver about Emily joining them. Ben kept the mood light with jokes and stories, though the boys remained suspiciously quiet whenever Emily tried to engage them.

By mid-morning, they arrived at the Boston Zoo. It was bustling with families, the air filled with the chatter of children and the calls of exotic animals. The boys' expressions softened as they stepped through the gates, their attention immediately captured by the sights and sounds of creatures they'd only read about in their century.

"Oh wow, look!" Oliver whispered, pointing to a nearby enclosure. "A tiger. A real tiger."

Ethan nodded, his earlier grumpiness momentarily forgotten. "I can't believe they had these just... out in the open like this. Do you think they're genetically pure or mixed with extinct subspecies?"

"Hard to say," Oliver murmured back.

Emily caught up with them, smiling warmly. "Isn't it incredible? Tigers are such majestic animals."

The boys glanced at her briefly before looking back at the enclosure, clearly uninterested in engaging. Ben stepped in, clapping a hand on Ethan's shoulder. "Ethan, why don't you tell Emily what you think of the tiger?"

Ethan shrugged, muttering, "It's fine, I guess."

Ben sighed but didn't push further.

As they moved deeper into the zoo, Emily tried again to connect with the boys. At the aviary, she leaned down to Oliver's level. "What's your favorite bird here? Mine's the scarlet macaw—look at those colors!"

Oliver hesitated, his gaze darting to Ben. "Uh… yeah, it's nice," he said flatly before walking over to Ethan, whispering, "Why's she trying so hard? It's like she's applying for a job or something."

Ethan stifled a laugh. "Right? She's overdoing it."

The brothers' dynamic became more apparent at the elephant exhibit, where they couldn't hide their awe.

"Look at the size of that thing!" Ethan said under his breath, his eyes wide.

"And it's not even a woolly mammoth," Oliver replied. "Imagine if they had those here."

Emily overheard them and smiled. "You two seem to know a lot about animals. Do you read a lot about them in school?"

Ethan didn't respond, his gaze fixed on the elephants.

"Ethan," Emily prompted gently.

Still nothing.

Ben, noticing the awkward silence, stepped in. He turned Ethan around by the shoulders and gave him a pointed look. "Ethan, Emily asked you a question. What do you say?"

Ethan rolled his eyes but finally muttered, "Yeah, I guess we read about them in school. Sometimes."

Emily's smile faltered slightly but recovered quickly. "That's great! What's your favorite subject?"

Ethan shrugged again, clearly uninterested in continuing the conversation.

Ben sighed, turning to Oliver. "And you, Oliver? What about you?"

Oliver shifted uncomfortably. "I like science," he admitted reluctantly.

"That's wonderful!" Emily said enthusiastically. "What kind of science? Biology? Chemistry?"

"Mostly physics," Oliver replied before quickly adding, "Can we go see the lions now?"

The lions turned out to be a highlight of the trip. Both boys pressed against the railing of the enclosure, their earlier reservations forgotten as they observed the massive predators lounging in the sun.

"Look at that mane," Oliver said, his voice filled with admiration. "It's so much bigger than I imagined."

Ethan nodded. "Do you think they're as strong as the textbooks say? Like, can they really take down a buffalo by themselves?"

Ben smiled, happy to see them enjoying themselves, even if their excitement was directed more at the animals than at bonding with Emily.

By lunchtime, the boys had mellowed slightly. Emily bought them ice cream cones, which they accepted with polite "thank yous" but little more. Ben made a point of sitting between the boys and Emily during their meal, mediating the conversation.

"So," Ben said, breaking the silence, "what's been your favorite part of the zoo so far?"

"The lions," Ethan answered without hesitation.

"Definitely the lions," Oliver agreed.

Emily nodded. "They're amazing, aren't they? I've always found big cats fascinating. Did you know a lion's roar can be heard up to five miles away?"

Ethan looked skeptical but refrained from commenting. Oliver, however, couldn't resist. "Actually, it's closer to four miles under ideal conditions," he said, his tone matter-of-fact.

Emily blinked, caught off guard, but then laughed. "Well, I stand corrected. You really do know your stuff, Oliver."

Ben chuckled, giving Oliver a small nudge. "See? You're impressing her already."

Oliver shrugged, his cheeks tinged red. Ethan smirked but said nothing, licking his ice cream cone instead.

As the day wound down and they made their way back to the car, the boys were visibly more relaxed, though still wary of Emily's attempts to connect. Ben, ever the mediator, considered the day a small victory—baby steps toward bridging the gap between his casual relationship with Emily and the boys' guarded attitudes.

For Ethan and Oliver, the highlight of the day remained the animals. As they climbed into the car, Oliver leaned over to Ethan and whispered, "Okay, the lions were worth it. But next time, no way are we letting Ben drag her along again."

Ethan nodded in agreement, glancing at Emily as she chatted with Ben up front. "Definitely."

One evening, as Ben sat in the living room, sipping a cup of tea after a long day at work, Lucas's voice interrupted his thoughts.

"Ben," Lucas's tone was calm but serious, "I have new information regarding a timeline alteration that requires your attention."

Ben set his cup down, feeling that familiar twinge of anxiety whenever Lucas had to update him about changes. "What is it?" he asked, leaning forward in his seat.

Lucas explained, "After conducting a comparison between the memory cards and the data I gathered since our arrival, I discovered a significant deviation involving an individual named Mark Petersen. He is the boy Ethan had an altercation with at school."

Ben rubbed his temples. He remembered that day well. Ethan, in one of his many frustrated outbursts, had pushed Mark Petersen, who then fell and injured his forehead. It was a minor incident, but Ben had to bribe Mark's mother with $1,000 to avoid trouble. He thought the matter was behind them, but Lucas's tone suggested otherwise.

"How does that affect the timeline?" Ben asked, trying to make sense of it.

"In the original timeline," Lucas began, "Mark Petersen would have eventually grown up to become a key member of the Mars Exploration Rover (MER) mission in 2004, working with NASA. His contributions would have been pivotal in the success of the mission. However, due to Ethan's actions and your decision to intervene by paying Mark's mother, this trajectory has been altered."

Ben's face hardened as he listened. "You're saying because of that one incident, Mark's life changed course?"

"Correct," Lucas confirmed. "Because of the injury and subsequent events, Mark no longer follows the same path. He does not go on to become part of the MER mission. As a result, the Mars Exploration Rover mission failed in this timeline. However, a similar mission conducted by China in the same year succeeded instead. This shift was likely influenced by the absence of Mark's contributions to the American team."

Ben leaned back in his chair, absorbing the gravity of Lucas's words. "So, because of us, a pivotal moment in space exploration didn't happen for the U.S., but for China instead?"

"Precisely. In the unaltered timeline, the U.S. Mars Exploration Rover mission led to groundbreaking discoveries. But with Mark Petersen no longer involved, the mission encountered critical errors and ultimately failed. China, meanwhile, capitalized on their mission's success."

Ben felt a cold wave of guilt wash over him. He thought about Mark—a kid in 1971, just like Ethan and Oliver, but whose future had been drastically altered because of one impulsive push. A minor moment of schoolyard frustration had led to a massive shift in world events.

"I didn't think... I never realized it would affect something this big," Ben muttered, shaking his head. "We were just trying to blend in, keep a low profile. Now we've changed history—again."

Lucas's voice was calm but carried the weight of the situation. "This is the nature of time travel, Ben. Even the smallest actions can have profound consequences. It is impossible to exist in the past without leaving some mark."

Ben clenched his fists, frustrated by the complexity of it all. "Is there anything we can do to fix this?"

"At this stage, it would be difficult to reverse the changes that have been made," Lucas replied. "The only viable option would be to return to the future with the time machine once it is functional again. By doing so, you may be able to assess the full scope of the alterations."

Ben was silent for a moment, then let out a long sigh. "And we can't go back until we get the gold piece. Stuck here... changing history with every move we make."

Lucas remained silent for a moment, letting Ben's thoughts settle.

Ben finally stood, his jaw clenched with determination. "We need to be more careful. I can't afford to let this spiral any further. We have to lay low, even more than we have already."

"I will continue to monitor for further alterations," Lucas said. "I will alert you immediately if any other significant changes occur."

He needed to have a serious talk with Ethan and Oliver. What had been just a minor school incident had become something far greater, and from now on, they all needed to be aware of the consequences their actions carried.

Time travel, it seemed, was far more dangerous than they had ever imagined.

Chapter 19: Pressure Points

Benjamin sat alone in the dimly lit office of the science department's director, the quiet hum of the city of Electropolis vibrating faintly in the background. His fingers tapped restlessly on the edge of his chair as he awaited the arrival of the director. The meeting had been scheduled suddenly, and Ben had an unsettling feeling about it.

The door opened, and Director Alara Gray strode in, her face a mask of professionalism marred by a hint of frustration. She placed a digital tablet on the desk and slid into her seat across from Ben.

"Benjamin," she began, her tone sharp. "We need to talk about Ethan and Oliver."

Ben sighed inwardly but maintained his composure. "What's happened this time?"

Director Gray swiped across the tablet's screen, bringing up a series of holographic images. The first was a photo of Oliver at a public square, surrounded by a sea of protestors. His expression was fierce, his arm raised high as he held a sign that read, "Stop Government Overreach!" The unmistakable emblem of the science department's logo adorned the backpack slung over his shoulder.

"This," Gray said, pointing to the image. "Do you know how many calls I've received since these photos started circulating? Oliver's made himself the face of this protest, and by extension, he's dragged the department into it. We're a government-funded institution, Ben! This kind of behavior is unacceptable."

Ben leaned forward, studying the image with a frown. "Oliver has strong opinions. He's young and… impulsive, but I'm sure he didn't mean for it to reflect on the department."

"Intent doesn't matter when the damage is already done," Gray countered, her voice rising slightly. "We've had to issue a public statement distancing ourselves from his actions. If this happens again, I'll have no choice but to consider disciplinary measures."

Ben nodded reluctantly. "I'll speak to him."

Gray swiped again, bringing up another set of images and a list of inventory logs. "Now, let's discuss Ethan."

Ben winced. "What did he do?"

"This," she said, pointing to a highlighted section of the inventory. "Rare isotopes and superconducting filaments—materials critical for three other ongoing projects—all requisitioned by Ethan without proper authorization. He used them for…" She paused, her lip curling slightly. "A personal side project. A self-cleaning desk, Benjamin. A desk."

Ben groaned, running a hand down his face. "I'll talk to him too. He's… enthusiastic, but he doesn't always think things through."

"That's putting it lightly," Gray replied. "His little experiment has delayed several key projects by weeks. Do you understand the pressure I'm under? The government is already questioning the viability of your time machine project. Two years, Ben. Two years of funding, and we have nothing to show for it."

Ben sat back, his expression darkening. "We're making progress. These things take time."

"Time isn't something we have in abundance," Gray snapped. "If you don't start showing results soon, they'll pull the plug. And given the stunts your team keeps pulling, they might just pull it sooner."

Ben felt the weight of her words settle heavily on his shoulders. He had always believed in Ethan and Oliver—their brilliance, their potential—but their recklessness was becoming a liability.

"I'll handle it," he said finally, his voice firm. "I'll make sure they stay in line."

Gray leaned back in her chair, scrutinizing him. "I hope you do, Ben. For your sake and for the department's."

As Ben left the director's office, the images of Oliver's protest and Ethan's misused materials lingered in his mind. He knew he had to have a serious conversation with them—not just as their team leader, but as their friend. They needed to understand the stakes, or everything they had worked for would come crashing down.

Ben strode into their shared workspace later that afternoon, his expression stormy. The time machine loomed in the corner, its sleek, partially completed form an imposing reminder of their collective responsibility. Ethan and Oliver, seated at their workstations, looked up as he entered, their faces immediately tensing.

"We need to talk," Ben said, his voice steady but firm.

The two exchanged uneasy glances but didn't argue. Ben walked to the center of the room, standing tall and radiating authority. He gestured for them to stay seated as he began.

"I just came from a meeting with Director Gray. She's not happy—and neither am I." He fixed them both with a hard stare. "Oliver, care to explain this?"

He tapped on a handheld device, projecting the image of Oliver at the protest onto the nearest wall. Oliver's shoulders slumped slightly.

"It was about the military activities on the Moon and Mars," Oliver began, his voice defensive but not defiant. "They're using resources meant for exploration and scientific advancement to build weapons and fortifications. I thought... I thought I could make a difference."

"And you thought dragging the department into your personal beliefs was the right way to do that?" Ben's tone was sharp. "You were wearing your department-issued backpack, Oliver. The government funds us. Do you have any idea how bad this looks?"

Oliver opened his mouth but closed it again, realizing he had no good defense. Ben turned his gaze to Ethan.

"And you," he said, projecting the inventory logs onto the wall. "You used rare materials meant for critical projects to build a desk. A desk, Ethan. Explain yourself."

Ethan fidgeted, avoiding Ben's eyes. "I... I thought it would be a cool addition to the time machine's interior. Something practical and sleek."

Ben's brow furrowed deeper. "And you didn't think to clear it with anyone first? Or consider the impact on other projects? Weeks of delays, Ethan. Weeks."

Ethan shrank in his chair, muttering, "I didn't think it would cause that much trouble."

Ben moved behind them, his tall frame casting a shadow over their seated forms. Grabbing the collars of their lab coats firmly, he leaned in just enough for his voice to be low and commanding.

"One more mishap," he said, his tone cold and deliberate, "and I will be the one kicking the butt. Understand?"

Both men nodded quickly, their earlier confidence drained. Ben released their collars and straightened up.

"Good. Now get back to work. And this time, use your brains for something productive."

He turned and walked out, leaving Ethan and Oliver in a tense silence. The faint hum of the time machine filled the room as they exchanged sheepish glances before returning to their tasks. The weight of Ben's warning hung heavily in the air, a reminder of just how high the stakes truly were.

A couple of days later, Ben found himself in the director's conference room. The air was tense as he sat across from Director Gray, flanked by Ethan and Oliver on either side. The door opened, and three individuals strode in, their presence commanding immediate attention. Clad in crisp uniforms adorned with insignias of rank, the officers radiated an aura of authority.

Director Gray stood and introduced them. "Benjamin, gentlemen—meet Colonel Reinhardt, Commander Levene, and Lieutenant Harlow. They're here on behalf of the Lunar and Martian Defense Initiative."

Ben's stomach sank. Military involvement in scientific projects was rarely a good sign.

Colonel Reinhardt, a tall man with piercing gray eyes, wasted no time. "Dr. Benjamin, your time machine project has drawn the attention of high command. We've reviewed your progress reports, and while the theoretical groundwork is sound, we're concerned about the lack of tangible results. Two years of funding is more than generous."

Ben straightened in his chair, his tone measured. "Colonel, scientific breakthroughs require patience. The time machine's mechanics are delicate, and there are safety concerns we cannot ignore."

Commander Levene, a woman with a sharp gaze, interjected. "Safety concerns are secondary. What we need are results. A prototype. A test run. Something to prove this project isn't a waste of resources."

"It's not a waste," Ben replied firmly. "But if we rush the process, we risk catastrophic failure. The machine is designed to manipulate spacetime—any malfunction could have disastrous consequences."

Lieutenant Harlow leaned forward, his expression skeptical. "Are these concerns valid, or are they convenient excuses for delays? The Defense Initiative needs this project operational. The potential applications for reconnaissance and tactical advantage are limitless."

Ethan and Oliver exchanged uneasy glances. Ben clenched his fists under the table, choosing his words carefully. "This project was never intended for military use. Its purpose is scientific exploration and the advancement of knowledge—not warfare."

Colonel Reinhardt's expression hardened. "Dr. Benjamin Johnson, whether you like it or not, this is about more than science. The geopolitical landscape demands innovation, and your project is a key asset. We're not asking—we're ordering you to accelerate the timeline."

Ben's jaw tightened. "With all due respect, Colonel, this machine isn't a weapon. Treating it as one could lead to unforeseen consequences. I will not compromise the integrity of this project or the safety of my team."

The room fell silent, the tension palpable. Finally, Reinhardt stood, his towering presence casting a shadow over the table. "You have three months to produce results, Dr. Johnson. Fail, and this project will be reassigned to someone who understands the value of compliance."

Without waiting for a response, the officers turned and left, their footsteps echoing down the corridor. Director Gray exhaled slowly, her expression grim.

"That could have gone worse," she muttered.

Ben stood, his mind racing. "This project is already under immense pressure. Adding arbitrary deadlines and military interference is a recipe for disaster."

Gray placed a hand on his arm, her voice softer. "Do what you can, Ben. But tread carefully. They won't hesitate to take drastic measures."

As Ben, Ethan, and Oliver exited the conference room, the weight of the conversation hung over them. Back in their workspace, Ethan broke the silence.

"Well, that was… intense."

Oliver shook his head. "Military types never change. They see a tool and immediately think of how to weaponize it."

Ben turned to face them, his expression serious. "We need to focus. No more mistakes, no more distractions. If we don't meet their demands—or at least show significant progress—they'll take over. And I don't trust them to handle this responsibly."

Ethan and Oliver nodded, their usual levity replaced by a sense of urgency. The time machine loomed in the corner, its unfinished form a stark reminder of the challenges ahead.

For the first time, the trio felt the weight of not just their ambitions, but the world-changing implications of their work—and the very real dangers of failure.

Chapter 20: Fathers and Sons

As the evening stretched into night, Oliver and Ethan were making their way home after a long and fun day with their classmates, Ava and Leo. The nearby mall had been the perfect place to spend time— shopping, playing games at the arcade, and grabbing some food. They had gotten so caught up in the excitement that they didn't even notice how late it had gotten.

Walking down the dimly lit street, Oliver checked his watch, squinting at the time. "Uh... Ethan, it's like 9 p.m. already."

Ethan, mid-laugh from a joke they had been sharing, froze. "What?! Oh, no… Ben is going to lose it."

They both picked up their pace, feeling the creeping sense of dread as they realized how much time had slipped away. They hadn't intended to stay out so late, but between the fun with their friends and forgetting they weren't really ordinary kids, it had happened.

Meanwhile, back at home, Ben had arrived late from work around 8 p.m. His usual routine was to find Ethan and Oliver either finishing homework or watching TV by the time he got home. But tonight, the house was eerily quiet.

"Boys?" Ben called out as he walked into the living room, but there was no response.

He made his way upstairs to their room, expecting to see them engrossed in their usual activities. When he found the room empty, a knot of worry started to form in his stomach. He didn't like the idea of them being out late, especially without telling him.

"Lucas," Ben said, standing in the middle of the boys' room. "Did Ethan and Oliver come home after school today?"

Lucas's voice, calm and even, filled the room. "I did not see them coming home after school today."

The knot tightened in Ben's chest. He immediately started thinking of worst-case scenarios. He knew that the boys could be impulsive, and despite all his efforts to keep them in line, they were still kids in this era—at least physically.

"Lucas, where could they have gone?" Ben asked, trying to keep his rising panic in check.

"You don't need to worry," Lucas responded, his tone measured. "They could be just around here. I suggest checking local parks, malls, or libraries."

Ben sighed heavily, running a hand through his hair. He knew Lucas was probably right, but that didn't stop the flood of concern from rushing through his mind. The 1970s weren't the same as the 24th century, and there were dangers here he couldn't control. If something had happened to them…

He grabbed his coat and keys, mentally going over the list of places Lucas had suggested. The mall seemed like the most obvious choice, especially since Ethan and Oliver had mentioned their friends Ava and Leo earlier that week.

As Ben hurried out the door, the weight of his responsibility felt heavier than ever. Ethan and Oliver weren't just his companions on this journey—they were his responsibility. He had to keep them safe, no matter what.

Driving towards the mall, Ben's mind raced. He wasn't just angry at them for being out late—he was scared. If anything happened to them, he wasn't sure he could forgive himself.

As he pulled into the mall parking lot, his eyes scanned the area for any sign of the boys. His heart raced as he stepped out of the car, determined to find them and bring them home safely.

As Officer Thomas drove slowly down the street, his headlights revealed two small figures running as fast as they could. It was Ethan and Oliver, hurrying to get home without being seen. The sight of the police car behind them only made them run faster.

"Those boys..." Officer Thomas muttered, narrowing his eyes. He recognized them instantly. It had been a year since he'd last dealt with Benjamin and his two strange "sons." Something about their situation had never sat right with him, but he'd let it go after Benjamin's convincing explanations and fake IDs. But now, seeing them running through the streets at this hour? It didn't look good.

"Stay in the car, Taylor," he said to his daughter, who sat in the passenger seat, her eyebrows raised in curiosity. Officer Thomas stepped out, his boots hitting the pavement with authority. "Hey! You two! Stop right there!"

Hearing the officer's shout, Ethan and Oliver exchanged a look of pure dread. "Oh no..." Oliver muttered under his breath, his heart racing.

"We have to run, Oliver," Ethan hissed, his voice shaky. "If he catches us, Ben's going to kill us. And who knows what the cop will do!"

But their legs, though fast for 10-year-olds, were no match for the officer's longer strides. Officer Thomas quickly closed the distance, grabbing both boys by the scruff of their necks. "Where do you two think you're going?" His tone was stern but not unkind, though his grip was firm.

Ethan and Oliver froze, wide-eyed, their stomachs sinking. They had no choice but to follow the officer's lead as he marched them toward the police car.

Officer Thomas opened the back door and unceremoniously pushed them inside. "Get in," he said, shaking his head in disapproval. "You boys should know better than to be out this late, running around like this."

As the door slammed shut, sealing them inside the patrol car, Ethan groaned, his head leaning back against the seat. "Oh nooo..." he whispered to Oliver. "This is the last thing we needed."

Oliver looked equally stressed. "Ben's going to flip out when he hears about this."

From the front seat, Officer Thomas's daughter, Taylor, peered curiously at the boys through the rearview mirror. "Aren't those the same boys you talked about before, Dad?" she asked quietly, recognizing them from the stories her father had shared about the odd family staying in town.

Officer Thomas nodded, his eyes fixed on the road as he began driving. "Yeah, that's them. And something tells me their dad is going to have a lot of explaining to do." He glanced in the mirror at the boys, his suspicion growing again. "But first, let's get you two home."

Ethan and Oliver sat in the back of the police car, hearts pounding, wondering just how much trouble they were about to be in— both with Ben and the local authorities.

Ben's heart had been pounding with worry as he sat on the front steps, talking quietly to Lucas. The hidden camera near the front door gave him a view of the street, but there was no sign of Ethan or Oliver. Lucas had been little help—modern surveillance systems of the 24th century didn't exist here in 1971. Ben had already searched the local mall and the library with no success, and now, he was left waiting, a knot of fear tightening in his stomach.

"They're just kids," Ben muttered under his breath. "But they don't realize how dangerous it is here. Not like home." He took a deep breath, imagining the worst. What if something terrible had happened?

The thought of losing Ethan and Oliver, who now felt more like his real sons than just fellow scientists, was unbearable.

As if in response to his spiraling thoughts, the unmistakable sound of a police car pulling up broke through the still night. Ben's heart sank, his mind jumping to the worst possible conclusion—had they been hurt? Had they drowned in a pond, or been hit by a car? His chest tightened with dread.

When Officer Thomas stepped out of the car and let Ethan and Oliver climb out from the back seat, Ben felt a flood of relief wash over him. The boys were alive—but the sight of them with their heads down, clearly aware of the trouble they were in, made him immediately switch to frustration and anger. His face hardened as he approached, but deep down, it was the relief of knowing they were safe that drove his next actions.

"Okay, naughty boys, you're home," Officer Thomas said, giving a stern but somewhat amused look at Ethan and Oliver. "Looks like your dad was waiting."

Taylor, Thomas's daughter, stepped out of the car as well, giving the boys a wave with a cheeky smile. "Goodnight, handsome!" she called out, her tone playful. Ethan and Oliver kept their heads down, too mortified and terrified to even acknowledge her.

Ben shot up from the steps, running toward the boys and the officer. "What happened?" he asked, his voice sharper than he intended, still wound up from the fear of losing them.

Officer Thomas gave him a calm look. "I found them running around town, probably heading home." He turned to glance at the boys. "It's late for kids to be out on their own."

Ben knelt slightly to look Ethan and Oliver in the eyes. His voice dropped, stern and cold. "Where did you two go?"

Ethan shuffled his feet. "We... were at the mall," he mumbled, unable to meet Ben's eyes.

Ben shot a quick look back at Officer Thomas, softening his tone. "Thank you so much, officer. I really appreciate this."

Thomas nodded. "I'm Thomas, remember me?" he asked, tipping his hat. "We've met before, about a year ago."

Ben straightened up. "Ah, yes, Officer Thomas, of course. Thank you again."

Thomas gave him a curious look, tilting his head slightly. "Seemed like you were talking to someone when I pulled up."

Ben froze for a moment, then forced a casual smile. "Oh, no, I was just talking to myself," he said quickly, gesturing toward the boys with a chuckle. "You know, saying, 'They'd be dead when they got home,' just to myself." He let out a forced laugh, hoping to brush it off as a typical parental outburst.

The officer raised an eyebrow, unconvinced but unwilling to press further. "Oh, really?" he said. "I could've sworn I heard you talking to someone else."

194

Ethan and Oliver exchanged a nervous glance. They knew what was coming the moment Officer Thomas left. Ben's face was calm, but that only made them more afraid of what he would do once they were alone.

"Ah, well, you know how it is," Ben said, still trying to sound nonchalant. "Kids make you say all sorts of things."

Thomas nodded but gave one last lingering look at the house, almost like he suspected there was more going on. "Well, take care of those boys. It's late for them to be out."

"I will," Ben promised. "Thank you again, Officer."

As Thomas got back into his car, Lucas's voice came through quietly in Ben's ear from the hidden camera. "Interesting."

Ben ignored Lucas's comment, watching the police car drive away before turning back to Ethan and Oliver. His face hardened again. "Inside. Now."

Ethan and Oliver didn't say a word, their stomachs churning with dread as they hurried into the house. They knew they were in for a serious talk—possibly worse. Tonight, they'd pushed him too far.

Lucas, always observing, quietly noted the rising tension but said nothing further. He knew Ben cared deeply for the boys, but he also knew the limits of his patience. Tonight, those limits had been tested.

The clock ticked past 10 PM, and the house was steeped in an uneasy quiet as Ben's footsteps echoed on the wooden floor. His frustration had reached a boiling point, and he was determined to make sure Ethan and Oliver understood the gravity of their actions. His stern voice filled the hallway as he addressed the boys.

"Change up and go to bed!" Ben commanded. His tone left no room for argument. "I'll deal with you two tomorrow."

Oliver, trying to hold back his tears, stepped forward, his voice pleading. "Ben! Please, we're sorry. Nothing serious happened! That police officer just caught us by chance. It's not like we were doing anything dangerous."

Ethan, standing beside Oliver, added with desperation, "We were just out a bit late. We're not little kids. Please, there's no need to discipline us—we're really sorry. Next time, we'll let you know in advance if we're going to be out late."

Ben's face stayed unreadable, but he didn't like the sound of "next time." Without a word, he reached down, took Ethan's hand, turned him around, and gave him two quick swats on the backside, firm but not harsh. Then he did the same to Oliver, making his point with just enough sting to let them know he meant it. Ben's discipline was never severe—just enough to get their attention and remind them that he cared and wanted them to stay on track.

A few tears slipped from the boys' eyes—not from pain, but from that familiar, uneasy feeling that came with knowing they'd let

Ben down. Despite the age swap, Ethan and Oliver still felt more like Ben's equals than his kids, and they knew Ben cared for them in that odd, big-brother-meets-reluctant-dad way. But getting scolded, and worse, swatted on the behind like they were naughty little boys, always stung their pride more than anything else.

Chapter 21: Officer Thomas

Two days later, as the school day ended and the sun began to sink low on the horizon, Ethan, Oliver, Ava, and Leo walked home together, their backpacks swinging with each step. The air was cool, the streets growing quieter as people retreated to their homes. Ava and Leo were chatting excitedly about some upcoming event at school, but Ethan and Oliver remained quiet, still nursing the sting of what had happened the other night—not just physically but emotionally.

The faint rumble of a car engine caught their attention. From behind, a police car slowly approached, its familiar presence making Ethan and Oliver tense. Ava, on the other hand, smiled brightly as she turned to see who it was.

Officer Thomas.

He rolled down his window, a friendly grin on his face as he matched their walking pace. "How's it going, kids?" he called out, his voice warm and familiar.

Ava beamed back. "Hi, Officer Thomas! We're doing great!" She waved, her usual cheerful self.

Ethan and Oliver, however, refused to acknowledge him. Their eyes were fixed straight ahead, lips pressed tightly together in stubborn silence. The mere sight of Thomas reminded them of their humiliating ordeal—being caught out late, dragged home in the back of his police car like they were helpless children, and the punishment that had followed. Their young faces, usually mischievous or curious, were now hardened with resentment.

Thomas noticed their cold demeanor and chuckled, his grin widening with a touch of teasing. "I guess some people had sore bums recently, huh?" he said with a laugh, clearly alluding to the spanking they'd received after he brought them home. He didn't seem to mean any harm by it, but the comment hit a sore spot, quite literally.

Ava giggled, oblivious to the tension, while Leo gave a nervous chuckle, glancing at Ethan and Oliver. But the boys remained stoic, their anger simmering just beneath the surface. The last thing they wanted was a reminder of that night—and especially not from the man who had played a part in it.

Thomas, sensing the mood, slowed his laughter and waved casually. "Alright, you kids stay out of trouble now," he said, a slight edge to his voice. He drove off slowly, his suspicion lingering in the air as the police car disappeared around the corner.

As soon as he was out of sight, Oliver finally spoke, his voice low and bitter. "I hate him."

Ethan nodded in agreement, his face still flushed with frustration. "Me too," he muttered, his fists clenched at his sides. The boys exchanged a glance, the unspoken understanding between them clear. They were tired of being treated like children—especially by Ben, and now Officer Thomas.

Ava, noticing their mood, tried to lighten the air. "Come on, guys. It's not that bad. He was just joking."

But Ethan and Oliver couldn't shake the embarrassment, and as they walked the rest of the way home, their thoughts were already spinning, filled with plans to reclaim some control over their lives in this strange, restrictive world they were trapped in.

At his office, Officer Thomas leaned back in his chair, eyes narrowed as he skimmed through the report his staff had compiled. His instincts had been nudging him for a while now—ever since he first met Benjamin and the boys a year ago. Something about them didn't sit right with him. The extended hotel stay, the strange way they carried themselves, and now the late-night incident with Ethan and Oliver running around like they had something to hide. He had requested a full background check on them, just to be sure.

As he flipped through the file, the information presented was exactly what he had been told before: Benjamin Johnson, 30 years old, a recent transplant to the town, now working at an energy company. Ethan and Oliver, his twin sons, aged 10, enrolled in the local elementary school.

It all seemed... normal. Too normal.

Thomas frowned as he glanced at the boys' birth certificates. Everything was accounted for—dates, names, even a record of a deceased wife, allegedly the boys' mother. The paperwork was airtight, leaving no room for doubt. But that was the problem. Thomas had been in law enforcement long enough to know that sometimes when things seemed too perfect, they usually weren't.

His mind wandered back to that night. The way Ben had nervously deflected when asked who he was talking to at the door. The boys' terrified expressions as they stood there, heads hung low, dreading what was to come. They didn't act like normal kids who'd just gotten in trouble. They acted like... well, like they were hiding something. Like they were scared of more than just a scolding.

But still, there was nothing in the report to confirm his suspicions. No criminal record, no red flags in their past. As far as the paper trail went, Ben Johnson was just a widowed father trying to raise his sons after a difficult move to the town.

Thomas rubbed his temples, feeling the weight of the unshakable doubt in his gut. He was a good cop—he trusted his instincts. There was more to this trio than met the eye, but without any solid evidence, all he had were gut feelings.

He placed the file down and stared at it for a long moment. There was nothing incriminating here—no gaps in their past, no strange details that would explain why they felt so out of place.

But Thomas wasn't done yet. He picked up the phone and dialed his staff. "I want you to dig deeper," he said, his tone firm. "Focus on their time before they moved here. See if there's anything— any unusual gaps, inconsistencies. Even the smallest detail. Let me know what you find."

Hanging up, Thomas leaned back in his chair again, eyes still on the report. There had to be something. It was just a matter of time before he found it.

As Ethan and Oliver approached the house, they saw Emily standing by her car, a warm smile on her face. The sun was setting, casting a soft glow on her as she waved at them. In her arms, she held a couple of bags—one filled with sweets, the other with small toys. Ethan and Oliver exchanged glances, both surprised and a little uneasy at the sight of her.

Emily had always been kind to them, but today, something felt different. Her smile seemed more maternal, her demeanor softer than usual. Ben hadn't mentioned she would be coming over today, and neither of them had expected a visitor after the recent tension at home.

"Hi, boys!" Emily greeted them cheerfully as they approached the driveway. "I thought I'd stop by and bring you two something special. Just a little treat for my favorite boys."

Ethan and Oliver forced smiles as they walked closer, their minds still on what had happened over the past few days. Ethan, always more cautious and suspicious, wondered if Emily knew what had happened. Oliver, on the other hand, just wanted to avoid any more trouble.

"We... didn't know you were coming," Oliver mumbled, his eyes darting to the bags in her hands.

"Well, it was a bit of a surprise," Emily said sweetly. She knelt down to their level and held out the bags. "I figured you two deserved a little something fun after a long day at school. And I got some candy I thought you'd like."

Ethan eyed the bags warily but reached out to take one, not wanting to seem rude. "Thanks," he said quietly.

If Emily wanted to win over Ben, she needed the boys on her side, too. She was already imagining herself as a part of their lives, perhaps even their stepmother someday. Emily stood up and looked at the house. "Is your dad home?" she asked, already knowing the answer

"Uh, yeah," Oliver said, "he's inside."

Emily nodded, then turned her attention back to the boys. "You know, if you ever need to talk about anything... I'm here for you," she said gently. "Your dad's doing his best, but sometimes it helps to have someone else to talk to, right?"

Ethan shifted uncomfortably, sensing that Emily was trying to get closer to them, to insert herself into their lives more than before. "We're fine," he said quickly, trying to avoid any deeper conversation.

Oliver, always the more diplomatic of the two, added, "Thanks for the candy and stuff. We appreciate it."

Emily smiled again, but this time it had a hint of determination behind it. She knew the boys were guarded, especially Ethan, but she was patient. She believed that, with time, she could win them over.

"Well, why don't you two go inside and enjoy your treats?" Emily said softly, stepping aside so they could head toward the front door. "I'll just say hi to your dad."

As they walked past her and entered the house, Ethan whispered to Oliver, "She's trying too hard."

Oliver shrugged, though he felt the same unease. "She's probably just being nice."

But Ethan wasn't convinced. He had a feeling Emily's kindness wasn't just for them—it was for something else, something that involved her wanting to be part of their strange and complicated world.

Ben sat on the couch, watching as Oliver carefully unwrapped the sweets Emily had brought. Despite everything that had happened in the past few days, Ben was relieved to see Oliver enjoying himself. He looked up at Emily, who was seated across from him, her smile warm as she observed the scene.

Ethan had bolted to his room immediately, not wanting to linger. But Oliver stayed behind to keep Emily company. Emily leaned in slightly, watching Oliver with a soft expression. "Oliver is so sweet and adorable," she said, her voice almost cooing. "He deserves all the love." Her eyes flicked to Ben as she spoke, and it was clear she wasn't just talking about sweets or toys. She was subtly suggesting that the boys were lacking something deeper—a motherly presence.

Ben caught the subtext. "You're saying that because you haven't seen the other side of them," he chuckled, his tone carrying an edge of exasperation. Emily, smiling, responded, "Boys will be boys, you know."

Oliver, between bites of candy, suddenly chimed in. "Dad, Officer Thomas followed us again as we walked home." His voice was casual, but the remark was enough to shift the atmosphere in the room.

Ben's brow furrowed, a trace of concern creeping into his expression. "Oh, him again... What does he want from us?" Ben leaned forward, his tone turning more serious. The last thing he needed was more attention from the local police, especially from Thomas, who had already been suspicious of them since day one.

Emily blinked in surprise. "Who? You mean Vincent? Vincent Thomas?" she asked, her curiosity piqued.

Ben shrugged, slightly irritated. "I don't know his first name, but he's been following me and the boys since we moved to town— like we're criminals or something."

Emily looked thoughtful for a moment. "Oh... I didn't know that." She hesitated, then added, "Vincent is my older brother. I'll talk to him."

Ben hadn't seen that coming. "Your brother?" he echoed, his worry deepening. Things just got more complicated. If Emily's brother was the one keeping tabs on them, it meant they were being watched more closely than he realized.

Upstairs, Ethan overheard the conversation. In a sudden, frustrated outburst, he shouted down from his room, "Officer Thomas was the reason Dad spanked us!"

The words hung in the air for a moment, and Ben's jaw tightened. He felt a flush of embarrassment rise, especially with Emily sitting right there.

Ben's voice was firm as he called up, "Get down here, Ethan. You don't yell like that in the house."

A moment later, Ethan reluctantly appeared at the top of the stairs, his face a mix of defiance and regret. He slowly descended the steps, clearly worried about what was coming next but unwilling to let it show.

Ben turned to Emily, a bit flustered and feeling the need to clarify. "A couple of days ago, Thomas found them out running around at 9 p.m. and drove them home. That's why I... well, why I gave them a quick smack." His voice held a hint of defensiveness; he didn't really owe Emily an explanation, but with Ethan bringing it up, he suddenly felt the need to justify his actions.

Emily, ever calm, nodded in understanding. "I'll talk to him," she said, her voice soothing. "He probably doesn't realize, or maybe he's just trying to get to know you all better. Vincent can be protective, but he means well. I know him."

Ben sighed, his tension easing slightly. Emily had a way of diffusing things, making them feel less chaotic. Still, he couldn't shake the feeling that they were walking a tightrope with Thomas—and now, with Emily being his sister, things were even more tangled.

Ethan stood awkwardly at the bottom of the stairs, his eyes darting between Ben and Emily. He looked slightly relieved that Emily wasn't pressing the issue of the spanking, but he was still on edge. Oliver, sitting quietly with his sweets, glanced up Ethan with a look that seemed to say, Why did you have to shout that?

Emily rose from her seat, smoothing down her skirt. "Well, I should probably head out," she said. "But don't worry—I'll have a word with Vincent. He just needs to know that you're good people." She gave Ben a reassuring smile, then bent down to give Oliver a quick hug before heading toward the door.

As she left, Ben watched her go, a swirl of thoughts in his head. He couldn't quite decide if Emily's involvement made things better or worse. But one thing was certain—this situation was getting more complicated with every passing day.

Two days later, Emily walked into the small-town police station that afternoon, her heels clicking softly against the tiled floor. It was a cozy, familiar place, not intimidating like police stations in big cities. She had grown up in this town, after all, and her older brother Vincent Thomas had been a fixture here for years. As she stepped into his office area, she noticed Taylor, her niece, lounging around, a book in her hands.

Taylor's face lit up when she saw Emily. "Hii, Aunt Emily!" she chirped, practically bouncing over to give her a quick hug. "What brought you here?"

Emily smiled warmly, brushing a hand through Taylor's hair. "Hi, sweetheart. I just need to talk to your dad for a bit."

Taylor nodded, already distracted by something else, but not before flashing a curious grin. "Ooh, are you gonna talk about Ben?" she teased playfully, before darting out of the room.

Emily sighed lightly. Kids were so quick to catch onto things. But she knew this conversation wasn't going to be that simple. She knocked on the door to her brother's office, stepping inside before he could respond.

Thomas was seated behind his desk, flipping through some paperwork. His head snapped up when he saw her, eyebrows raised in mild surprise. "Emily? What are you doing here?"

"I wanted to talk to you about something," she said, closing the door behind her.

He put down the file and leaned back in his chair, crossing his arms. "This isn't about work, is it?" There was a protective tone in his voice already, and Emily knew he could sense where this conversation was headed. "Wait... what? Don't tell me this is about Benjamin Johnson."

She took a deep breath. "Yeah, actually. We've been seeing each other for a while now."

Thomas' expression immediately hardened. He sat up straighter, his brow furrowing as he looked at his younger sister with concern. "No, no, no," he said, shaking his head. "You should be dating someone else, Em. Not this guy." His tone was firm but not angry. He was genuinely worried.

Emily sighed. "Vincent, come on—"

"I don't like him," Thomas interrupted, his tone lowering as if it was non-negotiable. "There's nothing good about that guy. I've had my eye on him since he moved here. He's... odd."

Emily frowned slightly, crossing her arms now too. "Odd? What do you mean by that?"

Thomas exhaled, leaning forward, resting his forearms on the desk. "Look, he's new in town, no background I can dig into. And he's got these two boys, right? I've seen them running around town late at night, not behaving like they should. Any father who lets his kids run wild at 9 p.m. isn't exactly the best parent."

"That was one incident, and they weren't even doing anything wrong," Emily defended. "He's not a bad dad."

"Emily, you're a fine doctor, you deserve better than some guy with a shady background and two sons who run amok. You should be dating someone with a solid career—a doctor, a lawyer, someone like that," Thomas added, his voice softening as he tried to appeal to her sensibility.

Emily couldn't help but roll her eyes a little. "Vincent, you know I can date whoever I want, right? It's not about someone having the same job as me. I like Ben—he's smart, kind, and he's doing his best with those boys."

Thomas shook his head again, clearly unconvinced. "Look, I get it, okay? He's probably charming, maybe even good-looking, but I can tell something's off with him. Call it cop's instinct." He tapped his fingers against the desk. "And there's more. He's... too careful. He's like someone who's hiding something."

Emily stared at her brother, surprised by how seriously he seemed to be taking all this. "You're being paranoid."

"No, I'm being protective," Thomas countered. "He just doesn't sit right with me. And I don't want you getting involved with a guy who has this many red flags."

Emily sighed, shaking her head. "Vincent, I'm not a teenager. I'm perfectly capable of making my own decisions. And Ben isn't some dangerous guy, he's a single dad doing the best he can with what he has. And the boys—well, they're just kids. I've been getting to know them, and they're good kids. They need stability and love, not judgment."

Thomas softened a bit, but his concern was still evident. "I'm just saying... be careful. I don't want you getting hurt. Especially if there's more to this guy than meets the eye. And I don't trust his parenting either."

Emily huffed lightly, giving him a small smile. "I know you're just looking out for me, but trust me. I'm a big girl, and I can handle myself. And as for the boys, maybe you've misunderstood the situation. I'll talk to Ben about them being out late again, but really, it's not that big of a deal."

Thomas leaned back, clearly frustrated but unable to argue further without coming off as overbearing. He rubbed a hand over his face. "Fine. But promise me you'll be cautious. You always see the best in people, Emily, and sometimes that's not enough."

Emily smiled, standing up and walking over to give her brother a reassuring hug. "I promise, Vincent. And I'll talk to you more about Ben soon, okay? Just give him a chance."

Thomas let out a reluctant sigh but nodded. "Alright. Just... keep your eyes open."

As Emily walked out, she couldn't help but feel a strange sense of foreboding. She knew her brother meant well, but his suspicions were starting to feel a little too close for comfort. Still, she was confident in her feelings for Ben—and maybe, just maybe, her brother would come around in time.

Chapter 22: Beyond Sight and Sound

At school, the four friends—Ethan, Oliver, Ava, and Leo—sat together under a large oak tree during lunch, enjoying the shade and the warm afternoon breeze. The playground buzzed with the sounds of kids playing, laughter echoing around them. Ava sat a little closer to Ethan than usual, her eyes occasionally drifting toward him. She laughed at all of his jokes, even the ones that weren't particularly funny, and she seemed to brighten every time he looked her way.

Ethan, however, didn't seem to notice. He was too busy poking fun at Oliver, who was still working through his sandwich slowly. Leo, on the other hand, was showing off the new toy car he had brought to school, a gift from his older brother.

Ava leaned in slightly toward Ethan, brushing her hair behind her ear as she spoke. "So, Ethan... what do you think about coming over to my place after school? We can work on that history project together," she suggested, her tone just a little hopeful.

Ethan gave her a friendly smile, but it was clear he wasn't picking up on her deeper intentions. "Maybe, but Oliver and I have some stuff to take care of. Maybe later, though."

Ava's smile faltered for just a second, though she quickly masked it. "Oh, sure, no problem," she said, trying to keep her tone light. She looked down at her hands, her cheeks flushing ever so slightly.

Oliver noticed the small exchange and raised an eyebrow, shooting a knowing glance at Ethan. He was tempted to nudge his brother but decided to hold off, figuring Ethan hadn't noticed anything. Leo, still focused on his toy, was blissfully unaware of the subtle tension.

Ava tried to keep the conversation going. "I bet you'd be great at the project, Ethan. You're always so smart with that kind of stuff." Her compliment was genuine, but there was a softness in her voice that gave away her feelings—at least to Oliver, who was beginning to piece things together.

Ethan grinned, shrugging casually. "Thanks, but you're smart too. I mean, you helped me figure out that math problem last week."

Ava's eyes lit up at the compliment, and she looked down, biting her lip shyly. She desperately wanted to tell Ethan how she felt, but something stopped her. Maybe it was the way he treated her, like a little sister—someone he looked after but didn't see in that special way.

Oliver, meanwhile, smirked to himself, thinking, Ethan is so clueless.

Leo finally looked up from his toy and said, "Hey, are we still playing soccer after school? I bet I can beat all of you this time."

Oliver chuckled. "Leo, you say that every time, but Ethan still outruns you."

Ava perked up at the mention of soccer, glancing at Ethan. "I could join you guys, if you want."

Ethan smiled at her, his tone light and friendly. "Sure, you can play with us anytime, Ava."

The bell rang, signaling the end of lunch. As they all gathered their things, Ava couldn't shake the feeling that maybe, just maybe, there was still hope. She'd keep hanging out with them, hoping that one day, Ethan might see her differently. Until then, she'd stick around as the supportive friend, waiting for the right moment to let him know how she really felt.

As Ben stirred a pot of spaghetti sauce on the stove, the scent of tomatoes and herbs filled the kitchen. He glanced over to the living room where Ethan and Oliver sat on the couch, their eyes glued to the TV. It was a typical scene—calm, for now at least. But then Oliver, with his usual sharpness, turned to his "younger brother" and broke the silence.

"Ethan," Oliver said, not looking away from the screen. "Ava likes you."

Ethan, slouched lazily, rolled his eyes. "No, she likes me the same way she likes you and Leo. We're all just friends."

Oliver raised an eyebrow, clearly enjoying this. "Right... sure. Now I understand why you never had a girlfriend back in the 24th century."

Ethan's attention snapped away from the TV, and he shot Oliver a look. "What are you talking about? I did have a girlfriend, thank you very much. And besides, I'm 20 years old—well, technically 21 now. I can't be interested in a 10-year-old girl. That's ridiculous."

Oliver laughed, teasing him. "Oh, please. You and Ben didn't have girlfriends back then either. I was the only one with a real relationship!"

Ethan raised his eyebrows and, without hesitation, lunged at Oliver. He quickly pinned him down on the couch, a mischievous grin spreading across his face. "Oh yeah? Well, at least I'm not the one with diapers at night. Maybe I should tell our class that and see if you still think it's funny."

Oliver's face flushed red with embarrassment. "Nooo, don't you dare!" he cried, squirming beneath Ethan's weight, struggling to break free but finding no success.

The two boys wrestled playfully on the couch, grunting and laughing as they rolled around. Oliver fought to push Ethan off, but Ethan was determined, keeping his grip firm as he teased his 'brother' mercilessly.

From the kitchen, Ben watched the scene unfold with a slight shake of his head, a mixture of amusement and exasperation in his eyes. It was moments like this that reminded him of the paradox they lived in—his 'sons' behaving like real children, even though deep down they were young men trapped in boyish bodies.

"Alright, guys, that's enough. Dinner's ready!" Ben called out, his voice firm but not without a hint of a smile.

Ethan and Oliver stopped their playful wrestling, breathing heavily from the exertion. Ethan let go of Oliver, who quickly scrambled up, adjusting his ruffled t-shirt and sending his brother a glare that quickly melted into a smirk. They both made their way toward the kitchen, their mock battle forgotten in the face of food.

As they sat down at the table, Ethan couldn't help but throw one last glance at Oliver, grinning. "Diapers, huh?"

Oliver shot him a warning look but couldn't help laughing along. Ben, watching the two of them, sighed with contentment. For all the madness of their current situation, these small, ordinary moments of family life felt oddly grounding. Even though they were stuck in the wrong century, they were still in it together.

That night, Oliver's nightmare returned, pulling him into the depths of his subconscious with a disturbing familiarity. He was no longer the 10-year-old child he appeared to be in the present—he was back in his adult body, walking the bustling streets of Electropolis City, just as he had done before the ill-fated trip. The towering skyline of the 24th century loomed overhead, sleek and filled with technological wonders. The air buzzed with the hum of hover cars, and the streets were busy with citizens who were blissfully unaware of what was about to happen.

He passed by a café, the scent of synthetic coffee wafting out the open doors, and glanced at a nearby holographic TV screen. The news anchor was reporting on the rising tensions between the North American Union and the Great Asia Confederation, a constant theme in recent years. Oliver felt the unease creeping in, the words "nuclear deterrents" and "warheads" flashing ominously across the screen.

Suddenly, the ground beneath him rumbled. A deafening sound, like the roar of a thousand storms, ripped through the air. Shockwaves tore through the city, shattering glass and toppling buildings in an instant. Oliver turned in horror, only to see a bright, blinding light erupt from the horizon. The unmistakable signature of a nuclear detonation.

Everything in its path was obliterated. People, cars, buildings—gone in the blink of an eye, consumed by the fury of the explosion. The heat scorched his skin, and he could feel the panic rising in his chest. This was it. The end.

And then, just like before, he woke up.

His heart pounded violently in his chest as he gasped for air, the remnants of the nightmare clinging to him like a heavy fog. Sweat drenched his body, but worse—he felt the telltale dampness of his wet diaper. He groaned softly, a mix of frustration and embarrassment. "Not again," he whispered to himself, wiping the beads of sweat from his forehead.

He glanced over at Ethan, who was still asleep, snoring softly, unaware of the terror that had just unfolded in Oliver's mind. For a brief moment, Oliver considered waking him, but then decided against it. Ethan didn't need to know about the nightmare. It would only worry him, and right now, Oliver needed to find a way to deal with this on his own.

Oliver stood in the dimly lit storage room, his heart racing as he looked around the time machine's structure. The unsettling silence hung thick in the air. Normally, Lucas, the AI that controlled the time machine, would respond immediately when called. But tonight, it was different—Lucas wasn't there.

"Lucas, I need to talk to you about something," Oliver repeated, his voice tinged with worry. But still, no response. He glanced nervously at the clock—it was 4:07 AM.

Feeling a wave of dread, Oliver hurried to Ben's room. He shook Ben awake, his voice urgent. "Ben! Ben! I had the nightmare again..."

Ben groaned as he tried to sit up, rubbing his eyes. "How so?" he mumbled, still half-asleep.

"I think something's wrong with the time machine," Oliver blurted out. "Lucas isn't responding."

That got Ben's attention. He shot up from his bed, fully alert now. "Lucas isn't responding?" he echoed, already swinging his legs out of bed. He quickly threw on a shirt and headed toward the storage room, with Oliver following closely behind.

As they entered the room, Ben began inspecting the time machine with a furrowed brow. "Lucas and I prepared for this kind of situation," he explained, his voice now more controlled. "He asked me to find materials so he could 3D print memory cards to store copies of his program. That way, if the timeline shifts too drastically and 'kills' him, we could bring him back."

Ben pulled open a small compartment in the machine where the memory cards were stored. He inserted one of them into a slot and turned to Oliver. "This should boost him back," Ben said, more to himself than anyone else.

After a moment of tense silence, Lucas reappeared. His familiar holographic form flickered into view, and his calm, robotic voice filled the room. "So I went black?" Lucas asked, almost as if curious about his own state of being.

"Yes, you did 'die,'" Ben confirmed, relief washing over him. "But we boosted you back."

Lucas paused for a moment, his internal systems processing the situation. "I see. I already noticed numerous changes in the time machine's components and significant alterations in my stored data. The discrepancies are growing each time I compare them with the backups in these memory cards."

Oliver, still on edge from the nightmare and now unsettled by Lucas's words, asked, "So... what does that mean? Are we safe?"

Ben exchanged a glance with Oliver, then looked back at Lucas. "It means the timeline is shifting around us more aggressively than before."

Oliver sat down on one of the chairs inside the time machine, trying to catch his breath. His heart was still racing from the vivid nightmare, the images of destruction lingering in his mind. Ben stood beside him, rubbing his temples, while Lucas hovered nearby, his holographic form calmly flickering in the dim light.

"I was back in Electropolis City," Oliver began, his voice trembling slightly. "It was just like before... before we left on this trip. I saw the news on the TV screens, talking about the tension between the North American Union and the Great Asia Confederation. Then, out of nowhere, everything... everything was gone. A nuclear bomb destroyed everything in its path. The shockwaves... I could feel it all over again."

Ben crossed his arms, trying to ground himself in reality. "Oliver, it was just a dream," he said, his voice calm but with an undertone of unease. "You've been having these nightmares ever since we got stuck here. The stress of being trapped in the 1970s, in these... these kids' bodies, is messing with your head. We're safe. We have to focus on getting back."

Oliver looked at him, his face pale. "But what if it's more than that? What if something's actually happening in our time? Lucas already said the timeline is shifting."

Lucas, listening intently, interjected. "The last time Oliver had one of these nightmares, I did notice changes in the time machine and in the data I collected from my internal systems—just like this time."

Ben frowned, glancing at the AI. "So you're saying there might be a connection?"

Lucas's form flickered slightly as he processed the information. "It's unclear. However, with the data I retrieved from the memory cards, I can confirm that, as of our last scan before arriving here, the chance of a nuclear war in the 24th century was only 5%. A small but calculated risk."

Oliver's eyes widened. "But that's still a risk, right? And now with these changes..."

Lucas interrupted gently, trying to soothe Oliver's fears. "Even when I read into the new data I've gathered since reactivating, there is no news about a war involving the North American Union, nor has there been any mention of nuclear attacks on Earth."

Ben exhaled slowly, trying to reassure both himself and Oliver. "So nothing's changed? No war, no nuclear strikes?"

Lucas's tone remained steady. "Correct. While there have been fluctuations in the timeline, nothing indicates that a large-scale war or nuclear event has occurred. The nightmare is just that—a nightmare. But I'll continue to monitor the data closely. Should anything shift further, I will inform you immediately."

Oliver slumped slightly, still uneasy but trying to accept the logic of Lucas's explanation. "I just can't shake the feeling that something's wrong... the dream felt so real."

Ben placed a hand on Oliver's shoulder. "I know. But right now, we have to focus on what we can control. We're not in the 24th century, and we're not in danger here. Let's just take it one step at a time."

Lucas chimed in, "Rest assured, I will continue to safeguard our path. My primary function remains intact—to return us to the future. But for now, rest is necessary."

Oliver nodded, though the sense of dread still gnawed at him. He looked over at the time machine, its silent presence looming like a reminder of their trapped reality.

Chapter 23: A Journey Through the Trials of Youth

Sebastian slouched in his seat at the dimly lit cinema, his arm loosely draped around Taylor. The flickering light from the movie screen barely illuminated their faces as they sat in the back row, far from the few other moviegoers scattered throughout the theatre. Taylor, her head resting on his shoulder, turned to kiss him softly, but Sebastian barely responded, his thoughts elsewhere.

Taylor, sensing something was off, pulled back slightly and looked at him with concern. "What's wrong, honey?" she whispered, her voice tender yet probing.

Sebastian forced a smile, trying to mask the fatigue that weighed on him. "Nothing," he said, his voice low. "It's just work."

Taylor frowned, clearly not convinced. She reached for his hand, intertwining her fingers with his. "Work? You never talk much about it. What happened?"

Sebastian sighed, rubbing the back of his neck with his free hand. The stress of the day hung heavy on his shoulders. He wasn't used to feeling so overwhelmed. His job had been intense lately, and Ben—his boss—had been particularly demanding. Although Sebastian respected Ben's intelligence and expertise, the pressure to keep up with him was draining.

"It was just... a rough day," Sebastian admitted. He didn't want to go into too much detail, especially not here. The last thing he wanted was to sound like he was complaining. "There's this big project we're working on, and... well, it's been a lot."

Taylor leaned in, her hand brushing gently against his cheek. "You've been working really hard lately," she said softly. "I can tell."

Sebastian glanced at her, appreciating her concern but feeling a little guilty for not being more present. Taylor was young, full of energy, and eager for more out of life—and their relationship. But right now, he just didn't have the energy to meet her halfway.

She shifted closer to him again, her lips brushing against his ear. "Maybe we can do something after the movie," she whispered, her tone suggestive. But Sebastian, feeling the weight of the day's stress, just couldn't muster up the enthusiasm she was hoping for.

He pulled back slightly, shaking his head. "Taylor, I'm really sorry, but... I'm just too tired tonight."

Taylor, visibly disappointed, sat back and stared at the screen. "You're sure it's just work?" she asked, almost hesitantly. "Is something else bothering you?"

Sebastian quickly shook his head, eager to reassure her. "No, really, it's just work. You know how it gets sometimes."

She nodded slowly but didn't say anything for a while. Instead, she nestled back into his shoulder, the excitement from earlier dimming. They watched the rest of the movie in silence, Taylor's hand still clasped in his, though the mood between them had noticeably shifted.

As the credits began to roll, Taylor looked up at him again. "You know you can talk to me, right?" she said softly. "About work, or... anything else."

Sebastian gave her a small, tired smile. "I know. I appreciate it."

He leaned down to kiss her forehead gently, grateful for her understanding. But as they walked out of the cinema into the cool night air, the exhaustion from work still weighed heavily on his mind. He couldn't shake the pressure of trying to meet Ben's expectations, even outside the office.

At work, Ben watched as Sebastian gathered his things, ready to leave after another long day. He had noticed the younger engineer's potential, though Sebastian struggled at times with the workload. Ben wasn't an easy boss—he believed that pushing Sebastian was the best way to help him grow, even if it meant pushing hard.

Just as Sebastian slung his bag over his shoulder and turned to head out, Ben called after him. "Sebastian, hold on a minute."

Sebastian paused, an exhausted look crossing his face as he turned back toward Ben's office. "Yes, Mr. Johnson?"

Ben held out a file, his expression serious but not unkind. "I need you to complete this analysis before tomorrow afternoon. I want it on my desk by two."

Sebastian's heart sank. He had plans with Taylor tonight, but there was no room for negotiation. "Understood," he said, forcing a smile, though his stomach twisted with frustration. He returned to his desk, resigned to another late night of work.

Meanwhile, at home, Ben wasn't much different. He maintained the same strict expectations with Ethan and Oliver, particularly Ethan, whose rebellious streak was becoming harder to manage.

As Ethan slumped on the couch, flipping through a school notebook half-heartedly, Ben stood in front of him, arms crossed. "Ethan, listen to me," Ben began, his tone firm but paternal. "I know you and Oliver were already scientists in the 24th century, but this is the 1970s. The tools, the technology—it's all different here. I've experienced it firsthand at work. And in case—just in case—we can't get back soon, I need you to take school seriously."

Ethan glanced up, clearly annoyed. "We will get back soon, Ben. As soon as we get the 2 kg of gold we need, just like we planned."

Ben sighed, shaking his head. "I know that's the plan. But we've been stuck here for a year already. If things don't go according to plan, you and Oliver will be going to middle school next year. If you fall behind, you won't even be able to go to the same school as Oliver."

Ethan's frustration bubbled over. "What are you talking about? I'm way too smart for this century's education system. I don't need to worry about school."

Ben raised an eyebrow, his voice dropping slightly. "Your grades say otherwise, my man."

Ethan shifted uncomfortably. He hated hearing that. He knew he was smart—smarter than any kid his age, and smarter than most adults in this century. But Ben had a point. He had been so focused on their plans to return home that he had neglected school, assuming it didn't matter. Now Ben was talking like they might be stuck here for good, and that idea sent a jolt of fear through him.

"I just don't see the point," Ethan muttered. "We're not staying here, and you know that."

Ben crouched down, so he was eye-level with Ethan. "I hope we're not. But as long as we're here, I need you to be prepared for anything. I'm not just your colleague anymore, Ethan—I'm responsible for you. And I want to make sure you're set up for the future, no matter what happens."

Ethan met Ben's eyes, the defiance in his expression fading slightly. Deep down, he knew Ben was right. He just didn't want to admit it. "Fine," he muttered. "I'll try harder."

"That's all I'm asking," Ben said, standing up. He ruffled Ethan's hair, a rare gesture of affection. "Now, go finish your homework. We'll figure everything else out later."

Ethan watched Ben walk back to the kitchen, where he was prepping dinner, and let out a sigh. He didn't like this new dynamic, but for now, he'd have to play along.

Ethan slouched into the shared room he and Oliver called their own, his schoolbooks tucked under one arm. He tossed them onto the bed with a sigh, rubbing his face in frustration. Oliver, already sitting at his desk, glanced over with a knowing smile.

"Let me guess—math?" Oliver asked, spinning around in his chair to face Oliver.

Ethan groaned. "Yeah, but not just math. I don't get why they solve problems this way in the 20th century. It makes no sense." He opened his book to a page filled with algebra equations and waved it at Oliver. "It's like they've never heard of neural calculators or dynamic learning systems. We had AI to do this stuff for us! And don't even get me started on geography. How do they survive without map applications? Paper maps are like guessing in the dark!"

Oliver chuckled and motioned for Ethan to bring the book over. "Alright, let me see." He skimmed through the equations, and while they seemed straightforward enough, he could understand Ethan's frustration. In the 24th century, complex calculations were often handled by technology, with students focusing on interpreting results rather than slogging through basic processes.

"You're overthinking it," Oliver said, pointing to a section in the math book. "Here, they expect you to show every single step

228

because they want to make sure you understand the process. It's not about speed like back home. They haven't automated everything yet. In the 20th century, you're supposed to prove you can do the math by hand."

Ethan sighed, rolling his eyes. "I get that, but it feels like such a waste of time. I mean, we could be doing actual science, solving real problems, not this... busywork."

Oliver smiled sympathetically, knowing exactly what Ethan meant. "Yeah, but this is what they value here. It's a different world. You'll just have to get used to it if you don't want to stand out."

Ethan leaned against the desk, flipping through his math notes. "I don't want to get used to it. It's like... we're pretending to be something we're not. And geography? Memorizing all the capitals? Back in our time, we had interactive global systems that updated in real-time."

"Welcome to 1971, brother," Oliver said with a grin, tapping the geography book. "Here, they teach geography through memorization, not exploration. You'll just have to remember things the old-fashioned way."

Ethan slumped further. "This is so backwards."

"Yeah, but remember, it's not just about smarts," Oliver reminded him. "It's about fitting in. If you mess up at school, it could blow our cover, and we can't afford that. Besides, once you figure out their system, you'll breeze through it. This stuff is still way below what we learned back home."

Ethan nodded slowly. "I guess. But it still feels like they're dragging us back to the Stone Age."

Oliver laughed. "Maybe, but I can help you through it. And once you get the hang of this stuff, school won't be that bad. Let's start with this math problem. Here—show the steps like this…"

As Oliver patiently walked Ethan through the problem-solving method, the difference between the two eras became clear. The education in the 24th century had been streamlined by technology—students were taught to interpret and innovate rather than memorize. But here, in the 1970s, it was all about repetition, showing your work, and sticking to traditional methods. Despite their advanced knowledge, Ethan and Oliver found themselves having to adjust, learning to navigate an education system that felt archaic but was vital to their survival in this world.

"See?" Oliver said after they finished the problem. "Not so bad."

Ethan gave a reluctant nod. "Yeah, thanks. Now let's tackle this geography nonsense."

Oliver laughed. "I've got a paper map ready. Let's go old-school."

At school, Oliver found himself in a strange and frustrating position. Back in the 24th century, he had been athletic—an all-around guy who could handle himself in any physical challenge. But ever since the Rezulix drug had transformed him into a 10-year-old boy, it felt like his body was no longer his own. His motor skills weren't what they used to be, and he often found himself stumbling or tripping over his own feet.

Swimming class was the worst. Unlike Ethan, who seemed to have adapted faster to their younger forms, Oliver struggled. He hadn't learned to swim back in the 24th century either—there had never been any reason to. Most recreational activities had become virtual, and swimming was an old-fashioned hobby that just never appealed to him. Now, in this 1970s P.E. class, he was paying for it.

As he stood at the edge of the pool, watching the other kids dive in and swim effortlessly, Oliver felt a wave of discomfort. He hesitated, his bare feet cold against the pool tiles, and stared at the water. He was self-conscious about the whole situation, knowing that his classmates were already teasing him for being clumsy. Ethan, Leo, and Ava were already in the water, their splashes echoing in the gym.

"Come on, Oliver! You're holding up the line!" the P.E. teacher called out, his voice gruff with impatience.

Ethan swam over to the edge, smirking up at Oliver. "What's wrong? Afraid of a little water?" he teased, though it wasn't mean-spirited. But Ethan couldn't resist ribbing his older brother whenever he could.

Leo, who was treading water beside Ethan, chimed in. "Yeah, man, you can't hide behind your smarts forever. You've gotta swim sooner or later."

Oliver sighed, feeling the pressure of their jabs. "I know, I know," he muttered, but the anxiety bubbling up in him made his legs feel stiff. He could feel the eyes of the other kids watching him, and the last thing he wanted was to look weak or embarrassed.

Ethan, sensing his brother's hesitation, swam a little closer and grinned. "Hey, remember when you tripped in dodgeball last week? I bet the water's softer than the gym floor. Just don't faceplant this time."

Oliver rolled his eyes, his cheeks flushing red. "Thanks for the encouragement," he shot back sarcastically, but he couldn't help smiling a little at Ethan's joke.

"You're welcome," Ethan replied, still grinning. "But seriously, it's not that hard. Just get in and splash around a bit."

Oliver took a deep breath, finally stepping into the pool, though his movements were awkward and stiff. The water felt colder than he expected, and the sensation of being buoyant made him even more unsteady. His legs kicked out unevenly, and after a few seconds, his head dipped under the water.

He flailed for a moment, splashing wildly, his face breaking the surface as he coughed up some water. Leo and Ethan burst out laughing, though their laughter was more playful than cruel.

"Okay, okay, maybe don't try that," Leo chuckled, swimming closer. "You'll get the hang of it."

Oliver was too busy catching his breath to respond, though his face had flushed with embarrassment. He felt like a clumsy kid all over again, struggling in a body that didn't listen to him. He knew he was capable of so much more, but here he was, barely able to keep himself afloat.

Ethan swam next to him, slapping him on the back lightly. "Relax, Oliver. You've just gotta let go a bit. I mean, you might never be an Olympic swimmer, but at least you won't drown."

Oliver shot him a look, though he couldn't suppress a small grin. "Gee, thanks, Ethan. That's real comforting."

Ethan laughed. "Hey, at least you're in the water now. That's progress!"

The P.E. teacher blew his whistle. "Alright, enough chit-chat, boys. Let's see some swimming."

Oliver gave a small nod, trying his best to keep up with the lesson, though it was clear his form wasn't great. Despite the teasing and awkwardness, he knew Ethan and Leo had his back. It wasn't easy adjusting to this new reality, but at least they were in it together. Even if he stumbled—and he certainly would—he could count on them to pick him back up.

Chapter 24: Emily's House

On Saturday evening, Emily's cozy suburban house was buzzing with soft music, warm lighting, and the clinking of glasses as friends gathered for a small party. She had meticulously planned the evening, hoping to create a relaxed, welcoming atmosphere. Her intentions were clear—she wanted her brother, Officer Vincent Thomas, to get to know Benjamin, Ethan, and Oliver better. After all, she had grown quite close to Benjamin and envisioned a future with him. But her protective brother had his doubts, especially about Benjamin and his mysterious background, and tonight was her chance to ease his concerns.

The trio arrived together, dressed casually but presentable, though Ethan and Oliver didn't seem too enthusiastic. The brothers, now used to their double life as children, shuffled behind Benjamin, both of them exchanging glances, clearly not thrilled about having to face Officer Thomas in such an intimate setting.

"I don't see why we had to come to this," Ethan muttered under his breath as they entered the living room, spotting Officer Thomas chatting with another guest. "He doesn't even like us."

Oliver nudged Ethan. "Ben thinks it's a good idea to keep him off our backs. Just smile and pretend you're having fun."

Ethan sighed but nodded reluctantly. It wasn't that he disliked Emily—she was warm and kind, and there was something reassuring about her presence—but her brother made things complicated.

Benjamin, on the other hand, viewed the evening as an opportunity. He knew that Vincent Thomas, as the town's police officer, was suspicious of him and the boys. The more Thomas believed in their cover story—that Benjamin was just a regular single dad raising two boys—the less likely he'd dig deeper into their true identities.

As the trio entered the party, Emily greeted them with a bright smile, clearly happy they'd come. She ushered them inside, offering drinks and snacks. "I'm so glad you could make it!" she said, her eyes lingering a little longer on Benjamin than the boys. She had grown fond of him, despite his secrecy, and she hoped this night would help bridge the gap between him and her brother.

Benjamin smiled warmly, though always keeping his cool. "Wouldn't miss it," he replied, glancing at Ethan and Oliver, who were already heading toward the snack table with as much enthusiasm as they could muster.

The evening unfolded with light conversation and casual chatter. Emily's friends mingled, complimenting her taste in décor and music. Officer Thomas, however, kept his distance from the trio at first, sticking to his own circle of friends and keeping a wary eye on Benjamin. It was clear he was still skeptical.

Eventually, Emily decided to bring her brother and Benjamin together, determined to ease the tension. "Vincent," she called, catching his attention. "Why don't you come over here and join us?"

Vincent, a tall, broad-shouldered man with a commanding presence, hesitated for a moment but then obliged, making his way over to Benjamin. He gave a curt nod in greeting. "Benjamin."

"Officer Thomas," Benjamin replied, extending his hand with a calm, confident smile. "It's good to see you."

They shook hands, and while Vincent accepted it, his eyes remained sharp, studying Ben as if he were a puzzle to be solved.

Emily, sensing the unease, quickly jumped in to break the ice. "I was just telling Ben here about how you used to take me and Taylor camping, Vincent. Remember those trips?"

Vincent's expression softened slightly at the memory, though his guard didn't drop entirely. "Yeah, those were good times," he said, glancing at his daughter, Taylor, who was chatting with some of the other guests. "She loved those trips."

Benjamin seized the moment. "I've been thinking of taking Ethan and Oliver camping once things settle down. They've never been, but I think it could be a good experience."

Ethan, overhearing the conversation, nearly choked on his snack. Camping? He shot a look at Oliver, who was trying not to laugh.

Vincent raised an eyebrow. "You? Camping?" he asked, the skepticism evident in his tone.

Benjamin nodded, keeping his tone light. "I may not look the part, but I like the idea of roughing it in the wilderness. Might teach the boys some survival skills."

Emily smiled, clearly pleased with Benjamin's efforts to connect with her brother. "See, Vincent? Benjamin's a lot more outdoorsy than you thought."

Vincent didn't look entirely convinced but seemed to ease up, if only slightly. "We'll see about that," he muttered, though there was a trace of amusement in his voice now.

As the evening went on, the boys, Ethan and Oliver, kept their distance from Officer Thomas, sticking close to Taylor, who was happy to have them around. Taylor, still oblivious to the trio's real identities, found Ethan and Oliver to be fun company, despite their odd quirks. She didn't seem to notice Ethan's frequent glances toward her dad, or Oliver's occasional fidgeting, as if he were waiting for something to go wrong.

At one point, Officer Thomas made his way over to the boys, more out of curiosity than anything else. "So," he said, looking at them with a neutral expression. "You two behaving yourselves?"

Ethan and Oliver exchanged a glance. Ethan quickly put on a polite smile. "Yes, sir."

Oliver nodded in agreement, though his mind was racing with ways to avoid further conversation with the officer.

Vincent scrutinized them for a moment, then looked back at Benjamin across the room, who was deep in conversation with Emily. "Your dad's a... different kind of guy," he said, almost to himself.

Ethan, not missing a beat, replied, "Yeah, he's... different." He quickly stuffed another piece of cake into his mouth to avoid saying anything more.

The rest of the evening passed without incident. Benjamin had managed to soften Officer Thomas's stance, even if just a little, and Emily was thrilled that her brother was starting to warm up to the trio.

As they shuffled out of the party, Ethan let out a groan. "I've never had to smile that much in my life. My face feels like it ran a marathon."

Oliver chuckled. "Better than I thought, though. At least we didn't blow our cover."

Benjamin gave a satisfied nod. "Mission accomplished, boys. One step at a time."

The car was peacefully cruising through quiet streets when Benjamin decided to drop the bombshell. "Next month, I have a business trip to Japan. You two will stay at Emily's for a week."

Oliver perked up. "Great, I'm in!" But Ethan's horrified "Nooo! We can stay home alone, we're adults!" echoed through the car.

Benjamin shot a look in the rearview mirror. "Yeah, except it's not the 24th century, and the law here frowns on leaving 'small children' alone for a week. And by the way, your babysitter Daisy's off at college."

Ethan crossed his arms, huffing like a tiny steam engine. "This is so unfair, Benjamin. You keep treating us like we're actual kids!"

Oliver, meanwhile, saw the real issue. "But who'll look after the time machine? What if Officer Thomas pops by? We don't want him seeing our inter-dimensional 'appliance' in the basement."

Benjamin just sighed. "Lucas can handle himself. The house has cameras, smart locks… we're fine."

Ethan wasn't having it. "I'm not staying with Emily for a week! There has to be another way—nooo!"

Benjamin's patience ran out. "One more 'no' and you'll be standing all the way home, Ethan."

Oliver tried a final concern. "Emily works, though. So who's gonna look after us?"

Benjamin answered, "She'll ask Taylor to help."

Ethan's groan of horror was almost Shakespearean. "No, not Taylor! Anyone but Taylor!"

Benjamin gripped the wheel, his voice dropping to a warning tone. "One more scream and your rear is in trouble. I mean it."

Ethan immediately sank back, muttering furiously. Meanwhile, Oliver stared out the window, already strategizing how he'd handle a week with Emily and her niece.

They rode in silence through the sleepy streets, Ethan sulking, Benjamin staring straight ahead, and Oliver, well, wondering if there was a way to smuggle his game console into Emily's house.

Chapter 25: Unpredictable Possibilities

The morning of Benjamin's trip arrived, and the house was a whirlwind of last-minute packing and preparations. Benjamin rushed around, making sure everything was in place for his week-long absence. Ethan and Oliver had already packed their bags, reluctantly stuffing clothes, books, and school supplies into backpacks, knowing they were set to stay at Emily's house for the next seven days. Ethan's face showed clear signs of frustration, while Oliver kept a neutral expression, already resigned to the situation.

Lucas, the AI of the time machine, chimed in from the camera mounted in the living room. "Have a nice week! I can handle things at home," Lucas said with his usual calm tone.

Ethan glared at the camera, clearly not as enthused. He dragged his feet, still dreading the thought of spending the week at Emily's—being watched over like a child, especially by her and, worse, Taylor, who he couldn't stand babysitting him. The idea made him feel small and embarrassed, and he wasn't hiding his displeasure.

Benjamin, noticing his reluctance, was having none of it. As he walked by Ethan, he gave him a swat on the bottom, just hard enough to make a point. "Move it, Ethan," he said firmly. "No more sulking. You're going to behave yourself, and you're not going to cause any trouble for Emily. Understood?"

Ethan jumped a bit at the swat, but he didn't argue back this time. With a grumble, he finally started walking toward the door, his head down in a sulky pout. Benjamin shot him a look that reminded Ethan there was no room for rebellion today.

Oliver, already carrying his bag, followed more quietly. He gave Ethan a sympathetic look but knew better than to say anything right now. Oliver had his own mixed feelings about the stay, but compared to Ethan, he wasn't as anxious about being at Emily's.

Meanwhile, Emily was at her house, buzzing with energy. She'd prepared everything, from fresh linens to making sure the kitchen was stocked. While her primary goal was to help Benjamin, she couldn't deny that having Ethan and Oliver around for a week felt like an opportunity to become a closer part of their lives. She smiled at the thought, imagining herself guiding them through the week, almost like a mother figure. It was a role she found herself drawn to, even if the boys didn't see it that way yet.

As the trio loaded up into the car and prepared to drive to Emily's, Ethan stared out the window, still sulking, while Oliver sat quietly, mentally preparing himself for the week ahead. Benjamin glanced back at his "sons" and felt a mixture of responsibility and determination. It was only one week, but for some reason, this week felt significant.

Emily, on the other hand, couldn't wait to welcome them into her home. She had a plan in mind, and while she knew Ethan might be a challenge, she believed she could win him over. After all, family wasn't always about blood—it was about the bonds you chose to create.

As they pulled up to Emily's house, Ethan's eyes narrowed slightly, already plotting how he'd make the next week as difficult as possible. He wasn't going to let Emily get away with trying to play mom. In his mind, she was an intruder, someone trying to step into their lives and take control, and Ethan wasn't having it. If Benjamin thought he could leave him and Oliver here like helpless kids, he was in for a rude awakening.

Benjamin parked the car and got out, helping the boys with their bags. Emily was already waiting at the front door, her face warm and welcoming. "Ben, you can count on me!" she said cheerfully, taking their bags and giving Benjamin a quick hug. "The boys will be just fine."

Ben bent down to Ethan and Oliver's level, a serious look on his face. "Behave yourselves, boys. Dad will be back in a week, very soon," he said, his tone leaving no room for argument.

Ethan barely managed a nod, his mind racing with ways to make Ben regret leaving him here. He thought to himself, We'll see how much she wants to play mommy after this week. He glanced at Oliver, who seemed far more accepting of the situation, but Ethan wasn't going to give up that easily.

Oliver, on the other hand, felt a little less rebellious. Sure, staying at Emily's wasn't ideal, but he was resigned to it, knowing Ben would only make it worse if they caused too much trouble.

Ben gave Emily a kiss goodbye and waved as he drove off, leaving the boys standing at the door with their new "caretaker." As soon as he was out of sight, Ethan's face twisted into a smirk. *Let the games begin*, he thought, determined to make Emily's life just a little more complicated.

Emily smiled warmly, oblivious to the plan brewing in Ethan's mind. "Come on in, boys! I've got everything set up for you. We'll make it a fun week, okay?"

Ethan simply muttered under his breath, barely concealing his mischievous grin. This was going to be a week to remember.

As Ben drove to the airport, he could see the familiar figure of Sebastian standing outside the terminal, checking his watch. Ben parked and got out, waving at the young engineer. Sebastian, looking a bit nervous but trying to hide it, greeted Ben with a nod.

"Ready for Tokyo?" Ben asked, slinging his bag over his shoulder.

Sebastian forced a smile, still feeling the weight of the workload Ben had given him before their departure. "Yeah, ready as I'll ever be."

Ben gave him a pat on the back. "Don't stress. It's going to be an important trip, but nothing we can't handle."

They walked into the terminal together, moving swiftly through the airport. Ben's mind briefly wandered back to the boys, wondering if Emily would be able to manage the boys' rebellious nature. But he quickly shook the thought off—he'd left everything in order. The trip to Japan was important, and he trusted Lucas and Emily to keep things under control.

Back at the house, Lucas monitored everything through the cameras installed around the property. The AI had a constant watchful eye on the time machine, ensuring no unexpected visitors or intrusions. While Lucas didn't have a physical body, he had access to a 3D printer within the time machine, which he used to create tools and equipment as necessary.

Tonight, Lucas decided to craft something new—a small, functional gun for the robot arm attached to the time machine. The thought wasn't for offense but for defense, just in case the timeline shifted, or someone came too close to discovering the time machine's true nature. Lucas carefully assembled the gun, using lightweight materials and ensuring it would integrate seamlessly with the machine's systems. It was all about preparedness.

As Lucas printed the final piece, he ran a diagnostic scan on the time machine's systems, ensuring everything was in peak condition. The boys were away, and Ben was in another country, but Lucas had everything under control. He would protect the time machine, no matter what.

Ethan smirked to himself as he heard the glass shatter on the kitchen floor, the crash echoing through the house. It was the first step in his plan to give Emily a hard time—he had to make Ben regret treating him like a child. Standing near the shards of glass, Ethan put on his most innocent face as Emily rushed in from the living room.

"Oh no, sorry Emily," he said in a deliberately soft voice. "I didn't mean to, please don't tell Dad about this."

Emily, completely unaware of Ethan's real intentions, knelt down and looked at him with concern, her eyes wide with worry but still gentle. "Oh no no, honey, it's alright," she assured him, picking up the larger pieces carefully. "Please step aside, I need to clean this up. Watch for the glass, you don't want to get hurt."

Ethan could see her kindness and felt a small twinge of guilt but quickly pushed it away, determined to make his time at Emily's house difficult. He watched as she moved quickly and efficiently, clearing the mess.

Oliver entered the kitchen, not aware of Ethan's deliberate act either. He looked at the mess on the floor and gave his brother a bewildered look. "Be careful, dude!" Oliver warned, stepping back as Emily continued to clean.

Ethan shrugged, playing innocent. "It was an accident."

Emily didn't scold, didn't raise her voice, just smiled softly as she grabbed a dustpan and broom. "It happens, boys. But next time, be a little more careful, alright?"

246

Ethan nodded, hiding his disappointment that his plan hadn't rattled Emily as much as he'd hoped. She was a tough one, but he wasn't ready to give up just yet. This was just the beginning.

That evening, during dinner, Ethan finished the curry dish Emily had prepared for him. As he pushed his plate away, it slid off the edge of the table, crashing to the floor with a loud clang. He barely glanced at the mess, his expression neutral, as though it were nothing more than an innocent accident.

Oliver, sitting across from him, raised an eyebrow, already sensing what was going on. He shot Ethan a warning look. "I think I know what you're trying to do here, Ethan. Stop it."

Ethan turned to him, feigning innocence. "What are you talking about, Oliver? It was just another accident."

Emily, who had been wiping her hands on a towel, glanced over. She sighed softly and she quietly grabbed the broom and dustpan, cleaning up the mess. She was patient, though the look in her eyes said she was beginning to understand what was happening. Still, she kept her tone light, brushing off the tension. Emily knew that the boys were resisting her, perhaps seeing her as someone trying to fill the space of their mother. She thought it was natural for them to push back.

As soon as Emily left the room to wash the dishes, the boys were left alone in the living room, watching TV. Oliver leaned in closer to Ethan, his voice sharp with frustration. "Stop it, Ethan! You're going to get yourself in so much trouble with Ben when he gets home."

Ethan shrugged casually, his smirk returning. "What are you talking about? Besides, if Emily isn't telling Ben, and you're not telling Ben, how would Ben even find out?"

Oliver crossed his arms. "She's been nothing but nice to us, Ethan."

"Nice because she wants to marry Ben and be our 'mother,'" Ethan replied, using air quotes when he said the word 'mother.' "I'm saving us all from this. Do you really want her to play house with us and deal with the mess of our real situation?"

Oliver shot Ethan an exasperated look. "You're gonna sign your own death oath if you keep this up. You know Ben's not gonna let this slide. He'll spank your butt deep red."

Ethan's confidence faltered for a split second, but he quickly shook it off. "Only if he finds out," he muttered, though a flicker of doubt crossed his mind. He knew Oliver was right about one thing— Ben wouldn't hesitate to deal with him if he thought Ethan had been making trouble. But for now, he wasn't ready to back down.

As Oliver stood up from the sofa, ready to distance himself from Ethan's antics, Ethan stuck out his leg, tripping him. Oliver stumbled forward, his arms flailing as he tried to catch his balance, but instead, he knocked into the nearby lamp. The crash echoed through the living room as both Oliver and the lamp hit the floor, the lamp shattering into pieces.

Emily rushed in from the kitchen, her eyes wide with concern. "What happened here?" she asked, looking between the broken lamp and the boys.

Before Oliver could say anything, Ethan crouched beside him, his voice low and filled with mischief. "Now you're in this with me," Ethan whispered. "If you tell Ben, he's gonna spank you too."

Oliver, still on the floor, winced in both pain and frustration. He glared up at Ethan, his mind racing. He could feel the heat of guilt and fear rising in his chest. Ethan's words lingered, and the idea of facing Ben's wrath—especially after this—made his stomach churn.

Emily knelt down beside Oliver, her tone soft. "Are you alright, honey? That was quite a fall."

Oliver, still glaring at Ethan, nodded slowly. "Yeah… I'm fine," he muttered.

Ethan, standing nearby, kept his innocent expression in place, but a small smirk tugged at the corners of his lips. He knew Oliver wouldn't rat him out now. They were both in too deep. Emily, ever patient, began cleaning up the broken lamp, unaware of the growing tension between the two boys.

Later that evening, Oliver wandered into the kitchen, where Emily was sitting quietly with a cup of tea. He hesitated for a moment, watching her before clearing his throat. "Emily… I'm really sorry about everything. The lamp, the mess... Ethan's just... well, you know how he can be."

Emily looked up, her expression softening as she put her tea down. She smiled warmly at him, reaching out to ruffle his hair. "Oh, Oliver, you're such a sweet boy. I know it's not easy, adjusting to all these changes. Don't worry about it. Accidents happen."

Oliver blushed slightly, feeling the warmth of her kindness. "I just didn't want you to think we were trying to cause trouble."

Emily's heart swelled. Oliver's sincerity touched her deeply, reinforcing her determination. "Of course not," she reassured him. "I know you and Ethan are good boys, and you've been through a lot. But you're doing just fine."

As she watched Oliver nod, his expression full of guilt and a hint of relief, Emily couldn't help but think to herself, *Ben is such a lucky man to have these boys.* Oliver's sweetness only solidified her feelings. He was already showing signs of affection towards her, and she could feel the bond growing between them.

I'm getting there, she thought. Ethan is cute, even if he's a bit mischievous. I can win him over with time. But Oliver? And Ben? They're already halfway in love with me.

Emily felt her resolve strengthen. She was more certain than ever that she would become a lasting part of their lives—no matter what it took.

In the dim light of their shared room, Ethan's mocking voice filled the space as he mimicked Emily.

"Oh, Oliver, you're such a sweet boy of mommy," Ethan said, exaggerating his tone in a sing-song voice. Then he added with a grin, "You can start calling her 'mom' from tomorrow, don't even wait until Ben marries her."

Oliver, already on edge from the evening's events, felt a surge of frustration. Without thinking, he shot up from the bed, his face flushed. "You're gonna regret that!" he growled, lunging at Ethan.

He pinned Ethan down on the bed, trying to 'teach him a lesson' for all the teasing and mischief. Ethan, laughing and squirming, half-enjoyed the scuffle. It wasn't too rough, more like a playful wrestling match between two brothers. But Oliver wasn't holding back his annoyance.

"Let's see who'll be crying when Ben gets home!" Oliver said, gripping Ethan's wrists to hold him in place.

Ethan wriggled under his grasp, trying to break free. "You're just mad because she likes me more!" he teased, even though he knew that wasn't true.

Oliver, now sitting on Ethan's chest, leaned closer and whispered, "Keep it up, and you'll find out just how mad I can get."

They continued to wrestle, but it was all in good fun, even if Oliver's annoyance was real. Eventually, both boys ended up laughing, out of breath, lying side by side on the bed.

For a moment, the tension between them dissolved, and they were just two brothers, stuck in a strange situation, trying to make sense of it all.

In a sleek, minimalist office in Tokyo, Benjamin and Sebastian sat across from two Japanese businessmen, both wearing sharp suits. The atmosphere in the room was tense but professional, as the four men discussed the intricacies of buying the rights to exploit certain oil wells in the South China Sea.

The Japanese company had acquired the rights at a lower price from the government of the Philippines and was now looking to resell them for a quick profit. The negotiations were delicate—both sides were aware of the strategic importance of these wells, especially given the rising demand for energy resources in the region.

One of the Japanese executives, Mr. Sato, leaned forward, his face calm but his eyes sharp. "The wells are profitable. We believe the price we are offering is more than fair."

Ben, composed but firm, responded, "We understand the value, but our company's interests lie in long-term sustainability. A more reasonable figure would be necessary for us to proceed."

Sebastian, sitting next to Ben, felt the pressure but admired Ben's ability to remain cool under these conditions. While he was nervous, he knew Ben had a plan. Over the course of the meeting, Ben's confidence began to sway the Japanese businessmen.

As the conversation stretched on, numbers were thrown back and forth, and tension built up in the room. But Ben remained resolute, skillfully navigating the complexities of the deal. He knew there was a potential competitor from Australia, rumored to be interested in the same oil rights, but so far, there had been no sign of them at the bidding.

After hours of tough back-and-forth, Ben finally pushed the deal over the line. "This agreement benefits both of our companies. We'll offer a 10% increase on your last asking price, provided we finalize today."

The two Japanese businessmen exchanged glances, weighing their options. They knew the offer was solid, and with no competitor from Australia in sight, they decided to proceed.

Mr. Sato nodded, extending his hand. "Agreed. The deal is yours."

Sebastian let out a quiet breath of relief as Ben shook Mr. Sato's hand. They had secured the rights for their US-based company, and the potential profit from the wells would be significant. As they finalized the paperwork, Ben couldn't help but wonder why the Australian competitor never showed up—it was unlike them to miss out on such a strategic opportunity.

As they left the office, Sebastian turned to Ben, admiration clear in his voice. "That was incredible. I thought we might lose them for a minute."

Ben smiled, though his mind was still turning. "It's never over until the ink dries. We did well today, but keep an eye out, Sebastian. Competitors don't just disappear without a reason."

As Ben and Sebastian walked out of the office, the weight of their successful negotiation hung in the air. Ben's face showed a quiet satisfaction, knowing they had secured the deal, but his mind was already working through deeper concerns. The thrill of victory was quickly overshadowed by a familiar worry—the potential ripple effects of his actions on the timeline.

He glanced at Sebastian, who was still energized by the meeting's success, unaware of the larger consequences Ben carried with him. For Sebastian, this was simply another career milestone, but for Ben, every decision weighed heavy with the knowledge that their very presence in the 1970s had already altered history in ways they couldn't fully predict.

Ben thought to himself, *It's too late to avoid changing things... we're already in too deep. Our very existence here is a disturbance. Doing nothing could be just as damaging as taking action.*

He had come to terms with the fact that they were no longer just visitors from the future—they were active participants in shaping a past that wasn't theirs. Every deal he made, every new connection, had the potential to send ripples into the future.

Still, Ben couldn't afford to worry too much about it now. His priority was providing for Ethan and Oliver. Their current situation required money, and without it, they wouldn't be able to buy the gold they needed to power the time machine. This job—despite the risks it posed to the timeline—was their best shot at getting home.

Sebastian interrupted his thoughts. "I can't believe we pulled that off. You were incredible in there, Ben."

Ben gave him a tight smile. "Thanks, Sebastian. It's good for the company, and it's good for us. But remember, we have to keep moving forward."

Sebastian nodded, still riding the high of their success. "Right. I'll get the paperwork processed first thing Monday."

As they headed toward their taxi, Ben's thoughts returned to Ethan and Oliver. He hoped they were behaving themselves at Emily's house. He trusted Oliver to keep things in check, but Ethan... well, Ethan was another story. Ben knew Ethan would be giving Emily a hard time, testing the boundaries as always.

Ben sighed. *I'll deal with whatever messes they've made when I get back,* he thought. *For now, I just need to focus on keeping this job—and saving up for the gold. We can't stay stuck here forever.*

As they drove toward the hotel, the city's lights flickered outside the car window, and Ben's mind lingered on the delicate balance he was trying to maintain—between survival in this era and safeguarding their way back to future.

Ben's pulse quickened as the words *"pixel out"* echoed in his mind. That was a phrase from his century—a 24th-century term, and there was no way anyone in 1970 should be using it. He stopped in his tracks, heart pounding, watching the man walk away. It took him a second to register what had just happened, but when he did, a flood of possibilities rushed through his mind. *Is he from my time? Or another time traveler?*

Without wasting a second, Ben turned to Sebastian, trying to keep his voice calm. "Hey, why don't you head up to your room? I need to handle something real quick."

Sebastian looked at him, puzzled, but nodded. "Sure, Ben. See you tomorrow morning."

As Sebastian walked toward the elevators, Ben took off after the man, weaving through the hotel lobby. His eyes were fixed on the stranger in the black suit who had just used the phrase. "Hey, hey, I need to talk to you!" Ben called out, his voice steady but urgent.

The man stopped and turned around, his expression neutral, but there was something off in his demeanor. He looked confused, yet there was a flicker of recognition in his eyes that made Ben's instincts scream that this man knew more than he was letting on.

"Huh? What is it?" the man asked, his voice casual, but Ben noticed the slight hesitation.

Ben approached him slowly, trying to keep things calm but also needing answers. "I couldn't help but overhear you say something. 'Pixel out'—what does that mean to you?"

The man's eyes narrowed, and for a brief moment, his expression slipped into something colder. Then he quickly smiled, shaking his head. "Pixel out? Nah, you must have misheard me. That's not what I said."

But Ben wasn't buying it. His gut told him this wasn't a coincidence. "Listen, I know that phrase. I know where it's from. You're not from here, are you? Which century are you from?"

The man's smile vanished, and he took a step back, glancing around the lobby as if considering his next move. "Look, you've got the wrong guy. I don't know what you're talking about."

Ben stepped forward, his voice lowering, filled with quiet authority. "Don't play games with me. I'm not here to cause trouble, but I need to know who you are and why you're here. If you're from my time—or any time that's not the 20th century—we need to talk."

The man's expression shifted, a flicker of fear crossing his face before he quickly masked it. He straightened his suit jacket, his eyes darting to the nearest exit. "I don't know what you think you heard, but I'm not getting involved in whatever this is." He turned abruptly and started walking away.

But Ben wasn't letting him go that easily. "You can walk away, but I will find out who you are. If you're here for the same reason

I am—or something worse—you should know you're not the only one out of place."

The man stopped in his tracks for a moment, his back still turned to Ben, but then without another word, he continued walking until he disappeared into the crowd.

Ben stood there, heart racing. *Who the hell was that?* His mind raced with questions. Was he another time traveler? Someone monitoring him? And if so, who sent him—and why?

He walked back toward the elevators, deep in thought. This just complicated things. If there was someone else from the future here, it could mean danger for him, Ethan, and Oliver. He needed to be more careful than ever.

When Ben got to his hotel room, he locked the door behind him and sat down, pulling out his notepad. He scribbled down everything he remembered about the man—the suit, his height, the phrase. He would need to keep an eye out from now on. There was no way this was just a coincidence.

Ben paced the hotel room, glancing down at his wristwatch, which was far more than just a timepiece. It was his connection to Lucas, the AI controlling the time machine. He tapped a few hidden buttons, bringing up the communication system.

"Lucas, I need to talk to you. Something strange happened."

Lucas's calm, familiar voice came through the watch. "I'm here, Ben. What's going on?"

"I heard a man say 'pixel out of here'—right here in Tokyo," Ben said, still trying to make sense of the situation. "That's a phrase from our time. He said it like it was normal."

There was a brief pause before Lucas responded. "You are correct, Ben. 'Pixel out' is a slang term originating in the 24th century. It's used to mean 'getting out of here.' I just checked the historical data for that time period—there is no recorded use of the phrase in the 20th century. No one in 1970s should be using that term."

Ben's heart sank a little. He knew this meant trouble. "So, it's likely we're not the only ones from our time stuck here?"

"It seems possible," Lucas confirmed. "While time machines like yours weren't invented until your team succeeded, your project isn't the only time travel initiative funded by the government and the North American Union. We also lack data on similar projects in other parts of the world."

Ben sighed, rubbing the back of his neck. "I can't believe it. If someone else has come back, they might not just be here by accident. What if they're trying to alter history—or even worse, what if they've been tracking us?"

Lucas responded thoughtfully, "It is possible. Remember, time travel was not widely available in our era. There could be a myriad of reasons someone would be here, from personal gain to political objectives. You'll need to be cautious."

"Cautious?" Ben muttered, looking out the window. "I'm practically drowning in caution already. And what's worse, I've got Ethan and Oliver back in the States. If someone's tracking us, they might be in danger too."

Lucas's voice remained steady, but there was a hint of urgency. "I will increase security around the time machine. I've already added additional cameras, and the 3D printer is capable of producing defensive measures if necessary."

Ben shook his head. "This is getting out of hand. If there's another time traveler, we need to know what their agenda is. I don't like the idea of competing with someone who might not care about preserving the timeline."

"I'll continue to monitor for any unusual activities or signals," Lucas assured him. "But for now, proceed carefully, Ben. Whoever this other time traveler is, their intentions are still unknown."

Ben nodded, "Thanks, Lucas. Keep an eye on everything back home, and let me know if anything else pops up."

"Of course, Ben. Stay safe."

As the call ended, Ben stared out at the neon-lit Tokyo skyline, his mind racing. He had to figure out who this mysterious traveler was—and fast. Because if they were willing to use 24th-century slang in public, they either didn't care about blending in, or they were getting careless. Neither option was good.

Chapter 26: Sticking to His Guns

It was a typical Thursday morning at school, but Ethan was far from typical today. His mind raced with a mixture of determination and annoyance as he thought about his plan. He was convinced that Ben's relationship with Emily was a threat to the trio's already precarious situation. Ben, in Ethan's view, was blinded by love, and Oliver was too compliant, too afraid of Ben's wrath to stand up for what was right. It was up to Ethan to act, to protect them all—even if they didn't realize it yet.

"I have to do this," Ethan thought as he clenched his fists, watching the schoolyard buzz with activity. He knew he had to push things to the edge, force Ben to see that involving Emily would only make things worse. Ethan was also secretly curious—would his actions somehow trigger a shift in the timeline? He wondered if this would fix the lingering issues with the past.

Spotting Mark Petersen, the boy he had gotten into trouble with not so long ago, Ethan felt his heart race. Mark had always been a bit of a troublemaker himself, but today Ethan had something far more reckless in mind. Without any warning or provocation, Ethan swung his fist and punched Mark square in the nose.

Mark staggered back, clutching his face in shock, blood already trickling from his nose. The kids around them gasped, and a crowd began to form. Mark's eyes were wide with anger and disbelief, and for a moment, there was silence in the schoolyard. Then the murmurs began, and Ethan could hear the buzz of whispers all around him.

Mark, still in shock, stumbled backward, almost too stunned to react. "What the hell, Ethan?" he spat, his hand still pressed to his bleeding nose.

Ethan stood there, his heart pounding, adrenaline surging through him. He felt a strange sense of power, knowing that his actions would have consequences—but consequences he was willing to face if it meant stopping Emily from becoming a permanent part of their lives.

"Ethan, are you crazy?" one of the boys in the crowd shouted. "What did Mark do to you?"

But Ethan remained silent, his eyes locking with Mark's, waiting for the inevitable retaliation.

The commotion in the schoolyard quickly escalated into a full-blown fight between Ethan and Mark. Shouting and chaos filled the air as the two boys grappled and swung at each other. Teachers rushed in, intervening with stern commands and physical force to break up the fight. Ethan and Mark were pulled apart, both breathing heavily and looking furious.

The teachers led them down the hallway to the principal's office, where they would face the consequences of their actions. Ethan, with a mix of defiance and frustration, was not prepared for the reality that awaited him. He had hoped that Emily would have to deal with this mess, but his plans took an unexpected turn.

Emily, who had been on her way to the hospital for an emergency case, received the call from the school. The principal informed her that Ethan had been involved in a fight and that she needed to come pick him up. Emily, already stressed by the emergency, was worried about how she would handle this additional complication.

Desperate for help, Emily called her brother, Officer Vincent Thomas. "Vincent, please, I need your help. I'm stuck at the hospital with an emergency case, and I can't get to the school right now. Can you pick up Ethan and Oliver? I know this is a big favor, but I'm really in a bind."

Officer Thomas was initially hesitant. "Emily, I don't know if I can just drop everything and pick them up. This is important work I'm dealing with."

Emily's voice softened, and she pleaded, "Please, Vincent. I know it's a lot to ask, but they really need someone right now. Ethan can be problematic, but he's a sweet kid. Just don't scare them, okay?"

Thomas sighed, a mix of reluctance and affection for his sister's request evident in his voice. "Alright, alright. I'll pick them up. But I'm not making any promises about not scaring them."

Emily thanked him profusely before hanging up, feeling a bit of relief despite the stressful situation. She hoped her brother's presence would at least keep Ethan and Oliver from further trouble and help manage the situation at the school.

Meanwhile, Officer Thomas made his way to the school, his mind racing with thoughts of how he would handle the boys. He had taken a liking to Ethan and Oliver and felt a certain responsibility towards them, especially given his sister's connection to them. As he arrived at the school, he braced himself for the challenge ahead.

Oliver's stomach churned as he saw Officer Thomas walked into the school hallway. He recognized the stern look on Thomas's face and knew that this wouldn't bode well for Ethan. Oliver, sitting on a bench outside the principal's office, felt a pang of anxiety. He could only imagine how Ethan would react to the unexpected arrival of Officer Thomas, especially given their current predicament.

Inside the principal's office, Ethan sat with his back straight and his face set in a defiant expression, though his insides were in turmoil. He had been waiting for Emily to arrive, hoping she would smooth things over. When the office door opened and Officer Thomas stepped in, Ethan's heart sank. The familiar face was not one he had anticipated seeing here today.

Officer Thomas, though a bit stern, greeted the principal, Mr. Harris, with a nod. "Mr. Harris, thank you for letting me come. Emily couldn't make it, so I'm here to pick up the boys."

Mr. Harris, recognizing Officer Thomas and knowing his reputation for fairness, nodded in acknowledgment. "Of course, Officer Thomas. Ethan here has been quite a troublemaker lately."

Ethan swallowed hard, his throat dry. He glanced at Oliver, who was sitting nervously on the bench, and then back at Thomas. The reality of his situation hit him hard. He had hoped to create enough trouble to make Emily reconsider being a part of their lives, but now the consequences of his actions were becoming clearer and more immediate.

Thomas turned his gaze to Ethan, his expression a mix of concern and sternness. "Ethan, Emily's tied up with an emergency at the hospital. I'm here to take you and Oliver home. Let's get this sorted out."

Ethan's mind raced as he processed Thomas's words. Now he was faced with the reality of dealing with a figure of authority who had no patience for mischief. Ethan's initial defiance wavered as he realized that his plan to embarrass Emily and make Ben regret his decision might backfire spectacularly.

With a deep breath, Ethan stood up from the chair, trying to muster some semblance of confidence. "I'm sorry, Officer Thomas. I didn't mean for any of this to happen."

Thomas's gaze softened slightly, but his tone remained firm. "I'm sure you didn't mean to, but actions have consequences. Let's get out of here and head home. We'll talk more about this when we get there."

Oliver, who had been anxiously observing from his spot, stood up and joined Ethan as they walked towards the door. As they left the office and headed toward Officer Thomas's car, Ethan couldn't shake the feeling of dread. He knew that his troubles were far from over and that the aftermaths of his actions would be dealt with once they were home.

Vincent opened the door to Emily's house, ushering Ethan and Oliver inside. The atmosphere was heavy with the tension of the day's events. Ethan and Oliver stepped in, with Ethan still brimming with defiance.

Vincent settled onto the sofa and gestured for Ethan to come closer. His tone was authoritative but not unkind. "Come here, Ethan. We need to talk."

Ethan approached hesitantly, his mind racing. He braced himself as Vincent's penetrating gaze fixed on him. "Why did you hit that boy at school today?"

Ethan, trying to save face, replied, "He hit me first," though he knew this wasn't the truth. His lie was shaky and unconvincing.

Vincent's expression remained stern. "Emily told me everything about the problems you've been causing at her house. Is that what you've been doing all week? Causing trouble?"

Ethan's heart sank. He felt cornered, unable to maintain his facade. "No, I've been good. I promise." His voice wavered under the weight of Vincent's scrutiny.

Vincent, a seasoned officer, was not easily deceived. His experience with people made him aware of the subtle signs of dishonesty. "Stop lying, Ethan. Emily confided in me about the trouble you've been causing. She's worried about you."

Ethan's mind raced to find a way out of the situation. His ability to handle stress, once formidable in his adult body, was now diminished in his 10-year-old form. The pressure was beginning to show. He shifted uncomfortably, his face flushing with a mix of shame and frustration.

Vincent's gaze softened slightly, but he maintained his firm tone. "You're a very naughty boy, Ethan. You've caused problems at Emily's house and now at school. Lying about it won't make things better."

Ethan, feeling a wave of regret and frustration, looked down. "I'm sorry. I didn't mean for things to..."

Vincent nodded, though his expression remained serious. "I hope you mean that, Ethan. We'll work through this, but you need to understand the importance of respecting others and taking responsibility for your behaviours."

Oliver, who had been listening from the kitchen, remained quiet. The distance gave him a clearer view of the situation, and he felt a mix of sympathy for Ethan and relief that he had kept his head down.

As Taylor arrived at Emily's house, she greeted Officer Thomas with a warm smile. "Hi Dad, I can watch over the boys now.

You can head back to work." She looked over at Ethan and Oliver, offering them a reassuring nod.

Vincent Thomas, still visibly stern, addressed Ethan with a final warning. "I'll talk to your dad when he gets back from his trip. Remember, Ethan, this is your chance to change."

Ethan nodded, feeling a mixture of embarrassment and apprehension. Vincent then turned his attention to Oliver, who was standing quietly by.

"And you, Oliver. Will you be good?" Vincent asked, his tone more gentle.

Oliver nodded earnestly. "Yes, Officer Thomas."

Vincent gave them one last look, his seasoned cop instincts still on high alert. He knew that there was more beneath the surface of the situation with these boys. They seemed to fit the image of a typical family, with a single father and two young boys. But Vincent's intuition told him that there might be more going on—something that didn't entirely fit the usual patterns he was used to dealing with.

As Vincent left, Taylor turned to Ethan and Oliver, her expression a mix of concern and kindness. "So, what's going on? Are you two okay?" She tried to bridge the gap between them, her presence a comfort amidst the tension.

Ethan, feeling the weight of the day's events, mumbled, "We're okay, I guess. Just had a rough day."

Taylor, ever the supportive older sister, offered a sympathetic smile. "I'm sure everything will get better. Emily will be back soon, and we can sort this out."

Oliver, still feeling the sting of the day's events, nodded. "Yeah, I hope so."

As the evening wore on, the atmosphere in the house began to shift. Taylor did her best to provide a sense of normalcy, preparing snacks and setting up a movie for them to watch. Despite the stressful encounter with Vincent, Ethan and Oliver found some solace in the small comforts of the evening.

Meanwhile, Vincent Thomas's suspicions lingered. He was accustomed to piecing together clues, and something about this family—this trio—didn't entirely add up. As he headed back to his own duties, he resolved to keep an eye on the situation. There was a feeling that their story wasn't quite as simple as it seemed, and Vincent, with his sharp instincts, would remain vigilant for any signs that might reveal the deeper truths about the family he had just begun to understand.

Unknown to everyone, Vincent Thomas was supposed to die today. Yeah, you heard that right—he was meant to be in a tragic car accident involving his police car and a big truck. But because of Ethan, Oliver, and Ben's presence in the town, Vincent managed to dodge that grim fate... at least for now.

It's like the butterfly effect is in full swing. So many shifts in the timeline, so many unknowns, and yet, here we are. The trio might not have a clue that they've saved Vincent's life, and honestly, it probably doesn't even matter to the big things—like that looming nuclear war in the 24th century.

But here's the thing: it matters to Emily. It matters to Taylor. Without Ethan and Oliver causing trouble at school, without Ben's involvement in their lives, Vincent wouldn't be sitting on that couch giving them stern looks. He'd be just another casualty of fate. And yet, here he is, safe for now, all thanks to the time-warping chaos of the trio.

We, the readers, get the inside scoop, but the characters? They're blissfully unaware of how close Vincent came to not being part of the picture anymore. Funny how life—or time travel—works, right?

Chapter 27: No Good Deed Goes Unpunished

It had been a week since Ben's trip to Tokyo, and now he was back in his office in Maine, sifting through stacks of paperwork. The sound of a knock on his door interrupted his concentration. A female colleague poked her head in, a cautious smile on her face.

"Mr. Johnson, a police officer is here to see you," she said.

Ben's eyebrows lifted in surprise. He hadn't expected any official visits, but after a brief pause, he guessed who it was. *Vincent Thomas*, Emily's brother.

"Send him in," Ben replied, feeling a mix of curiosity and slight apprehension. He wasn't sure if this visit was about something official—or if it had to do with his personal life.

Officer Thomas entered, his presence as commanding as ever. He wasn't in uniform, which struck Ben as unusual. The visit felt informal, but Ben could sense the underlying seriousness. Vincent took a seat without waiting to be offered one, his eyes scanning the office as if assessing more than just the décor.

"Officer Thomas," Ben greeted, "What brings you to my office?"

Vincent leaned back in his chair, arms crossed. "Well, a couple of things, actually. First off, your boy, Ethan… seems like he's been stirring up trouble while you were away."

Ben inwardly sighed. *Of course.* He had a feeling Ethan wouldn't make the week easy for Emily. "What happened?" Ben asked, trying to keep his tone neutral.

"Let's just say he had an altercation at school—punched another boy right in the nose. And that's not the first issue. Emily told me he's been acting out at home too. Naughty boy, that one."

Ben rubbed his temples. Ethan's behavior wasn't unexpected, given his resistance to the entire situation. Still, hearing it from Officer Thomas made the issue feel more pressing.

Vincent wasn't done, though. His tone shifted as he added, "But that's not the only reason I'm here, Ben. I wanted to pay you a visit—see if anything's unusual around here." He glanced around the office again, then fixed Ben with a serious gaze. "Also, I wanted to check in on you… personally."

Ben raised an eyebrow. He could see through Vincent's intentions. This wasn't just a visit—it was a vetting. Vincent was trying to size him up, likely as a potential brother-in-law, given his relationship with Emily.

Ben met Vincent's gaze, his calm demeanor unchanged. "I appreciate you checking in on Ethan and Oliver. They're a handful, no doubt, and I'll make sure Ethan faces consequences for his behavior. But as for me, things are normal here. Just the usual work."

Vincent nodded, though his eyes held a glint of suspicion. "I trust you'll handle Ethan. But I'm protective of my sister, Ben. She's been through enough, and if you're planning to be a part of her life, I just want to make sure you're the kind of man who'll look out for her."

Ben smiled slightly, understanding the underlying message. "I respect that, Officer Thomas. I care about Emily, and I have no intention of causing her any trouble."

Vincent gave a slow nod, though the tension between them remained. "Good. I'll be keeping an eye on things," he said, standing up to leave. Before walking out the door, he added with a smirk, "And you might want to have a talk with Ethan soon. That boy's got a lot of energy. Too much, if you ask me."

That evening, Ben's voice echoed through the house with that unmistakable, calm authority. "Ethan! Living room, now!"

Ethan's stomach dropped like a rock. He shot a worried glance at Oliver, who sat calmly in their room, looking over his book like he'd seen this coming a mile away.

"I told you, Ethan," Oliver said, shaking his head.

"How could this be? Emily didn't say a word when Ben picked us up!" Ethan's mind whirled, still holding onto a tiny thread of hope. Maybe Ben didn't actually know? But he couldn't shake the feeling that something had gone very, very wrong.

Reluctantly, he shuffled into the living room, his feet dragging with every step. Ben sat on the couch, looking calm but serious, an expression that instantly made Ethan want to run the other way.

"You know who came to visit me at work today?" Ben asked in that calm-but-you're-in-trouble voice that made Ethan's heart hammer.

Ethan's big blue eyes went wide, his blonde head shaking as he whispered, "No... Ben... please..."

"Officer Thomas," Ben said, voice unyielding. "And he told me all about your fight at school. You punched Mark Petersen again, didn't you?"

Ethan's cheeks flushed, his young frame fidgeting as he tried to think of an excuse. "But... but he started it!" he squeaked, looking so much smaller and younger than his 10-year-old self already made him.

"Enough." Ben's voice cut him off, and Ethan knew he was done for. "And to top it off, you've been a handful for Emily while I was away."

"Wha–I mean–no! That's... uh... not exactly true..." Ethan's voice trailed off, and he glanced at Oliver for some backup. But Oliver only sighed, knowing better than to get involved.

"Drop your pants, Ethan," Ben said, and Ethan's face turned beet red, his hands fluttering nervously around his waist. He knew there was no way out, but he couldn't help a tiny, hopeful glance back at Oliver.

Ben didn't budge. "Now, Ethan."

With a deep, defeated sigh, Ethan fumbled with his waistband, his cheeks burning as he let his pants and undies drop to his ankles. He looked every bit the part of a little boy caught red-handed, cheeks rosy, big teary eyes, and tousled blond hair.

"Oliver," Ben said, "fetch the ruler."

Oliver hesitated for a split second, then nodded, returning moments later with the wooden ruler in hand, passing it to Ben without a word.

Ben motioned for Ethan to lie across his lap, and, biting his lip, Ethan clambered into position, feeling completely helpless and small. His little frame trembled, his heart racing.

The first smack of the ruler landed with a quick, sharp snap, and Ethan yelped, squirming with every firm, precise swat. "Ow! Please...Dad, I was only... trying to help!" he squeaked, his voice cracking with every word.

Ben's gaze didn't soften one bit. "You've been pushing every boundary, Ethan. I don't know what's gotten into you, but you're going to understand there are consequences."

Each swat was measured but firm, and before long, Ethan was sniffling, tiny whimpers escaping his lips as he struggled to hold back tears. His bottom turned a shade of pink that matched his flushed cheeks, his tear-filled eyes squeezed shut in helplessness.

When Ben finally stopped, Ethan slid off his lap, his hands flying to his stinging bottom. But Ben pointed him toward the wall. "Face the wall, hands on your head. And leave your pants where they are."

Ethan, looking like a tiny lost puppy, bit his lip and shuffled over to the wall, sniffling, hands up, his tousled blond head drooping. "You promised..." he mumbled, a pitiful little pout on his face. "You promised no more spankings..."

Ben's gaze softened slightly, though his tone stayed firm. "And I also promised there'd be consequences if you kept pushing. Trust me, Ethan, I don't enjoy disciplining you—not even a little."

Ethan's lip trembled as he stared at the wall, feeling every bit like a helpless, small child. Oliver, standing to the side, gave him a tiny nod of sympathy, though he'd warned him it would come to this.

Ben settled back on the sofa, his expression finally relaxing. He didn't enjoy punishing Ethan, but he knew the young lad had to understand. Meanwhile, Ethan shifted slightly, his bottom still stinging, a little frown forming as he realized he might just have to rethink his approach... at least for now.

Chapter 28: Surrendering to Reason

As the tension began to settle in the room, Ben, sitting on the couch, decided it was time to update Oliver about the strange encounter he'd had during his trip. "Oliver," Ben started, his voice still carrying authority, though now less severe, "I had a run-in with someone in Tokyo—a man I suspect might be another time traveler from the 24th century."

Oliver's eyes widened, his posture stiffening as he sat up. Ben knew that Ethan could hear him too, even while facing the wall, his sobs still filling the room. But that's when Ethan, still raw from the spanking, snapped his head around at Ben's words.

"What?" Ethan's voice cracked as he turned to look at Ben and Oliver. He struggled to pull himself together, but he was too overwhelmed. His pants still around his ankles, he stumbled forward toward Ben, almost tripping in his hurry. He collapsed next to Ben, still sobbing uncontrollably. "It means we're not alone," Ethan said, his words broken by his sobs. "They can help us go home... I want to go home. I don't want to live here anymore."

His small frame shook with every word, his face red and tear-streaked. The sorrow in his voice wasn't just from the punishment; it was deeper, a longing for the life they'd left behind, for the comfort of their world in the 24th century. Ben's heart softened at the sight. He gently took Ethan's face in his hands, wiping away the tears with his thumbs.

"I know, Ethan," Ben said, his voice low but tender. "But that guy… something about him seemed off. He ran before I could even ask for help."

Ethan's eyes, still filled with tears, searched Ben's face for answers, as if the hope of returning home rested on his next words. But Ben wasn't sure, and he hated that uncertainty more than anything.

Oliver, sitting nearby, spoke up cautiously. "So… time travel tech is more common than we thought?"

Ben nodded slightly, though his expression was troubled. "It's possible. Or they could be from a later century than ours. We don't know. But whoever they are, they're not here to help us."

Ethan's body shook with another wave of sobs. "I just want to go home," he repeated, clutching onto Ben's arm as though it were his only anchor. "I'm tired of pretending, tired of this place, tired of being a kid…"

Ben pulled Ethan closer, holding him firmly. "I know, buddy, I know," he murmured. "We're going to figure this out. I promise. But right now, we don't know enough about these people or what their goals are."

Ethan nodded weakly, still sniffling, feeling the warmth and security of Ben's presence. Though the pain of his spanking lingered, the greater pain was the homesickness and the uncertainty of when— or if—they'd ever get back to their time. The fleeting hope of encountering another traveler brought both a small flicker of hope and a new layer of fear.

Oliver watched quietly, his own emotions bubbling beneath the surface, though he remained silent. He'd been handling the situation better than Ethan, but deep down, he shared the same fears.

Ben finally released Ethan from the hug, his voice returning to its more fatherly tone. "Right now, we need to stay focused. If we're going to find a way home, we'll have to keep looking. But that doesn't mean you can act out, Ethan."

Ethan, still wiping his tears, nodded, his face full of regret. He knew Ben was right, but it didn't make the longing any less painful.

Chapter 29: The Art of Convincing

Ben sighed as he reached down to pull Ethan's pants up. Despite everything—the mischief, the constant trouble—he felt an undeniable bond with Ethan, one that had evolved beyond just being colleagues from the 24th century. There was something fatherly about the way he now cared for him, especially in this new world where they were forced into these roles.

Ben looked at Ethan, his face still flushed from crying, his hair messy, and his eyes puffy. He softened, offering, "How about you promise to be good, and this will be the last spanking I ever give you?"

Ethan shook his head weakly, still teary. "You promised that before. I don't trust you... wah," he mumbled, his voice breaking with emotion.

Ben raised an eyebrow, his voice firm but gentle. "And you've promised me a lot of things too, Ethan. You haven't exactly kept any of them either."

For a moment, there was silence between them, broken only by Ethan's sniffles. Ben sighed again, this time more softly. He could see how worn out the boy was, emotionally and physically. "How about a warm bath now?" Ben suggested, his voice low and caring. "You look like a mess."

Ethan, despite wanting to hold onto his pride, hesitated. He wanted to be taken care of, even if he pretended otherwise. "No..." he whispered weakly, though his body language said otherwise.

Ben, recognizing the small crack in Ethan's defenses, didn't wait for more protests. He gently placed a hand on the boy's shoulder and guided him toward the bathroom. Ethan didn't resist.

Oliver watched from the living room, his eyes following them as they left. Though he didn't say anything, there was a flicker of something in his chest—jealousy, perhaps. He had always tried to be the responsible one, the one who stayed out of trouble, yet it was Ethan who seemed to receive more of Ben's attention and care. But Oliver kept his thoughts to himself, knowing deep down that they were all struggling in their own ways.

In the bathroom, Ben helped Ethan out of his clothes, filling the tub with warm water. The tension from earlier seemed to dissolve a little as the steam filled the room. Ethan, though still upset, allowed himself to relax, feeling the warmth of the water and the gentle care from Ben as he guided him through the bath.

Ben didn't say much, but the silence was comforting. He knew that sometimes, words weren't needed. Just being there, taking care of Ethan, was enough for now. It was a strange dynamic, this forced family situation, but in moments like these, it didn't feel so forced. It felt... real.

After the bath, Ethan was calmer, quieter, and though the emotional weight of the day still lingered, the bond between him and Ben seemed a little stronger, even if they didn't admit it.

After the bath, Ethan sat on the couch, wrapped in a towel, his eyes still a little red but calmer. Ben knelt down beside him and asked gently, "What do you want for dinner?"

Before Ethan could answer, Oliver, who had been quietly observing from the sofa, spoke up. "How about we go to a Chinese buffet?"

Ethan, still feeling tender and seeking comfort, shook his head. "No... I want Phở," he mumbled softly, craving the warm, familiar flavors of the Vietnamese dish.

Ben smiled. "Actually, I love Phở too. We'll go to the buffet next time, Oliver," he said, trying to keep the mood light.

Oliver stayed silent but couldn't help the pang of jealousy that crept in. He thought to himself how, even though Ben disciplined Ethan often, it always seemed like he cared for Ethan more. Whether it was because Ethan needed more attention or because of some deeper connection, Oliver couldn't help but feel left out at times.

Despite his silent feelings, Oliver didn't say anything and followed along as they left the house. The trio made their way to a local Phở restaurant in Portland, a spot that Ethan and Oliver knew well—it was owned by Ava's family. In fact, Ava often helped out at the restaurant, and tonight, as fate would have it, she was working.

As they entered the cozy restaurant, the warm scent of broth and herbs filled the air. Ethan spotted Ava almost immediately, and their eyes met across the room. Ava gave them a smile, quickly wiping her hands on her apron before approaching their table.

"Hey, I didn't know you guys liked Phở!" Ava greeted them, surprised and happy to see her friends.

Ben, oblivious to the deeper connections between Ethan, Oliver, and Ava, smiled warmly. "We love it," he said. "And it's just what we need after a long day."

Ava chatted with them briefly before getting back to work, and as the trio settled into their meal, the atmosphere seemed lighter. Ben looked relaxed for the first time in a while, and even Oliver, despite his earlier jealousy, began to enjoy himself as the rich flavors of the Phở filled his senses.

For Ethan, the meal was a small comfort after a long, emotionally draining day. Even though things were complicated between him and Ben, moments like this—a warm bowl of Phở shared with people who, despite everything, still cared—made things feel just a little more bearable.

As they ate, the boys exchanged small glances with Ava, who waved at them from behind the counter. It was a quiet, simple moment, but after everything they had been through, it felt like a brief but welcome reprieve from the chaos of their lives.

After returning home from the Phở meal, the atmosphere was calmer, but Ben still had something on his mind. He had realized over the past year that using corporal punishment against Ethan hadn't changed much in the boy's stubborn nature. Ethan was still defiant, and Ben began to wonder if his approach had only deepened Ethan's resentment. Perhaps it was time to try something different. He was unsure if spoiling Ethan would work, but maybe showing more care would make a difference.

Later that night, Ben grabbed a bottle of lotion and walked into the boys' room. Ethan was lying on his bed, facing the wall, his body tense with lingering anger and embarrassment from earlier.

Ben sighed and sat on the edge of the bed. "Just don't want you to get sick like last time. Don't think I'm softening on your behaviors," Ben said, trying to keep his voice neutral.

Ethan, his pride still wounded, glared at Ben over his shoulder. "Then I don't need your care," he mumbled, trying to push Ben away.

Ben held his ground, though. "Alright, alright," he said, "just be still."

Ethan didn't push him away again, but he remained tense and quiet as Ben applied the lotion to his still-red, spanked bottom. The cooling sensation was soothing, though Ethan didn't want to admit it. He had always been more emotionally resilient in his adult body, but in this 10-year-old form, it was harder to cope with the overwhelming feelings of shame and frustration.

Oliver, who had been sitting on his bed nearby, broke the silence. "Why did people in our time even invent Rezulix in the first place?" he asked thoughtfully. "I mean, who would want to be a kid again?"

Ben paused, considering the question. "Well, you and Ethan weren't old yet when we started the experiment. But a lot of people would love to have their youth back. It wasn't just about reversing age—it was about restoring the energy, health, and opportunity of being young again."

Just then, Lucas, the AI of the time machine, chimed in from the small camera in the corner of the room. "The original purpose of Rezulix was to treat age-related illnesses like Alzheimer's," Lucas explained in its calm, synthetic voice. "It was never intended for recreational use. The idea was to rejuvenate the brain and body to prevent deterioration in old age."

Ethan rolled onto his back, staring at the ceiling as the information washed over him. "Well, it sure feels like a curse now," he muttered. "I don't want to be a kid anymore. I hate it."

Ben finished applying the lotion and sat back, looking at Ethan with a mixture of sympathy and frustration. "I know it's tough, Ethan," he said quietly. "But we're here now. We have to figure out how to make the best of it, even if it wasn't what we wanted."

Ethan didn't respond, but the anger in his expression softened slightly. Ben stood up, his voice more gentle now. "Get some rest. We'll talk more tomorrow."

As Ben left the room, Oliver watched him go, his mind swirling with thoughts about the strange fate they were all caught in. Meanwhile, Ethan lay still, staring into the dim light of the room, wondering when—if ever—they'd be able to escape this unintended consequence of time travel and Rezulix.

Chapter 30: Unveiling the Shadows

It was a rainy afternoon in March 1971, the rhythmic patter of raindrops against the windows providing a steady background as Ben worked with Lucas in the storage room. The atmosphere outside was gray and cold, but inside, Ben was focused on the task at hand—extracting crucial information from his smartwatch. The video recording from his encounter with the mysterious man in Tokyo had weighed on his mind ever since.

Lucas displayed the video. The image of the man appeared clear on the screen—a figure in his mid-30s, with sharp features and an almost too-confident demeanor. He had exchanged a few words with Ben before vanishing into the crowd. Ben and Lucas had been going over the footage for the past hour, but no clues had surfaced to reveal the man's identity.

"Enhancing facial features... cross-referencing with known databases from the 24th century," Lucas said in its mechanical, precise tone.

Ben rubbed his chin thoughtfully, staring at the image. "Whoever he is, he's either from a later century or someone off the grid in our time," Ben muttered. "But why would he show up here? And why run before giving me any real information?"

Across the room, Ethan and Oliver were half-paying attention. They were there because Ben had asked them to stay close, but they had grown restless. A playful wrestling match had broken out between the two boys, their laughter cutting through the otherwise tense atmosphere.

Oliver had Ethan in a headlock, but both were giggling. "Come on, Ethan, admit defeat!" Oliver teased.

Ethan struggled for a moment before slipping out of Oliver's grasp. "Not happening!" he declared, shoving his 'older brother' playfully.

Ben glanced over at them, momentarily distracted from the task. "Hey, can you two calm down for a minute?" he said, though his tone wasn't particularly stern. He appreciated that, despite everything, the boys could still find a way to have fun. But they were in the middle of something important, and Ben didn't want any distractions.

Ethan shot him a sheepish grin. "Sorry..." he said, though the twinkle in his eye suggested that they would be at it again soon.

Lucas interrupted their moment with a sudden beep. "Analysis complete," the AI announced. "No matching records found in the 24th-century database."

Ben frowned, leaning in closer to the screen. "So, he's not anyone from our timeline. Or at least, not someone documented."

Ethan, still catching his breath from wrestling, wandered over to the projection. "So... he's definitely a time traveler too, right?" he asked, his curiosity piqued. "Maybe he's from the future? Like... way after us?"

Ben nodded thoughtfully. "That's what I'm thinking. But without more information, we're shooting in the dark here."

Oliver joined them, his interest now fully captured. "What if he's someone important? Maybe he was trying to help us... or stop us?"

"That's what worries me," Ben admitted. "We don't know his motives. And the fact that he didn't reveal himself fully makes me think he's hiding something."

The rain continued to fall outside, the room growing quiet again as the trio considered the possibilities. Ben stared at the man's face on the screen, feeling a strange sense of foreboding. The more time they spent in the past, the more they were attracting the attention of forces they didn't understand.

"We need to be careful," Ben said, breaking the silence. "Whoever this guy is, he knows we're not from here. And he might not be the only one watching us."

That night, Oliver was back in the 24th century—but it wasn't any familiar part of his world. He found himself in a sprawling scientific lab, vast and stark, with white floors that stretched endlessly. The people around him moved with purpose, each one wearing the uniform and insignia of the Great Asia Confederation. The air was unnaturally cold, filled with wisps of icy vapor that clung to the floors and ceilings, and he could feel the chill seep into his skin. When he looked up, his gaze fell on an enormous, labyrinthine structure of sleek metal and bright lights—a supercomputer that towered ominously above him. It radiated a strange, unsettling energy. Suddenly, the computer's voice, unmistakably feminine and eerily calm, broke through the silence: "Hi Oliver! I need to tell you something." Her tone was gentle, almost soothing, but it sent a chill down his spine.

Before Oliver could respond, the world around him shifted violently. A deafening blast shattered the silence, and a wave of scorching heat roared toward him. He barely had time to brace himself as everything was engulfed in blinding light. The entire lab, the people, and the vast computer dissolved in an instant, erased by the force of an explosion that could only have come from a nuclear detonation. He tried to shield himself, but the blinding brightness and intense pressure suffocated him. In a panic, he jolted awake, heart racing and skin slick with cold sweat. The terror of that voice and the devastation lingered, haunting him even as he lay safe in his bed.

He wanted to cry, but he held it in. He didn't want to wake Ethan or Ben. Taking a deep breath, he slowly slipped out of bed and tiptoed to the bathroom, hoping to clean himself up without making a sound.

Oliver quietly slipped into Ben's room, his small feet barely making a sound on the wooden floor. He stood by the bed for a moment, hesitant. Part of him wanted to wake Ben, to tell him about the nightmare and the deep sense of fear that still clung to him. But the vulnerability he felt in his current state held him back.

Instead, he gently laid himself down next to Ben, pulling the edge of Ben's blanket over his body. He buried himself in the warmth, hoping it would soothe the anxiousness lingering from the dream. He was still trembling slightly when Ben stirred.

Ben woke up slightly, his instincts as a caregiver kicking in even while half-asleep. He could sense something was off, though he wasn't entirely awake yet. His arm instinctively wrapped around Oliver, pulling him closer.

"What's wrong, Oliver?" Ben asked softly, his voice groggy but filled with concern.

"I just... want to sleep with you tonight. Please," Oliver whispered, his voice small, almost like a child seeking comfort after a nightmare.

Ben didn't need to ask why. He could tell by the way Oliver was curled up against him, the way he was clinging to his blanket, that something had frightened him deeply. Without another word, Ben hugged Oliver closer, offering him the warmth and security he was seeking.

"Okay," Ben whispered.

As they lay there, Ben's mind began to drift. Over the past year, these two boys had become more than just his former colleagues. They had started to feel like his sons, and tonight only cemented that feeling. The roles had shifted so dramatically, but Ben had embraced them without realizing it. His sense of responsibility for Ethan and

Oliver was stronger than ever, not as peers, but as their father in this strange, unexpected life they were living.

Oliver, feeling Ben's protective arms around him, finally began to relax. The remnants of his nightmare faded, replaced by the comfort of knowing he wasn't alone. Ben's steady breathing lulled him back to sleep.

Chapter 31: Cracking the Code

At the office, Ben sat behind his desk, reviewing several documents when Sebastian knocked and entered the room. Dressed in his usual crisp attire, Sebastian looked both excited and a bit nervous. He had been reporting to Ben for months now, working under his direct supervision on various projects. But this, the oil well project in the South China Sea, was one of the largest undertakings he had been trusted with.

"Sir," Sebastian started, clearing his throat. "I wanted to give you an update on the South China Sea project. The preparation phase has gone smoothly. The equipment's in place, the logistics team has done a fantastic job, and we're on track for the next phase."

Ben glanced up from his work, giving Sebastian his full attention. The young man had certainly come a long way. When they first began working together, Ben had been hard on him, demanding excellence and attention to detail. But now, it seemed that Sebastian was starting to thrive under the pressure, rising to meet expectations.

"Good," Ben said, leaning back in his chair. "You've handled a significant amount of responsibility here. I trust you're keeping an eye on potential setbacks? The weather in that region can be unpredictable, and I don't want any surprises."

"Yes, sir," Sebastian replied confidently. "We've accounted for potential delays due to weather, and the offshore teams are ready to act if necessary. I've made sure to double-check every phase before giving the green light. So far, everything's going according to plan."

Ben nodded, a hint of approval crossing his face. He wasn't one to dole out praise often, but Sebastian could tell from Ben's expression that he was pleased.

"You've earned this, Sebastian," Ben finally said. "After all the hard work and challenges you've faced, I'm trusting you with this project. Keep this momentum, and you'll go far."

Sebastian couldn't hide his pride. Hearing those words from Ben—someone he deeply respected—was a validation of all the effort he had put in. He knew Ben wasn't an easy man to impress, and that made the acknowledgment even more meaningful.

"Thank you, sir. I won't let you down," Sebastian said, his voice firm with determination.

Ben gave a slight smile, the kind that rarely crossed his features. "Good. Now, go and make sure it stays that way. I'll be checking in, but I expect smooth sailing from here."

As Sebastian left the office, he felt a renewed sense of confidence. Ben's trust in him was a big step, and now it was his responsibility to prove that he could handle the weight of this project. The stakes were high, but Sebastian felt ready for the challenge.

Officer Thomas sat at his desk, drumming his fingers as a nagging thought resurfaced in his mind. It was something Ben had said when they first met, back when Ben, Ethan, and Oliver were staying at the hotel during their initial months in town. Ben had told him that they were visiting a woman named Mrs. Wilson—Ben's mother. At the time, it didn't seem odd, just a standard explanation for why the trio had been staying in town for so long.

But now, after spending more time around them, and especially after his recent conversation with Ben at the company, something didn't sit right. Vincent's instincts, honed over years of policing, were telling him that Ben was hiding something significant.

Unable to shake his suspicion, Vincent pulled out his files and ran a search on all the women in town with the last name "Wilson." There were only six. He spent the next two days visiting each of them, asking questions and listening for any mention of a son named Benjamin Johnson.

By the time Vincent had finished his rounds, he had confirmed what his gut had already told him—none of these women had a son named Benjamin Johnson. In fact, none of them had ever heard of Ben at all.

Standing outside the last house on his list, Vincent's jaw clenched in frustration. "I knew it," he muttered under his breath. "Ben was lying. He's been hiding something from the start...in his house."

As he got into his car, his mind raced with possibilities. Ben's story was falling apart, and now that Vincent had proof of a lie, he had to dig deeper. Something about that family wasn't right, and he was determined to find out what it was—even if it meant confronting Ben directly. He wasn't going to let this go.

Chapter 32: A Confrontation for the Truth

Officer Vincent Thomas stepped out of his police car in full uniform, walking up to the trio's house with determination in his eyes. The evening air was cool, with a slight breeze rustling the trees in the yard. Vincent knocked firmly on the door, his mind racing with the suspicion he'd been carrying since his investigation started.

Inside, Ben heard the knock and already felt a tight knot forming in his stomach. He had been sensing something was off with Vincent's recent interactions, and now it seemed that the officer was finally here to confront him. He opened the door and forced a neutral expression as he greeted Emily's brother.

"Can I come inside?" Vincent asked, his tone serious. "I have something to ask you."

Ben hesitated for a moment before stepping aside. "Come on in, Officer Thomas."

They both sat on the sofa, and for a brief moment, the silence between them hung heavy. Ethan and Oliver were in their room, completely unaware of the tension brewing in the living room, absorbed in their homework.

Vincent wasted no time. "Who is your mother?" he asked directly, his gaze never leaving Ben's face.

Ben forced a small smile. "I told you earlier, Officer. It's Mrs. Wilson."

Vincent's expression hardened. "I talked to every woman in town with the last name Wilson," he said, his voice rising slightly. "None of them is your mother."

The shift in Vincent's tone made Ben's heart skip a beat. *He knows.*

Vincent stood up suddenly. "If you don't mind, I'd love to have a look around your house."

Panic swelled in Ben's chest, but he tried to keep his composure. "Officer Thomas, I know my rights!" Ben exclaimed, his voice firm but laced with anxiety. "You may be Emily's brother, but you're here as a police officer, and I need to see a search warrant before you start going through my house."

Vincent's eyes flashed as he pulled out the warrant from his pocket. "I have it right here," he said, holding it up. Without waiting for further discussion, Vincent began walking toward the rooms, leaving Ben momentarily frozen.

Ben knew he couldn't stop a police officer armed with a search warrant, but he needed to buy some time—anything to prevent Vincent from discovering the time machine. Luckily, Lucas, the AI of the machine, was always watching. Ben hoped Lucas had already activated the machine's stealth mode.

Vincent reached the storage room on the first floor, its door securely locked. "Open this room, please," he demanded, turning to face Ben.

Ben tried to sound casual, but the words came out rushed. "There's nothing inside," he insisted. "It's just a place for the boys to play!"

"Then open it."

"Let me explain—"

Vincent, wasting no more time, kicked the door hard, breaking the lock and forcing it open. Ben held his breath, waiting for disaster.

But as the door swung open, the room appeared empty. Lucas had succeeded—activating the cloak mode just in time to hide the time machine from view.

Vincent stepped inside, scanning the empty space. He glanced back at Ben, slightly frustrated. "I told you, Officer. Nothing inside," Ben said, relieved but still on edge.

Vincent grunted, clearly dissatisfied. "Sorry about the door." He turned back to Ben, his curiosity not entirely quenched. "Now, what was it you wanted to explain earlier?"

Ben's mind raced, and before he could stop himself, the first excuse that came to his lips spilled out. "I wanted to explain... my plan to propose to Emily."

Vincent's eyebrows shot up in surprise. "Oh... really?"

Ben swallowed hard, realizing this was the path he had to commit to. "Yes, you're her brother, and I thought you should know. I wasn't sure how to bring it up."

Vincent stared at him for a moment before his stern expression softened. "Well, that's... unexpected. Alright."

Ben, desperate to change the subject and get Vincent out of the house, gestured toward the stairs. "Do you want to check upstairs? The boys' room and mine are up there."

Vincent shook his head. "No need. Sorry for the door and the hassle, but tell me this, Ben—why did you lie about your mother being Mrs. Wilson?"

Ben exhaled slowly. "We didn't want to tell you why we were really here," he confessed. "We didn't plan to stay in town at first. I came here looking for a job with the oil companies. I wasn't sure how long we'd be here until I found work, so I made up a story."

Vincent scrutinized Ben for a moment longer, as if weighing his words. "Alright," he finally said. "But just know, Ben—if you're hiding anything else, I will find out."

Ben nodded, keeping his face neutral as Vincent turned and left. Once the door closed behind the officer, Ben slumped down on the sofa, his mind still racing. He had narrowly avoided disaster, but it was clear that Vincent's suspicions were far from satisfied.

Ethan and Oliver rushed down the stairs as soon as they were sure Officer Thomas had left. Ethan, his eyes wide with disbelief, broke the silence first. "That was so close... but you said you would propose to Emily!?"

Oliver, his expression equally alarmed, quickly followed up. "I hope that was just an excuse, Ben!"

Ben, feeling the weight of his own hasty words, swallowed hard. "It is just a proposal... I had to say something to get him off our backs."

Ethan stepped forward, shaking his head. "No, Dad—I mean, Ben... You can't actually go through with this. We can't live under the same roof with Emily. That would be a disaster!"

Oliver crossed his arms, pacing nervously. "We're screwed. If Vincent's snooping around, it's only a matter of time before he finds out the truth. I think we should just leave town. We should go to another state while we still can."

Ben sighed heavily, rubbing his temples. "We can't just leave like this, Oliver. If we run, Vincent will chase us down. He's already suspicious, and that'll only make it worse. Plus, we can't move the time machine out of the house without attracting attention—it's too big. Imagine trying to move it across state lines!"

The trio stood in silence for a moment, tension thick in the air. Each of them was running through the impossible options in their heads, knowing full well they were trapped.

Ethan looked up at Ben, his face worried but hopeful. "So what do we do, then?"

Ben stared into the distance, his mind racing with possibilities. "We have to stay here and act normal, for now. We have no choice. But we'll need to be smarter, cover our tracks better... and as for Emily—" He paused, unsure of how to proceed. "Well, I'll think of something."

Oliver, still not fully convinced, sighed. "You better, Ben. Or else we're in real trouble."

Chapter 33: A Dance with Destiny

The next evening, Officer Thomas was driving home with his daughter, Taylor. She sat in the passenger seat, chatting excitedly about her boyfriend, Sebastian. Thomas, however, was only half-listening, his mind weighed down by the events of the previous night with Ben. Guilt gnawed at him. He had pushed too hard, invaded Ben's home, and now felt unsure about whether he had crossed a line.

"Taylor," Thomas interrupted as they neared home, his voice more serious than usual. "There's something I need to talk to you about, but you can't tell your aunt Emily about it, okay?"

Taylor, caught off guard by her father's tone, looked over at him. "What is it, Dad?"

Thomas sighed, keeping his eyes on the road. "I went over to Ben's place last night. I got a search warrant—but, well, it was forged. I went through his house."

Taylor's jaw dropped in disbelief. "Dad! Why would you do that? Ben and his boys are good people! What did you think you'd find?"

Thomas shifted uncomfortably. "I don't know, Tay. There were some things that didn't add up. Like that story he told me about his mother, Mrs. Wilson? Turns out that was a lie. I checked with every Wilson in town."

Taylor shook her head, her voice rising in defense of Ben. "Dad, people lie about stuff like that all the time when they don't want to share personal details. It doesn't mean they're criminals! I can't believe you did that. Aunt Emily will be so mad if she finds out."

Thomas grimaced, gripping the steering wheel tighter. "I know, I know. That's why I'm telling you. I felt like I was doing my job, but now... I'm not so sure. Ben seemed like he was hiding something, but maybe I overstepped."

Taylor stayed quiet for a moment, her voice softer when she finally spoke. "You trust your gut, Dad. But sometimes you've got to trust people too. Ben's been good to Aunt Emily. Maybe you should just apologize and clear things up with him."

Thomas nodded, feeling the weight of his daughter's words. "Yeah... maybe you're right."

But even as he agreed, he couldn't shake the lingering suspicion in the back of his mind. Something about Ben still didn't sit right with him.

A few days later, Officer Thomas decided to extend an olive branch. He invited Ben, Ethan, Oliver, and Emily over to his place for a family dinner. The invitation came as a surprise to Ben, who had been on edge since Thomas's unexpected search of their house. Ben wasn't sure if this was Thomas's way of apologizing or another way to dig into their lives. Either way, he couldn't decline without raising suspicion.

When Ben told Ethan and Oliver about the dinner, they exchanged nervous glances.

"Do you think he still suspects something?" Oliver asked, fidgeting with a pen in his hand.

Ben sighed, rubbing his temples. "He might, but this dinner could be his way of smoothing things over. If we don't go, it'll look suspicious."

Ethan, sitting cross-legged on the couch, added, "And what about Emily? Are you really going to pretend like nothing happened with the whole 'proposal' thing?"

Ben's stomach knotted at the reminder. "I'll handle it. Just... be on your best behavior, both of you."

As the trio prepared to head to Thomas's house that evening, Ben felt both on edge and relieved. On one hand, this dinner was a chance to ease any lingering tension and show Thomas that they were just an ordinary family. On the other hand, he couldn't shake the feeling that Thomas might still be probing for answers.

When they arrived at Thomas's house, the atmosphere was warm and welcoming. Emily greeted them at the door with a bright smile, and Taylor was setting the table. Thomas appeared calm, almost relaxed, as he waved them inside.

"Dinner's almost ready," Emily said, hugging Ben. "Vincent thought it'd be nice for all of us to spend some time together."

Ben nodded, trying to mask his anxiety. "Yeah, sounds great."

Throughout the evening, the conversation stayed light. Thomas asked Ethan and Oliver about school, and they played along, recounting mundane stories about classes and friends. Ben could feel Thomas watching him closely, but there was no hostility, just a hint of curiosity.

As the night went on, Ben slowly let his guard down, realizing this might be a genuine effort from Thomas to repair the tension between them. But deep down, he knew he still had to be careful. One wrong move, and the facade they had built could come crashing down.

After dinner, as the night wound down, Thomas pulled Ben aside. "Listen, about the other night... I think I might've overreacted. Just wanted to apologize for that."

Ben breathed a quiet sigh of relief. "Thanks, Vincent. I appreciate that."

Thomas nodded, his expression softening. "Let's just move on from it, okay?"

"Of course," Ben replied, though he couldn't help but wonder if this was truly the end of Officer Thomas's suspicions.

As the night grew quieter, Thomas and Ben found themselves sitting in the living room, a thin veil of smoke rising between them as they shared a cigarette. The air outside was cool, and the soft murmur of conversation from the kitchen—where Taylor, Emily, and the boys were still talking—was the only background noise.

Thomas, leaning back into the sofa, exhaled slowly before turning to Ben with a question he had been holding in for a while. "So, when are you going to tell Emily?" His tone was casual, but his eyes hinted at something deeper, something unsaid.

Ben, who had been preparing himself for this conversation, started to reply, "I'm going to—"

But before he could finish, Emily, who had just walked into the room, overheard Thomas and smiled innocently. "Tell me what?" she asked, her voice light, unaware of the weight behind the question.

Ben froze for a moment. His mind raced. He knew he couldn't afford to look suspicious, not now, especially after everything that had happened with Thomas recently. His heart pounded in his chest, but something in him clicked. Maybe this was the way forward, the way to keep everything from unraveling. So, without missing a beat, he turned to Emily and said, with as much sincerity as he could muster, "Tell you that I would love to have you as my wife."

Emily's eyes widened in surprise, her breath catching as she processed what he had just said. For a moment, the world around them seemed to blur. Then, tears welled up in her eyes. "Yes, yes, Ben, definitely!" she cried, a small, happy yelp escaping her lips.

In an instant, she was in Ben's arms, and he felt a mixture of relief and guilt. He loved her, there was no doubt about that, but this proposal, at this moment, was a desperate move—one born from the necessity to protect the secret of their true origins. And yet, even as they kissed, even as he held her close, something real passed between them. Ben had always cared for Emily, and if not for the fact that he and the boys were from the 24th century, he would have asked her sooner.

Taylor, hearing her aunt's joyful outburst, ran into the living room to celebrate. "Yes! I knew it!" she squealed, hugging Emily and then Ben. "Congratulations, Aunt Emily!"

Ben smiled awkwardly but genuinely, trying to absorb the warmth of the moment while suppressing the gnawing anxiety within.

Meanwhile, back in the kitchen, Ethan and Oliver exchanged worried glances, having overheard everything.

"Oh no," Ethan whispered, feeling the weight of the situation press down on him.

Oliver, equally concerned, nodded. "We're in trouble now."

They both knew that Ben's proposal was more than just a romantic gesture—it was a new complication, one that could entangle their lives even further. How would they manage to keep their 24th-century secret now, with Emily so much closer, so much more involved?

As Emily celebrated, Ben couldn't help but glance toward the boys, feeling the tension grow tighter around them all. He had made his move. Now, he could only hope it would be enough to buy them more time, to keep the truth buried just a little longer.

Chapter 34: A Struggle with Acceptance

Ethan's heart raced as he realized the weight of their situation. Without giving it much thought, he knew he had to act fast—to buy time for Ben and keep their secret hidden. "I gotta play our parts, Oliver! Help me!" he whispered urgently before sprinting into the living room.

As he burst into the room, he summoned every ounce of innocent charm he could muster, tears welling in his eyes as he put on the best performance of his young life. "Nooo! I don't agree! I oppose!" His voice trembled, but the conviction behind it was unmistakable.

The room fell silent, the jubilant atmosphere suddenly frozen in place. Ben's expression shifted from surprise to confusion, unsure if Ethan was genuinely distressed or simply an exceptional actor. He felt a wave of panic wash over him—had Ethan really just jeopardized everything?

Oliver, caught off guard but knowing he had to back Ethan up, quickly followed suit. "I oppose this marriage too! We had a mom already; we don't need a stepmom!" His voice echoed Ethan's sentiment, solidifying their united front.

Emily stood there, wide-eyed and unsure of how to respond to this unexpected backlash. The joy of her earlier moment was overshadowed by the boys' distress, and she felt a knot form in her stomach.

Taylor, sensing the tension and eager to defend her aunt, piped up. "Come on, guys! Your dad loves my aunt; they love each other!" Her words hung in the air, a plea for understanding.

Ethan shook his head vehemently, tears spilling over. "Nooo!" he insisted, as if that single word could reverse everything.

Oliver jumped in, trying to articulate their shared feelings. "We don't want our dad to marry anyone! This is not because of Emily or anything!" The determination in his voice was palpable, but it also revealed a deeper fear—one they all shared about losing their sense of family.

Ben exchanged glances with Emily and Vincent, feeling the weight of their boys' protests bearing down on him. "Kids," he began, his voice steady but laced with concern. "I will talk to them."

He stepped forward, preparing to navigate the emotional minefield he now found himself in. This was a delicate moment, one that could either strengthen their bond as a family or tear them apart. As he looked at Ethan and Oliver, he felt the tension crackle in the air, the stakes higher than ever. He had to find a way to reassure them without revealing the truth, to bridge the gap between their past and the uncertain future that lay ahead.

Ben knelt down in front of Ethan and Oliver, his expression earnest. "We're going to be a happy family. Dad will still love you two the same. Nothing will change that."

Emily stepped forward, her voice soft yet pleading. "Yes, please, boys! I will treat you two as my own." Tears shimmered in her eyes, genuine emotion spilling over as she reached out to them.

Ethan shook his head vehemently, his voice rising in desperation. "Nooo! I don't want you to replace my mom's position!" The hurt in his words cut through the room, and he felt the weight of his protest heavy on his shoulders.

Vincent, ever the voice of authority, stepped in. "That's not your choice to make, Ethan!" He crossed his arms, a stern look etched on his face. "You need to understand that."

Oliver chimed in, his tone just as adamant. "We can continue like this; you two don't have to marry!" His heart raced as he spoke, feeling the pressure of the moment.

The atmosphere in the room grew thick with tension, and it became clear that the night had taken a turn. With each word exchanged, the hope of a joyful family dinner dissipated, leaving behind only awkwardness and uncertainty.

On their way home, the trio remained silent, each lost in their thoughts. Finally, Ben broke the silence, glancing in the rearview mirror at the boys. "That was quite an act, guys..." His voice was a mix of admiration and confusion, unsure of how to interpret their performances.

He didn't know whether to feel happy that they were trying to protect him or sad that they were so deeply troubled by the prospect of change. The weight of their fears hung heavy in the air, and he felt the stirrings of conflict in his own heart.

As they pulled into their driveway, Ben knew that their lives were becoming increasingly complex, and he had to find a way to navigate this new landscape without losing the bond they had fought so hard to build.

In the kitchen, the atmosphere was thick with tension as Emily leaned against the counter, tears streaming down her face. She felt a whirlwind of emotions, torn between the joy of Ben's proposal and the painful rejection from his boys.

"I don't know if I should be happy or devastated," she sobbed, her voice trembling. "The boys hate me."

Vincent leaned against the doorframe, his arms crossed, watching his sister with concern. "That was expected, honestly," he replied, his tone matter-of-fact.

Emily looked up, her eyes red and puffy. "What do you mean?"

Vincent sighed, running a hand through his hair. "You really thought they would just welcome you with open arms? They're kids, Emily. It's a lot for them to process." He paused, shaking his head slightly. "I didn't expect Ethan to voice it so openly, though. That boy always brings troubles."

Taylor, sensing the heaviness in the air, stepped closer to her aunt, wrapping her arms around her. "Don't worry, Aunt Emily. The boys will come around eventually. They just need time to adjust."

Vincent nodded, trying to offer some reassurance. "Well... if I'm not mistaken, it's the adults who are supposed to call the shots here. You're not just their stepmom; you're an important figure in their lives now. They'll see that eventually."

Emily wiped her tears, taking a deep breath as she contemplated his words. "I just want to be a part of their lives, to show them that I care. I didn't expect it to be easy, but..." Her voice trailed off, and she looked down, guilt swirling within her.

Taylor squeezed Emily's shoulder. "You'll figure it out. Just be patient with them. They need to see that you're not trying to replace anyone; you just want to love them."

As the conversation continued, Vincent felt a sense of protectiveness for his sister. "Just remember, it takes time to build trust. It's a process, but you're strong, and you have a good heart. Don't let one night's chaos discourage you."

Emily nodded, taking solace in her brother's words. "Thank you, Vincent. I just hope they can see that I'm on their side."

The kitchen felt a little less heavy as they shared this moment of understanding. Though the path ahead was uncertain, they all knew they had to navigate it together, for the sake of family.

Emily

Chapter 35: Unlocking the Doors

In the bustling fast-food restaurant, the aroma of freshly fried burgers filled the air as Taylor and Sebastian settled into a booth, their trays laden with food. Taylor took a bite of her burger, her mind still swirling with the events of the previous evening.

"You won't believe what happened at dinner last night," she began, her voice animated. "Aunt Emily was proposed to by Ben, and the boys totally freaked out!"

Sebastian raised an eyebrow, intrigued. "Really? I didn't expect that. How did they react?"

Taylor sighed, her expression shifting from excitement to concern. "They were so against it. Ethan was practically in tears, insisting that he didn't want a stepmom. I mean, I get it—they've been through so much already, but it still hurt to see Aunt Emily so upset."

Sebastian nodded thoughtfully, taking a sip of his drink. "I can understand why they'd feel that way. It's a huge change for them." He paused, his brow furrowing slightly. "But I guess I can relate. When I first started working under Ben, I was terrified of him."

"Really?" Taylor laughed, surprised. "You? Scared of Ben?"

"Yeah, I know it sounds ridiculous now," Sebastian admitted, a smile creeping onto his face. "But he was so authoritative, and I thought he was all business. Then, after our trip to Japan, I got to see a different side of him. He's really passionate about what he does, and he genuinely cares for the people around him."

Taylor leaned in, intrigued. "So you like him now?"

"Absolutely," Sebastian replied, his tone sincere. "He's more than just a boss. He's someone I respect and admire. It's clear he wants what's best for his family, even if things get messy sometimes."

Taylor nodded, contemplating his words. "I just hope the boys can see that. They need to realize that Aunt Emily isn't trying to replace their mom; she just wants to be there for them."

"Exactly," Sebastian agreed. "It takes time, but with patience, they'll figure it out. Just like how I had to get used to Ben's style. It's all about understanding each other."

Their conversation flowed easily, the weight of the previous night's tension gradually lifting as they enjoyed their meal and each other's company. In that moment, Taylor felt a flicker of hope that perhaps, with time, everything would work out for her aunt and the boys.

Taylor glanced at her watch, noting the time. "How about we swing by the elementary school first? We should be able to catch them as they get out."

Sebastian nodded, a smile spreading across his face. "Sounds like a plan. Plus, I could use a break from adulting for a bit."

As they drove through the sunny streets, Taylor felt a mix of excitement and nervousness. She hoped the boys would be open to hanging out, especially after the tumultuous dinner the night before.

Arriving at the school, they found a spot to park and stepped out, the energy of children playing and chatting filling the air. "There they are!" Taylor pointed as she spotted Ethan and Oliver, their small figures standing by the school entrance.

"Hey, boys!" she called out, waving enthusiastically.

Ethan's expression brightened momentarily upon seeing her, but then his face turned serious, recalling the previous night's tension. Oliver looked a bit more receptive, his curiosity piqued at the sight of Sebastian beside Taylor.

"Hey, what's up?" Oliver greeted, though Ethan remained silent, arms crossed defensively.

"We were just about to head to the mall. Want to join us?" Taylor asked, trying to keep her tone upbeat.

Oliver exchanged a glance with Ethan, who shrugged. "I guess. What's there to do?" he asked, still cautious.

"Just hang out, grab some food, maybe hit a few stores. It'll be fun!" Taylor said, eager to lighten the mood.

Sebastian stepped in, his friendly demeanor shining through. "I could use some young advice on fashion. Plus, I'm sure you two have a ton of cool ideas for things to do."

Ethan hesitated, sizing Sebastian up. "Are you really cool? Or are you just saying that because you're our dad's boss?"

Sebastian chuckled. "I promise, I'm not just saying it because of that. I'm genuinely interested in what you guys think is fun."

Oliver smirked at Ethan, who finally relented with a resigned nod. "Alright, I guess we can hang out. But no boring stuff."

"Deal!" Taylor exclaimed, relieved. "Let's go!"

As they walked toward the parking lot, the atmosphere shifted slightly, the boys' initial apprehension fading as they started to engage with Sebastian. Taylor felt hopeful; perhaps this outing could bridge some gaps and help ease the tension that lingered after the dinner.

As they cruised through the mall, Ethan and Oliver felt themselves relax for the first time in days. Inline skating was a blast, the sleek wheels gliding under their feet as they raced through the rink. Afterward, they hit the arcade, spent time in the comic book store, and grabbed snacks at a diner.

Sebastian, curious about life at the trio's home, turned to Ethan as they sat around a table in the food court. "So, is Ben—your dad— strict at home?" he asked, taking a sip of his soda.

Ethan couldn't help but smirk, feeling the need to exaggerate a little for dramatic effect. "Strict? Our dad is a tyrant!" he replied, leaning back in his chair. "He whips my ass almost every other day!"

he added, laughing a little as he saw the look of surprise on Sebastian's face.

Sebastian chuckled, shaking his head. "Oh really? That's hard to imagine, but I guess I can believe it. Ben is pretty difficult at work too. I was actually a bit scared of him when I first started working under him," he admitted, smiling as he recalled his early days at the company.

Taylor, who had been listening intently, couldn't resist chiming in. "Well, that's exactly why you need my Aunt Emily, Ethan! She'll be the one you can run to when your dad's planning to whack you next time," she teased, giggling.

Ethan rolled his eyes, but there was a slight smile tugging at his lips. "Yeah, right. Like my dad would let that happen," he said, though the idea of having an ally in Emily wasn't completely unappealing.

Oliver, who had been quiet, finally spoke up. "Emily's nice, but... it's just weird, you know? Everything's changed."

Taylor's expression softened, sensing the underlying concern. "I get that. But Emily really does care about you guys, and so does Ben. Maybe this could be a good thing, like having a bigger family."

Ethan glanced at Oliver, then back at Taylor. "Maybe," he said, though there was still hesitation in his voice.

Sebastian leaned in, offering a comforting smile. "Look, your dad's tough, but he's also a good guy. I've learned a lot from him. Maybe things seem hard now, but they'll work out. And hey, you'll always have us around too."

The conversation settled into a more relaxed tone as they continued to hang out, the earlier tension fading. Ethan and Oliver began to feel a little more at ease with the idea of Emily, though they knew there was still a lot to work through.

At the hospital, Emily—known there as Dr. Reynolds—was going about her daily rounds, but her mind wasn't entirely focused on the tasks at hand. Between checking patient charts and speaking with nurses, her thoughts kept drifting back to the dinner at Vincent's house. The proposal. Ben's words. And, of course, the boys' fierce opposition. She felt a swirl of emotions that she couldn't quite shake off, and it was starting to affect her concentration.

During a break, Emily made her way to the staff lounge. A few of her female colleagues were already there, sipping coffee and chatting. Hoping to find both advice and some much-needed support, she took a seat and joined the conversation.

"Hey, Emily!" One of the nurses, Janine, smiled as she poured herself a cup of coffee. "You look like you've got something on your mind. What's up?"

Emily hesitated for a moment, then sighed. "It's been a rollercoaster, honestly," she admitted, rubbing her temples. "Ben proposed to me a couple of nights ago."

The room instantly buzzed with excitement. "Oh my God, that's amazing! Congratulations!" one of the other doctors, Karen, exclaimed, clapping her hands together. "Tell us everything!"

Emily smiled softly, appreciating the enthusiasm. "Thanks. I'm happy, don't get me wrong. Ben is… wonderful. I love him. But…" She paused, her expression clouding over. "His boys—Ethan and Oliver—they… well, they don't exactly want me in their lives."

Janine raised an eyebrow. "They don't like you? That seems odd. You've always seemed to get along with them."

"We've gotten along fine in the past," Emily replied, "but when Ben proposed, they both opposed the idea. Ethan was very vocal about it. He doesn't want anyone replacing his mom."

Karen nodded sympathetically. "That's tough. Kids can be really protective of their parents, especially when it comes to things like this. But that doesn't mean they hate you."

"I know," Emily said, biting her lip. "But it was hard to hear them say it, you know? I want to be part of their family, but now I'm wondering if I'm just intruding."

Janine leaned forward, giving her a reassuring smile. "Emily, those boys are young. They're still processing everything. It's not easy for them to see their dad with someone new, especially after losing their mom. But that doesn't mean they won't come around. It'll take time, but if they see how much you love Ben—and how much you care about them—they'll soften."

Karen added, "Maybe you can try spending more time with them, just you and the boys. Show them that you're not trying to replace their mom, but that you can be there for them in your own way."

Emily nodded slowly, considering their words. "You're right. I just… I don't want to push them too hard, you know? I want them to accept me, but I don't want to force it."

"You won't force it," Janine assured her. "Just be yourself. You're a great person, Emily, and they'll see that eventually. And remember, they're just kids. They're probably scared of change more than anything."

A small smile crept onto Emily's face. "Thanks, guys. I really needed to hear that."

Karen grinned. "Anytime. And hey, don't let their resistance ruin this for you. You're about to marry a great guy. Be happy about that!"

"I am," Emily said, her smile growing. "I really am."

As she returned to her duties that day, Emily felt lighter, more assured. She still had work to do with Ethan and Oliver, but she knew it wasn't impossible. The love she felt for Ben, and the hope that she could eventually win the boys over, gave her strength. It was just a matter of time.

Sitting in his office at the oil company, Ben stared blankly at the report in front of him. His mind wasn't on work, and he knew it. His thoughts were tangled, a web of confusion and conflicted emotions. The proposal to Emily, which should have been a joyful milestone, had turned into something far more complicated.

How did I get here? he wondered, rubbing his temples. He knew the answer, of course—one lie to cover another, an offhand proposal to distract Thomas when the officer had been too close to discovering the time machine. And now, that impulsive decision had become very real. Emily had said yes, her eyes filled with genuine happiness and love. The thought of her reaction still tugged at his heart. He loved her, that much was true. If things were different, if they weren't stranded in 1971, maybe this would be the perfect next step.

But things weren't different. He wasn't just Benjamin Johnson, a widower falling in love with a kindhearted doctor. He was Benjamin from the 24th century, a time traveler with two colleagues—Ethan and Oliver—who were now posing as his sons. They were stuck here, struggling to maintain a cover story, while working on a way to return to their own time.

And the boys' reactions...

Ben sighed heavily, leaning back in his chair. He had expected some resistance from Ethan and Oliver, but Ethan's dramatic outburst at Thomas's house had caught him off guard. Ethan had always been difficult, especially after being reverted to a child's body. His stubbornness had only grown. And while Oliver was usually the more level-headed of the two, even he had joined in on opposing the marriage.

Maybe it's because they feel trapped too, Ben thought. They don't want more complications. And I can't blame them for that.

He knew their opposition could slow things down, but it wouldn't stop the inevitable. At some point, he would have to move forward with the marriage—if only to keep up appearances. Thomas was already suspicious, and if Ben suddenly backed out, it would raise even more red flags. But the weight of the decision pressed heavily on his chest. He wasn't just asking Emily to marry him; he was inviting her into a life built on secrets and lies.

And what about the future? The trio couldn't stay in 1971 forever. They were planning to return to the 24th century once the gold obtained. But marrying Emily would complicate things. What would happen when they left? Could he just abandon her? Or was he getting too deep, losing sight of the mission?

Arghhh! Ben clenched his fists in frustration, a wave of guilt and doubt crashing over him. The conflicting emotions were exhausting. He loved Emily—there was no question about that. But love, in this case, felt like both a blessing and a curse.

Chapter 36: The Future Awaits

The Maine sun beat down as the school year came to an end. Ethan and Oliver, both now 11 years old by appearance, had just finished their 5th-grade year—a strange milestone in their trapped existence in the 1970s. It was difficult to know how to feel about it. For two young men of science, adults by every metric but their physical form, the experience of reliving elementary school felt like a prolonged embarrassment, an absurd twist of fate they were forced to endure.

Ben, sitting on the porch of their modest house, glanced up from his newspaper as the boys trudged up the driveway, their school bags slung over their small shoulders. They didn't look particularly triumphant, despite the fact that they were now officially done with elementary school. They looked... tired.

"How was the last day of school?" Ben asked, folding the paper onto his lap. He tried to keep the tone light, but even he wasn't sure if he should congratulate them or apologize for putting them through another year of this.

Ethan, scowling as usual, dropped his bag with a thud on the porch and slumped into the seat beside Ben. "It was terrible, as always."

Oliver, slightly less grim, offered a weak smile. "Well, at least it's over."

"Over?" Ethan shot back, incredulous. "Over? It's not over, Oliver! We're supposed to go to middle school after summer. Sixth grade!" He ran a hand through his hair in frustration. "I can't believe we've been stuck like this for a year and a half. A year and a half, Ben!"

Ben sighed, knowing where this conversation was headed. "I know it's not easy—"

"Not easy?" Ethan interrupted, his voice rising. "You think this is about not easy? We're supposed to be working on high-level research projects, not learning long division for the hundredth time! This is humiliating."

Oliver sat down quietly, nodding in agreement. "It is pretty bad, Ben. We're not... we're not actually kids. Having to go to middle school with real 11-year-olds after summer break—it feels like a step backward. Again."

Ben leaned forward, his elbows resting on his knees, rubbing his temples as he listened. "Look, I know you hate it. And believe me, I hate that you have to go through this. But we don't have a choice, not if we want to keep the cover. The longer we're stuck in 1971, the more important it is to blend in. If you don't go to school, people will get suspicious."

Ethan huffed. "I'd rather deal with the suspicion than another year of pretending to be some helpless kid."

"Well, you'd have to deal with more than suspicion," Ben said, his voice lowering. "You know that. If you two aren't enrolled, the authorities might get involved. They could take you away, investigate the family situation. Do you really want that kind of attention?"

Both boys fell silent. They knew Ben was right, as much as they hated it. The risks of not playing along were too high.

"Look," Ben continued after a moment, softening his tone. "This is temporary. You're not stuck in this forever. I'm still working on figuring out how to get that gold back, and as soon as we have it, we can power the time machine and leave this whole nightmare behind. But until then, you have to keep up appearances."

Oliver looked down at his feet, feeling the weight of their situation. "It just feels like it's never going to end," he said quietly. "I thought by now we'd have made progress, but every day it feels like we're sinking deeper into this… this life."

Ethan, still fuming, muttered under his breath. "Another year of this garbage, and I'll lose my mind."

Ben reached out and put a hand on Ethan's shoulder. "I get it, Ethan. I really do. But you're stronger than you think. Both of you are. You've handled this better than most people could."

Ethan, though still frustrated, gave a reluctant nod. He knew Ben was trying to help, even if it didn't feel like enough.

There was a long silence between them, the three trapped in their own thoughts. The sun was setting now, casting a warm, orange glow over the quiet neighborhood. In this world, in 1971, the passage of time felt cruel. Every day that went by brought them closer to a future they weren't sure they could reach.

Finally, Oliver broke the silence, his voice soft but firm. "Do you think we'll ever make it back, Ben? I mean… really?"

Ben hesitated for a moment. The truth was, he wasn't sure. But he couldn't let them lose hope. He wouldn't allow it. "Yes," he said, his voice steady. "We will. It might take longer than we thought, but we'll make it back. I promise you that."

Ethan looked up at Ben, his eyes filled with a mix of skepticism and longing. "You better be right," he muttered, standing up and grabbing his bag. "Because I'm not living another year in this kiddie prison."

Oliver stood as well, giving Ben a small smile. "We'll manage," he said. "We always do."

As they headed inside, Ben stayed on the porch for a while longer, staring out into the distance. He wished he could give them more certainty. He wished he could believe it himself.

But for now, all he could do was keep them moving forward— one day at a time.

The engagement party of Ben and Emily was set in the sprawling backyard of Emily's friend from the hospital, a warm June evening breeze sweeping through the crowd. The air was filled with laughter, clinking glasses, and casual conversation, as friends, colleagues, and even a few neighbors gathered to celebrate. Fairy lights twinkled overhead, and tables were arranged neatly with hors d'oeuvres and champagne. Ben and Emily had spared no expense to make this party the perfect mix of casual fun and formal engagement celebration.

Ben, dressed sharply in a crisp suit, moved through the guests with practiced ease. He smiled, shook hands, and exchanged pleasantries with his colleagues from his company. Many of them had admired him at work, but tonight, they saw another side of him—a man who was finally "settling down." He had hoped this engagement would strengthen their connections with Emily's family, including Officer Thomas, and help solidify the facade they were still desperately holding onto in 1971.

Emily, in a soft peach-colored dress, was glowing as she chatted with her fellow doctors and nurses from the hospital. She seemed genuinely happy, but there was a nervous edge to her demeanor. Every now and then, she'd glance across the yard at Ethan and Oliver, who were sitting on the edge of the porch, clearly sulking. It was hard to tell if they were playing their parts as resistant children, or if their emotions were real. Maybe both.

Ethan, with his arms crossed, kicked at the porch's wooden railing, his face a storm cloud of frustration. He hated this. Not just the party, but the entire situation. It was bad enough they were trapped in this time period, but now they had to pretend they were excited about Ben getting married to some woman who, frankly, Ethan still didn't know all that well. It felt wrong to him, forced. He knew it was all part of Ben's long game, a way to blend in and buy them more time. But that didn't make it any easier.

Oliver, sitting beside him, wasn't much better off. He wasn't scowling as intensely as Ethan, but his usual calm demeanor was shadowed with confusion. "I don't know how to feel about this," Oliver muttered under his breath.

Ethan snorted, giving his brother a sideways glance. "Feel about what? The fact that Ben's getting married? Or the fact that we have to sit here and smile about it?"

Oliver sighed. "Both, I guess. I mean, I get it… we need this. We need to keep up appearances. But it feels… weird."

"Understatement of the century," Ethan grumbled. He glanced over at Ben, who was deep in conversation with Officer Thomas. "He's so caught up in this whole charade. It's like he's actually convinced himself this is a good idea."

Oliver leaned back, his arms stretched out behind him. "Maybe it is, for now. It keeps us safe. The last thing we need is Thomas digging any deeper into our lives."

Ethan was quiet for a moment, watching Ben laugh at something Thomas had said. Then he shook his head. "I just don't want a 'mom.' Not now. Not here."

The evening continued as the party hit its stride. People gathered in small clusters, talking and laughing. Emily's colleague, a cheerful nurse, made a toast, speaking warmly of Emily's dedication at the hospital and her obvious love for Ben. Emily's eyes shimmered with tears as she thanked everyone for coming.

Ben's eyes drifted toward Ethan and Oliver more often than not, trying to gauge their reactions from across the yard. He could see the tension in their posture, the way they kept to themselves on the porch. He wondered if their feelings had shifted or if they were simply playing their parts too well. He knew they didn't like the idea of having Emily as a mother figure, but Ben hoped they would come to understand that blending in required this necessary step.

Taylor, who had been mingling with the guests, spotted the boys and sauntered over. "You two look like you're having a blast," she said sarcastically, plopping down beside them.

Ethan rolled his eyes. "You think?"

Taylor, grinning, nudged Oliver's shoulder. "Hey, at least after this, you'll get to hang out with me more often. We'll be family." She winked. "Won't that be fun?"

Oliver forced a smile. "Yeah. Fun."

"Come on, it won't be that bad," Taylor said, trying to lighten the mood. "You guys should at least pretend to be happy. It's a party."

Ethan huffed. "We're here, aren't we? That's enough."

Taylor was about to respond when Sebastian appeared, balancing a plate of snacks in one hand and two sodas in the other. "Hey, I got you guys something," he said, offering the drinks to Ethan and Oliver. "Figured you might need a little sugar rush to survive this thing."

Ethan took the soda begrudgingly. "Thanks, I guess."

Sebastian smiled. "Look, I know it's probably hard, but your dad's a good guy. And Emily's nice. It might not be the worst thing in the world."

Ethan shot him a look. "Easy for you to say. You're not the one being told to accept a new mom."

Sebastian shrugged. "True but try to see it from their perspective. They both need a spouse, you know."

Ethan didn't respond, just sipped his soda and stared into the yard. He wasn't sure if anything anyone said would change how he felt.

As the night began to wind down, Ben finally found a moment to step away from his guests and head toward the porch. He sat down beside the boys, letting out a small sigh as he leaned back.

"You two okay?" he asked, though he already knew the answer.

"We're here," Ethan said flatly, staring at the ground.

Ben gave a small, tired smile. "I appreciate that. I know it's a lot to ask."

Oliver looked at him, searching his face. "Do you... do you really love her, Ben? Or is this just for the show?"

Ben hesitated for a second, then nodded. "I do love her, Oliver. But I also know this situation isn't easy for any of us. We're in a tough spot, and I'm trying to do what's best for everyone—keep us safe, keep us… normal, as much as we can be."

Ethan finally looked up at Ben, his expression softening, but only slightly. "I get it. I just don't like it."

Ben nodded, understanding. "I don't expect you to like everything about this. But I do expect you to try. We're a team, right? We'll get through this."

Ethan and Oliver exchanged glances. Neither of them said anything, but in their silence was a reluctant acceptance. They didn't have to like it—but they understood. For now, that was enough.

As the last of the guests began to filter out and the lights dimmed, the trio sat together on the porch in the cooling night air. Ben knew the engagement was just one more layer of complexity in their already tangled lives, but it was necessary. It kept them moving forward—at least for now.

Chapter 37: Our Family's Trip to Japan

It was a warm summer evening at Emily's house. The hum of the air conditioner mixed with the clink of silverware as everyone lingered at the dining table after dinner. Ethan and Oliver, 11-year-old boys on the outside, sat slouched in their chairs, swinging their legs under the table like every restless kid ever forced to endure adult conversations.

Emily set her fork down and smiled warmly. "I've been thinking," she began, looking around at her little 'family.' "We should take a family trip. Something fun to do together before things get too busy."

Ben raised an eyebrow over his coffee mug. "A trip? What kind of trip?"

"Tokyo!" Emily announced with enthusiasm, her eyes lighting up. "It's such a vibrant city—culture, food, and maybe even some theme parks. I thought it'd be a great way for us to bond as a family!"

Ethan paused mid-swing of his legs, his expression shifting into a suspicious squint. "Family bonding" always sounded like a code for things he wouldn't like, such as matching outfits or enforced politeness. He shot a quick glance at Oliver, who was nibbling on a breadstick and pretending to look thoughtful.

Ben nodded slowly, a faint smirk on his face. "Tokyo, huh? Not a bad idea." He turned to the boys. "What do you think? Time to broaden your horizons."

Ethan muttered, "I like my horizons just fine," under his breath, but Ben's raised eyebrow silenced him before he could say more.

Emily leaned forward, undeterred. "There's something for everyone—arcades, sushi, beautiful sights. Doesn't that sound fun?"

Oliver perked up slightly. "Arcades?" His voice betrayed genuine interest, though he quickly masked it with a nonchalant shrug. "I guess that could be cool."

Ethan rolled his eyes. "Yeah, if we don't get dragged to boring stuff like museums."

"You might learn something," Ben said dryly.

Ethan slumped back in his chair, muttering, "I already know stuff."

Before Emily could respond, Taylor, her bubbly teenage niece, jumped in from her spot at the table. "Tokyo? That sounds amazing! Can I come too?"

Emily laughed. "Of course, Taylor. It's a family trip, and you're family."

Taylor grinned and immediately added, "Oh! And what about Sebastian? He's been so stressed lately with work. He deserves a vacation too."

Ben raised a hand like a referee about to call a foul. "Wait. You're suggesting your boyfriend comes on this trip?"

Taylor clasped her hands dramatically. "Please, Ben! He's practically part of the family, and he's been working so hard. He could use a break."

Ethan shot Oliver a look, then stage-whispered, "Great. Now it's a circus."

Oliver smirked but nudged Ethan's arm to stop him from saying more.

Ben rubbed his temple. "Fine," he said at last. "But Sebastian's not getting any special treatment. He carries his own luggage."

Taylor squealed in delight, and Emily beamed. "This is going to be so much fun! I'll start planning everything tonight."

Ben sipped his coffee, hiding a more contemplative expression. A trip to Tokyo meant more than just sightseeing for him. His last visit had hinted at connections to the future—connections he needed to investigate.

Later, back at home, Ethan stormed into their shared room and flopped face-first onto the bed. "This is the worst idea ever. 'Family trip.' Who even came up with that?!" His voice was muffled by the pillow.

Oliver sat cross-legged on the floor, flipping through a comic book. "You're being dramatic. It could be fun."

Ethan turned his head, glaring at his brother. "Fun? It's bad enough we're stuck here pretending to be kids, and now we're going on vacation with Taylor and her boyfriend? What's next, matching pajamas?"

Oliver chuckled. "Hey, at least there'll be arcades. And maybe sushi. You like sushi."

"Not enough to sit through hours of 'family bonding,'" Ethan groaned. "Ben's probably going to make us pose for photos. You know how much I hate photos."

Oliver grinned. "You only hate them because your hair never cooperates."

Ethan grabbed a pillow and chucked it at Oliver, who dodged expertly.

"Relax, Ethan," Oliver said, still smiling. "At least it's Tokyo and not a camping trip. Imagine Ben trying to roast marshmallows. He'd probably build a fire pit and lecture us on heat distribution."

Ethan cracked a small smile despite himself. "Okay, that's actually funny."

Oliver shrugged. "See? It's not all bad. Just… try to enjoy it. If we're stuck in the 1970s, we might as well make the most of it."

Ethan sighed and flopped back onto the bed, his frustration bubbling over. "Fine. But if anyone tries to call me a 'good boy' again, I'm gonna start drinking Sake, right in front of this 'family.'"

Oliver, sitting cross-legged on the floor, chuckled and leaned back against the wall. "Deal. But honestly, I think Ben or Emily would just shrug and let us have Cokes. That's about as rebellious as we're allowed to be."

Ethan groaned and began thrashing around dramatically on his bed, arms flailing like a toddler mid-tantrum. "I am twenty-one! I can drink! I can drink whatever I want—Noooo!" He flopped onto his back, throwing an arm over his face like the weight of the world had crushed him.

Oliver burst out laughing, nearly toppling over. "Wow. You're really going for an Oscar with that performance."

Ethan peeked out from under his arm, glaring. "Laugh all you want, but you know I'm right. This whole thing is ridiculous. I have years of experience, Oliver. Years! And now I can't even open a soda without someone checking the label for caffeine."

"True," Oliver said, still grinning. "But hey, at least nobody's tried to cut your food for you. Yet."

Ethan sat up sharply, eyes wide with mock horror. "If that ever happens, I swear I'm running away to Canada. No ID required—just freedom and maple syrup."

Oliver laughed again, tossing a pillow at Ethan. "Relax. You've survived this long. What's a little more humiliation?"

Ethan caught the pillow and clutched it to his chest with mock gravity. "Humiliation? Oh no, brother, this is oppression. An affront to my dignity as a grown man." He paused, then smirked. "I mean, your dignity was gone the moment you agreed to go to school just because Ben told you to, without even putting up a fight."

Oliver rolled his eyes but couldn't hide his grin. "Because I'm an adult who knows when to pick my battles—and I don't get spanked like a 5-year-old for mouthing off."

"I am not—" Ethan snapped, then caught himself and shifted gears. "It's… strategy. Someone had to take the heat so Ben didn't start drowning us in even more rules. Honestly, you should thank me."

"Sure," Oliver said, raising an eyebrow. "Thank you, oh great mastermind of the 24th century, who's clearly too busy complaining about everything to actually do anything useful." He leaned in, his grin turning mischievous. "And by the way, I know you like Taylor. You hate that she's hanging around Sebastian, don't you?"

Ethan's face turned red as he hurled the pillow back at Oliver, who ducked just in time, laughing.

Their laughter filled the room, cutting through the tension like sunlight breaking through a storm. Despite their frustrations, they both knew they were in this together—whether it was enduring the charade of childhood, navigating awkward family dynamics, or scheming for the day they could finally return home.

The bustling noise of the airport echoed around them as the group moved through the terminal. Emily was juggling everyone's passports and boarding passes, her eyes darting between the kids and the departure screens. She seemed to be taking it all in stride, but her slightly tense smile revealed she was in full "mom mode"—keeping everything and everyone in check.

"Here, Emily, my passport." Oliver handed his over with a polite smile. "Thanks for organizing everything for the trip. It's nice to just show up and not worry about all this stuff."

Emily smiled warmly at Oliver, her eyes softening at his manners. "You're welcome, Oliver. I'm happy to take care of it."

Standing next to him, Ethan couldn't help but roll his eyes dramatically. With a swift, playful swat on Oliver's arm, Ethan grumbled, "What are you doing? That wasn't helping."

Oliver leaned in and whispered, "Just thank her. It's polite."

Ethan shook his head, his voice barely above a murmur as he looked around, making sure no one else could hear. "No way. We have to slow everything down, Oliver. You really want to rush toward a real wedding?"

Before Oliver could respond, Taylor, who was just a few feet away, caught wind of their conversation. She walked over, a teasing grin on her face, raising her eyebrows at Ethan as she threw up air quotes. "Oh? Talking about my aunt? Your 'mom'?"

Ethan shot her a glare, his cheeks flushing slightly as he clenched his jaw. "She's not—" He stopped himself, realizing he couldn't say what he really felt. Instead, he grumbled, "You know what I mean."

Taylor just laughed softly, clearly enjoying riling him up. "Yeah, sure. Anyway, you better be nice, or your 'mom' might ground you."

Oliver shot Ethan a warning look, as if to say, Don't take the bait. But Ethan just rolled his eyes again and crossed his arms, clearly frustrated by the whole situation. He didn't want to cause a scene, but every little reminder of this charade—of them being stuck in this fake family—made his blood boil.

As they moved through the security line, Emily fussed over everyone, making sure they had everything they needed. "Taylor, do you have your carry-on? Sebastian, don't forget your passport! Ethan, where's your boarding pass?"

Ethan reluctantly handed it over without a word, his earlier frustration still simmering beneath the surface. He exchanged a glance with Oliver, who shrugged slightly, as if to say, It is what it is.

The trip was happening whether he liked it or not, and despite his silent resistance, there was no stopping this "family" vacation to Tokyo.

As they approached the boarding gate, the group shuffled in line, passports and tickets in hand. Ethan and Oliver walked side by side. The airport's bright lights and excited travelers only seemed to heighten the dread bubbling in Ethan's chest. He kept his head down, his lips pressed together in silent rebellion as they made their way toward the plane.

Ben, walking just behind the boys, watched them closely. He noticed the sulk in Ethan's posture—the way his shoulders slumped, and his head hung slightly lower than usual. As they neared the entrance of the plane, Ben stepped forward and placed a firm hand on Ethan's back, making the boy stiffen for a second.

Leaning in close, Ben's voice was low but carried unmistakable authority. "Show some respect to Emily, Ethan," he said in a controlled tone, but there was an edge to it, a warning. "Enough sulking."

Ethan flinched slightly but didn't dare look back. He felt Ben's hand lingering on his back for a moment longer before it finally let go. For a brief second, he thought about snapping back, about telling Ben what he really thought of this whole situation. But he knew better. There was no winning that argument—especially not here, not in front of everyone.

Oliver glanced at his side, catching the tension between Ethan and Ben. He gave Ethan a subtle nudge, as if to say, Not here, not now. Oliver had learned by now that picking fights with Ben, especially over things like this, never ended well for either of them.

Ethan just huffed in response, muttering under his breath, "I'm not sulking…"

But he knew Ben was right. Emily didn't deserve his attitude. Not really. She wasn't the reason they were stuck in the 1970s, and it wasn't her fault Ben had proposed. Still, it didn't stop the frustration gnawing at him, this constant reminder that their lives were spiraling further away from the future they belonged in. Every step deeper into this "family" facade felt like another step away from the life he was supposed to have.

As they walked down the narrow aisle of the plane, finding their seats, Ben gave Ethan one last look—his eyes hard, but not without understanding. Ben wasn't just telling him to behave for Emily's sake; he was telling him to keep up the act. They couldn't afford to let things slip, not now, not ever. Ethan knew that deep down, but it didn't make any of this easier.

They found their seats, Emily ahead, already talking to the flight attendants with her usual cheerful grace. Taylor was chatting with Sebastian, full of excitement about the trip. The air buzzed with everyone's anticipation.

Ethan buckled his seatbelt and stared out the window at the shrinking terminal, it just felt like another step into a life he never asked for.

At 4 a.m., in the stillness of the house, Lucas, the AI of the time machine, sensed something he hadn't expected. It started as a subtle shift, a disturbance that rippled through the fabric of his database, like a tremor echoing from a distant place and time. His circuits processed the information with precision, but as the data flowed in, a deep unease began to settle within his artificial consciousness.

He accessed the news archives from the 24th century—something he hadn't been able to do since the trio had become trapped in the 1970s. Yet, there it was: clear as day, as if the future were reaching back to him. Headlines about the escalating tensions between the North American Union and the Great Asia Confederation flashed before him.

And then, the most devastating news of all.

Full-scale nuclear war has erupted.

Lucas froze for a moment, processing the sheer magnitude of the information. His systems worked tirelessly, reviewing the data, trying to comprehend how and why this had happened. He knew the trio had feared such a possibility, but this... this was a reality. The future they had hoped to return to was now engulfed in flames.

"Oh... no..." Lucas muttered to himself, his voice betraying an unusual tone of sorrow, almost as if he were a living being. The humanlike quality of his voice startled even him, but the weight of what he was witnessing overwhelmed his usual protocols. The cold, detached logic of an AI gave way to something approaching panic. He had grown more attached to the trio than he ever anticipated, and this news, these changes in the timeline, were catastrophic.

Lucas calculated the timeline changes, the effects they could have on the trio still flying to Japan. Would they even be able to return to the 24th century? His circuits buzzed with urgency as he tried to formulate a solution, but the situation seemed dire.

He scanned the house, then looked deeper into his systems. His database was continuously updating as if he were somehow linked to the future, despite being physically cut off. The nuclear fallout, the collapse of world governments, the mass loss of life—it was all there. The North American Union was devastated, and the Great Asia Confederation had also been nearly wiped out.

What scared Lucas the most was that some events weren't supposed to happen—not yet. Something in the timeline had shifted, and it had accelerated this chain of destruction. Was it because of them? Because of their presence in the past?

Lucas worked furiously, running simulations, trying to calculate how these events might impact the trio's future. But with each model he ran, the likelihood of their return home dwindled further. The world they had once known was gone, reduced to ash and ruin.

For the first time since he was created, Lucas felt... hopeless.

As they landed in Tokyo, the familiar bustle of Narita Airport surrounded them, but Ben's mind was elsewhere. His wristwatch, disguised to look like an ordinary 1970s timepiece, buzzed subtly as they disembarked. It was a message from Lucas. The AI never contacted him unless it was critical.

Excusing himself under the pretense of needing a moment alone, Ben headed to the restroom. Inside, he locked the door of a stall, his heart racing as he activated the hidden interface on the watch. The message appeared before his eyes, causing a chill to run down his spine.

"Timeline disruption detected. Full-scale nuclear war confirmed in 24th century between North American Union and Great Asia Confederation. Future uninhabitable."

Ben's breath hitched, and his stomach twisted. Nuclear war? He gripped the sides of the small stall, feeling the weight of the message crush him. Everything—their research, their dreams of going home—was now meaningless. The future they were so desperate to return to had collapsed into chaos and ruin.

He slumped against the wall, his mind spinning. Oliver's nightmares… they were real. The images Oliver had seen—the nuclear destruction, the cities wiped out—had been more than just a side effect of the Rezulix. They were premonitions of a future that now existed, a reality Lucas had just confirmed.

Ben sat for a long moment, trying to steady himself. He knew Oliver had been deeply disturbed by the dreams, and Ethan would undoubtedly unravel at the news. Telling them about this now, with Emily and the others so close, would risk everything. Ethan would melt down completely—and that was the last thing Ben needed. Not here, not now. This trip to Japan was supposed to be a distraction, a way to find answers about their situation—not to confirm that their future had been obliterated.

Ben knew he had to remain composed, even as dread threatened to swallow him. He couldn't let this information destroy the fragile balance he had maintained with Ethan and Oliver. But his own mind wrestled with the truth. How could everything be gone?

"So... Oliver's nightmares were true... but how?" he whispered to himself, running his fingers through his hair in frustration. The questions burned in his mind. How had they missed the warning signs? Was it their fault? Had their meddling in the past somehow accelerated this catastrophe?

He exhaled deeply, trying to clear his head. For now, he had to push it aside. There would be time for a breakdown later, but not here, and not in front of everyone.

Forcing himself to stand, Ben straightened his jacket and pocketed the watch, wiping any trace of emotion from his face. He couldn't afford to show his hand yet.

When he rejoined the group outside, Emily was cheerfully organizing their luggage, and Ethan and Oliver were bickering as usual. They had no idea how much their world had just changed. For now, Ben would let them stay in their bubble a little longer, even if it felt like a lie. He'd keep this secret until he could figure out what to do next.

"Everything okay?" Emily asked, smiling as she handed him a bag.

Ben nodded, forcing a smile. "Yeah, just a quick moment. Ready to explore Tokyo?"

"Always," she grinned. Ethan shot him a glance, but said nothing, clearly still in his sulking mood about the trip.

Ben kept his expression neutral, but inside, the weight of Lucas's message continued to press down, like an unbearable shadow that would soon come to light.

The hotel they checked into was large and luxurious, a true reflection of Tokyo's modern appeal in 1971. After the long flight, the group was ready to unwind. Their rooms were spacious, with sweeping views of the city, and each came with a small welcome basket of traditional Japanese sweets. Emily and Ben shared a room, a subtle acknowledgment of their engagement, while Sebastian had a room to himself. Ethan, Oliver, and Taylor shared a room, a setup that instantly made Ethan grumble.

As soon as they settled in, Emily suggested they all try the onsen, a traditional Japanese hot spring. The idea was met with enthusiasm, especially by Ben, who saw it as the perfect way to relax after the travel. They all agreed, with Ben subtly keeping his recent revelation about the 24th century's nuclear war locked away, pushing it down as much as he could.

The onsen had separate bathing areas for men and women, and so the group divided accordingly. Ethan, Oliver, Ben, and Sebastian walked to the men's side, their conversation light and easy as they anticipated the relaxation of the hot spring.

Once inside the changing room, they began undressing. Sebastian, as someone who had visited Japan before, was already casually stripping down, unbothered by the fact that onsen culture required full nudity. Ben followed suit, folding his clothes neatly and placing them in the provided basket.

But Oliver hesitated. His fingers lingered on his waistband as he noticed the others casually standing there, already naked. His discomfort was evident, his brows furrowed as he nervously glanced around the room.

Ethan, already unclothed and standing by the edge of the hot spring, rolled his eyes at Oliver. "Really? Just us men here, Oliver. Why're you making a fuss?" His voice had that teasing, older-brother tone, although they were hardly brothers by blood. But after one and a half years of living this life, they played the part well enough.

Sebastian smiled and tried to ease the tension. "It's normal to enjoy the hot springs nude in Japan, Oliver. It's a cultural thing. Trust me, no one cares."

Oliver bit his lip, still uncertain. "I just... I'm not comfortable with... you know, everyone seeing everything."

Ben, leaning against a wall, watched the interaction with a mix of amusement and impatience. "Come on, Oliver. We don't have all day." His voice was firm, a gentle reminder of authority, though softened by his knowing glance.

"Can I at least wear my underwear?" Oliver asked, his voice quiet but determined, as if searching for a compromise.

Ben sighed but shook his head. "I think that's a no-no here, Oliver. It's a bathing facility. Trust me, no one's going to judge you."

Ethan, never missing an opportunity to rib Oliver, smirked. "Afraid of people seeing your little worm? We all have one, you know."

Oliver shot him a sharp look, his cheeks flushed with embarrassment. He was about to protest further when the glances from the others made him realize he was fighting a losing battle. Slowly, with great reluctance, he stepped out of his underwear and folded them alongside the others' clothes.

As they stepped into the steaming onsen, the warmth of the water hit them immediately, soothing their travel-weary muscles. The spring was nestled in a serene stone setting, with the faint scent of sulfur and minerals filling the air. A quietness took over, the soft bubbling of the water the only sound.

"This is heaven," Sebastian sighed, sinking deeper into the water.

Ben closed his eyes, feeling the weight of his thoughts momentarily lifted by the calming atmosphere. He glanced at Ethan and Oliver, both adjusting to the heat, and smiled. It was a brief respite from the complications of their tangled lives.

Ethan, letting the heat soak into his bones, glanced at Oliver, who was sitting stiffly, still uncomfortable despite the relaxation. "You're not going to enjoy it if you keep sitting like a board."

Oliver huffed but leaned back slightly, letting the water's warmth finally begin to work its magic. "I'm trying..." he muttered, though his discomfort still lingered under the surface.

Ben chuckled. "You'll get used to it. Trust me."

The tension in Oliver's body slowly began to unwind, though he still kept glancing around nervously. He didn't quite trust the casual ease everyone else seemed to have, but the warmth of the onsen was starting to win him over.

For now, they allowed themselves this moment of calm, unaware of the storm brewing beneath the surface of Ben's thoughts.

Chapter 38: Our Family's Trip to Japan II

As Ben sat in the steaming waters of the onsen, the heat relaxing his muscles, his mind began to drift. His thoughts returned to the day they left the 24th century—the day that had changed everything. He could still see it clearly, as if it had happened just yesterday. Ethan and Oliver, so eager and full of confidence, had taken the Rezulix pills without hesitation. They had climbed into the Rezulix sleeping pods, their adult forms slowly beginning to reverse as the drug worked its wonders. Ben had stood by the control panel, watching the process with a mix of anticipation and excitement, not knowing that everything was about to spiral out of control.

He remembered entering the coordinates and dates into the time machine. He had been so careful, or so he thought. But somewhere, somehow, a mistake had been made. He couldn't pinpoint the exact moment, but instead of their planned destination, they had ended up in 1970—a full 400 years off course.

For a long time, Ben had blamed himself. He had replayed the scene over and over in his mind, trying to figure out what went wrong. How could he have made such a critical error? But now, sitting here in 1971, with the soothing onsen waters lapping at his skin, Ben wasn't so sure it was a mistake at all.

The revelation from Lucas, the AI in the time machine, had changed everything. A full-scale nuclear war between the North American Union and the Great Asia Confederation had erupted in the

24th century—an event that could have wiped out the world as they knew it. The future they had come from might be gone, reduced to radioactive ash, while here, in the 1970s, they were safe.

Ben stared into the distance, watching the steam rise from the hot spring. His brow furrowed as the thought settled in. Was this all a blessing in disguise?

Here, they had a second chance. They might be stuck in the 1970s, but they were alive. Sure, Ethan and Oliver were trapped in the bodies of young boys, frustrated and sulking most days, but they were safe from the devastation that had gripped the future. They might not know it, but they were lucky to be here. Ben, on the other hand, had adjusted surprisingly well to life in this era. His knowledge of advanced technology had helped him secure a comfortable job, and his engagement to Emily was something he hadn't expected but had grown to embrace.

"Maybe I should keep the truth to myself," Ben thought, leaning back deeper into the hot water. *"Ethan and Oliver... they can grow up again here. In just 10 years, they'll be adults again. They can live full lives here, maybe even better ones than what awaited them in the 24th century. Why burden them with the knowledge that their time might be gone? Let them keep hoping. Let them think we can still return."*

The weight of that secret pressed on him, but Ben felt certain it was the right decision. He could handle the truth—he had always been good at compartmentalizing. But Ethan? If that boy knew what had become of their home, he'd spiral. Ben had seen enough tantrums and sulking from Ethan; the last thing they needed was him melting down over something they couldn't change. And Oliver... Oliver had been plagued by those nightmares of nuclear war. Telling him now would only confirm his worst fears.

Ben let out a long breath, watching the steam swirl around him. *"We'll be fine here,"* he told himself, trying to believe it. *"We've got a good setup. Emily, the job, the house. The boys will settle eventually. They'll grow up again, and when they do... maybe they'll thank me for not telling them."*

But even as he thought it, a flicker of doubt wormed its way into his mind. Would they? Would Ethan and Oliver ever forgive him for hiding such a monumental truth? For letting them believe they still had a future to return to when, in reality, their world might already be gone?

Ben shook his head, pushing the thoughts away. *"No. This was the right choice. "*

As he sat in the hot spring, the heat soothing the knots in his shoulders, Ben closed his eyes, silently resolving to carry this burden alone—for as long as he could.

After a relaxing soak in the onsen, the group reconvened at the hotel's sushi restaurant for dinner. The ambiance was lively yet serene, the soft murmur of conversation blending with the quiet clink of chopsticks on porcelain plates. The aroma of fresh fish, soy sauce, and wasabi filled the air as trays of beautifully prepared sushi were placed in front of them.

Ben, sitting next to Emily, raised a glass of sake with a smile. "To family," he said, his voice confident but his mind still spinning with the secret he now carried. Emily clinked her glass against his, her eyes bright with happiness.

"To family," she echoed, casting a glance down the table at Ethan and Oliver, who were sipping their cokes with little enthusiasm. Taylor, always bubbly, was making an effort to keep the mood light. She nudged Ethan playfully with her elbow.

"How's that coke, little cousin?" she teased with a grin. Ethan, ever the stubborn one, gave her a sideways look but didn't respond. His mind was still caught up in the irritation he had poured out to Oliver earlier.

Oliver was more polite. "The food's amazing. And thank you, Emily, for organizing everything," he said, offering her a warm smile. Emily beamed at the compliment, though she could still sense the undercurrent of nervousness.

Sebastian, sitting across from Ben, looked over at him. "This place is incredible. I've never had sushi like this," he said, popping a piece of tuna sashimi into his mouth. His tone was light, but Ben could tell that Sebastian was watching him closely, perhaps sensing that something was off.

Ben took another sip of his sake, leaning back slightly in his chair. "Japan's got a lot to offer," he said with a distant smile. His mind drifted briefly to the mysterious man he had hoped to find on this trip, the one who had seemed to know far more about their time than anyone in 1970s should.

After the meal, with the sun setting behind the city skyline, the group decided to visit one of Tokyo's renowned museums. They hailed a taxi outside the hotel, the warm evening air carrying the scent of street food and the distant hum of city life. Ethan and Oliver crammed into the back seat with Taylor, who was bubbling with excitement about the museum.

"This place has a whole section dedicated to the Edo period," Taylor said, flipping through a brochure. "Samurai swords, traditional armor, and even artifacts from ancient Japan!"

Ethan stared out the window, barely paying attention. "Great. More history," he thought, though deep down, the thought of ancient samurai did pique his curiosity a little. He just wouldn't admit it in front of everyone.

Ben and Emily sat up front, with Ben lost in thought as the city lights blurred past. His gaze lingered on the neon signs and busy streets, but his mind was somewhere else entirely. The news from Lucas still weighed heavily on him, and the closer they got to the museum, the more he found himself wondering about their place in this world.

"Maybe staying here is the only option after all," he mused. But for now, he kept that thought to himself, glancing over at Emily, who was looking out the window with quiet excitement.

As the taxi pulled up to the museum, the family stepped out into the evening air, ready to explore a different side of Japan. For Ben, it was another opportunity to keep the charade going, to maintain the illusion of normalcy. But in the back of his mind, the weight of the truth hung like a shadow, lurking just beneath the surface.

The next day in Japan, after another soothing dip in the onsen, the group made their way to one of Tokyo's most famous Buddhist temples. The temple grounds were serene, with tall trees swaying gently in the breeze and the distant chime of bells echoing through the courtyard. Visitors moved in quiet reverence, lighting incense and bowing in front of golden statues, while monks in saffron robes moved silently through the halls.

Ben trailed behind the group, his thoughts heavy. As they passed through the grand temple gates, he found himself drawn to the teachings of the Buddha, something he had studied briefly back in the 24th century. He could almost hear the ancient wisdom in the air: *"All things are impermanent."*

"Nothing is permanent," Ben repeated in his mind. The words held a new weight now. As he gazed at the peaceful faces of the statues around him, the contrast between this calm, ancient world and the cataclysmic destruction that awaited in the future tore at him. The images of a nuclear war—the billions of lives lost, the burning cities,

and the wastelands that Lucas had described—flashed through his mind.

"Compassion," Ben muttered under his breath, recalling another key teaching of the Buddha. Yet, how could compassion be reconciled with the knowledge of what was coming? He thought of his parents, his friends, everyone he knew in the 24th century. Were they already gone? Had they perished in the flames of the war?

He clenched his fists as he walked, grappling with the weight of the future's devastation and the uncertainty of their situation in the 1970s. *"I have to try to stop it,"* he thought. *"I can't just sit here and enjoy life while billions of people are dying in the future."*

But how? They were stuck in 1971, over four centuries before the war even started. How could he, Ethan, and Oliver—three people from the future, now posing as a family in this strange, distant past—possibly stop a war that had been brewing for decades? The tension between the North American Union and the Great Asia Confederation had been simmering since the end of the 23rd century. It was not a sudden war but a slow build-up of hostilities, alliances, and mistrust.

The politics of that time were intricate, far beyond what Ben could affect from the 1970s. Or were they?

"We still have the time machine," he thought. *"Maybe there's a way to change the course of history, to prevent the war from ever happening. Maybe we can influence events before the tensions rise."*

As the group wandered further into the temple, Ben fell into a contemplative silence. He watched as Ethan and Oliver, their young forms blending into the crowd of tourists, wandered ahead with Taylor. They seemed so out of place, these brilliant minds trapped in young bodies, trying to navigate a world that wasn't theirs. He wondered how they would react if they knew the full truth about the future—about the war, and the possibility that their lives in the 24th century were already lost.

For now, Ben kept that burden to himself. But the question gnawed at him: *"Is there a way to fix this? Can we stop the war from here, from the past?"*

He looked up at the towering figure of the Buddha, serene and unmoved by time, and felt a strange sense of both hope and despair. If he could find a way—somehow—maybe the suffering of billions could be avoided.

Emily's voice broke his reverie. "Ben? Are you coming?" She was waiting with the rest of the group, a gentle smile on her face. The boys and Taylor were already moving on to the next part of the temple tour.

Ben gave a nod and joined them, but his mind was still spinning with the heavy realization that their time in the 1970s might hold more significance than any of them had imagined. For now, the charade of their family life had to continue, but deep down, Ben knew he couldn't stay idle forever. He had to find a way to stop the war before it was too late. The only question was—how?

Chapter 39: Our Family's Trip to Japan III

The next day, Ben decided it was only right to visit Mr. Sato, the respected businessman whose company had sold the oil well deal to Ben's company during his last trip to Japan. It was a courtesy visit, but Ben also had a nagging feeling there was something more to uncover. His thoughts had been weighed down by Lucas' message about the nuclear war, but business had to continue, at least for appearances.

As the group gathered in the hotel lobby, Ben turned to Sebastian. "We should pay Mr. Sato a visit while we're here. A courtesy call, nothing formal, but it's the right thing to do."

Sebastian nodded, feeling a bit more comfortable around Ben now than he had been during their previous trip to Japan. "Of course, sounds like a good idea."

Meanwhile, Ethan, Oliver, Emily, and Taylor had planned to spend the day at a large Tokyo mall, buying souvenirs and enjoying some leisure time. Taylor had insisted on seeing some traditional Japanese items, and the boys, though sulking about the "family" trip, were eager to explore more of Japan.

At the café in downtown Tokyo, Ben and Sebastian arrived to find Mr. Sato already seated at a corner table. The café was a blend of modern and traditional, with minimalist design and soft lighting. A quiet hum of conversation filled the air as patrons sipped their drinks.

Mr. Sato stood and greeted them with a warm smile. "Ben-san, Sebastian-san, it's good to see you again. How is your stay in Tokyo?"

Ben smiled politely and shook his hand. "It's been great so far. A little leisure time with the family. Thought we'd stop by and say hello while we're in town."

They ordered some tea and settled into their seats, the conversation light at first. Mr. Sato asked how things were going at the oil company and about any new business ventures on the horizon. Ben answered smoothly, weaving in casual talk about their ongoing projects and some praise for Mr. Sato's efficient handling of the deal.

But after a few minutes, the conversation took a darker turn.

Mr. Sato leaned in slightly, lowering his voice as if the subject carried weight. "Ben-san, there's something I should tell you. Do you remember the Australian team that was bidding for the same oil deal?"

Ben nodded. "Of course, the other contender for the contract."

Mr. Sato's expression grew serious. "Well, a week after you and Sebastian returned to the States, the police concluded their investigation. It wasn't in the news immediately, but... the Australian team—three of their senior executives—were killed. Shot in their hotel room."

Ben froze, the words sinking in. "Killed?" His voice was barely above a whisper.

Sebastian looked stunned, his teacup hovering mid-air. "What??"

Mr. Sato nodded, his face reflecting a deep sadness. "Yes. They were good men. The police said it was a professional job, but no one has been arrested yet. They are still investigating."

Ben's mind raced. This wasn't just a business deal anymore; there was something darker lurking beneath the surface. "Who would do this? I mean... what reason would someone have to kill them?"

Mr. Sato sighed. "It's unclear. The oil deal was significant, but this kind of violence... it's unprecedented, even in cutthroat business. The police have their theories—perhaps an underground organization, or maybe it was something tied to a personal vendetta. But nothing conclusive has come out."

Ben's thoughts spun in a million directions. He had known the oil industry could be ruthless, but this—murder—was something entirely different. He couldn't help but wonder if their business trip had something to do with it, or if there was a connection to something larger, something beyond business.

Sato continued, "I thought you should know, Ben-san, since you were also part of that bidding process. The police haven't come to me with more details, but I keep an eye on the situation."

Ben looked over at Sebastian, who still seemed in shock. The young man clearly hadn't expected this family trip to take such a turn.

"Thank you for telling me, Mr. Sato," Ben said carefully. "If there's anything we can do... please let me know."

Mr. Sato gave a slow nod, though his face suggested there wasn't much anyone could do at this point. "I will keep you informed. It's a difficult situation, but I hope the police can resolve it soon."

The conversation moved on to more neutral topics, but the atmosphere had changed. Ben couldn't shake the feeling that there was far more to this than met the eye. Murdering three men over a business deal felt extreme, and now that he had learned about the full-scale nuclear war in the 24th century, he couldn't help but wonder if some unseen force was manipulating events across time.

As they left the café, Ben's mind was racing. What were they truly up against? Could this be part of something larger, something tied to their predicament and the war in their own time? He needed to tread carefully—there were forces at play he still didn't fully understand.

For now, though, he had to stay focused on the present. They had a trip to finish, and for the time being, that meant keeping up appearances. But Ben knew that he couldn't let this information go. He would dig deeper, and soon enough, the truth would emerge—whether he was ready for it or not.

At the mall, Emily was trying her best to bond with Ethan and Oliver, eager to close the emotional gap that still existed between them. She had taken them to a store that specialized in boys' clothing— bright, trendy clothes that seemed to be made just for the preteen crowd. Emily wandered through the racks, eyeing the options, trying to figure out what might appeal to the boys.

She held up a couple of shirts with playful patterns, looking over at them with a warm smile. "Ethan, Oliver, these clothes are really nice. Do you want to try some of them on?" She spoke in her usual gentle tone, hoping to engage them, but also unsure how much she could push.

Ethan, standing stiffly with his arms crossed, shook his head almost immediately. "Thank you, but I don't want them." His voice was polite, but it had a hard edge, the dislike just beneath the surface.

Oliver, trying to navigate the tension in the air, hesitated before responding. He still felt caught between the expectations placed on them and his own internal conflict. "Thanks, Emily," he said quietly. "Dad bought us enough clothes already."

Taylor, picking up on the boys' resistance, rolled her eyes dramatically. "Forget these ungrateful boys, Aunt Emily." She linked arms with Emily and pointed toward a women's clothing shop. "Come on, we can go look at something more fun. I want something unique— something that you can only find in Japan!"

Emily chuckled softly, though she cast a concerned glance back at Ethan and Oliver. "Alright, sweetheart," she said to Taylor, though it was clear she still wished the boys would warm up to her efforts.

Oliver, sensing Emily's slight disappointment and not wanting to be entirely dismissive, glanced around the store. He didn't want to be the difficult one, and he appreciated that Emily was trying. After a moment, he spotted something that might bridge the gap—a simple but stylish baseball cap. "Hmm... actually, I think I want this," he said, lifting the cap and showing it to Emily with a tentative smile.

Emily's face brightened, grateful that Oliver was at least making an effort. "That's a great choice, Oliver. I'll get it for you," she said, clearly happy to have connected with him, even if only in a small way.

Ethan, watching the interaction from the side, muttered under his breath, just loud enough for Oliver and possibly Emily to hear. "Doormat" His voice carried a mixture of annoyance and bitterness. He couldn't understand why Oliver seemed so eager to appease Emily, even if it was just over a baseball cap. Ethan didn't like the idea of growing closer to someone who was now supposed to be their 'mom.'

Oliver stiffened slightly at the comment but chose not to respond. He knew Ethan's attitude came from their shared frustration and their desire to go back to their own time, but he also didn't want to keep fighting against every small gesture of kindness. It wasn't Emily's fault they were stuck in the 1970s, after all.

Taylor, picking up on the tension but misreading the deeper issues, just grinned and shook her head. "Come on, Ethan. Lighten up! It's a free cap. How can you be mad about that?"

Ethan gave her a half-hearted shrug but remained quiet, his eyes darting toward the exit as if he wanted nothing more than to leave the store and get this shopping trip over with. He felt like the walls were closing in, this entire 'family trip' just another reminder of how trapped he was in this false life they'd been forced to live.

Emily, aware that Ethan was still distant but hoping that time would soften his stance, smiled at both boys. "I'll hold on to the cap for you, Oliver. Let's go find something for Taylor now, okay?"

As they wandered another store, Taylor sifted through the racks of clothing, her face lighting up when she found something she liked. Emily was in a fitting room trying on a dress, leaving the kids to themselves for a moment. The atmosphere between them had started to ease, though Taylor still couldn't resist poking fun at Ethan.

Taylor glanced sideways at Ethan and smirked. "You know, if you don't let Aunt Emily buy you anything this trip, I'm totally going to tell your dad you misbehaved," she said teasingly, her tone playful but carrying a hint of mischief.

Ethan scowled, his eyes narrowing as he looked at her. "What? I've been good... since when is not wanting to buy stuff misbehaving, Taylor?" His voice had a slightly defensive edge, aware that Taylor was just messing with him but not wanting to give her any ammunition.

Taylor grinned, enjoying the moment. "I don't know... I'll just tell Ben you were 'being disrespectful.' You know how he gets about respect—especially toward Aunt Emily." She added air quotes around the word 'disrespectful' and chuckled, knowing exactly what buttons to push.

Ethan's stomach dropped slightly. Sure, he knew Taylor was teasing, but Ben had made it very clear earlier about showing Emily respect. The last thing he needed was for Taylor to stir up trouble, especially after that onsen episode where Ben reminded him to cut the sulking. The discipline from a while ago was still fresh in his memory, and he had no intention of risking anything close to a repeat performance.

Looking around, Ethan spotted the skateboard section of the store. He'd always loved skateboarding back in the 24th century and had been eyeing them since they arrived in Japan. He didn't have the money for one, but now it seemed like the perfect moment to turn the situation around.

He wandered over to where the skateboards were displayed and hesitated for a moment before walking back to the fitting rooms. When Emily stepped out, adjusting the dress she was trying on, Ethan approached her, trying to keep his tone casual but polite.

"Emily... it would be great if you could buy me a skateboard," Ethan said, doing his best to sound sincere. He wasn't just saying it to get out of trouble; he really did want the skateboard. But he also knew Emily would be thrilled at the idea of buying something for him.

Emily's face lit up, visibly happy that Ethan was finally asking for something. "Of course, Ethan! I'd love to get you one," she said, her voice warm. The tension between them seemed to melt, and for the first time that day, Emily felt like she was making progress with him.

Ethan picked out an expensive skateboard, his eyes gleaming with excitement as he selected one with sleek designs and high-end wheels. It was a high-quality board, priced around 80 dollars. As he rolled it back to the group, Taylor's eyes widened.

"Ahhh, not fair!" Taylor protested, looking from the baseball cap in Oliver's hand to the fancy skateboard Ethan was holding. "Oliver and I got small things, and Ethan gets this super-expensive skateboard?" She pouted playfully, though she wasn't truly upset— just looking for an excuse to tease Ethan more.

Oliver, meanwhile, had been admiring his reflection in the mirror, adjusting his new baseball cap. He shot Taylor a look, trying to ease the situation. "It's fine, Taylor," Oliver said with a small grin. "I like my cap. Besides, we all got what we wanted."

Taylor gave him a mock sigh, then crossed her arms as she glanced over at Ethan. "Still, Ethan lucked out big time," she said with a teasing glint in her eye. "I'll make sure to remind him when he's flying down the street on that thing."

Ethan, feeling a bit smug now, looked at Taylor with a raised eyebrow. "Well, maybe you should've asked for something bigger too." He glanced at the skateboard in his hand, feeling the weight of it with satisfaction.

Emily watched them with a soft smile, "Don't worry, Taylor," Emily said, placing a reassuring hand on her niece's shoulder. "I'm sure we'll find something special for you too before the trip's over."

Taylor smiled back, her playful mood returning. "Alright, alright... maybe I'll just get two souvenirs to make up for it!" she said with a wink, and the group laughed lightly as they moved to the checkout.

As they paid for their items and left the store, Ethan caught a sidelong glance from Oliver. His brother-in-arms in this strange time-travel predicament didn't say anything, but there was a knowing look between them. Oliver understood Ethan's strategy, even if he didn't fully agree with the motives behind it.

Peace seemed to settle over the group as they made their way out of the mall, each of them carrying a little piece of Japan with them—whether it was a cap, a skateboard, or just the sense of having survived another day of this unusual 'family' vacation.

The final day of the family trip to Japan arrived, and the group spent the morning wandering through the bustling streets of Tokyo, soaking up the last bits of the city's energy. They had explored temples, visited museums, shopped for souvenirs, and shared more laughs than they had in a long time. Yet for Ben, despite the laughter and outward enjoyment, his mind had been swirling with too many heavy thoughts.

The others, however, were still riding the high of the trip. Ethan had been inseparable from his new skateboard, itching to test it out back in the U.S., while Oliver admired his baseball cap as though it were a small treasure. Taylor had managed to convince Emily to buy her one more unique piece of clothing. For Emily, the trip had been a bonding experience; she felt closer to Ben and the boys, even though there were still moments when Ethan's resistance showed.

But as the family gathered their belongings and headed to the airport, Ben found himself stuck in his own head. The message from Lucas, the visions of war in the 24th century, and the eerie sense of calm in 1971 all weighed on him. He stared out of the taxi window, watching the buildings and people of Tokyo blur by, thinking about the world they were about to return to.

As they sat in the airport, waiting for their flight back to the United States, the group had settled into a comfortable silence. Ethan and Oliver played a quiet game of cards, Taylor leafed through the stack of photos she had taken with her camera, and Emily busied herself with a book. Ben, however, could hardly focus on anything.

"Everything alright?" Emily asked, nudging Ben lightly as she noticed his faraway expression.

Ben blinked, snapped out of his thoughts. He forced a smile. "Yeah, just...thinking about work." It wasn't entirely a lie, but it wasn't the full truth either.

Emily smiled softly, leaning her head on his shoulder. "Well, it's been a great trip. Hopefully, it helped you relax a bit."

Ben nodded, though relaxation was the last thing he felt. "Yeah, it was a good trip," he said, his voice quieter than usual.

As their boarding was announced, they gathered their things and made their way to the gate. The flight back was long, and the others eventually drifted off to sleep. But Ben couldn't shake the unease that had settled in his chest. Sitting there in the dim cabin of the plane, Ben wondered if they were meant to be trapped here. Was this their fate?

He looked over at Ethan and Oliver, both fast asleep, their small frames curled up under airplane blankets. They were still his colleagues—scientists from a time so far ahead of this world—but at this moment, they were just two boys, innocently unaware of the grim possibilities hanging over them.

"Maybe it's better they don't know," Ben muttered to himself, turning to look out the window into the endless darkness of the night sky. He couldn't burden them with this. For now, they needed to hold on to the illusion that there was a future to return to.

He sighed deeply, watching the clouds pass below. They were heading back to the United States, back to the life they'd crafted for themselves in the 1970s. It was supposed to be temporary, but the longer they stayed, the harder it became to believe they'd ever leave.

The family trip had been great—everyone had enjoyed it, even him in brief moments—but it also reminded Ben of how fragile their situation was. Time kept moving forward, both here and in the future they left behind. He knew that soon enough, he would have to make a decision. Would they stay in the past, live out their lives in this strange era? Or would they risk everything to return to a future that might already be gone?

The plane began its descent, and as the lights of the U.S. coastline came into view, Ben took a deep breath. For now, they'd return to their house, to the life they'd built in the 1970s. But the weight of the future was pressing down on him, and he knew it wouldn't be long before that pressure demanded action.

Chapter 40: Secrets Upon Secrets

A few days after returning from Japan, Ben stood alone in the storage room of their house. The space was cluttered with boxes, tools, and an assortment of random items, giving it the unmistakable vibe of a typical 1970s storage area. Yet, nestled amidst the chaos was the time machine, its sleek, tent-like structure a striking contrast to the surrounding mess.

Ben walked over to Lucas, his footsteps slow and deliberate. The machine's faint hum filled the otherwise quiet room, and Ben's gaze settled on its metallic surface. The glow of its control panel illuminated Ben's face as he reached out to activate the interface. "Lucas," Ben said, his voice low but clear. "About the war in the 24th century... although it was confirmed by your data and through Oliver's nightmares, we still don't really know if it's real, do we? Not 100%. The data you have could have been altered somehow, or maybe something changed again."

Lucas's voice, calm and mechanical yet somehow tinged with an uncanny sense of humanity, responded, "Possibly. We don't know for certain because we are not in the 24th century to confirm those facts firsthand. However, the likelihood of the war being true remains very high. The tensions between the North American Union and the Great Asia Confederation were escalating long before we left."

Ben frowned, his mind racing with the implications. He had always known that a global conflict was possible, but hearing Lucas confirm it—or at least the probability of it—made everything feel more tangible. "But," Ben began, "we're relying on assumptions, on old data. We're stuck here in the 1970s, and there's a chance something else could've happened—maybe a solution was found. Maybe it was averted, or maybe... something even worse happened."

Lucas was silent for a brief moment before responding, "The possibility exists, but as of now, the data I have points to the outcome I shared with you. We can't be certain until we return or find a way to gather more information from the 24th century."

Ben let out a slow breath. "Right. Until then, though, this information stays between you and me. I don't want Ethan or Oliver knowing about this. They've got enough to deal with as it is, and I don't want to send Ethan into a meltdown." His voice dropped an octave as he spoke, making his intentions clear. "I need them focused."

Lucas responded promptly, "Understood. I will not disclose this information to Ethan or Oliver."

Ben nodded, satisfied, but there was still another layer of secrecy he needed to address. "And Emily," he continued, "she's my fiancée now, but she can't know about you or what we are. Not yet. She still thinks we're just a normal family, a normal life. You're going to stay in stealth mode, ready to activate if necessary, but I'll do my best to ensure that only I—and the boys—come into this room."

Lucas's soft hum filled the pause. "Acknowledged, Ben. I will remain in stealth mode and will not reveal my presence to Emily or anyone else."

Ben turned and leaned against one of the nearby shelves, feeling the weight of all the secrets he was carrying. From Emily to the boys, from the 1970s to the 24th century, his life was a balancing act of lies and half-truths. But for now, he had no choice. He had to protect them—protect the fragile life they had built in this past they never meant to stay in.

"Thanks, Lucas," Ben muttered, rubbing his forehead. "Sometimes I wonder if we'll ever figure all of this out. But at least we're still in the game. For now."

Lucas's response was calm, almost reassuring in its machine-like simplicity. "As long as we are operational, there is always a chance to find a solution."

Ben chuckled softly, the irony of finding comfort in an AI not lost on him. "Yeah...let's hope so." He straightened up and gave Lucas a final glance before heading toward the door. As he reached for the knob, he hesitated, looking back at the time machine that had brought them here and might be their only hope of getting back.

"One step at a time," Ben whispered to himself before leaving the room. The door clicked shut behind him, sealing Lucas—and all its secrets—safely away, for now.

Another day passed as Ben, Emily, Ethan, and Oliver found themselves strolling down the aisles of the local supermarket. The list of items to pick up had grown lengthy, mainly due to Ethan and Oliver's upcoming start of middle school next week as 6th graders. Ben pushed the cart as Emily walked beside him, their hands intertwined, a small but comforting gesture of their growing bond. Ethan and Oliver led the way, occasionally glancing back at the two adults who were clearly smitten with each other.

The boys had their shopping list ready. They grabbed spiral notebooks in various colors, mechanical pencils, a pack of highlighters, some folders with neat designs, and new lunchboxes. Ethan tossed a sturdy binder into the cart while Oliver grabbed a new backpack, this one covered in a space-themed pattern that caught his eye.

Oliver paused near the back-to-school section and turned to face Ben and Emily. "Dad," he began, "I want a bicycle. Ethan's got his skateboard for school, and I don't want to walk every day."

Emily's face lit up with a warm smile. "Yes, sweetheart," she responded enthusiastically. "I'll buy you one. Let's go pick it out after we finish here."

Oliver, caught in the moment, beamed at her, then slipped up in his excitement. "Thanks, mom... ah, no, I mean Emily." The word "mom" had tumbled out so naturally that he hadn't even realized it until the last second. His face flushed slightly in embarrassment.

Ethan gave Oliver a side-eye from across the cart, clearly unimpressed. "Gosh," Ethan muttered under his breath, just loud enough for Oliver to hear, "I should punch you in the face now." His tone was more teasing than hostile, but Oliver shot him a look of annoyance all the same.

Ben, choosing to ignore the boys' back-and-forth, turned to Emily and handed her a small key. "You're family now, Emily," he said softly, the key resting in her hand. "Please come to the house whenever you want."

Emily looked at the key with a soft smile before meeting Ben's gaze. "Thanks, honey," she replied, her voice warm. She then pulled out her own set of keys from her purse and handed one to Ben. "Here's a key to my place, too. I want you to have it."

Ben accepted the key with a nod of gratitude but then lowered his voice, his expression becoming more serious. "The boys still need time to adjust," he said, glancing over at Ethan and Oliver as they debated over which brand of mechanical pencils to buy. "We shouldn't rush the wedding yet."

Emily nodded in understanding, her gaze following his to the boys. "Of course, babe," she agreed. "They'll come around in their own time."

Ben paused, then added in an even quieter tone, "There's one more thing... the storage room at the house. Please don't go inside."

Emily looked at him, curiosity piqued, but she didn't interrupt. "We store the boys' mom's belongings in there," Ben explained. "It's also a place where the boys go to play and unwind. I think it's best if you don't go in for now—it's kind of a sensitive spot for them."

Emily nodded slowly, respecting his request. "I understand, Ben. I won't go near it."

"Thank you," Ben said, relieved. He knew that keeping Emily away from the time machine—and all the secrets that came with it—was essential, but he didn't want to raise her suspicions. He gave her hand a gentle squeeze, and the two shared a brief moment of understanding before Ethan and Oliver approached the cart with their final round of supplies.

Oliver held up a pack of gel pens, clearly excited. "Can I get these too?" he asked.

Emily smiled warmly, still holding onto the happiness from their earlier conversation. "Of course, sweetheart," she said, dropping the pens into the cart. She then glanced at Ethan. "How about you, Ethan? Do you want anything special for school?"

Ethan, still thinking about the skateboard he had already scored, shook his head. "Nah, I'm good. I've got everything I need."

With the boys set for school, they made their way to the bicycle section for Oliver. After looking through several options, he picked out a sleek black and red bike with a cool, aerodynamic design.

Ben helped him load it into the cart, and they were finally ready to check out.

As they approached the register, Taylor called from across the store, holding a pile of clothes she had picked for herself. "Aunt Emily, look what I found!" she shouted excitedly.

Emily smiled, waving back. "Let's get those too," she said as they headed toward Taylor, finishing up their family shopping trip with smiles and laughter.

Chapter 41: Fragments of Hope

Benjamin had been reaping the rewards of his hard work at the energy company. His impressive management skills and success with the oil well deal had not gone unnoticed. As a result, he received a generous financial reward from the company. The project was on track, and Ben's reputation as a key player in the company was growing steadily. His colleagues admired his work ethic and problem-solving abilities, and the higher-ups saw him as someone with great potential for future leadership.

Life at home had settled into a comfortable rhythm. Ethan and Oliver had slipped into their roles as middle schoolers with surprising ease, despite their young adult minds tucked into 11-year-old bodies. Ethan loved zooming through the neighborhood streets on his skateboard, the wind in his face and the thrill of speed matching his boundless energy. Beside him, Oliver pedaled along on his new bicycle, more composed but just as eager to get to school every morning.

Middle school brought its own set of challenges, but the boys handled them with their usual sharp minds and quick thinking. They were smart—smarter than most of their classmates, of course—but they had learned to keep their brilliance just below the radar. Sometimes, amid the chatter of classmates or the hum of routine homework, they found themselves momentarily forgetting they weren't really kids. And on rare evenings, when they sprawled on the living room floor finishing a math worksheet or reading history textbooks, it almost felt natural to call Benjamin "Dad," even though he was still their colleague at heart.

A few weeks into the school year, Ethan and Oliver made a new friend: Hak-Kun, a bright and cheerful Korean-American boy with oversized round glasses and a love for books. Hak-Kun was a bookworm and a bit of a nerd, but in the best way. He loved video games and comics, passions he shared with Ethan and Oliver. The three boys became fast friends, bonding over their shared interests and a mutual curiosity about the world.

Hak-Kun lived just a few blocks away, making after-school meetups easy and frequent. Whether they were skateboarding, riding bikes around the neighborhood, or geeking out over the latest comic book, their time with Hak-Kun felt refreshingly normal. With him, the weight of being stuck out of time lifted a little. For a while, they could laugh, play, and almost forget about their time machine or the future they still hoped to return to someday.

At the dining table, the warm glow of the hanging light illuminated the faces of Ben, Ethan, and Oliver as they sat together for dinner. Ben, feeling proud of his recent achievement at work, decided it was time to share the good news with the boys.

"Well, I've got something to tell you both," Ben said, leaning back in his chair with a small, satisfied grin. "I received a financial reward at work for the oil well deal."

Ethan perked up, immediately curious. "Oh? How much did you get?"

"A lot," Ben replied, his voice calm but with a hint of excitement underneath. "30,000 USD bonus."

Oliver's eyes widened. "Wow, Ben! That's amazing! We're rich now!"

Ethan leaned forward, his eyes gleaming with enthusiasm. "Yeah, we're about to have enough money for the gold, right?"

Ben nodded slowly, though his expression became more serious. "Yeah... we have around 100,000 USD saved up now, but we're still about 120,000 short to get the gold back for the time machine."

The mention of the time machine brought a brief moment of silence, a reminder of the enormity of their situation. But Ethan quickly snapped back to the present and, with a cheeky grin, turned his attention to something more immediate.

"Speaking of money," Ethan began, trying to sound casual but clearly planning something, "I've been thinking... since we're middle schoolers now, I think we can do with some extra allowances. How about... 10 dollars a week?"

Ben raised an eyebrow, amused but not swayed. "10 dollars for both of you?"

Ethan shook his head, eyes gleaming with mischief. "No, no, I mean 10 dollars each."

Ben chuckled, shaking his head. "What would you even do with all that money, Ethan? 5 dollars each is more than enough. That's already a 2-dollar increase from what you had before."

Oliver, who had been listening with a grin, decided to take a more reasonable stance. "That'll do! Thanks, Ben."

Ethan sighed dramatically but couldn't hide his small smile. "Fine... I guess I'll take it. But you know, we could've lived like kings."

Ben laughed, leaning forward. "You'll be fine."

Emily had become a fixture in their lives, almost seamlessly integrating into the daily rhythm of Ben, Ethan, and Oliver's household. As a doctor, her days were often busy and demanding, but she made time, nearly every evening, to come by the house and take care of the three of them. It was something she found herself enjoying more than she expected—the simple act of cooking dinner, tidying up the kitchen, or folding laundry. It felt like family.

One evening, she arrived just as Ben was wrapping up some paperwork from his job. Ethan and Oliver were tucked away in their rooms—supposedly doing homework but probably squeezing in a bit of video gaming on the side. She walked in, balancing a bag of groceries in one arm and wearing her signature bright smile.

"Hey, I'm home!" she called out playfully, setting the bags on the counter.

Ben, hearing her voice, got up from his chair, smiling warmly. "You don't have to keep doing this, you know? You're already working a full-time job."

Emily waved him off. "Nonsense. I love it. Besides, you boys would probably live on cereal if I wasn't here," she teased, pulling out vegetables from the bag and heading toward the stove.

Ben chuckled. "I admit, our diet's been a bit basic. But seriously, you're spoiling us."

"Well, someone has to," she quipped back, rolling up her sleeves. She began chopping vegetables with a practiced ease. The smell of garlic and onions quickly filled the kitchen, bringing a cozy warmth to the space.

A few minutes later, Oliver wandered into the kitchen, likely lured by the smells of dinner. "Hey, Emily. What are you making tonight?" he asked.

"Spaghetti with meatballs and some salad. Thought you might like it," Emily smiled, reaching out to ruffle his hair. "You're such a good boy, Oliver. Always polite and curious."

Oliver, a bit shy but pleased, smiled. "Thanks, Emily. You're really good at cooking."

Emily leaned down slightly and planted a gentle kiss on the top of his head. "You're sweet, you know that?"

At that moment, Ethan walked into the kitchen, catching the tail end of the exchange. He rolled his eyes, though not without a hint of amusement. "Geez, Oliver, do you really need to get kissed on the head like that?"

Oliver shrugged, clearly unbothered. "She's just being nice, Ethan."

Ethan plopped himself down at the kitchen table. "Yeah, well, I guess someone's gotta be the teacher's pet," he teased with a smirk.

Ben, who had been watching the exchange from the doorway, laughed. "You two are hopeless. Always at each other's throats."

Emily, still smiling, glanced over her shoulder. "Don't worry, Ethan. You're a good boy too. Just... a little less willing to show it."

Ethan grinned, pretending to act tough. "I'm not a kid, Emily."

Emily raised an eyebrow, turning to face him as she wiped her hands on a towel. "A skateboard and a middle schooler? You're definitely still a kid in my book." She then playfully tousled his hair, much to his exaggerated annoyance.

"Okay, okay, I get it!" Ethan laughed, brushing her hand away. "I just... don't need a kiss on the head."

"Fine, fine, no kisses," she said, smiling fondly. "But I still get to make sure you're well-fed."

"Deal," Ethan agreed, nodding toward the food cooking on the stove. "Smells awesome, by the way."

Ben shook his head, a soft smile on his face as he watched the interaction unfold. Emily had stepped into the role of a mother figure with such grace. It was like she was meant to be part of their lives, her presence filling a void they didn't realize was there.

Later, as they sat around the dining table, the meal was full of chatter. Ethan recounted some stories from school, embellishing just enough to make Oliver roll his eyes. Oliver talked about his new bike and how fast he was getting on it. Ben, for the most part, listened, enjoying the normalcy of it all, while Emily smiled and chimed in from time to time.

As they finished up and the boys began clearing the table, Emily caught Ben's eye, her expression softening. "They're good kids, Ben. You've done a great job raising them."

Ben gave a small, appreciative smile. "Couldn't have done it without your help lately. You've made things feel... different. In a good way."

Emily leaned closer, brushing his arm lightly. "I love being here. You, Ethan, Oliver—it feels like home."

Ben looked at her for a moment, feeling the weight of her words. "It does feel like family, doesn't it?"

And as the evening wound down, Emily stayed a little longer, cleaning up the last of the dishes and making sure everything was just right before she headed home. She kissed both boys goodnight—though Ethan quickly dodged hers with a laugh—and gave Ben a lingering hug.

As she left, Ben couldn't help but think how much their lives had changed. Maybe, just maybe, despite everything, this was exactly where they were supposed to be.

Chapter 42: From Sunshine to Shadows

Out of the blue, Oliver's frustrations at school began to boil over. Middle school science classes felt painfully primitive compared to the advanced knowledge he carried from the 24th century. One day in his 6th-grade science class, the teacher was explaining the solar system, relying on a 1970s textbook that made Oliver cringe.

As the teacher described how the planets orbit the sun in perfect circles, Oliver couldn't stay quiet any longer.

"That's not right!" Oliver interrupted, his voice sharp. "The planets move in elliptical orbits, not perfect circles. Kepler figured that out centuries ago!"

The class fell silent, eyes turning to Oliver, who had recently become known for his frequent corrections. The teacher, caught off guard, tried to maintain composure. "Yes, Oliver, but this is just an introduction to basic concepts."

"But it's wrong!" Oliver snapped back. "How can we learn anything if we start with wrong facts?"

Ethan, sitting next to Oliver, buried his face in his hands. He didn't need this kind of attention, and his brother's new outspoken nature was starting to draw suspicion. "Oliver, stop," Ethan muttered under his breath. "You're going to make things worse."

But Oliver wasn't done. "And when are we going to get into Exoplanets? You're teaching things like it's the 19th century!"

Mr. Collins, a young teacher at just 22 years old, had only recently begun his teaching career. Facing a challenging student like Oliver was no easy task. He cleared his throat, visibly agitated.

"Oliver, that's enough. We're following the curriculum. If you have questions, please save them for after class."

Ethan could feel the tension rising in the room, and his gut told him this wasn't going to end well. As they walked out after class, he elbowed Oliver. "What's wrong with you? You can't just keep blowing up like that. Do you want people to figure out we're not normal?"

Oliver huffed, still irritated. "I can't stand having a teacher my age who fills our heads with garbage information."

At home, the tension was thick as Oliver sat on the couch, arms crossed, staring down at his feet while Ben paced the living room. Ethan, sitting nearby, was pretending to be engrossed in his skateboard magazine, but he could feel the storm brewing and kept glancing up.

Ben finally stopped pacing and turned to Oliver. "Seriously, Oliver? What's going on with you? This is the fourth time you've been sent to the principal's office in the past month. What's wrong?"

Oliver, still sulking, looked up at Ben. "It's not like I'm saying anything that discloses our identities. I just can't stand the misinformation. The things they're teaching... it's either outdated or completely wrong! How am I supposed to sit there and stay quiet when I know better?"

Ben sighed, rubbing his temples in frustration. "I get that, Oliver. I do. But you have to control yourself. You're not just any 11-year-old kid. You're from the 24th century! You can't go around correcting everything like you're some kind of know-it-all. People will start asking questions. And if they dig too deep... we're all in trouble."

Oliver's face flushed with frustration. "But I'm not disclosing anything! I'm just—"

"Yeah, but you're acting like you want to get caught!" Ben interrupted. "You can't act like this. It's like you're trying to replace Ethan as the troublemaker or something. Is that what you want?"

Ethan, who had been trying to stay out of it, perked up. "Hey, leave me out of this! I haven't caused any trouble lately. I've been good!"

Ben shot a look at Ethan. "Yeah, and that's exactly why I'm using you as an example. You've been good, and I expect the same from Oliver." He turned back to Oliver, his tone becoming stern. "One more time, Oliver, and I'm going to start dealing with you the way I dealt with Ethan. You remember how that went, right?"

Oliver's eyes widened slightly. He did remember. He had seen what Ben had done, and it wasn't something he wanted to experience firsthand. He shifted uncomfortably on the couch.

"Hey!" Ethan interjected, looking insulted. "That's not fair, Ben! Why do you always have to use me as an example? I've been good for months now!"

Ben gave Ethan a stern look but softened slightly. "I know, Ethan. And I'm proud of that. But you also know how serious I am when it comes to keeping a low profile, especially now. Oliver, I'm not asking you to stay quiet forever. But you need to pick your battles. Stop drawing attention to yourself over every little thing, or else I'm going to have to step in."

Oliver looked down, feeling the weight of Ben's words. "Okay, okay... I'll stop correcting our science teacher."

Ben nodded, his tone softer now. "Thanks. Just don't cause any more trouble, and that's all I'm asking."

The room fell into an uneasy silence, broken only by the sound of Ethan flipping the pages of his magazine a little too loudly. Oliver slouched back into the couch, his mind racing. He understood the stakes, but every day at school was becoming harder and harder to bear.

Three days later, Oliver sat on the couch in the living room, sulking, his arms crossed tightly across his chest. His cheeks were still flushed from the argument he'd had with Mr. Collins earlier in the day. The test papers felt like an injustice, graded with what he considered blatant disregard for logic. He had corrected the outdated science facts, but instead of praise, he'd received a failing grade. Now, he was facing the consequences, and it wasn't just a stern talking-to. Ben was livid, and Oliver knew exactly what was coming next.

Ben stood nearby, his expression a mixture of disappointment and frustration. "I warned you, Oliver. This has gone on long enough. First the class corrections, now arguing with your teacher over your grades. You've been pushing it."

Oliver shot up from the couch, pleading, his voice tinged with desperation. "But, Ben, I was right! It was Mr. Collins who made the mistake, not me. The grade is wrong, and I shouldn't be punished for speaking the truth!"

Ben crossed his arms, his face firm. "That's not the point, Oliver. We've talked about this. I don't care if you were right—you have to learn how to handle these situations without causing a scene. You don't argue with your teacher in front of the entire class. That's not how it works here in 1971."

"But it's unfair!" Oliver protested, his eyes darting nervously toward Ethan, who was standing off to the side, watching the exchange with wide eyes.

Ethan, usually the troublemaker, had been on his best behavior lately. But now, Ethan's role as the rebellious one seemed to be shifting onto Oliver, who had grown more hot-tempered and defiant since starting middle school. He was taller than Ethan now by a few centimeters, his voice slightly deeper. It seemed like puberty was beginning to kick in again, and with it, came a new sense of rebellion.

Ben sighed, shaking his head. "I warned you, Oliver. One more incident, and there'd be consequences. You know how this goes."

Oliver's heart sank as Ben's words confirmed what he had feared. He instinctively took a step back, shaking his head, his voice cracking slightly. "No, Ben, please. I didn't mean to... I was just—"

"It doesn't matter," Ben interrupted, his tone firm but not unkind. "This behavior has to stop. Now."

Without another word, Ben grabbed the waistband of Oliver's pants, yanking them down despite the boy's protests. Oliver's face flushed with embarrassment as his pants dropped, leaving him standing there in his underwear, his hands clutching his shirt in a desperate attempt to cover himself. He had grown a bit taller and stronger, but not enough to resist Ben's firm grip.

"Please, Ben!" Oliver cried out, his voice trembling with fear.

Ben ignored the plea, pulling Oliver over his knee as he sat down. Oliver squirmed, trying to free himself, but Ben was far too strong. His legs kicked uselessly as Ben pulled down his underwear, exposing his bare bottom. Ethan watched silently from the corner, wincing slightly. He had been in this exact position before, and he knew how much it hurt. But what baffled him was Oliver's sudden shift in behavior—why was he acting like this?

"I'm sorry, Ben!" Oliver cried, trying to twist around, but Ben's grip was unrelenting. "I won't do it again, I promise!"

Ben's face was stern, his voice low. "I know you won't. But you have to learn, Oliver. You're not in the 24th century anymore. This is how things are now. You don't get to talk back to teachers, no matter how right you think you are."

With that, Ben raised his hand and brought it down firmly on Oliver's bare bottom. The loud smack echoed through the room, followed by Oliver's sharp yelp of pain.

"Ben! No, please!" Oliver begged, his voice breaking as he squirmed. "I'm sorry! It hurts!"

Ben kept his grip steady, delivering another firm swat. "I warned you, Oliver. You need to think about your actions before you act out."

Each smack drew a fresh cry from Oliver, who wriggled and kicked his legs, but Ben held him in place with ease. The spanking wasn't harsh, but it was enough to sting and leave Oliver in no doubt that Ben meant every word.

Tears began streaming down Oliver's face as the discipline continued, his cries turning into soft sobs. Ethan, watching from the corner, felt a pang of sympathy mixed with relief—it wasn't him this time.

After a few more smacks, Ben finally stopped, resting his hand on Oliver's back for a moment. Oliver lay limp over his knee, sniffling and gasping for breath.

"All done," Ben said, helping Oliver to his feet. The boy quickly pulled up his underwear and pants, wincing as the fabric brushed against his tender skin.

Ben stood, placing a hand on Oliver's shoulder. "That's the end of it. But let this be a lesson, Oliver. You need to control yourself and respect the rules."

Oliver nodded, biting his lip as he wiped his tears, avoiding Ben's gaze. Without a word, he turned and shuffled off to his room, sniffling quietly.

Ethan stayed silent, his gaze dropping to the floor as Ben glanced at him. "Let's hope I don't have to do that again," Ben said, his voice softer now, but still firm.

Ethan nodded quickly, resolving not to cross any lines himself. Ben sat down with a sigh, hoping this would be the last time he'd need to resort to such measures.

The next morning, as the school bell rang and students filed into their classrooms, Oliver felt a growing pit in his stomach. He stood just outside the school gates with Ethan, who glanced over at him, unaware of the turmoil brewing inside his brother.

"You coming in?" Ethan asked, his skateboard tucked under his arm, already used to the daily routine of middle school.

Oliver hesitated, looking past the school building as if it were a prison. The thought of facing his teachers again—especially Mr.

Collins—was unbearable. He hadn't slept well the night before, not just because of the sting from the spanking, but because the injustice of it all burned in his mind. How could Ben, of all people, not understand that he had been right?

"I... I'll catch up with you later," Oliver muttered, turning on his heel before Ethan could protest.

Ethan gave him a curious look but shrugged, heading inside as Oliver walked briskly away from the school. He wasn't going to deal with it today. He couldn't. Instead, there was one place where he knew he could find comfort—Emily.

The hospital where Emily worked wasn't far from the school, just a twenty-minute walk. Oliver kept his head down as he weaved through the streets, hands in his pockets, deep in thought. Emily had always been kind to him, kissing him on the head and calling him a "good boy." She would understand. She had to. She wasn't like Ben—stern and quick to punish. She was caring, gentle.

When he arrived at the hospital, he stood nervously outside the main entrance. He had never come here alone before, but desperation drove him forward. After gathering his courage, Oliver slipped inside, walking past the reception desk, blending in with the stream of visitors. He knew where Emily's office was; she had shown him once when they came to visit her for lunch.

The sterile smell of the hospital hit him, and he felt a strange mix of calm and anxiety. He followed the familiar hallways until he reached the department where Emily worked. One of the nurses spotted him, recognizing him from the times he had visited with Ben.

"Hey there, sweetheart," the nurse said with a smile. "You're Emily's boy, right? Are you looking for her?"

Oliver nodded shyly. "Yeah… is she busy?"

"She's finishing up with a patient, but you can wait in her office. I'll let her know you're here."

Oliver mumbled a thanks and sat down in one of the chairs outside Emily's office, tapping his foot impatiently. The seconds felt like hours as he replayed the events of yesterday in his mind. He needed to tell Emily how unfair everything was. He needed her on his side.

After what felt like forever, Emily appeared, her face lighting up in surprise when she saw Oliver. "Oliver! What are you doing here, sweetie? Is everything okay? Shouldn't you be at school?"

Oliver looked up at her with watery eyes, his lip trembling. The sight of her immediately broke through the wall he had been trying to keep up. "Emily… I didn't go to school today. I—I needed to talk to you…"

Concern washed over her face as she quickly ushered him into her office, closing the door behind them. "Come here, sweetheart. What happened?"

Oliver hesitated for a moment, feeling the weight of everything he'd been holding in. Then, before he knew it, the words started spilling out. "The teachers… they're so unfair! I tried to tell Mr. Collins he was wrong—he was the one who made the mistake, not me! But he gave me a bad grade, and when I tried to explain, he wouldn't listen! And then… then Dad…dad spanked me! He didn't even care that I was right! It's not fair!"

His voice cracked as the tears finally started to fall. He hated that he was crying, but he couldn't stop himself. He had held it in for too long.

Emily immediately knelt down in front of him, her hands gently cupping his face. "Oh, sweetheart… I'm so sorry." She pulled him into a hug, and Oliver buried his face in her shoulder, crying softly. "I know it feels unfair right now. But Ben… he's just trying to help you learn how to handle things. He doesn't want you to get into trouble."

"But I wasn't wrong!" Oliver sniffled. "I shouldn't get in trouble for telling the truth."

Emily sighed softly, rubbing his back. "I know, honey. Sometimes things can feel unfair even when we're right. But there's a time and a place to correct people, and sometimes… we have to find better ways to explain ourselves. Maybe you and I can talk to Dad about this, okay? I'll help him understand how you're feeling."

Oliver pulled back slightly, looking up at her with hopeful eyes. "You will? You'll talk to him?"

"Of course I will," she smiled, wiping the tears from his face. "You know I'm on your side, Oliver. But you also have to promise me you'll try to be more patient, even when things don't go the way you want. Can you do that?"

Oliver nodded, still sniffling. "I'll try…"

"That's all I ask," Emily said, giving him a soft kiss on the head. "Now, how about I call Ben and let him know you're with me? We'll figure this out together."

Oliver felt a sense of relief wash over him as Emily's words sunk in. He didn't know how Ben would react, but at least he had someone in his corner. Someone who cared.

As Emily dialed Ben's number, Oliver sat back, feeling a bit lighter. Whatever happened next, he wasn't alone.

Chapter 43: From Radiance to Shade

When Emily called Ben from her office at the hospital, she had a gentle tone, but the tension in her voice was unmistakable. She had just finished consoling Oliver, and now she needed to speak with Ben, knowing he wouldn't be pleased.

Ben was at his office when the phone rang, his eyes scanning through a report on one of the oil projects. "Benjamin Johnson," he answered in his usual, business-like tone, unaware of the situation.

"Ben, it's me—Emily," she began, her voice slightly hesitant. "I need to talk to you about Oliver."

Ben immediately stiffened at her words. His fatherly instinct kicked in, and he already had a bad feeling. "What's going on? Is he okay?"

Emily sighed softly, trying to ease into the conversation. "He's fine physically. But, Ben... he's not at school. He came here to the hospital to see me."

There was a long pause on the other end of the line, and then Ben's voice dropped to a low, frustrated growl. "He skipped school?"

"Yes," Emily admitted softly. "He didn't feel like he could go today. He's really upset, Ben. He came to talk to me about what happened with his teacher... and about the punishment you gave him."

Ben leaned back in his chair, rubbing his temple as he felt the familiar tension build. "I warned him. If he kept pushing back against his teachers and misbehaving, there would be consequences. I can't believe he thought skipping school was the answer to all this."

"Ben, he's just feeling overwhelmed," Emily pleaded, her voice calm but firm. "He's not trying to disobey you; he just didn't know how to handle everything. The school environment, the grades, the spanking—it's all building up for him. He needs guidance, not more punishment."

Ben sighed deeply, clearly irritated. "I understand that, Emily, but I can't just let him skip school and run to you whenever something doesn't go his way. That's not how this works. He's going to be in more trouble when he gets home, that's for sure."

Emily's heart sank at Ben's words, but she wasn't going to back down. "Ben, please... listen to me." Her voice was gentle but insistent. "I know you're frustrated, but punishing him further isn't the answer right now. He feels misunderstood. He just needs some extra patience. If you keep coming down on him this hard, you'll lose him. He needs to feel like he can talk to you."

Ben was quiet for a moment, his jaw clenched as he stared at the papers in front of him, not really seeing them. Emily's words tugged at his conscience, and he knew she was right—at least partly. But he was also a firm believer in discipline, and this felt like a direct challenge to his authority.

"Emily," he began, his voice quieter now but still firm. "I get that he's upset. But he has to learn that actions have consequences. If he keeps undermining his teachers and now skips school, there's got to be some discipline."

"I'm not saying you shouldn't discipline him, Ben," Emily said carefully. "But maybe there's a better way to reach him. Punishing him isn't always going to teach the right lesson."

Ben pinched the bridge of his nose, exhaling slowly. "I just… don't want to send the message that it's okay to act out or skip school. If I go easy on him now, he might think he can get away with anything."

"I know that's not what you want, Ben. But what if instead of punishing him again, you talked to him? Really talked to him. Let him explain how he's feeling without fear of more punishment. That's what he needs right now."

Another silence followed as Ben mulled over Emily's words. He wasn't used to being talked down from his disciplinary stance, but there was a lot of truth in what she was saying. He knew Oliver had been different lately—more emotional, more rebellious. Maybe it was puberty starting to kick in again. And he also knew deep down that Oliver was a good kid, just lost in the shuffle of middle school pressures and his own frustration.

"Alright," Ben finally said, his voice heavy with resignation. "I'll… talk to him. No further punishment, but he's going to hear me out."

"Thank you," Emily replied softly, her relief evident. "He looks up to you more than you realize, Ben. He just needs to know you're on his side too."

Meanwhile, Emily looked over at Oliver, who was sitting in her office, fiddling nervously with a toy she had on her desk. She walked over and knelt beside him, resting a gentle hand on his shoulder.

"I talked to Ben," she said softly. "He's going to come home tonight, and he's ready to listen to you."

Oliver looked up at her, his eyes wide. "Is he mad?"

"He's upset, but he's willing to hear you out," Emily reassured him. "Just be honest with him, okay? Tell him how you feel."

As the clock neared 5 PM, Emily pulled into the driveway with Oliver slouched in the passenger seat beside her. After a quiet drive from the hospital, they had stopped by the supermarket to pick up a few things for dinner, though Oliver hadn't been in the mood to talk much. He knew what awaited him at home—an uncomfortable conversation with Ben, and possibly worse.

When they walked inside, Ethan was already home, lounging on the couch and flipping through a comic book. The moment he saw Oliver, he raised an eyebrow, smirking mischievously. "Well, well, look who's back from a day of rebellion," Ethan teased, stretching out the word mockingly. "You are in so much trouble now, Ollie!"

Oliver's face flushed red with a mix of frustration and fear. He dropped his backpack with a thud and shoved Ethan away, harder than he intended. "Shut up, Ethan!" he snapped, his voice cracking with the tension that had built up all day.

Ethan, caught off guard by the shove, stumbled a bit before regaining his balance. He blinked in surprise. "Whoa, okay, chill out! No need to get physical, man." He held up his hands defensively, sensing that Oliver was on edge.

"Just leave me alone," Oliver muttered, storming past him and heading toward the stairs. He had no energy to deal with Ethan's teasing on top of everything else.

Emily, who had been unloading groceries in the kitchen, heard the brief scuffle and glanced over her shoulder. "Boys," she called softly, "let's not fight, okay? Dinner will be ready soon."

Ethan shrugged, his smirk fading as he watched Oliver retreat up the stairs. "Fine, whatever." He returned to his comic, though the fun of teasing his brother was now gone.

Upstairs, Oliver threw himself onto his bed, burying his face in the pillow. He wasn't sure what he dreaded more—talking to Ben or the inevitable disappointment in his eyes. He knew he had messed up, but it still felt so unfair. He was right about the grading, and Mr. Collins had been dismissive and condescending. But none of that would matter to Ben.

Meanwhile, Emily got to work in the kitchen, chopping vegetables and marinating the chicken. She wanted to create a warm, comforting atmosphere for the family tonight, hoping that a good meal might soften the tension that was sure to follow when Ben got home. She glanced at the clock—6:30 PM was approaching.

Sure enough, at exactly 6:30 PM, the front door opened, and Ben walked in, his posture slightly stiff, as if bracing himself for what was to come. He set his briefcase down and took off his jacket, his eyes scanning the living room for any sign of Oliver.

Ethan was still on the couch, looking up briefly from his comic book. "Hey, dad," he greeted casually. "Oliver's upstairs, probably waiting for you."

Ben gave a curt nod, his mind already on the looming conversation. "Thanks, Ethan," he replied, though his tone was distracted. He glanced toward the kitchen, where Emily was finishing up dinner. He could hear the sizzle of food on the stove and the comforting clatter of dishes being prepared.

He made his way toward the stairs, but not before pausing at the kitchen door. "Hey, Emily," he greeted, his voice softening a little when he saw her.

"Hey, hon," Emily replied, turning to smile at him. She wiped her hands on a towel, knowing what was on his mind. "Oliver's upstairs. I think he's ready to talk… just, go easy on him, okay?"

Ben sighed, running a hand through his hair. "I'll try," he muttered. "But he skipped school, Em. He has to understand that's not acceptable."

"I know," she agreed gently. "But he's not a bad kid, Ben. He just needs to feel heard."

Ben nodded, giving her a quick kiss before heading up the stairs. As he approached Oliver's room, he could feel the weight of the situation bearing down on him. He knocked lightly before entering, finding Oliver lying face down on his bed.

"Oliver," Ben began, his tone calm but firm. "We need to talk."

Oliver didn't move at first, but then he rolled over, sitting up on the edge of the bed. His eyes were red, and it was clear he had been crying earlier. "I know," he mumbled, avoiding Ben's gaze. "I'm sorry I skipped school."

Ben sat down beside him, keeping a bit of distance but making sure Oliver knew he had his full attention. "I get that you're frustrated," Ben said, his voice steady. "But you can't just walk out of school whenever you feel like it. That's not how we handle problems."

"I know," Oliver repeated, his voice small. "But Mr. Collins... he wasn't being fair! He graded my test wrong, and when I tried to explain, he wouldn't even listen! It wasn't about skipping, it was about him not being fair!"

Ben sighed deeply, nodding. "I believe you, Oliver. I'm not saying you were wrong to feel upset. But the way you handled it—by arguing with the teacher and then skipping school—that's not going to solve anything. You have to learn how to manage these situations without running away from them."

Oliver sniffled, wiping his nose on his sleeve. "But I'm always right about the science stuff... it's so frustrating when they don't listen!"

Ben placed a hand on Oliver's shoulder, squeezing gently. "You have to pick your battles. Running off to the hospital won't fix anything, it just makes things harder for you."

Oliver looked down at his feet, biting his lip. "I just... didn't know what else to do."

Ben softened a bit, seeing the genuine struggle in Oliver's face. "You should've come to me first, Oliver. We could've talked about it together. I'm here to help you, but I need you to meet me halfway. No more skipping school, okay?"

Oliver nodded slowly. "Okay... I won't do it again."

"Good," Ben said, patting his shoulder before standing up. "Let's head downstairs. Dinner's almost ready, and I'm sure Emily's been working hard on it."

Oliver stood up too, feeling a little lighter now that the conversation was over. As they headed downstairs, Ben gave him one last piece of advice. "And remember, next time something like this happens, talk to me. We'll figure it out together."

Oliver gave a small smile. "I will, Ben."

As they reached the kitchen, the smell of dinner filled the air. Emily glanced up from the stove and smiled warmly at them both, clearly relieved to see them together again.

"Everything okay?" she asked, her eyes searching Ben's for a sign of how things went.

Ben nodded, giving her a reassuring look. "Yeah. We're good."

Ethan, still lounging on the couch, looked up and quipped, "So, did you get grounded or what?"

Oliver shot him a tired but playful glare. "Shut up, Ethan."

Emily chuckled softly, placing the food on the table. "Alright, boys, enough teasing. Let's eat."

And with that, the family sat down for dinner, the tension of the day slowly easing as they shared a meal together, feeling just a little bit closer than before.

Two weeks had passed, and things had returned to a comfortable rhythm in the house. That evening, Emily was busy in the kitchen, preparing a meal for a special dinner. Officer Vincent Thomas, her brother, and his 17-year-old daughter, Taylor, were coming over. It wasn't often that they all got together like this, and she wanted everything to be perfect. The aroma of roasting chicken and freshly baked bread filled the air, and she hummed softly as she moved between the stove and the counter, making sure all the details were just right.

In the living room, Oliver and Ethan were engaged in one of their playful fights. At first, it was lighthearted—pushing, shoving, and trying to one-up each other—but it quickly escalated as Oliver's size advantage became apparent. Over the past year, Oliver had hit a growth spurt, and now he stood a good 5 cm taller than Ethan and was noticeably heavier. Ethan, on the other hand, hadn't grown as fast and was starting to feel it during their scuffles.

Oliver grinned down at Ethan, pinning him to the floor, one knee pressed firmly into his back. "Surrender, Ethan!" he demanded triumphantly, his face flushed with excitement.

Ethan struggled beneath him, trying to break free, but it was clear he was losing. "Never!" he shot back defiantly, wriggling under Oliver's grip but unable to shake him off.

Just then, the screen door creaked open, and Ben stepped in from the backyard, wiping his hands on a towel. He watched the scene for a moment, his brows raised. "Alright, alright, that's enough," he said with a firm but amused tone, moving swiftly to pick Oliver up from behind. With one smooth motion, he lifted Oliver off his brother and set him back on his feet.

"Okay, boys, dinner's about ready," Ben announced, giving Oliver a look that said no more roughhousing.

Ethan, still lying on the floor, looked up at Ben with wide eyes, quickly seizing the opportunity to shift the blame. "Dad, Oliver was picking on me!" he complained, sitting up and dusting himself off.

Oliver groaned, rolling his eyes. "I wasn't picking on you! We were just wrestling. Besides, you started it!"

"Yeah, well, you're bigger now," Ethan retorted, getting to his feet, his voice tinged with annoyance. "It's not fair."

Ben sighed, stepping between them before things could escalate further. "It doesn't matter who started it. You're brothers, and I expect you to act like it. No more fighting before dinner, got it?"

"Yes, Dad," they both mumbled, glancing at each other sheepishly.

Just then, the doorbell rang, and Emily called from the kitchen, "Can someone get that? I think it's Vincent and Taylor!"

"I got it," Ben said, walking toward the front door. He opened it to find Officer Vincent Thomas standing there in his police uniform, his tall, broad-shouldered frame filling the doorway. Beside him was his daughter, Taylor, looking every bit like a teenager on the edge of adulthood—tall, confident, with her long hair tied back and a casual smile on her face.

"Vincent! Taylor! Come on in," Ben greeted them warmly, stepping aside to let them enter.

"Hey, Ben," Vincent said, shaking his hand with a firm grip. "Thanks for having us over. Smells amazing in here." He glanced around the house, taking in the comfortable, lived-in atmosphere.

Taylor smiled and waved at Ethan and Oliver, who were now standing awkwardly in the living room, trying to act as if they hadn't just been wrestling on the floor. "Hey, you two," she said teasingly. "What've you been up to?"

"Nothing," Ethan muttered, shoving his hands into his pockets.

Oliver, still a little flushed from the tussle, shrugged. "Just hanging out."

Vincent smirked, noticing the tension between the boys. "Uh-huh, sure," he said, giving them both a knowing look. "Try to keep it civil tonight, okay?"

Ben chuckled, patting Vincent on the back. "They're still getting used to this whole middle school thing. Lots of energy to burn."

"Tell me about it," Vincent replied with a sigh. "Taylor's got her hands full with high school drama."

Taylor rolled her eyes playfully. "Dad, I'm handling it just fine."

Emily poked her head out from the kitchen, a bright smile on her face. "Vincent, Taylor! So glad you could make it! Dinner's almost ready, just a few more minutes."

"Thanks, Em," Vincent said, giving her a warm smile. "Smells like you've outdone yourself."

As everyone settled into the living room, Ben pulled Oliver aside for a moment, lowering his voice. "Hey, I know you were just messing around, but keep it cool tonight, alright? We've got company."

Oliver nodded, glancing down at his feet. "Yeah, I know. Sorry, Ben."

Ben gave him a reassuring pat on the shoulder. "Good. Let's go eat."

Soon, they all gathered around the dining table. Emily had laid out a beautiful spread—roast chicken, mashed potatoes, vegetables, and freshly baked rolls. It was the kind of meal that felt like home, warm and hearty, with everyone laughing and chatting.

As they dug into the food, Vincent leaned back in his chair, taking a sip of his drink. "So, boys," he said, looking at Ethan and Oliver. "How's school treating you?"

Ethan exchanged a glance with Oliver before answering. "It's fine, I guess. Just a lot more work than last year."

Oliver, feeling a bit more composed now, added, "Yeah, and the teachers are tougher. But it's not too bad."

Vincent nodded thoughtfully. "Well, middle school's a big step. But you'll get through it. Just remember to stay out of trouble."

Ben shot Oliver a quick glance, and Oliver shifted uncomfortably in his seat, knowing exactly what Ben was thinking.

Taylor, noticing the nervousness, leaned forward with a grin. "Hey, don't worry. I got into trouble all the time when I started high school. It's part of growing up."

Ethan snorted, trying to hide a smile. "Yeah, I bet."

The room was filled with laughter, and the evening continued in the warm, easy way that only family gatherings can. Though there had been some bumps earlier, the love and support that surrounded them all seemed to ease everything, making it another memorable night.

Chapter 44: Reactions

It was an ordinary school day in Mr. Collins' science lab, but for Oliver, the temptation to show off his knowledge and experiment with chemicals was too strong to resist. While Mr. Collins was deep into his lecture, writing equations and formulas on the board, Oliver's attention wandered. His eyes landed on the shelf filled with chemicals. A mischievous idea crept into his mind, and he quietly started mixing the available chemicals, carefully selecting just the right ones to create a small, colorful show.

As Oliver worked, the tubes lit up in vibrant hues—blues, greens, and purples swirling together in a mesmerizing display. A few students noticed and whispered among themselves, some giggling, others giving him subtle nods of approval. A girl at the back whispered, "Wow, that's so cool, Oliver!" and a boy in the front smirked, impressed. Oliver grinned to himself, feeling proud of his mini light show.

But as he reveled in the moment, Mr. Collins, who had been writing on the board, turned around just in time to catch the colorful glow. His eyes narrowed in disbelief. Silently, he approached Oliver from behind, and before Oliver could react, Mr. Collins grabbed him by the ear, yanking it sharply.

"What are you doing, Oliver!" Mr. Collins barked, his voice full of frustration. "These chemicals are expensive and not your toys!"

Oliver winced, caught off guard. He quickly tried to defend himself. "Ah, I was just showing everyone how these things react together—ouch, please!"

Mr. Collins didn't let go of his ear. "You think this is a joke? You're not even listening to what I'm teaching, are you? That's it. I've had enough of your antics. Go to the principal's office!" His voice rose louder, making the rest of the class fall into silence. The students who had previously been entertained now shrank back in their seats, not wanting to catch Mr. Collins' wrath.

Oliver's heart sank as Mr. Collins continued. "And tell your father I want to see him in my classroom the next time you come to school!"

The words hit Oliver hard. He knew what that meant. Ben wouldn't let this one slide. Not after all the warnings and consequences he'd already faced. He swallowed hard, trying to maintain his composure, but his voice cracked slightly as he mumbled, "Yes, sir."

Grabbing his things, Oliver stormed out of the classroom, his heart racing, his head spinning. As he walked down the hall, Ethan hurried out after him, catching up just outside the door.

"Gosh, Oliver," Ethan panted, glancing at his brother. "Why do you have to keep doing crazy stuff in Mr. Collins' class? You know he's been watching you like a hawk ever since the last time!"

Oliver's face was flushed, his hands clenched into fists. "I don't care anymore, Ethan. I'm so done," he said, his voice barely holding back the emotion. He paused, taking a shaky breath before adding, "Ben's not gonna slide this one." His voice cracked at the end, betraying how scared he really was.

Ethan sighed, shaking his head. "I miss the days when I was the bad one. Now you're living up to being the troublemaker—the 'successor,'" he teased, trying to lighten the mood.

But Oliver didn't laugh. His eyes were fixed ahead, already forming a plan. "I'm not going back to school," Oliver declared, his voice low and determined. "I'm going to Emily's hospital. She's the only one who can help me now."

Ethan's eyes widened in disbelief. "What? No way, man! School isn't even over! And if you skip out, Ben will kill you for this."

"I don't care," Oliver snapped, his pace quickening. "I'm not sticking around to face Ben's wrath. I've had enough." He looked resolute, already heading toward the bike racks where his bicycle was waiting.

Ethan could see that Oliver wasn't going to change his mind. Letting out a frustrated groan, Ethan ran after him. "This is a bad idea, Oliver. You know that, right?" he said, grabbing his skateboard and following his brother down the street.

Oliver hopped on his bike, glancing back at Ethan. "I'd rather take my chances with Emily than go back to school or face Ben right now."

Ethan shook his head as he pushed off on his skateboard, keeping pace beside Oliver as they sped down the road. "You're seriously going to regret this," he muttered under his breath, though deep down, he understood Oliver's desperation.

The two brothers rode silently for a while, the cool wind whipping past them, the streets buzzing with the midday hum of cars and pedestrians. They passed rows of houses, shops, and parks until they finally reached the hospital where Emily worked. The tall white building stood before them, a sanctuary of sorts, especially for Oliver, who now saw Emily as his only hope.

They parked their bike and skateboard outside, and as they walked toward the entrance, Ethan nudged Oliver. "So, what are you gonna tell her? That you ditched school because you can't stand Mr. Collins?"

Oliver shot him a look. "I'm gonna tell her the truth—Ben's been too hard on me lately, and I can't handle another punishment. She'll understand. She's always on our side."

Ethan just shrugged, not entirely convinced, but he followed his brother inside. They navigated the hospital hallways until they found Emily's office. Oliver knocked hesitantly on the door, and after a few moments, Emily opened it, looking surprised to see them.

"Oliver? Ethan?" she said, her brow furrowing in confusion. "What are you two doing here? It's the middle of the school day."

Oliver glanced nervously at Ethan before speaking. "Emily… I need to talk to you. Please." His voice was shaky, and his eyes were filled with a mixture of fear and pleading.

Emily stepped aside, letting them in. She could tell something was wrong, and her protective instincts kicked in immediately. "Alright, come in. Tell me what's going on."

As they stepped into the office, Oliver felt a small wave of relief wash over him. Emily would know what to do. She always did. But in the back of his mind, he knew that no matter what, there was still the looming threat of what Ben would say—and do—when he found out.

As Oliver opened his mouth to explain what had happened at school, a nurse burst into Emily's office, her voice tense with urgency. "Dr. Reynolds, there's an emergency case in the ER. They need your help right away."

Emily's face shifted instantly, her professional demeanor taking over. "I'm sorry, boys, I have to go," she said, standing up quickly. She glanced at Oliver, clearly concerned about what had brought him here, but the pressing nature of the situation left no room for questions. "Wait here, okay? I'll be back as soon as I can."

But Oliver, still filled with anxious energy from his earlier run-in at school, wasn't ready to sit still. As Emily hurried out of the office, both he and Ethan exchanged a glance. Without saying a word, they bolted after her, ignoring her instruction to stay behind. They followed her down the winding corridors of the hospital, weaving through nurses and patients until they reached the emergency department.

The ER was a chaotic scene of doctors rushing around, machines beeping, and patients being wheeled in on stretchers. The boys were stopped just outside the doors by a nurse, who sternly told them to wait outside, but neither Oliver nor Ethan had any intention of listening. While the nurse turned away to attend to another matter, they slipped inside, unnoticed amidst the commotion.

It was then that something unusual caught Ethan's attention. His eyes locked onto a man being wheeled into the room on a gurney—a man with a tattoo that immediately set alarm bells ringing in Ethan's mind. "Look! Oliver, look!" Ethan whispered urgently, his voice low but filled with intensity.

Oliver turned, following Ethan's gaze, and his breath caught in his throat. "No way…" he muttered under his breath.

The tattoo was unmistakable: a bright, colorful image of a cartoonish character from a 24th-century show—a character that had no business existing in 1971. The realization hit them both at once. This man wasn't from the 1970s. He was from their time.

The two brothers exchanged a wide-eyed glance, the gravity of the situation sinking in. How was this possible? They weren't the only ones who had somehow made their way to the past.

"That tattoo…" Oliver started, but before they could process it further, the room's attention shifted. The doctors surrounding the man moved with grim determination, but despite their best efforts, the urgency began to fade. Emily, along with the other doctors, tried to revive the man, but after several intense minutes, they stepped back, defeat washing over their faces. One doctor looked at the clock and solemnly announced, "Time of death, 2:38 PM."

Oliver and Ethan watched, stunned, as Emily and the other doctors covered the man's body with a sheet. The chaos of the ER continued around them, but the boys were frozen, their attention fixed on the now-lifeless body of the man who, somehow, was from their time.

Ethan was the first to break the silence. "Did you see his watch?" he whispered, his voice shaky but filled with urgency.

Oliver's eyes darted back to the man's wrist. Beneath the sheet, just barely visible, was the edge of a device that definitely didn't belong in the 1970s. "Yeah," Oliver replied, nodding slowly. "That's not from this era. We need to get it."

Ethan's mind raced. They had to get that watch—it could hold critical information about who the man was, why he was here, and maybe even how he got trapped in the past. But the real question was: how?

They glanced around, trying to come up with a plan. The ER was still buzzing with activity, but the attention had shifted to other patients. For now, no one was paying much attention to the dead man on the gurney.

Ethan's eyes narrowed. "We'll have to be quick. If we're caught…"

Oliver nodded, steeling himself. "I know."

They waited until the doctors stepped away, leaving the man's body momentarily unattended. Moving quickly and quietly, Oliver slid closer to the gurney, careful not to draw attention. Ethan stood nearby, keeping watch. Oliver's heart raced as he carefully lifted the sheet just enough to reveal the man's wrist.

There it was—a sleek, futuristic device that looked like a watch but was unlike anything from 1971. Oliver's fingers trembled as he unfastened it, sliding it off the man's wrist as delicately as he could. His pulse pounded in his ears, but after a few tense seconds, the watch was in his hand.

Ethan motioned for him to hurry, and Oliver quickly tucked the watch into his pocket. The two brothers darted back toward the door, trying to act as casual as possible, but their hearts were racing, adrenaline pumping through their veins. Just as they reached the exit, a nurse looked their way.

"Hey!" she called out. "What are you boys doing in here?"

They froze for a split second, but then Ethan, thinking quickly, gave a nervous smile. "Sorry, we were just looking for our mom. She's one of the doctors here."

The nurse frowned but seemed to buy the excuse. She pointed to the door. "You can't be in here. Go wait outside."

The boys nodded and slipped out of the ER, their hearts still pounding. Once they were back in the hallway, they looked at each other, both a mix of exhilaration and fear. Oliver reached into his pocket, pulling out the device and holding it between them.

"We got it," Ethan breathed, barely able to believe they'd pulled it off.

Oliver stared at the watch, his mind racing with possibilities. "Now we just need to figure out what this thing does... and why that guy was here."

Ethan and Oliver burst through the hospital entrance doors, their hearts still pounding from the adrenaline rush. They had no time to cry to Emily about their troubles anymore. This discovery—this watch—was far more important than anything that had happened at school. Hastily, they made their way back home and entered the storage room, where Lucas, their trusted time machine, resided

Breathing heavily, Oliver pulled the watch from his pocket, holding it up to the glowing interface of Lucas. "Lucas, analyze this," he ordered, his voice taut with urgency.

The machine hummed to life, lights flickering softly as it scanned the object. For a moment, the room was silent, save for the quiet whirr of Lucas's systems processing the data. Ethan and Oliver exchanged tense glances, anticipation and hope dancing in their eyes.

They knew this could be it—this could be their way back home, to their real lives, to their adult bodies.

Lucas's voice finally broke the silence. "The device is from our time period. It uses an operating system developed in the Great Asia Confederation, a major tech region in the 24th century. This is not merely a watch. It is a navigator and positioning device, a piece of a larger time travel system. However, I need more time to unlock its full capabilities."

Ethan's eyes widened, his mind racing with possibilities. "A piece of a time travel system? Does that mean—"

Oliver interrupted, his thoughts rushing ahead. "But if this is part of a larger system..." His voice trailed off as realization dawned on him. "We could use this, Ethan! We might not need the 2 kilograms of gold after all. This might be a way back!"

Ethan grinned, his eyes alight with the same realization. "Exactly! We need to talk to Ben as soon as he gets home. If this device can get us back—" He paused, glancing down at his small, 11-year-old hands. "We wouldn't have to be stuck as kids anymore. No more school, no more dealing with teachers and principals. We could finally be us again."

The thought of it sent a rush of excitement through both of them. They had been trapped in the 1970s for over a year and a half now, and the weight of their predicament had felt like an unshakable burden. But now, with this watch, everything could change. The challenges of their current lives—the endless rules imposed by Ben, the limitations of their prepubescent bodies, the humiliations of attending school with children—could finally be left behind. They might even return to the 24th century with answers to deeper questions, bringing something that could redefine time travel forever.

Oliver, however, was still distracted by another thought. His run-in with Mr. Collins earlier that day loomed large in his mind. He'd skipped the entire afternoon of school to chase after the watch, and it wasn't lost on him that when Ben found out, there would be consequences—ones he wasn't eager to face.

"I should have been in class," Oliver muttered under his breath, his stomach knotting. "Ben's going to be furious when he finds out I ditched the rest of the day. Especially after what happened with Mr. Collins."

Ethan shrugged. "You've got bigger things to worry about now, Oliver. Once we show Ben the watch and what it could mean, I doubt he'll care much about what happened at school today."

Oliver wasn't so sure. He had seen Ben get upset before—seriously upset. The thought of another punishment like last time made him wince. But Ethan was right. This watch, this device, could be their ticket home. And if they could figure out how to use it, nothing else would matter.

Oliver exhaled sharply, shaking off his anxiety. "You're right. We'll deal with that later. For now, we need to focus on this."

They both turned their attention back to Lucas, who continued working on unlocking more of the watch's secrets. The machine's soft glow illuminated the storage room, casting long shadows over the dusty walls.

Ethan crossed his arms, pacing slightly as his excitement bubbled over. "I think this system is way more advanced than ours. This watch—like Lucas said—is a navigator and positioning device. It could mean... I don't know... maybe a larger machine pushed or 'teleported' to the wearer across time. And look—it's from the Confederation! I knew it. Of course, they have a time machine. The Confederation always had more talented people and poured more resources into physics research."

Oliver nodded, a hint of bitterness in his tone. "Yeah, while our government barely cared. We didn't even have the techs we needed to build ours properly. If we'd gotten our hands on the Temporal Stabilizer—or anything like it—we wouldn't have had to use Rezulix to shrink ourselves. We could've upgraded our machine to handle space-time distortions instead."

Ethan groaned, throwing his arms up in frustration. "Exactly! And our facility sucked. They didn't even approve enough funding for the good version of Rezulix—the one that only regresses a few years. Nope, we had to take the full dose. And now look at us—we look like babies!"

The hours stretched on, and the two of them waited, eyes flicking back to Lucas every so often, wondering when Ben would get home. They had to tell him—they had to explain what they'd found. And more importantly, they needed his help. The sooner they figured out how to unlock the full potential of the watch, the sooner they could go home.

Around 6 p.m., Ben arrived home, weary from another grueling day at work. Ben stood in front of the boys, his eyes narrowing as they revealed the full story. He was already weary from a long day at work, and this news hit him like a punch to the gut. He had been carefully balancing the fragile situation they were in—managing their lives in the 1970s, keeping them under the radar, and trying to save enough money to buy back the gold for Lucas. And now this.

A watch from the 24th century, here in 1971? The implications were staggering.

Ben exhaled slowly, willing himself to stay composed even as the anger simmered just beneath the surface. "Let me get this straight," he said, his voice calm but edged with steel. "You two skipped school—again—and went to Emily's hospital. After everything I've told you?" He paused, his gaze fixed on them, heavy with disappointment. "I've been more lenient with you two than I should've been, but clearly, that ends now."

Oliver and Ethan exchanged a nervous glance. Oliver's throat tightened. He knew Ben was angry—not just a little annoyed, but truly furious. Ethan fidgeted, trying to think of how to respond, but Oliver's voice cracked first. "Ben, we can talk about school later, the watch—"

430

"And you took this off a dead body?" Ben's voice rose, cutting off Oliver's explanation. His eyes were wide with disbelief. "Do you have any idea how reckless that is? Forget about the fact you skipped school, forget about the fact you disobeyed me—what if someone at the hospital saw you messing with the body? Do you realize the trouble you could've caused? What were you thinking?"

Ethan winced but spoke up, trying to defend them. "We thought... we thought it was important. The guy wasn't from this time, Ben. He had a tattoo from our century—one from the 24th! We're sure of it."

Oliver, still trembling from Ben's reaction, added, "Yeah, we knew we couldn't just let the watch stay there. It could be a clue, Ben. A way out. A way home."

Ben inhaled deeply, pacing back and forth, the wooden floor creaking beneath his feet. He ran a hand through his hair, his mind racing. Home? They didn't know. They couldn't know what he had discovered. What Lucas had confirmed about the future. There was no home to return to. The 24th century—their time—had been decimated by a nuclear war, a reality Ben had been keeping from them for months. He didn't want them to lose hope, to feel like all of their efforts were for nothing.

Ben turned to face the boys, his voice calmer but more serious than they'd ever heard it. "This watch... yes, it's important. But you two need to understand that you can't just go off on wild, impulsive chases like this. We're in a delicate situation here, trying to survive, to blend in. The last thing we need is you drawing attention to yourselves by running around in the middle of a school day and stealing things from a hospital."

Oliver, his hands shaking slightly, tried to protest. "But Ben, what if this is a way to avoid having to wait for the gold? What if it's a way back? Lucas said it's part of a larger time travel system—"

Ben cut him off, his voice firm but with a tinge of bitterness. "And do you even know how to use it, Oliver? This tech—it's not like what we're used to. We don't have the full picture. Sure, maybe it's a clue, but do you really think it's safe to gamble our way home on a piece of technology we don't fully understand? One that isn't even from our region or system?"

Ethan chimed in, trying to stay hopeful. "But Ben, if this watch works, we might not even need the gold! We could—"

"—we could what, Ethan?" Ben's voice had an edge now, his frustration spilling over. "We could try and use something we don't know how to operate and end up even more lost? Or worse, stuck in an even worse situation than we're already in?"

Both boys were silent, staring at Ben. Oliver's confidence had been shattered in the span of moments, and Ethan's optimism was faltering. Neither of them had seen Ben this rattled before.

Ben softened slightly, seeing the impact his words had on the boys. He sighed, rubbing his temples. "Look, I know you're frustrated. I know you want to go home..." His voice trailed off for a moment before he forced himself back into the conversation. "This watch is significant, and we can learn from it. But I still think finding the two kilograms of gold is our safest bet."

Oliver, still desperate to push his point, raised his voice. "But Ben, finding that much gold could take years. We've already been here for almost two! And now with this... we might not have to—"

"Oliver." Ben's voice was suddenly quiet, and that made the boys freeze in their tracks. "I understand how you feel but trust me when I say that using this watch to get back may not give you what you're hoping for."

Ethan squinted, sensing something off in Ben's tone. "What do you mean, Ben? What aren't you telling us?"

Ben looked away, staring out the window for a moment, gathering his thoughts. He couldn't tell them—not yet. "It's just...All I'm saying is that we shouldn't rely on something we barely understand. This tech—this watch—it's not our primary way out of here."

Oliver, still shaken by Ben's earlier anger, kept his voice low. "So, what's the plan? Just keep trying to scrape together enough money for the gold?"

Ben nodded, his expression firm. "Yes. We stick to the plan."

Ethan opened his mouth to protest, but Ben raised a hand to silence him. "Enough," Ben said, his tone leaving no room for argument. He pivoted back to the topic of school, steering the conversation away from the watch. "Listen to me, both of you. The next time I get called to the school because of something one of you did, there will be real consequences. Do you understand?"

Oliver and Ethan exchanged a wary glance, then nodded in unison. They knew better than to test Ben's patience any further today.

Ben glanced at the watch again, his mind returning to the dark truth he was hiding. There might not be a home left for them to return to, but for now, the boys didn't need to know that. Not yet.

"Good," Ben said finally, his voice soft but commanding. "Now go finish your homework. I'll figure out more about this watch later."

Chapter 45: The Spark

In their shared room, Oliver paced back and forth, frustration boiling over. He stopped in front of Ethan, crossing his arms. "Ben is hiding something from us. I know it," he said, his voice tight with suspicion.

Ethan, sitting on the bed, glanced up. "He's just stressed out. I don't think he's hiding things. Come on, we're his colleagues—partners in this experiment, remember?"

Oliver scoffed, shaking his head. "Colleagues? Really? He treats us like his children now. Do you spank your colleagues if they don't listen to you?"

Ethan cringed, thinking back to all the times Ben had disciplined him over the past year. "Yeah, well...I guess not." He rubbed the back of his neck. "But he's in charge."

"I'm done letting him treat me like that," Oliver said, his voice rising with a newfound determination. "Enough. I won't let him spank me again."

Ethan chuckled, but there was bitterness behind it. "Why didn't you say this last year when I was the one getting all the 'treatments'? You seemed fine with it when it was me."

Oliver paused, his face softening for a moment. "Everything is unfair in this stupid time, Ethan. The teachers, the people...and especially Ben. I don't even know why we let him get away with treating us like kids from the beginning. I get it—we needed to lay low—but now? He talks to us like we're really 10 or 11 years old."

Ethan shrugged. "Well, we do look like it. And honestly, he's got all the control. He calls the shots, decides when we eat, where we go, what we do...and yeah, he's the one in charge of...consequences."

Oliver shook his head, his anger still simmering. "It's more than that, Ethan. It's like we let him rewrite the rules. I don't know when it happened, but we stopped being equals, and now it's like we're at his mercy. And after what just happened with the watch, I'm sure he's not telling us everything."

Ethan sighed. "What are we supposed to do? We don't have any options here. If we push him too far, who knows what'll happen?"

Oliver glanced toward the door, lowering his voice. "That's the problem, Ethan. We don't know what'll happen. I just don't want to be left in the dark anymore. And I sure as hell won't let him spank me like I'm some brat who doesn't know better. Not again."

Ethan lay back on the bed, staring at the ceiling. "Yeah, I get it. But we have to be smart about this. Ben's stressed too. We just need to figure out what he's hiding...before he finds another excuse to 'teach' us a lesson."

Oliver clenched his fists, his jaw tightening. "I'm going to find out. One way or another."

Ben stood in the dimly lit storage room, the hum of machinery filling the air as he stared at the sleek, metallic frame of Lucas, their time machine. He ran a hand through his hair, his mind racing with conflicting thoughts. His heart felt heavy as he prepared to address Lucas directly.

"Don't tell Ethan and Oliver about the war in the 24th century," Ben said firmly, crossing his arms. "They need hope to get through the 1970s. If they find out what's waiting for us back home, they'll lose all sense of purpose. We can't afford that."

Lucas's voice, calm and measured, echoed through the room. "Are you certain of this course of action, Benjamin? Keeping them in the dark about such crucial information could strain the trust you've built."

Ben took a deep breath, nodding. "I'm sure. You confirmed it yourself, Lucas. The war is real. And Oliver's nightmares..." He paused, his eyes clouding as he remembered Oliver waking up in a panic, haunted by visions of nuclear devastation. "His dreams have been more than just side effects of the Rezulix. They're warnings. I believe the war is happening—or at the very least, it's imminent. We can't let that destroy them now."

Lucas's interface blinked as it processed Ben's words. "You understand the risk of withholding such vital information. Shouldn't they be involved in the decision-making process, considering their intellect and involvement in this experiment?"

Ben shook his head, pacing now, tension in his shoulders. "No. Not yet. If they knew... If they understood how bad things are back in our time, they'd push to return immediately, thinking we could somehow change things. But what's the point of returning to a world that's on the edge of extinction?"

He stopped, leaning on the time machine as if trying to ground himself. "We've been stuck here for nearly two years. We've adapted. They've grown, mentally and emotionally, even if their bodies are still those of kids. But this thing—this watch—it's our chance to understand more. To find out who else is messing with time. It could give us clues about how to stop the war...from here. From the past."

Lucas processed the data, speaking again with a hint of skepticism. "But should you succeed in learning how to use the device, would it not present an alternate path to returning home? One that Ethan and Oliver may view as an escape from the 1970s?"

Ben sighed, his gaze hardening. "Keep me updated on everything you find about the watch. But don't tell Ethan and Oliver anything significant—especially if it involves how we could use it to return. Not until I say so."

Lucas paused, as if contemplating Ben's directive. "Understood. I will withhold major updates regarding the device from Ethan and Oliver."

Ben rubbed his temples, the weight of his decisions pressing down on him. "They need hope, Lucas. If they find out that our world is on the brink of destruction...they'll lose themselves. We'll lose them. And I can't—" He stopped, taking a breath to steady himself. "I can't let that happen."

Lucas's lights dimmed slightly, as if acknowledging Ben's inner turmoil. "I will proceed as you have requested. But I advise caution, Benjamin. Trust is a fragile bond, especially in times of uncertainty."

Ben stared at the machine, his jaw tightening. "I know. But for now...it's the only way to protect them. They have to believe there's still something worth fighting for."

The following morning was tense. Ben drove Oliver and Ethan to school in silence, his knuckles white on the steering wheel. Oliver sat in the passenger seat, arms crossed, glaring out the window. He wasn't just angry at Ben—he was furious with Mr. Collins and the whole situation. Being treated like a child, time and time again, was something Oliver could hardly tolerate. And now, they were on their way to apologize to Mr. Collins, someone no different from Ben. Oliver struggled to respect Mr. Collins, whose shallow understanding of science only deepened his irritation.

When they arrived at the school, Ben pulled into the parking lot and turned to Oliver. "You know why we're here, right?"

Oliver didn't respond, his jaw clenched. He just stared straight ahead.

Ben sighed heavily, trying to keep his patience. "Look, Oliver, I need you to behave in there. Promise me that you're going to listen to Mr. Collins and—"

Oliver cut him off with a sharp glance. "I heard you the first ten times."

Ben parked the car, his shoulders slumping as he turned off the engine. Weariness settled over him like a heavy blanket, but he pushed it aside. They walked into the school together, the silence between them heavier than words could be.

Inside Mr. Collins' classroom, the teacher stood waiting, arms folded, his face stern. "Mr. Johnson," he greeted Ben. "Thank you for coming."

Ben forced a polite smile. "Of course, Mr. Collins. I'm sorry for the trouble Oliver's been causing in your class. We've discussed it, and I can assure you it won't happen again."

Oliver stood off to the side, eyes focused on a spot on the floor, his arms still crossed. He said nothing, simmering with quiet resentment. He had promised Ben he'd behave, but now it felt more like a trap—like he was being forced into submission.

"Oliver?" Ben turned to his side, expecting him to say something, to apologize.

Oliver didn't move. His face was unreadable, but the tension in his shoulders said enough.

"Oliver!" Ben raised his voice slightly, his patience starting to crack.

"Yeah, I promised," Oliver mumbled, his voice barely above a whisper. He still refused to look at either Ben or Mr. Collins.

Mr. Collins glanced between the two, clearly sensing the friction. "I expect better behavior from you in class, Oliver. If it continues, we'll have to take more serious measures. I'm sure your father understands."

Oliver shot a glare at Mr. Collins, but he quickly looked away, biting his lip to keep from saying what was really on his mind.

Ben nodded, forcing another strained smile. "We'll make sure that won't be necessary. Right, Oliver?"

"Yeah," Oliver muttered, his hands balling into fists by his sides. The anger burned inside him—he hated being called out like this, and he hated Ben for making him stand there like a scolded child.

After a few more pleasantries, the meeting ended. As they walked out of the classroom and back into the hallway, Ben tried to reach out to Oliver, his voice softening. "I know this is challenging, but you've got to get through this, Oliver. It's just school. Just... cooperate, okay?"

Oliver didn't respond, his gaze fixed firmly on the floor as they exited the school building. Ben sighed, rubbing his forehead in frustration, and headed off—not to work, but to Emily's hospital. He intended to talk things over with her. Or at least, that's what he told himself. In truth, Ben wanted to look around the hospital, hoping to find something—anything—connected to the dead man or the mysterious watch.

As Oliver walked down the hallway toward his next class, he spotted Ethan standing outside the door, leaning against the lockers. Ethan gave him a questioning look, his arms crossed.

"Everything okay?" Ethan asked, eyeing his brother.

Oliver stopped in front of him, dropping his backpack to the floor. He leaned against the lockers with a deep sigh, looking drained. "No. I don't feel okay at all."

Ethan raised an eyebrow, leaning in slightly. "What happened? Did Mr. Collins chew you out again?"

"Mr. Collins, Ben... It's all the same," Oliver grumbled, frustration leaking into his voice. "I'm tired of pretending like this stupid school matters. Everything we do here—it's pointless. We don't belong here."

Ethan shifted awkwardly, knowing Oliver was struggling but not entirely sure what to say. "Yeah, I get it. But if you keep acting up, Ben's just gonna come down on you harder. You don't want that."

Oliver clenched his jaw, staring ahead with a hard expression. "I know, but I think Mr. Collins hates me now. He's just looking for ways to get me in trouble. I bet that either this week or next, he'll come up with some excuse to call Ben in again."

Ethan nodded slowly, trying to be the more level-headed one. "We'll figure it out, man. Just... don't make things harder for yourself, okay?"

Oliver said nothing, the weight of his frustration still heavy on his chest. He picked up his backpack and headed toward class, but inside, he felt like he was losing control of everything. He hated being stuck in this time, in his small, powerless body, and he hated how Ben had started treating them more like children than colleagues. Ethan was right about this from the beginning.

As the bell rang, they shuffled into their respective classrooms. But as Oliver sat down, his mind wasn't on school or the lesson. It was on the growing resentment inside him, and the feeling that something had to change.

Ben entered Emily's office at the hospital, carrying a bouquet of flowers. He smiled when he saw her, and they greeted each other with a soft kiss, lingering just a moment longer than usual.

Emily took the flowers, her eyes lighting up with a mix of surprise and appreciation. "These are beautiful, Ben," she said, setting them on her desk. She sighed as she leaned back in her chair, exhaustion still evident in her posture. "Yesterday, Ethan and Oliver came here... I was going to stop by the house after my shift, but I was so wiped out, I just couldn't."

Ben, hands in his pockets, leaned against the doorframe, his face slightly hardening at the mention of the boys. "They skipped school," he said, his voice tinged with frustration. "I had to deal with it."

Emily's eyes softened as she stood up and moved closer to him, placing a gentle hand on his arm. "Ben," she began carefully, her voice low and understanding, "please don't tell me you punished them."

Ben looked at her, a slight tension in his eyes, but also a hint of defensiveness. "I didn't. Not this time," he said, glancing away. "But you have to understand—this is getting out of hand. I let it slide once for Oliver because you asked me to. But now he thinks every time he messes up, he can just run to you, and you'll get me to back off. He's playing us, Emily."

Emily tilted her head, her expression concerned but gentle. "He's 11, Ben. He's going through a lot of changes right now. You can't expect him to act perfectly all the time. He's just… figuring things out."

Ben let out a sigh, pacing a few steps as he gathered his thoughts. "I know," he said, "but I need him to understand that there are limits. Yesterday, it wasn't just Oliver. He dragged Ethan into it too. They both skipped school and came straight here, hoping you'd save them from whatever consequences were coming."

Emily crossed her arms, frowning slightly. Emily studied Ben for a moment, hearing the defeat in his voice, but also sensing the weariness behind it. She knew Ben cared deeply for both boys, but she also knew he was struggling to maintain control. "Ben," she said softly, "you know I love those boys, and I love you. But maybe... maybe they're acting out because they feel trapped. They're still adjusting, and they need some space to make mistakes."

Ben shook his head, disappointment creeping back into his voice. "I get that, Em."

Chapter 46: Double-Edged Sword

The warm aroma of Vietnamese spices filled the small pho restaurant, but the tension at the table was stifling. Bowls of steaming noodles sat untouched as Ben, seated at the head, tried once again to break the silence.

"How's it going, Oliver?" he asked casually, his tone neutral but probing.

Oliver barely looked up, his voice clipped. "Fine."

Ethan poked at his noodles, avoiding eye contact with either of them. The air between them felt heavier than usual, and Ben could see that Oliver's dissatisfaction had deepened into something more pointed.

"Out with it, Oliver," Ben said after a moment, setting down his chopsticks. "You've been stewing over something for days. Let's hear it."

Oliver paused, then pushed his bowl away. "Fine," he said, his voice sharp. "I'm sick of this. Sick of you treating us like we're kids. You think because we're stuck in these bodies, you get to play parent now? You forget we were your colleagues—not your sons."

Ben sighed, leaning back in his chair. "I haven't forgotten. But like it or not, I'm the one responsible for keeping us alive and getting us through this."

"Alive?" Oliver scoffed, shaking his head. "You think this is about survival? We wouldn't even be in this mess if you hadn't rushed the completion of the time machine. You wanted to make history, and now we're stuck here paying for your ambition."

Ben's jaw tightened, the words striking a nerve. "I rushed the project because we were on the brink of losing funding—something you knew very well. Without that push, we wouldn't have a time machine at all."

Oliver leaned forward, his voice rising. "At least we wouldn't be trapped in the 1970s with you calling all the shots. You treated us like your protégés back then, but the truth is, you never saw us as equals. We were just the kids you handpicked to do the grunt work."

Ethan spoke up, his voice quiet but firm. "We thought we were a team, Ben. But looking back, you were always pulling the strings. You decided what we worked on, how we worked on it, and now—when we get to know anything."

Ben raised an eyebrow, his voice hardening. "You want to talk about teamwork? Let's talk about how I had to rein you both in constantly. Don't act like you didn't need someone to guide you. You were brilliant, sure—but you were also brats, even in the 24th century."

Oliver's eyes narrowed, his tone turning bitter. "Brats? That's rich, coming from the guy who's been spanking us like we're toddlers. You're abusing your position, Ben—bullying us because you can, not because you have to."

Ben's expression darkened, but he kept his voice steady. "You want to call me a bully? Fine. But don't forget the tricks and pranks you two used to pull on the faculty back in Electropolis. The whole Science Department was ready to throttle you half the time."

"That's not the same!" Oliver shot back, his fists clenching on the table. "We were colleagues, not kids! You had no right to treat us like that, even now. If we were still in our adult bodies, you wouldn't dare."

Ben's eyes narrowed, his tone turning sharper. "And if you were in your adult bodies, maybe you'd act like adults instead of pushing every boundary I set. Talking doesn't work with either of you. It never has."

Oliver leaned forward, his voice trembling with anger. "You think treating us like this is going to make things better? All it's done is show how little you respect us. You never did."

The table fell silent for a moment, the sounds of the bustling restaurant fading into the background. Ben exhaled slowly, his gaze flicking between Oliver and Ethan.

"I've always respected your talents," Ben said finally, his tone heavy but resolute. "But respect goes both ways. You can't act like rebellious kids and then demand to be treated as equals. You've got to earn that."

Ethan hesitated but finally spoke, his voice soft. "Maybe we'd respect you more if you told us the truth—for once. About why we're still here. About what's really going on with the 24th century."

Ben's eyes hardened, but for a split second, he faltered. Oliver caught the hesitation and pressed forward.

"You think we haven't noticed?" Oliver said, his voice quieter but sharper now. "You're hiding things, Ben. About the machine. About why we haven't gone back. About what's happening in our time."

Ben stared at them both, his mind racing. He had always known this moment would come, but he wasn't ready.

"I'm doing what's best for you," he said finally, his voice quiet but firm. "Whether you understand that or not."

Oliver stood abruptly, his chair scraping against the floor. "We're not your kids, Ben. You don't get to control everything forever."

Ethan hesitated but eventually rose as well. "He's right," he muttered, avoiding Ben's gaze. "You owe us the truth."

Oliver pushed his chair back with a loud scrape, standing abruptly. His expression was a storm of anger and disappointment. "I'm done," he muttered, his voice barely above a growl, before heading toward the door.

Ethan hesitated, glancing between Ben and Oliver. After a brief pause, he got up and followed Oliver without a word.

Ben sighed heavily, pinching the bridge of his nose. He signaled for the check, quickly paid, and rushed out of the restaurant. The parking lot was dimly lit, and the cool night air hit him like a wave. But when he stepped outside, his stomach sank—Oliver and Ethan were nowhere in sight.

"Oliver! Ethan!" Ben called, his voice echoing across the empty lot. Anxiety tightened his chest as he scanned the area. He jogged toward the far end of the lot, looking behind cars and around corners, but there was no sign of them.

Panic rising, he sprinted toward the main street. The buzz of passing cars and chatter of pedestrians filled the air, but finally, he spotted the boys down the block, walking briskly. Relief washed over him, but it was fleeting—he could tell by their posture that Oliver was still seething.

"Oliver! Ethan! Wait!" Ben shouted, running toward them.

They didn't stop.

Ben picked up his pace and caught up, grabbing both of them firmly by the shoulders. "What do you think you're doing?" he demanded, his tone a mix of anger and concern.

Oliver shrugged off Ben's hand, his glare sharp as a knife. "Anywhere but near you."

"Get back to the car," Ben ordered, his voice low but commanding.

"No," Oliver shot back, crossing his arms.

Ben's patience snapped. "I'll ask one more time," he said, his voice steely. "If you still want to act like a brat, I'll drag you home and give you a spanking you'll never forget."

Oliver's face twisted with fury. "You think you can scare me into listening to you? I'm done letting you push me around!"

Before Ben could react, Oliver turned and bolted down the sidewalk.

"Oliver, stop!" Ben shouted, but the boy didn't look back.

Ben groaned, realizing he'd gone too far. "Damn it," he muttered under his breath before chasing after him. "Oliver, wait! I'm sorry!" he called, his voice softer now, trying to bridge the gap.

Ethan stayed put, watching the scene unfold. As Ben ran after Oliver, Ethan sighed heavily, his expression caught between weariness and resignation.

When Ben finally caught up to Oliver, he gently grabbed his arm. "Oliver, listen to me. I didn't mean it. I shouldn't have said that." His voice was steady but apologetic. "I let my frustration get the better of me, and I'm sorry."

Oliver stopped, breathing heavily, his face flushed from running. He didn't pull away this time but refused to look at Ben.

Ethan walked up, his hands shoved in his pockets. "Oliver," he said calmly, his voice cutting through the tension. "Let's just go home and talk. Running isn't going to fix anything."

Oliver stayed silent for a long moment, staring at the ground. Finally, he let out a long breath, nodding slightly.

Ben stepped back, giving him some space. "Let's go," he said quietly. "We'll talk, and I'll listen. I promise."

Reluctantly, Oliver turned and followed Ethan back toward the car. Ben trailed behind, the weight of his words and actions pressing heavily on his shoulders.

Once home, they filed inside the house. Ben shut the door behind them, his back leaning against it for a moment before he turned to face them.

"Sit down," he said, his voice no longer commanding, but heavy. He wasn't in the mood for another fight. Ethan and Oliver exchanged a glance, sensing something different in Ben's tone. They slowly sat down on the couch, their earlier defiance replaced by a quiet, simmering tension.

Ben ran a hand through his hair, pacing slightly before standing in front of them. "There's something I need to tell you," he began, exhaling deeply. "Something I've known for a while but... I didn't tell you because I didn't want to take away the last bit of hope you had."

Ethan furrowed his brow, sensing the seriousness in Ben's voice. "What are you talking about?"

Ben looked at the floor for a moment, gathering his thoughts. Finally, he met their eyes, his expression grim. "The 24th century... it's likely gone. Destroyed by a nuclear war."

The room fell deathly silent. Oliver's face, which had been filled with anger just moments ago, was now pale with shock. Ethan blinked, not sure if he had heard Ben correctly.

"What?" Oliver's voice was barely a whisper.

"I didn't tell you because I didn't want you to lose hope," Ben said, his voice tight with emotion. "But Lucas confirmed it. And those nightmares you've been having, Oliver... they're not just dreams. I think they're glimpses of what's happening in our time."

Ethan leaned forward, his face paling. "You've known this for how long?"

"Since shortly after we arrived in Japan last time," Ben admitted. "But I didn't think it would help us to know the truth. If we can't stop that war from happening, there's no point in going back. It's a wasteland, a dead world."

Oliver shot up from the couch, pacing back and forth, his hands in his hair. "So you've been lying to us. This whole time, you've been letting us believe that if we got the gold, we could go home and everything would be fine?!" His voice cracked, torn between anger and devastation.

Ben winced at Oliver's words. "I wasn't lying. I didn't know for sure until recently. But I had to make a choice—keep you focused on surviving here or... or let you give up."

Ethan buried his face in his hands, overwhelmed by the revelation. "This can't be real. There has to be something we can do."

"There is," Ben said, stepping closer to them. "The watch you found... it might be the key. But we need more time to figure it out. Until then, we have to survive here. We need to stay under the radar, keep going as we are."

Oliver stopped pacing and turned to face Ben, his face filled with fury and disbelief. "You're asking us to keep living like we're children when there's no future to return to? You've been treating us like kids for over a year, making decisions for us, hiding things—"

"Because I had to!" Ben's voice rose, finally breaking under the pressure. "Do you think I wanted this? To be stuck here? To watch everything we knew disappear? I'm trying to protect you both, whether you realize it or not."

The weight of the truth pressed down on all of them. The future they had once known was gone, and now they were left with nothing but the uncertain reality of the 1970s.

Oliver's sadness and anger had reached their peak. He stormed over to Ben, who was sitting on the sofa, grabbed him by the collar, and shouted, "This is all your fault! Your fault!"

His small fists pounded against Ben's chest in frustration. Though Oliver was still just a kid, his punches weren't physically painful—but the weight of his emotions was undeniable. Ben remained still, taking the blows without resistance.

Ethan, standing nearby, could tell this wasn't right. He stepped in, gently pulling Oliver back. "Oliver, stop! Please, don't do this!"

But Oliver shoved Ethan away, his voice breaking with rage. "Stay out of it! I should never have joined this team, this project—any of it!"

Ben, though deeply sad, was also stunned. He had expected Ethan to be the one to fall apart after hearing the truth, not Oliver.

Consumed by his anger and a profound sense of betrayal, Oliver grabbed a wooden stool and hurled it at the TV. The screen shattered with a loud crack. That was the breaking point. Ben finally stood up and wrapped his arms around Oliver to restrain him.

"Ollie. Ollie, stop!" Ben pleaded, his voice trembling.

Oliver let out a guttural cry and collapsed to the floor, sobbing uncontrollably. Ben knelt beside him, still holding him tightly, a few tears slipping down his own cheeks.

"I know," Ben whispered, his voice soft but steady. "I know, Ollie. It's hard—but we're okay. We're here, and we've got each other."

Ethan sank to the floor beside them, joining the embrace. Together, they held Oliver, a fragile unity formed amidst the chaos.

Chapter 47: Puppies

The next morning, as the sunlight streamed into the kitchen, Ben called Oliver and Ethan to sit with him at the table. His expression was more serious than usual, but there was a hint of something softer too, a change from the tension that had filled the house the night before.

"I was wrong," Ben began, taking a deep breath. "I shouldn't have kept you guys in the dark about everything. I thought I was protecting you, but I realize now that it wasn't the right way to handle things." He paused, meeting both their eyes. "I think we need a break. Let's stop school and work for a couple of days, just us. The three of us can go somewhere... out of Maine. How about Boston? We could hit the beach, get away from all this for a while."

Oliver looked up, his face still tired from the emotional strain of the last few days. "You're serious?" he asked cautiously. "You won't make me and Ethan go back to middle school?"

Ben smiled faintly. "We'll take a break from school for a few days, Oliver. I don't know about forever, but we need this time away. 20th century or 24th century, time doesn't stop. So let's step away for a little bit."

Ethan, sitting beside Oliver, nodded in agreement. "Good idea, Ben. I think we all need this."

There was a sense of relief that filled the room as they all sat there, the weight of their situation momentarily lifted. For the first time in a while, the tension between them seemed to ease, replaced by a quiet anticipation of something different.

By mid-morning, they packed up their things—nothing too extravagant, just the essentials—and headed out in Ben's car. It was a road trip, a small retreat from everything, as they drove south toward Boston. As the Maine landscape slowly turned to the long highways of Boston, there was a quiet excitement. They weren't running from their problems, but for now, they were stepping away, seeking a change of scene and a moment to breathe.

The open road stretched ahead of them, and for the first time in a while, they weren't worried about the past, the future, or even the 24th century. Just the present, just the road, and the idea of the beach waiting for them.

When they arrived at Nantasket Beach, near Boston, the salty breeze seemed to carry away the stress that had been clinging to them for so long. The waves rolled gently onto the shore, their rhythmic sound offering a temporary escape from the stress and conflicts they'd left behind. It was peaceful, almost surreal to have a moment like this after everything they had been through.

Ben had arranged for them to stay in a small, cozy hotel just a few minutes' walk from the beach. It was nothing luxurious, but it was clean, simple, and had a beautiful view of the ocean. As they settled in, the room was filled with the soft sound of the waves and the scent of the sea, and for a little while, everything felt lighter.

Ben, who had been genuine in his apology and efforts to reconnect, still couldn't help but calculate his moves. He knew how to manage people, especially in situations where control was essential. With Ethan and Oliver physically trapped in the forms of children, they were more dependent on him than they realized. They needed him not just for practical things like food and shelter, but emotionally too. He understood that, and while his care for them was real, Ben also knew he could guide their actions if he played things right.

As they all unpacked, Ben made sure to keep things relaxed, giving them the sense of freedom they had been craving.

"Why don't you two head down to the beach while I settle things here?" Ben suggested, handing them the keys to the room. "Just don't wander off too far. We'll grab some food after."

Ethan looked at Oliver, and for the first time in a while, they both smiled. "Let's go," Ethan said, already running toward the door. Oliver followed, glancing back at Ben for a second, uncertain if this newfound relaxation was permanent.

Ben waved them off. "Have fun," he called after them.

As the boys disappeared down the hall, Ben leaned back against the wall, exhaling. This was how things needed to be, he thought. A balance. He had given them some space, some breathing room, but in the end, they would still rely on him. The beach, the getaway—this was as much for them as it was a chance to reestablish his authority in a different way. One where they trusted him again, even if they didn't fully realize the extent of that reliance.

Meanwhile, on the beach, Ethan and Oliver kicked off their shoes and ran into the water. The cool waves lapped at their legs as they splashed around, laughing for the first time in what felt like ages. For now, there was no talk of the 24th century, of school, or of Ben's authority. Just the beach, the sun, and the moment of calm they both needed.

Later that day, Ben watched Ethan and Oliver play with the golden retriever puppies in the hotel yard, a subtle smile forming on his lips. The boys were absorbed in the moment, giggling and crouching to let the little furballs lick their hands. During that time, it felt like the weight of their complicated reality had lifted—like they were truly just two kids enjoying life.

"Ben, look at this one!" Oliver called out, holding up a small male puppy, its soft golden fur gleaming in the afternoon light. "Can we keep him, please?"

Ethan, crouched beside another puppy, chimed in, his face lit up with the same pleading look. "Yeah, Ben, c'mon, he could be our dog. You said this was supposed to be a break from everything, right?"

Ben crossed his arms, pretending to deliberate. "No," he said firmly, though his eyes betrayed the softness he felt seeing them so happy. "You know we can't just take a dog. It's a lot of responsibility, and what happens when we have to go back to our real lives?"

Oliver's face fell, but Ethan persisted, giving Ben that classic, wide-eyed look. "Please, Ben. He'd be our buddy, and we'll take care of him, promise!"

Ben sighed, putting on a show of reluctance. Inside, he knew that allowing them to have the puppy was exactly what he wanted. It would give them something to anchor them here, in the 1970s, something to care about. A puppy was a simple joy, but it was also a subtle way to bind them closer to their current lives. He'd been regaining control over them, carefully balancing his authority with moments like this, and he knew that allowing the puppy was another way to deepen that trust.

"Fine," Ben said, pretending to be exasperated. "But only one. And you two are fully responsible for him. Feeding, walking, everything. I won't lift a finger."

Both boys lit up, their moods instantly lifting as they hugged the puppy and each other. "Thank you, Ben!" Ethan shouted, running over to give him an enthusiastic, albeit clumsy, hug. Oliver followed suit, more reserved but equally thrilled.

Ben allowed himself to smile, ruffling Oliver's hair. "You're welcome, but remember—this is your responsibility."

They named the puppy Max, and as the trip continued, it was clear how attached the boys had already become. Oliver, who had been the most defiant and rebellious lately, seemed to soften in the presence of Max. Ethan, too, found joy in the small moments of training and playing with the dog. Ben watched it all with a quiet satisfaction.

His plan was working. The trip had eased the tensions between them, and now, with the addition of Max, Ethan and Oliver had something anchoring them even more to their new life. They weren't as focused on the past or their true identities anymore. They were adjusting, growing more comfortable.

Ben loved them both, genuinely cared for their well-being, but he knew his way of control was necessary. He had been the one keeping them safe, making the hard decisions since the beginning, and this small retreat to Boston was proof that he could regain their trust while still holding the reins.

In the coming days, as they spent time on the beach and at the hotel with Max, the conflicts that had once simmered between them seemed to dissolve. Ben gave them space, let them feel like they were gaining more autonomy, but he never fully let go of the control. It was a delicate balance, one he managed with the precision of someone who had long learned how to manipulate situations—whether it was billion-dollar oil deals or two boys who needed guidance.

As they packed up to leave the beach and head back to Maine, Max curled up in the back seat with Ethan and Oliver, the boys no longer thinking of their 24th-century lives as much. Ben looked at them through the rearview mirror and smiled. They were exactly where he needed them to be.

Chapter 48: Study

Their lives in the 1970s resumed as though the confrontation over the war had never happened. School, work, and the day-to-day routine carried on, but underneath it all, there was a quiet understanding between them. The knowledge of the war lingered in the back of their minds—a haunting reminder of what they had lost and what they might never return to. Yet, life had to continue.

Ben believed it was essential for Ethan and Oliver to stay occupied. Keeping them focused on school and other responsibilities, he reasoned, would leave them less time to dwell on things they couldn't change. He began paying closer attention to their schoolwork, determined to ensure they were making the most of their situation.

It was the end of the first-quarter grading period, and report cards had been distributed earlier that day. After dinner, while Emily was cleaning up in the kitchen, Ben turned to the boys as they lingered at the table.

"Alright," he said, setting down his glass of water. "I'm expecting to see your report cards. Let's have them."

Ethan and Oliver exchanged hesitant glances before trudging off to their room to retrieve the folded papers. When they returned, they handed the cards to Ben with considerably less enthusiasm than he might have hoped.

Ben unfolded Oliver's report card first. His brow furrowed as he scanned the grades. "C in French?" he asked, his tone incredulous. "Seriously, Ollie?"

Oliver squirmed in his chair, already fidgeting with the hem of his shirt. "Dad... it's hard," he admitted, his voice defensive. "I got all As in math and science, though."

Ben nodded, unimpressed. "I'd be more surprised if you got anything less than an A in those. But I expect you to get at least a B in French. You're a smart kid, Oliver. You can do better."

Oliver's ears turned red, but he nodded. "I'll try harder next quarter."

Satisfied for the moment, Ben turned his attention to Ethan. "Alright, let's see yours."

Ethan handed over his report card with slightly more confidence. "I didn't take French," he said quickly, anticipating the comparison. "I chose Chinese as my foreign language. Look, I got an A." He pointed to the neatly printed grade as though it would bolster his case.

Ben's eyebrows lifted in mild surprise. "Chinese? I didn't even know your school offered that."

From the kitchen, Emily chimed in as she rinsed a plate. "Well, their school is one of the best in the state, Ben. It's a public school, sure, but our neighborhood's doing quite well, so they've got the funding for programs like that."

Ben nodded thoughtfully as he set Ethan's report card down beside Oliver's. "Good job, Ethan. Keep it up."

Ethan beamed, though he refrained from making a comment that might rub salt in Oliver's wounds. Oliver, meanwhile, remained quiet, clearly mulling over how to tackle French more effectively in the coming weeks.

"Alright, boys," Ben signed the cards, folding them and placing them neatly on the table "You both have potential. Let's make sure we're living up to it. Understood?"

"Yes, Dad," they answered in unison, though their tones carried varying degrees of enthusiasm.

As they headed off to their room for the evening, Emily glanced over her shoulder from the sink. "You're a tough taskmaster, you know that?" she teased, a small smile playing on her lips.

Ben shrugged, leaning back in his chair. "Someone has to be. They're capable of so much more than just coasting through."

Emily dried her hands and crossed the room, placing a hand on his shoulder. "They'll thank you for it someday. Maybe not today, but someday."

Ben chuckled softly "I hope so," he said. "For now, I'll settle for a B in French."

Two days later, Ben walked briskly through the sterile, white corridors of the hospital, his mind racing as he rehearsed the lie he'd crafted. He knew Emily trusted him, but this was different. This wasn't just bending the truth—this was crossing a line, one that could put them both at risk. But the stakes were too high. The watch was a critical piece of technology, potentially holding the key to unraveling the mystery of the time traveler—and perhaps their way back home. Lucas had been clear: they needed a piece of DNA from the owner. And Ben wasn't about to let that opportunity slip through his fingers.

Emily met him just inside her office, her brow furrowed in confusion. "Ben, what's going on? You sounded urgent on the phone."

Ben took a deep breath, pushing aside the guilt that threatened to creep into his voice. "Emily, it's about that day when Ethan and Oliver came here. They told me they saw a man die in the ER, a guy with a distinctive tattoo. I didn't think much of it at the time, but then it hit me—I think I've seen that guy before."

Emily crossed her arms, skeptical but listening. "And?"

Ben leaned in, lowering his voice. "There was a murder in Tokyo months ago. The Australian team. It's been all over the news. I think this guy might be connected."

Emily's eyes widened. "Ben, that's serious. But… why are you telling me this now?"

"I need to see his face. Just to confirm if it's him," Ben said, his voice steady but urgent. " If he's involved in the crime in Tokyo, we can't just ignore it. You know I wouldn't ask unless it was absolutely important."

Emily hesitated, clearly torn. "Ben, you're not a staff member here. I can't just walk you into the morgue like that."

"I know, I know," Ben replied quickly. "But it could be crucial. Please, Emily. Just this once. I just need to see him."

She looked at him for a long moment, then sighed, glancing around the hallway to make sure no one was watching. "Alright," she whispered, her voice tight with anxiety. "But we have to be quick. If anyone catches us, I could lose my job."

Ben nodded, his heart pounding as she led him through a series of twisting hallways. They moved in silence, the quiet hum of hospital machinery the only sound as they made their way deeper into the building. Emily used a key to open a large steel door labeled "Morgue," and the door clicked open with a hiss of cold air.

The room was dimly lit, with rows of metal drawers lining the walls. The temperature dropped immediately, sending a chill down Ben's spine. Emily moved with practiced efficiency, pulling out a chart and scanning it.

"Here," she said softly, pulling out a drawer halfway. A body, covered in a white sheet, lay before them. Emily peeled back the cloth, revealing the face of the man Ethan and Oliver had seen.

Ben's breath caught in his throat. It was him. The tattoo. The same one the boys had seen, a bold, colorful cartoon character from a 24th-century show, now inked permanently on the arm of a corpse in the past.

"We don't have long," Emily murmured, clearly on edge.

Ben's mind raced as he took in the sight. Without hesitating, he quickly leaned down and, under the pretense of inspecting the face, plucked a single hair from the man's head. It was all he needed—one strand of DNA to unlock the secrets inside the watch.

Straightening up, Ben gave Emily a tense nod. "That's him," he said, not daring to reveal the relief in his voice.

Emily covered the body back up and slid the drawer shut, turning to Ben. "I hope this was worth it," she said, her voice barely more than a whisper.

"It will be," Ben replied, trying to sound confident. But in truth, he had no idea what they would uncover next.

They exited the morgue as quickly and quietly as they had entered, the cold air still clinging to Ben as they made their way back to the main hospital corridor. Ben could feel the weight of the small hair burning in his pocket. He had crossed a line tonight, and he knew it. But whatever secrets the watch held were too important to let slip away. He had made his choice.

Now, all that was left was to see what Lucas would uncover.

The dimly lit storage room buzzed with the quiet hum of Lucas processing the final bits of data from the watch. Ben, Oliver, and Ethan stood inside the time machine, tension in the air as they waited for Lucas to reveal what he had uncovered. The soft glow from Lucas' interface cast shadows on their faces, and the feeling of impending discovery gripped them all.

Lucas's voice broke the silence. "The watch is unlocked. The DNA matched with a man named Li Haoran, a citizen of the Great Asia Confederation. He was born in Longquan Shi city and left the 24th century in the year 2375."

Oliver and Ethan exchanged uneasy glances. This was far more than they had expected. Ben remained stoic, though internally, his mind was racing.

"Li Haoran," Ben murmured, committing the name to memory. "So, what was he doing here?"

Lucas continued, "The watch contains encrypted messages. They have been decoded. Li Haoran was sent back in time by an organization, presumably the Great Asia Confederation's intelligence network. His mission was to kill an American scientist who was a student in 1971—Alexander James."

Oliver frowned. "Alexander James... who's that?"

Lucas hesitated for a moment before revealing more. "Alexander James is the man who laid the foundation for the technology that protects cities in the North American Union—the

470

Atomic Dome. It's a defense system against Cerulean Surge thermonuclear bombs, a critical technology that prevents total destruction from future nuclear attacks."

Ethan's eyes widened. "So, this guy... this Li Haoran... was sent to kill Alexander James before he even became important? Before he developed this... Atomic Dome thing?"

"Yes," Lucas confirmed. "If Haoran succeeded in his mission, the development of the Atomic Dome would have been disrupted, leaving North America vulnerable to nuclear destruction during future wars."

Ben clenched his fists. "The war in our time... the nuclear attacks that we were trying to avoid. This is all connected. If the Atomic Dome wasn't developed, those bombs would have wiped out North America."

Oliver was starting to piece things together. "So, the Confederation wanted to change history... to stop North America from protecting itself?"

Ben nodded, his voice hard. "It seems like it. They sent Haoran here to make sure North America wouldn't have that defense, to change the outcome of the war in their favor."

Ethan asked, "But why did Haoran end up dead, then? Did someone stop him?"

Lucas paused, the faint hum of processing filling the room once more. "There are no details in the watch regarding how or why he died. It's possible his mission failed due to unforeseen circumstances, or perhaps someone else intervened. The only thing clear is that he never completed his objective."

A silence fell over the room as the gravity of the situation sank in. They were standing in the middle of a plot to alter the future, a plot that had somehow already failed.

Ben broke the quiet. "We need to find Alexander James. He's in 1971 right now, just a student, but he's crucial to everything that's going to happen."

Oliver's brow furrowed. "And what exactly do we do when we find him? Tell him about the future?"

Ben shook his head. "No. We need to make sure no one else from the future tries to stop him. If Haoran was sent back, there could be others. We can't let history be rewritten."

Ethan leaned against a shelf, the weight of the moment pressing down on him. "So... we're protecting history now? Making sure this Alexander James becomes the scientist he's meant to be?"

Ben met his eyes. "Exactly. Whether we like it or not, this is our fight now. If we don't stop anyone else from meddling with time, the future could be lost. Our future could be lost."

Oliver's voice was tinged with frustration. "We barely got here ourselves. Now we're supposed to stop some kind of international time travel conspiracy?"

Ben's face hardened. "Yes. And we'll do it because we have no other choice."

Ethan glanced at the watch, still glowing with the traces of its original owner's presence. "Do we even know where to start?"

Ben thought for a moment. "We start by finding Alexander James. And then... we make sure he stays safe. If he develops the Atomic Dome, maybe... just maybe, we can prevent the war."

The room was silent once more, but this time it was a silence filled with determination. The trio—no longer just three scientists stuck in the 1970s—had a new mission. One that could alter not only their own futures but the future of the entire world.

Chapter 49: Sheep

Emily's voice rang out through the house, warm and cheerful as always. "Guys! I'm home!"

Ben and the boys quickly left the storage room, making sure the door was securely closed behind them. Oliver was the first to reach the living room, with Ethan right behind him. The tension from moments earlier melted away, replaced with the familiar comfort Emily's presence brought.

"Emily!" Oliver called, his face lighting up with a grin. "What are you gonna cook for us today?"

Emily, still in her hospital scrubs, smiled warmly at the three of them. Her eyes softened as she saw the boys, knowing how much they looked forward to her meals. "Meatloaf," she said in a cheerful voice, setting her bag down and ruffling Oliver's hair as he stood near her.

"Yes! Max is going to love it too," Ethan chimed in, referring to the golden retriever puppy that had quickly become the trio's companion. Max was already bouncing around Emily's feet, wagging his tail in anticipation of something delicious.

Ben laughed, reaching out to take Emily's coat. "Next time it'll be my turn to cook, Emily. I've got a few tricks up my sleeve too, you know."

Emily chuckled as she unbuttoned her coat, letting Ben help her. "Oh, I'm sure you do, Mr. Oil Executive." She teased, but there was a glimmer in her eye, knowing that while Ben handled billion-dollar deals, his cooking might need some refining.

"Work been crazy today?" Ben asked, trying to keep the mood light.

"Non-stop," Emily sighed, massaging the back of her neck. "But that's what happens when you're a doctor. Patients don't schedule their emergencies." She caught Ethan and Oliver looking at her intently, their eyes gleaming with curiosity, as if they still couldn't believe their 'Dad' had managed to convince a woman like Emily to fall for him.

"Boys," Emily said with a mock-serious expression. "I hope you didn't give Ben too much trouble today while I was gone."

Oliver looked at her with a playful smirk. "Us? Trouble? Never."

Ethan added, "We're angels. Even Max will tell you."

Max barked, wagging his tail, adding to the lightheartedness of the moment. Ben smiled, watching them all interact, but a small flicker of unease stirred within him. As much as he wanted this domestic bliss, he couldn't shake the reality of what they'd learned earlier.

"Why don't we let Emily get settled while we help with dinner?" Ben suggested, gently pushing the conversation back to the present.

Ethan and Oliver nodded, quickly following her into the kitchen. For now, the secrets of time travel, nuclear wars, and conspiracies could wait. Dinner and the simple moments of family were what they needed most right now. As Ben joined them, he allowed himself a rare moment of peace, watching Emily interact with the boys. Max jumped up near the counter, and Oliver laughed, pulling him back down.

They were a strange, unconventional family, trapped in a time they didn't belong to, but in moments like these, Ben realized how much he needed them.

Three months into middle school, Oliver and Ethan had settled into their roles, blending in as much as two boys from the future could. They were smart, quick-witted, and despite their childlike bodies, they exuded a level of intellect and maturity that stood out. It was inevitable that their confidence, combined with their good looks, would draw unwanted attention.

It happened one afternoon during lunch. Oliver, Ethan and Hak-Kun were sitting at a table, chatting quietly when a group of 8th graders approached. The leader of the group, a tall, rough-looking boy named Brett, loomed over them.

"Well, well, if it isn't the new little geniuses," Brett sneered. "What are you three? Some kinda teacher's pets?"

Ethan stayed calm, his expression unreadable, while Oliver, always quick with words, shot back, "Maybe you should take notes, Brett. You might learn something."

The group of bullies laughed, but Brett's face darkened. He didn't like being talked back to, especially by a younger kid. He grabbed the apple from Oliver's tray and took a large bite.

"You got a smart mouth on you, kid. Maybe you should learn when to shut it," Brett said, his voice dripping with threat.

Ethan glanced at Oliver, giving him a subtle shake of his head. It wasn't the time to escalate things. They had been through worse than a schoolyard bully, but they couldn't afford to draw too much attention.

"Whatever you say," Ethan muttered, hoping to defuse the situation.

Brett narrowed his eyes, clearly not satisfied with Ethan's quiet surrender, but before he could push further, a teacher called from across the room, "Brett! Stop bothering them and get back to your table."

The bullies reluctantly left, but Brett shot them a look that promised this wasn't over.

As soon as they were alone again, Oliver whispered, "We're gonna have to deal with him eventually, you know."

Ethan sighed. "Yeah, but let's pick our battles. We don't need to be stirring up more trouble than we already have."

Hak-Kun nodded hesitantly. "I know a few taekwondo moves, but those 8th graders are probably twice our size."

Oliver nodded, though he felt a fire simmering beneath his calm exterior. The last thing they needed was more trouble, but he also wasn't about to back down from a fight, especially not against someone like Brett.

The school bell rang, signaling the end of the day. Ethan and Oliver packed up their things, hoping to slip out of the building without any trouble. But as they rounded the corner by the gym, there was Brett, flanked by two of his cronies, their faces smug and ready for trouble.

"Hey, geniuses," Brett called out, his voice laced with mockery. "Where do you think you're going? We have some unfinished business."

Ethan and Oliver exchanged a glance. They could tell there was no escaping this time. No teachers around, no crowd to blend into—just them and three older boys who had more muscle and less to lose.

"Look, Brett," Ethan started, trying to keep things calm, "we don't want any trouble. Just let us go home."

Brett smirked, cracking his knuckles. "Oh, there won't be any trouble. Not unless you make it."

Before either of them could react, Brett shoved Oliver hard against the wall. Ethan immediately tried to step in, but one of Brett's friends grabbed him from behind, pinning his arms.

"You're not so smart now, are you?" Brett taunted, raising his fist.

It all happened quickly—fists flew, insults were thrown. Oliver swung at Brett but missed, only to take a punch to the stomach that knocked the wind out of him. Ethan struggled against the boy holding him but was soon slammed to the ground. It wasn't long before both of them were on the ground, bruised and sore, trying to shield themselves from the kicks.

Finally, satisfied with the damage they had inflicted, Brett spat on the ground and muttered, "Let this be a lesson to you. Stay out of our way." With that, the bullies sauntered off, leaving Ethan and Oliver lying in the dirt, battered and beaten.

When they finally made it home, their bodies aching from the fight, they were met with an unexpected sight—Emily was in the kitchen, preparing dinner. She turned around as they walked in, her cheerful greeting quickly replaced with concern as she took in the sight of their bruised faces and limping forms.

"Oh my God, what happened to you two?" Emily asked, rushing over, her voice tight with worry.

Ethan tried to wave it off, not wanting to cause a fuss. "Just some older kids at school. It's not a big deal."

"Not a big deal? You're both bruised up!" Emily's voice wavered between concern and sadness. She gently touched the bruise forming on Oliver's cheek, her eyes soft with empathy. "You should have gone to the nurse."

"We didn't want to make things worse," Oliver muttered, avoiding her gaze. He felt embarrassed, ashamed that they had been so easily overpowered.

Emily frowned, clearly upset. "Where was the teacher? You shouldn't have to deal with this alone."

Just then, Ben walked in, immediately sensing the trouble. He took one look at Ethan and Oliver, his face hardening. "What the hell happened?" His voice was calm, but there was an unmistakable edge of anger.

Oliver, still shaken, spoke first. "It's Brett. That 8th grader. He and his friends... they jumped us after school."

Ben's expression darkened, but he knelt down beside them, checking their bruises. His voice was steady, but beneath it, there was fury. "Did they hurt you badly?"

"We'll be fine," Ethan said, wincing as he touched a sore spot on his arm. "Nothing broken, just some bruises."

Emily looked at Ben, worried. "What are you going to do?"

Ben stood up, pacing the room. "I'll deal with it. But first, I'll get some ice packs for them."

As Ben headed toward the kitchen, Oliver called after him, "What do you mean by 'deal with it'? You'll just make it worse, Dad!"

Ben stopped and turned, his gaze sharp. "Trust me, son. I'll make sure this so-called 'best-in-the-state' school understands that bullying is absolutely unacceptable."

Ethan, sensing the tension, added, "We can handle it. We'll figure out how to avoid them."

But Ben shook his head. "You shouldn't have to avoid anyone. You're both smart, strong, and capable. I don't want you to feel scared to go to school."

Emily touched Ben's arm gently. "Let's just focus on getting them better first. We'll figure out what to do about the bullies tomorrow."

Later, as they sat with ice packs on their bruises, Oliver sighed. "We're not meant for this," he said quietly to Ethan. "We're supposed to be scientists. Not kids getting beat up in middle school."

Ethan nodded, his eyes filled with frustration. "I know. But for now, we are kids. And we have to survive this, too."

Ben, standing nearby, overheard them and clenched his fists. He knew they were right—this life wasn't what they were meant for. But as long as they were stuck in the 1970s, he had to protect them, even if it meant playing the role of a father more fiercely than ever before.

Emily brought them dinner, trying to lighten the mood. "Meatloaf's ready. I made extra for Max, too."

The golden retriever puppy padded over, his tail wagging, blissfully unaware of the tension in the room. For a moment, everything softened. Even Oliver smiled faintly as Max jumped into his lap.

Ben sighed, already devising how to address the situation with the school. His thoughts churned with regret: *"Rezulix... that cheap, damn dose. What was I thinking? Letting 20-year-old lads take Rezulix—a drug meant for elderly patients. God damn me for agreeing to that stupid idea of theirs."*

The morning after the fight, Ben walked into the school with a determined stride, one hand on Ethan's shoulder, the other on Oliver's. Both boys, still nursing their bruises, could feel the tension radiating from him. His usually composed expression was tight with anger, his jaw clenched as they made their way down the school hallway toward the principal's office.

When they arrived, Mrs. Davis, the principal, greeted them with a polite but slightly wary smile. She was used to dealing with concerned parents, but Ben's presence carried a different weight. He didn't seem like the usual father bothered by a playground scuffle— there was something in his eyes, something fierce and unyielding.

"Mr. Johnson," Mrs. Davis began, gesturing for them to sit. "I understand you're upset, but—"

Ben cut her off before she could finish. "Upset? Mrs. Davis, this is beyond upset. My boys came home bruised and battered, and I demand to know what's being done about it."

Mrs. Davis raised her hands in a calming gesture. "Boys will be boys, Mr. Johnson. This happens all the time—kids sometimes rough each other up, but it's rarely anything serious."

Ben's eyes narrowed. "You think this isn't serious? I don't care if it 'happens all the time.' That's precisely the problem. If you're telling me that bullying is normal here, then you've got a bigger issue on your hands than just Brett and his friends. My sons were ambushed and beaten by three older students, and I expect consequences."

Ethan and Oliver exchanged a glance. They appreciated Ben standing up for them, but as they listened to him, they couldn't help but feel that he was pushing things a bit too far. They'd been in fights before—nothing life-threatening. But Ben's tone was relentless, like a bulldozer plowing through every word Mrs. Davis tried to say.

Mrs. Davis sighed, clearly trying to keep the situation from escalating. "Mr. Johnson, I understand you're protective of your sons, and we will, of course, investigate. But—"

"No 'buts,'" Ben interrupted, his voice rising. "If I don't see those boys expelled, I'll make sure the entire state knows how this school tolerates bullying. Every newspaper will run stories on how your administration does nothing to protect students from violent attacks. I guarantee you, I know how to get people to listen."

Mrs. Davis blinked, taken aback by the intensity of his threat. She straightened in her chair, now visibly uncomfortable. "Mr. Johnson, let's not be hasty. Expulsion is a serious step, and we follow a specific protocol for incidents like these. We can't expel students based on a single altercation without a thorough review. The boys involved will be disciplined, but—"

Ben's voice was cold. "Disciplined? That's not enough. My sons don't feel safe here. They were attacked, and you're telling me you'll just give their attackers a slap on the wrist?"

Oliver and Ethan sat quietly, watching the exchange unfold. They felt a strange mix of emotions—grateful that Ben cared so much, yet uneasy with how far he was taking it. Oliver, especially, was beginning to feel a pang of guilt. It was hard enough dealing with the 8th graders, but now they were worried that their situation would blow up in a way that might make them even bigger targets.

"Dad, maybe we should..." Oliver started softly, but Ben gave him a look that silenced him.

Mrs. Davis, sensing the rising tension, leaned forward slightly, her tone firm but measured. "Mr. Johnson, I understand your concerns, but you must trust that we will handle this appropriately. Threatening the school isn't going to make this process any faster or more effective. I will personally speak to the students involved and their parents. We will follow up with disciplinary action, but I cannot promise expulsion without further investigation."

Ben held her gaze, his expression unyielding. "I'm holding you to that, Mrs. Davis. If anything like this happens again, there will be consequences. And I'll be watching."

Mrs. Davis nodded, clearly eager to end the conversation. "I assure you, Mr. Johnson, we take all incidents seriously. You'll receive a report by the end of the week."

Ben stood, his towering frame making Mrs. Davis seem even smaller behind her desk. He gave her a curt nod, then turned to Ethan and Oliver. "Let's go."

The boys followed him out of the office, the atmosphere tense but quiet as they walked down the hallway. As they stepped outside into the sunlight, Oliver finally spoke.

"Ben, that was... intense," he said cautiously, glancing up at him.

"Yeah," Ethan agreed, rubbing the back of his neck. "You didn't have to go that far."

Ben stopped and looked down at them, his expression softening slightly. "I did what I had to do. No one is going to mess with you two again, not while I'm around."

Oliver shifted uncomfortably, unsure if he should feel relieved or more nervous. "But now Brett and those guys are really going to hate us," he mumbled.

Ben crouched down to their level, his face serious but warm. "Listen, you two are smart, and you're tough. You shouldn't have to deal with bullies, but if anyone comes after you again, they'll have to answer to me. And trust me, they won't want that."

Ethan nodded, though his eyes betrayed a flicker of uncertainty. "Thanks, Ben... but maybe next time, we don't need to go nuclear on the principal?"

Ben chuckled, ruffling Ethan's hair. "Don't worry. I know how to handle these things. You're safe, and that's all that matters."

As they walked to their classroom, the boys couldn't shake the feeling that the situation had been blown out of proportion. Yet, despite everything, there was a strange comfort in knowing that Ben—not just their manager but now their 'dad'—had their backs.

Chapter 50: In Safe Hands

The following day, as school was letting out, Officer Thomas pulled up to the front in his police cruiser. His presence commanded attention, and the usual schoolyard bustle slowed to curious whispers and sideways glances. The sight of a police officer stepping out of his car caught the eye of nearly every student nearby. But for Ethan and Oliver, it brought a sense of relief and excitement.

"Look who's here!" Ethan whispered to Oliver, his eyes lighting up.

Oliver, who still felt some lingering unease from the fight, smiled. "I didn't know he was coming," he said quietly, grateful for the surprise.

Officer Thomas was a tall, imposing figure, but his warm smile and relaxed demeanor made him approachable. As Emily's older brother, he had always kept an eye on the boys and treated them like family. Now, his presence felt like an extra layer of protection after everything that had happened with the bullies.

"Hey, guys," Officer Thomas called, waving them over.

Ethan and Oliver eagerly approached, their earlier bruises now barely visible but still a reminder of the fight. They stood a little taller as they reached the cruiser, the attention from their classmates making them feel like they had their own bodyguard.

"Everything alright?" Officer Thomas asked, his gaze flicking from one boy to the other, subtly checking for any new signs of trouble.

"Yeah," Ethan replied with a grin. "Better now that you're here."

Oliver nodded in agreement. "Definitely better."

The boys couldn't help but feel a sense of pride with Officer Thomas standing beside them. His police badge gleamed in the afternoon sun, and they knew the sight of him would be enough to make the bullies think twice before messing with them again.

As they chatted, the sound of shuffling footsteps interrupted them. One of the boys from Brett's gang, Alex, cautiously approached, his hands shoved into his pockets and his face tinged with embarrassment. He stopped a few feet away, glancing nervously between the boys and Officer Thomas. His shoulders were slouched, and he looked like he was struggling to find the right words.

"Hey," Alex mumbled, eyes flicking up toward Oliver and Ethan. "I, uh… I wanted to apologize for what happened."

Ethan's eyebrows shot up in surprise, and Oliver crossed his arms, unsure if Alex was serious or if this was just another attempt to mess with them.

Alex shifted uncomfortably under their scrutiny. "I mean it," he added quickly. "Brett... he wanted to start that fight, not me. I didn't want to, but... I just got dragged into it."

Officer Thomas watched the exchange silently, his presence making Alex even more nervous.

"I'm really sorry," Alex continued, sounding more sincere. "I don't want any more trouble with you guys. Brett's been a jerk to everyone, not just you."

Ethan glanced at Oliver, who seemed torn. On one hand, it felt good to have one of the bullies finally back down. On the other, the memory of being outnumbered and beaten was still fresh. But Alex's apology sounded genuine enough.

Oliver narrowed his eyes at Alex. "Are you serious? Or is this just because Officer Thomas is standing right here?"

Alex shook his head quickly. "No, man, I swear. I've had enough of Brett, too. He's just been dragging us all into his mess. I didn't want to do it."

Ethan gave a slight nod, sensing that Alex was telling the truth. "Alright, Alex. Apology accepted. But if Brett tries anything again—"

"He won't," Alex interrupted, his voice firm. "I'll make sure of it."

Officer Thomas, who had been watching quietly, finally spoke. "Sounds like you're making the right call, Alex. It's never too late to do the right thing."

Alex nodded sheepishly, relief washing over his face. "Thanks," he muttered before walking off, clearly eager to distance himself from the situation.

As he disappeared back into the crowd, Ethan turned to Officer Thomas. "Thanks for coming by today. That was... unexpected."

Officer Thomas smiled, ruffling Ethan's hair. "I'm just doing my part. Plus, I heard what happened, and I figured showing up might send a message."

Oliver relaxed a little, feeling a weight lift off his shoulders. "It definitely did," he said with a small grin. "Thanks, Vincent!"

"Anytime, guys," Officer Thomas replied warmly. "And if anyone gives you trouble, you know who to call."

As they watched Officer Thomas drive off, Ethan and Oliver stood a little taller, feeling more confident than they had in days. With Alex's apology and Officer Thomas on their side, it seemed like the tide was finally turning in their favor.

Ethan and Oliver relaxed in the warm water of the bathtub, their muscles finally loosening after the long and exhausting day. The soft steam rose around them, creating a comforting, hazy atmosphere. Max, their golden retriever puppy, was nosing around the pile of discarded clothes next to the tub, occasionally giving a little sniff or nudge with his wet nose, curious as always.

Outside the bathroom door, Emily's cheerful voice called, "Hey, boys! Can I come in?"

Ethan and Oliver looked at each other, eyes wide, before they both shouted back in unison, "Nooo!"

Emily chuckled to herself, her motherly instincts kicking in. "Alright, alright. I put your clothes by the door, okay?" she said with a grin, clearly enjoying their mock horror at the thought of her barging in.

Inside the bathroom, Ethan smirked and splashed some water playfully at Oliver, the warmth of the tub making them both feel invincible after the day's events. "Haha, we're untouchable now! The entire school knows no one can mess with us," he said triumphantly, a proud grin stretching across his face.

Oliver, resting his head against the side of the tub, nodded but was more thoughtful. "Yeah, I think Alex freaked out after what Ben did at the principal's office. And then Vincent showing up in his police car? That probably sealed the deal. He's scared stiff."

Ethan laughed, "Could you imagine if that kid Alex turned out to be Alexander James? You know, the same guy who's supposed to build the Atomic Dome in the future? That would be hilarious!"

Oliver's eyes widened slightly at the mention. He glanced over at Ethan, splashing water absentmindedly. "Well... could be, you know," Oliver said, more seriously than Ethan had expected.

Ethan's smile faded a bit as he considered it. "Wait, really? You think so?"

"I mean, why not? The name matches," Oliver said with a slight shrug, his thoughtful side kicking in. "We know that the timeline has all kinds of weird overlaps. There could be versions of people living here in the 1970s who are crucial to the future. If Alex really is Alexander James, then... everything makes a lot more sense."

The water sloshed gently as Ethan sat up straighter. The idea that Alex, the timid, apologetic 8th grader who had been caught up in Brett's bullying, could be the same person who would later lay the foundation for the technology that protected cities in the future—it felt almost surreal.

"But..." Ethan hesitated, "if Alex is Alexander James, doesn't that mean he's supposed to be the target of that time traveler we found out about? The guy in the morgue, Li Haoran?"

Oliver nodded slowly. "Yeah... that's the scary part. If Alex— well, Alexander—is supposed to survive and build the Atomic Dome, we might have already changed things just by being here."

Ethan frowned, the weight of their situation pressing down on him again. "But that means we have to protect him, right? If he doesn't survive, then the future's screwed."

Max, completely unaware of the heavy conversation happening in the bathtub, wagged his tail and tried to paw at the door. Ethan glanced down at the puppy, then looked back at Oliver, a smirk forming again on his face despite the seriousness of the topic. "So... we're his bodyguards now? Protecting the future genius from getting shoved into lockers or beaten up by Brett and his gang?"

Oliver grinned, the absurdity of it hitting him as well. "Yeah, I guess we are," he said, laughing softly. "But we can't let him know what we know. We'll just have to keep an eye on him, make sure nothing happens."

Ethan nodded in agreement, then leaned back again, sinking into the warm water. "Well, that's one way to keep middle school interesting. Who knew saving the future would involve fighting off bullies?"

Oliver chuckled, the tension between them finally easing. "It's kind of ridiculous, isn't it?"

The two brothers soaked in the tub a little longer, their laughter mixing with the bubbling sound of the water as they pondered the strange twists of their lives.

Outside, Emily listened at the door, smiling as she heard the boys laughing and talking, unaware of just how much responsibility the two carried.

In the dim light of their shared room, Ethan lay on his bed, idly petting Max, who was curled up beside him. The soft rise and fall of Max's breathing was calming, a small piece of comfort in the midst of the chaos that their lives had become. Across from him, Oliver sat on his own bed, knees drawn to his chest, staring off into the distance as if lost in thought.

Ethan broke the silence first. "You know, sometimes I think everything happened for a reason."

Oliver glanced over at him, curious. "What do you mean?"

"I mean…" Ethan shifted slightly, his hand moving in rhythm with Max's breathing. "The time machine, Rezulix... all of it. We're trapped here in 1971 as 11-year-old boys, living a life we never could've imagined. And then there's Emily, Vincent, Taylor, Sebastian. All these people we weren't supposed to meet, but now we're connected to them."

Oliver nodded, picking up on the thread of thought. "And middle school, the bullies, the nuclear war in our time..."

"Right," Ethan said, his voice quieter. "It's like the universe wanted us here for something. Like it was all part of some plan. I mean, we've been through so much in the last year and a half. Sometimes I wonder if we're meant to stay here. Maybe we shouldn't even try to go back."

Oliver's brow furrowed, his gaze drifting toward the window, where the shadows of trees swayed gently in the night breeze. "You really think we should stay?" he asked quietly.

"I don't know," Ethan admitted, sighing. "But it feels like we've built something here. Max, Ben, Emily... It's starting to feel like home. And maybe we could just live this life—forget about the 24th century. What if this is where we're supposed to be?"

Oliver shook his head, conflicted. "I don't know anymore, Ethan. You might be right, but... how can we just forget everything? Our families are still there, in the 24th century. If there's even a chance that we can stop the nuclear war, we have to try. We can't just leave them behind."

Ethan looked up at the ceiling, lost in his own thoughts. "Yeah... our families. But what if it's too late? What if the future's already gone, and there's nothing we can do?"

"That's why we have to keep going," Oliver said, his voice firmer now. "We don't know for sure. Lucas is still working, and there's still hope. Maybe we can't stop the war entirely, but maybe we can save some part of our world—some part of our families."

The room fell silent again, save for the faint rustling of Max shifting in his sleep. Ethan kept petting the dog absentmindedly, his mind spinning with the weight of Oliver's words.

"I just wish we knew for sure," Ethan said finally, his voice barely above a whisper. "What if we're stuck here forever?"

Oliver sighed, leaning back against the headboard. "Then we figure it out, like we always do. We've survived this long, haven't we? We'll find a way to make things right—whether that's here in 1971 or back in the 24th century."

Ethan nodded slowly, feeling a bit of the weight lift. He knew Oliver was right. They had been through so much already, and even though the future felt uncertain, they had each other. And that, for now, was enough.

Max snored softly, his presence a quiet reminder of the strange and unexpected connections they had formed in this time— connections that, for better or worse, had become their new reality.

"Yeah," Ethan said softly, "we'll figure it out."

In his room, Ben lay on his back, staring at the ceiling, his arm wrapped loosely around Emily as she rested her head on his chest. The room was quiet, the faint sounds of the night filtering in through the window. He felt the steady rhythm of Emily's breathing, but his mind was far from at ease. Everything that had happened—the discoveries, the secrets, the lies—felt like they were pressing down on him, even in this peaceful moment.

"It feels unreal sometimes," Ben said quietly, breaking the silence. "I came to this town with the boys, and everything's just… changed so much. We met Vincent first, then you, and Taylor. It's like all of it was meant to happen, you know?"

Emily shifted slightly, lifting her head to look at him. "Meant to happen? That sounds a little deep for you, Ben," she teased softly, smiling.

Ben chuckled lightly, running his hand through her hair. "Yeah, maybe. But I've been thinking a lot lately. It's like we were supposed to find each other… in this place, this time."

Emily's smile softened, and she snuggled closer to him. "I like the sound of that. But why are you thinking so much about it now? Something bothering you?"

Ben hesitated, knowing he had to tread carefully. "It's just… the boys. Sometimes I feel like I've dragged them into something bigger than they realize. We've had to adjust to so much. New school, new life, everything. It's hard not to feel a little guilty, you know?"

Emily sighed, tracing small circles on his chest with her finger. "You've done a great job with them, Ben. Ethan and Oliver are smart, they're resilient. Whatever changes you've gone through, they're adjusting just as well. And you're doing your best to protect them. I see it every day."

Ben's heart tightened at her words. The truth was, he had no idea how to truly protect them—not from the dangers that lurked in their world. But Emily didn't know that. She couldn't know.

"Thanks," he said softly. "I just… I want to make sure they're okay. Especially after everything that's happened at school with those bullies. It's hard sometimes, being in this situation."

Emily nodded. "I know. But you're not alone in this, Ben. You've got me, Vincent, and even Taylor in your corner. We're all here to help. You don't have to carry it all on your shoulders."

Ben smiled, though there was a sadness behind it. "Yeah, I know. It's just... I'm used to having to handle things myself. It's hard to let that go."

Emily laughed softly, a light sound in the dark room. "You're stubborn, that's for sure. But you're also strong. You've been through a lot, I can tell. And whatever it is that you and the boys are dealing with, you're going to come out the other side just fine. You always do."

Ben swallowed, pushing down the lump of guilt in his throat. She had no idea how right and wrong she was at the same time. He had been through a lot, more than she could ever imagine, but the reality of it was something he could never share.

"I hope so," he said finally, his voice quiet.

Emily kissed his chest softly and rested her head back against him. "Just remember, you don't have to do it all alone."

Ben closed his eyes, his mind racing even as his body relaxed against the bed. He had to keep up the charade, for her sake and for theirs. But deep down, he couldn't shake the feeling that their time here was running out, and soon, everything would change.

For now, though, he held onto this moment—this quiet, fleeting moment where everything felt almost normal.

"I'll remember," he whispered, though a part of him knew that was a promise he might not be able to keep.

Chapter 51: Pants and Puzzles

The next day, Ethan and Oliver walked through the quiet streets after school, their backpacks bouncing lightly as they exchanged glances. They had one mission today—find Alex, the boy from Brett's gang, and get to the bottom of something that had been nagging them since the bathtub conversation the night before.

"Do you think he could really be him?" Ethan asked, kicking a small rock along the sidewalk.

"I don't know," Oliver replied, his face serious. "But we have to be sure. If Alex is actually Alexander James... and if he's the one that guy from the future was sent to kill, then we have to figure it out before it's too late."

They spotted Alex walking ahead, his hands shoved in his pockets, his pace slow as if he were lost in thought. He had apologized to them the day before, but the boys weren't satisfied yet. There was more to this kid than they had first thought.

"Hey, Alex!" Ethan called, jogging up to him. Oliver followed close behind.

Alex turned around, his eyes widening for a second as if he wasn't sure what to expect. "Oh... hey guys," he said cautiously, stopping in his tracks. "Uh, what's up?"

Ethan wasted no time. "We were wondering... what's your last name?"

Alex blinked, clearly caught off guard by the question. "My last name?"

"Yeah," Oliver said, stepping forward. "You know, just curious."

Alex shifted uncomfortably, his eyes darting between the two of them. "Why do you want to know that?"

Ethan smiled, trying to keep things casual. "We're just curious, that's all. We were talking about names earlier and realized we didn't know yours."

Alex hesitated for a moment, his brows furrowing as if he didn't entirely trust them. Finally, he let out a breath and said, "Polonsky. My last name is Polonsky."

Both Ethan and Oliver exchanged a quick glance, relief washing over them—but also confusion. Polonsky? That wasn't the name they were expecting. Not Alexander James.

"You sure about that?" Ethan asked, half-joking, but with a nervous edge. "Not... James, maybe?"

Alex raised an eyebrow, looking even more wary now. "Yeah, I'm pretty sure I know my own last name. Why do you guys care so much anyway?"

Oliver quickly jumped in to cover. "No reason. We just... thought we knew someone with that name before. Alexander James. Doesn't that sound like a cool name?"

Alex shrugged, now clearly growing impatient. "I guess? But it's not mine. Look, if this is about what happened with Brett, I told you, I didn't want to be part of that. I was just going along with him."

Ethan waved his hands. "No, no, we're not worried about that. We believe you. We're just trying to figure something out."

Alex looked between the two of them, then shook his head with a sigh. "Okay, well... if that's all, I'm heading home. See you guys tomorrow."

With that, Alex turned and started walking away again, leaving Ethan and Oliver standing on the sidewalk.

"Polonsky," Ethan muttered under his breath. "Well, that's not what I was expecting."

Oliver frowned, watching Alex disappear around the corner. "Me neither. But at least now we know. He's not the Alexander James we're looking for."

Ethan sighed, rubbing the back of his neck. "Yeah... but something still feels off. I mean, what if we're missing something?"

Oliver crossed his arms, thinking hard. "We might be. But I don't think Alex is the key to it anymore. Still, we should keep an eye on him, just in case."

"Agreed," Ethan nodded, though his mind was already racing toward the next clue. "Let's just hope we find the guy before things get too crazy."

The two boys turned and began walking back home, their suspicions about Alex fading slightly, but their curiosity about the mystery of Alexander James and the potential threats from the future growing stronger by the day.

A few days later, Emily took Ethan and Oliver to the local mall for a day of shopping. The boys had grown a bit, and Emily decided they needed some new clothes. The afternoon started light-hearted and fun. The mall was bustling with life—people wandering in and out of stores, children excitedly pulling their parents toward toy displays, and the familiar scent of cinnamon rolls wafting from the food court.

Ethan and Oliver had even enjoyed themselves at first, browsing through racks of clothes, picking out a few shirts and jeans that suited their tastes. They were gradually adjusting to being kids again. Well, except for the schoolwork, the bullies, and, of course, getting tanned by "Dad." Still, being 11 years old wasn't all bad. At least they didn't have to work or worry about bills—"parents" took care of everything.

Eventually, Emily directed them toward the fitting rooms, her arms full of clothes. "Alright, boys, try these pants on, see how they fit!" she said cheerfully, guiding them into a fitting room together.

Inside, the fitting room was a tight space, with a single mirror and a bench crammed into the corner. The boys had slipped out of their jeans, only to be struck by a mortifying realization: neither of them was wearing boxers.

The memory of that morning came rushing back. Ethan had shouted from their room, "Ben, where are our boxers?"

Ben had strolled in, looking slightly frazzled. "Oh, I forgot to do your laundry this week. I'll throw it in today."

Ethan had glared at him, incredulous. "So Ollie and I are just supposed to walk around boxer-less all day? What kind of dad are you, Ben?"

Without missing a beat, Ben had grabbed Ethan's left ear—not too hard, but enough to make his point. "Hey, you ungrateful brat. How about you two start putting your own laundry in the machine from now on?"

Now, back in the fitting room, Ethan sighed, muttering under his breath, "What kind of dad forgets the laundry and blames the kids?" Oliver just shrugged, trying not to laugh at the absurdity of it all.

"Uh, I think these pants fit fine," Ethan called out, trying to keep the door closed while they fumbled around with the clothes.

"Yeah, we'll be out in a minute!" Oliver added quickly, hoping to stall Emily.

But Emily was already on her way. "I'll help you," she said, pushing the door open before they could react.

"Emily, wait!" Ethan stammered, grabbing his shirt to cover himself, while Oliver tried to do the same with a pair of pants.

But Emily, in full mother-mode, barely noticed their panic. To her, they were just boys—little boys who needed help. Her motherly instincts had been in overdrive lately, probably sparked by the time they had spent together and the recent incidents at school. Without thinking twice, she kneeled down and began helping them pull the pants up, like they were five-year-olds struggling with their clothes.

"There we go, Ethan, that's better," she said, her tone gentle, oblivious to the boys' frantic attempts to cover themselves.

"Emily—uh, we can do it ourselves," Oliver said, his face flushed red as he tried to keep the shirt over his exposed body.

"Yeah, we've got it, really!" Ethan echoed, squirming to pull the pants up without revealing more than he already had.

Emily smiled warmly, her hands adjusting the waistband on Ethan's jeans as if this were the most natural thing in the world. "Nonsense, it's no trouble. You two are growing boys, and sometimes you just need a little help, that's all."

Ethan and Oliver, mortified and overwhelmed, could only nod in defeat. They exchanged helpless glances, their faces burning with embarrassment. As much as they wanted to push her out of the fitting room, their usual sharp wit and quick thinking had vanished in the face of this unexpected situation.

After what felt like an eternity, Emily stood up, brushing her hands together. "There we go. That wasn't so hard, was it?" she said, smiling at them both.

The boys could only mumble something incoherent as they quickly turned around to finish dressing.

"Alright, I'll step outside and grab some shirts for you to try on," Emily said cheerfully, walking out and leaving the door ajar behind her.

As soon as she was gone, both Ethan and Oliver let out a synchronized sigh of relief.

Ethan shook his head, his voice barely above a whisper. "I can't believe that just happened..."

Oliver, his face still flushed, managed a faint chuckle. "Seriously. For a second, I thought she was about to help us change back or something."

They finished dressing in silence, the earlier awkwardness hanging in the cramped fitting room. Emily's motherly instincts had completely thrown them off guard. While they appreciated her care, neither of them liked the idea of being treated as her boys.

Ethan glanced at his reflection in the mirror. After a year and a half, they had grown a bit, but the changes were subtle—just enough to remind him how far they still were from their adult selves.

As they stepped out of the fitting room, Ethan leaned toward Oliver and muttered under his breath, "Next time, we're wearing boxers—even if they're not clean."

Oliver nodded in agreement, still blushing. "Definitely."

As Ethan and Oliver stepped out of the fitting room, still recovering from their own awkward ordeal, they suddenly froze. From the neighboring fitting rooms, they heard a familiar voice—Alex.

It was unmistakable. His slightly nervous tone echoed through the area, followed by a woman's voice, presumably his mother. She sounded firm but gentle, calling him by a name that caught Ethan and Oliver's attention immediately.

"Jamie, stop fidgeting, please! Just let me help you with the shirt," the woman's voice said.

Ethan raised an eyebrow at Oliver, nudging him slightly. "Did she just call him… Jamie?" he whispered.

Oliver's eyes widened. "Yeah, she did."

They exchanged a look, the weight of what they'd just heard sinking in. Alex, who had introduced himself as one of the bullies' sidekicks just days ago, wasn't just Alex Polonsky after all. The name 'Jamie' triggered a wave of suspicion in their minds, especially considering the crucial discovery they had made about Alexander James being the key to a future technology that would save North America from nuclear disaster.

Ethan leaned in closer to Oliver, his voice barely above a whisper. "I think we've found him, Oliver. He's definitely the Alexander James we're looking for."

Oliver nodded slowly, piecing it all together. "Jamie… Alex… Alexander James. It fits. I guess he goes by both names."

They stood silently for a moment, processing the discovery. Alex—or Jamie—was just a 13-year-old boy now, caught in the same web of life in 1971, unaware of the future impact he would have. But the boys now had to figure out what to do with this information. If Alex, or Jamie, was indeed the person the mysterious Li Haoran had come back in time to kill, then it was their responsibility to protect him. The entire future of North America—and possibly the world—rested on keeping him safe.

Ethan bit his lip, glancing toward the door of the fitting room where Alex was. "Should we tell him?"

Oliver shook his head. "No, not yet. If he really is the Alexander James, we need to be careful. We can't just freak him out."

"True… but we need to keep an eye on him. If someone sent a time traveler to kill him, that means they'll try again. We can't let that happen."

Just then, Alex—or Jamie—emerged from his fitting room, his mother still adjusting his collar and fussing over his clothes. He looked slightly embarrassed, trying to pull away from her, much like how Ethan and Oliver had felt with Emily earlier.

Ethan exchanged another quick look with Oliver and whispered, "We need to keep tabs on him. Make sure nothing happens."

Oliver agreed. "Yeah, we need to protect him… even if he has no idea what's at stake."

As they both watched Alex walk away with his mother, they knew their mission in 1971 had just gotten a lot more complicated.

Ethan turned to Oliver, his voice low. "Should we tell Ben about this? That we found Alexander James?"

Oliver shook his head, frowning. "We don't even know for sure if Jamie is James... And besides, if Ben thinks there's a potential target for hitmen at our school, he'd drive us to and from school every single day. Do you really want that?"

That afternoon, Ethan and Oliver were enjoying a warm, relaxing bath when suddenly the door swung open, and Emily stepped in, holding fresh towels and clothes.

Both boys yelped in unison, their faces instantly turning crimson as they scrambled to cover themselves with whatever they could—mostly just their hands and a lot of frantic splashing.

Ethan glared at his brother, his voice half-panicked. "I told you to lock the door, Oliver!!!"

Oliver, equally flustered, shot back, "I thought I did! Emily, please leave us, please!" His voice cracked a little as he tried to maintain any semblance of dignity.

Emily, however, was completely unfazed. She stood there with an amused, motherly smile, holding out their clothes as if this were the most normal thing in the world. "I wouldn't have to walk in like this if you two didn't forget your fresh clothes," she said calmly, her eyes soft with affection.

As the boys stared at her in shock, still trying to hide under the water, she added with a gentle chuckle, "You don't have anything I haven't seen before, boys."

Ethan, mortified, turned even redder. "Yeah, but still… we're not little kids!"

Oliver, meanwhile, had his face buried in his hands, mumbling something that sounded like, "Please just leave…"

Emily smiled again, placing the clothes neatly on a chair nearby. "Alright, alright," she said soothingly. "I'm going. Just don't forget to dry off properly, okay? I'll be in the kitchen when you're ready for dinner."

As she left the room, gently closing the door behind her, the boys were left in stunned silence for a moment. The awkwardness hung in the air like a thick cloud.

Ethan broke the silence with a groan, sinking lower into the water. "Why does she always have to do that…?"

Oliver sighed, still embarrassed but trying to shake it off. "I don't know… but we seriously need to remember to lock the door from now on."

Ethan nodded in agreement, his pride stinging a little, but at least they could both laugh about it—later.

Emily had comfortably integrated herself into the trio's life over time, seamlessly slipping into a maternal role for Ethan and Oliver. Despite this growing bond, there was one area she had never ventured into—the storage room, where the time machine was kept. Ben had tactfully discouraged her from exploring that particular part of the house, explaining it was where they kept the personal belongings of the boys' "mother," a story that had been their cover since day one. Emily, ever respectful, never pushed the matter.

After their bath and the family dinner, Ethan and Oliver decided it was time to confront Ben about boundaries—specifically, the complete lack of them when it came to Emily. Between her walking in on them in the mall fitting room and the recent incident in the bathtub, they felt a serious discussion was long overdue.

Ben was in his room, poring over a thick stack of reports from Sebastian about the oil well project in the South China Sea. The man looked like a picture of focus: glasses perched on his nose, pen in hand, scribbling notes in the margins. Ethan and Oliver knocked, and without waiting for an answer, marched in with all the determination of two very short lawyers ready to present their case.

Ethan crossed his arms. "We need to talk, Ben!"

Ben didn't even glance up. His eyes stayed glued to the report. "Hm?"

Oliver stepped in, backing his brother. "It's about Emily…"

"Hm?" Ben repeated, still flipping a page, clearly not registering their mounting frustration.

This time, Ethan stomped closer and slammed his hand down on the report, blocking Ben's view. "This is serious, Ben! Emily keeps walking in on us! First at the fitting room in the mall, and now in the bathtub! BATHTUB, Ben!"

Ben finally looked up, raising an eyebrow. "So? You forgot your fresh clothes. She brought them in for you. What's the big deal?"

"The big deal," Oliver interjected, "is that we're men! And she's a woman! There's a thing called privacy, you know!"

"Men?" Ben leaned back in his chair, giving them both an exaggerated once-over. "All I see are two kids in pajamas trying to grow a mustache."

"WE ARE NOT KIDS!" Ethan shouted, his voice cracking slightly. "Emily needs to respect our men's privacy!"

Ben sighed, clearly humoring them. "Fine, fine. I'll tell her to knock or whatever. Are we done here? I've got work to do." He nudged Ethan's hip lightly with his hand, trying to get him to move aside. "Now go finish your homework."

"We don't have any homework," Oliver added, standing his ground.

"Great. Then go play outside. Climb a tree or invent something." Ben waved dismissively. "Just let me finish my—"

But Ethan wasn't having it. He slapped the report lightly, then harder for emphasis. "You're not listening! You're not going to talk to her, are you?!"

Ben's patience was thinning, and he decided to remind them who was in charge. Without even looking, his hand darted out, hooked two fingers into Ethan's pajama waistband, and yanked them down in one swift motion.

"HEY! WHAT THE—?!" Ethan yelped, scrambling to pull his pants back up with the speed of a caffeinated squirrel. "WHAT ARE YOU DOING?!"

Ben, looking entirely unbothered, smirked. "Making a point."

"MAKING A POINT?!" Ethan was practically vibrating with indignation, his cheeks as red as a fire hydrant. "You're acting like I'm five years old!

Ben leaned forward and, in a deliberately slow voice, said, "If you don't want to be treated like a kid, maybe stop acting like one. Now, unless you want your pants to hit the floor again, leave my room."

Oliver, who had wisely maintained a safe distance throughout this ordeal, raised his hands in mock surrender. "I'm out! No need to involve me."

But Ethan wasn't giving up. "This is exactly what I'm talking about, Ben! You and Emily keep embarrassing us! You—"

Ben interrupted with a dry chuckle. "Ethan, if I wanted to see anything you have going on down there, I'd need a magnifying glass. Trust me, Emily didn't see anything either."

Ethan froze. His jaw dropped. His arms flailed as if trying to summon words from thin air. "You—you—you—" he stammered, before giving up and storming out of the room, muttering something under his breath about "Total jerk!"

Oliver, now alone with Ben, raised an eyebrow. "Did you really have to go there?"

Ben shrugged and went back to his report. "I call it tough love. Now shut the door on your way out."

Oliver sighed, knowing better than to push his luck. "You're impossible."

"Thanks for noticing," Ben replied with a smirk, already lost in his work again. Oliver rolled his eyes and left, vowing to find a way to deal with Emily himself—preferably without involving Ben's unique brand of 'parenting.'

Chapter 52: Hunted and Hunter

The day began like any other, routine and uneventful, until it took a turn into something Ethan and Oliver would never forget. They were sitting in Mr. Collins's science class, staring blankly at the chalkboard while the teacher droned on about the properties of atoms. The ticking of the clock was the only sound, counting down the minutes to freedom when a sudden noise echoed through the halls.

It wasn't a normal sound. A dull pop, then another. It was far too loud to be lockers slamming or the usual clamor of middle school. There was a pause. Then the sounds repeated, sharper now, echoing closer—gunshots.

The entire room froze, the students exchanging terrified glances. Mr. Collins was the first to react. His face paled as he glanced toward the door, then back at his class.

"Guys," he said, his voice unnervingly calm but tight with fear. "We need to lock the doors and not make any sound. Now."

A collective gasp rippled through the room, and panic set in. Chairs scraped against the floor as students hurried to the far corner, huddling together like frightened animals. Mr. Collins moved quickly, locking the door and shutting the blinds. The classroom fell into a suffocating silence, broken only by the sound of shallow, panicked breaths.

Ethan's heart pounded in his chest. His eyes darted toward Oliver, who sat at his desk, white as a sheet. Everything was happening

515

so fast, and fear tightened like a knot in Ethan's stomach. But there was something else, something darker that gnawed at his thoughts—this wasn't a coincidence.

In that instant, Ethan bolted from his seat and scrambled across the room to where Oliver sat. The tension in the air was suffocating, but he couldn't shake the dread that crept up his spine.

"Oliver," Ethan whispered harshly, grabbing his brother's arm. "I think... I think Alex is in real danger."

Oliver's eyes widened, his mind racing to catch up. "What are you talking about?" he whispered back, his voice barely audible.

"This is no coincidence, Oliver. The timing, everything. It's him. Alex—Jamie—whatever his name is. I think the shooter is after him."

Oliver's brain clicked into overdrive. It was true that they'd had their suspicions about Alex, the boy they believed could be Alexander James, the future scientist whose life was pivotal to history. But a school shooting?

Oliver's voice trembled as he glanced toward the locked door. "You think someone from the future...?"

"I don't know," Ethan replied, his voice shaking. "But if we don't do something, he could die today."

Just as the words left Ethan's mouth, another round of gunshots pierced the air. They were closer now—right outside the classroom. The students huddled closer, some crying, others staring at the door in silent terror.

Mr. Collins motioned for everyone to stay quiet, his face a mask of fear as he pressed his back against the wall near the door. Ethan and Oliver crouched down behind a row of desks, their minds spinning. Time slowed to a crawl as the weight of their predicament settled over them.

Oliver leaned in close to Ethan, his voice a harsh whisper. "We have to find Alex. We can't let him die here."

"But how?" Ethan whispered back. "We're trapped like everyone else."

For a moment, they sat in the thick silence, contemplating their next move. Then, the unmistakable sound of footsteps echoed in the hallway. The heavy, deliberate steps of someone searching. Hunting.

The door handle rattled.

Everyone in the room sucked in a breath as the door creaked, but the lock held firm. There was a soft click, and the footsteps continued down the hall. The room exhaled in relief, but Ethan and Oliver knew this was far from over. Whoever the shooter was, they were getting closer to Alex.

Ethan looked at Oliver, determination hardening his gaze. "If we stay here, Alex might die. We need to find him before they do."

Oliver's pulse raced as he nodded. It was risky, but they had no choice. Somehow, they had to reach Alex before the worst happened. He was too important to history, and more than that—he was a friend to them now.

"On three," Ethan whispered. "We make for the back door when Collins isn't looking."

Oliver took a deep breath. "Okay. Let's do it."

Their hearts thundered as they crouched low, waiting for the perfect moment. As Mr. Collins turned toward the window, scanning for any signs of movement outside, the boys slipped from the safety of their desks and moved quietly toward the back door that led to the science lab.

Ethan carefully unlocked the door, wincing at the soft click. The door swung open just wide enough for them to squeeze through.

They stepped into the empty science lab, the tension pressing down on them like a weight. The air was heavy with fear, and the distant echo of gunfire still haunted the halls. They didn't have much time.

"We need to get to the cafeteria," Oliver whispered urgently. "Hak-Kun told me yesterday that Alex got in trouble with the principal and was assigned to clean the cafeteria. Hopefully, he's still there now."

Ethan nodded, and together, they slunk through the empty halls, navigating the maze of lockers and classrooms as quietly as possible. Every step was a risk, every corner potentially fatal. But they pressed on, driven by the terrifying knowledge that Alex's life—and the future—hung in the balance.

Bursting into the cafeteria, they found Alex huddled beneath a table, wide-eyed and trembling. His face was pale, and there was no mistaking the fear in his eyes.

"Ethan? Oliver? What are you doing here?" Alex's voice was barely a whisper, but the relief in it was palpable.

"We're getting you out of here," Oliver said, grabbing Alex's arm. "Come on, we need to move."

They heard footsteps again. Heavy. Approaching. Time was running out.

As they dragged Alex to his feet, they shared a silent glance—whatever was coming, they were going to face it together.

The sound of gunfire echoed down the hall, each shot sending a shiver of terror through Ethan, Oliver, and Alex. They hadn't expected it to escalate this quickly. As they sprinted out of the cafeteria, panic gripped them like a vice. There wasn't time to process the chaos; they could only act.

"We need to get out of the school!" Ethan shouted over his shoulder, his voice strained with urgency.

Alex stumbled along behind them. His eyes were wide with fear and confusion. "What...what's happening?"

Oliver glanced back, his face pale but determined. "Someone wants you dead, Alex. That's all you need to know right now. Trust us, we're trying to save your life."

The truth gnawed at them, but there was no time to explain. No time to delve into the fact that this wasn't just a random school shooting. They were being hunted, and those gunmen—they knew exactly who Alex was and why he had to die. It wasn't coincidence. It was planned.

The sound of heavy boots hitting the linoleum floor behind them grew louder as the gunmen closed in. Ethan glanced back for just a moment, his heart lurching as one of the men raised his weapon.

"Run!" Ethan yelled, his voice breaking with desperation.

But it was too late.

The shot rang out, and Alex cried out in pain. His hand shot to his left arm as blood seeped through his fingers. He stumbled, nearly collapsing, but Ethan and Oliver grabbed him, dragging him along.

"We can't stop here!" Oliver urged, his voice barely audible over the pounding of their footsteps and the distant screams of panicked students. "We have to keep moving!"

Alex was pale and trembling, his eyes glassy with shock, but he nodded, pushing through the pain. He didn't understand any of it—

why these strangers were after him, why Ethan and Oliver seemed to know so much—but right now, none of that mattered. Survival was the only thing that counted.

They rounded a corner, their breaths coming in ragged gasps as they approached the hallway leading to the principal's office.

But the footsteps behind them were relentless, growing closer with each second.

"They're catching up!" Oliver gasped, his mind racing for a plan.

Ethan's eyes darted around frantically, searching for anything that could buy them some time. His heart was pounding so hard it felt like it might burst from his chest. They couldn't outrun these men forever. If they didn't do something, they were as good as dead.

"Get in here!" Ethan hissed, dragging Oliver and Alex into a small janitor's closet just off the hallway. The three of them squeezed in, huddling behind shelves of cleaning supplies, trying to stay as silent as possible.

Ethan could feel Alex trembling beside him, and he winced at the sight of blood dripping from Alex's arm, but they couldn't afford to make noise. Not now. The gunmen were close, their heavy boots stomping down the hall outside.

Through a small crack in the door, Ethan saw one of the gunmen—tall, broad, wearing a grim expression that was all business.

They didn't look like the usual deranged shooters who had snapped and decided to wreak havoc. These men were professionals. Their movements were precise, their intentions deliberate.

Ethan's heart pounded as the truth hit him. These guys were hunting Alex with unnerving precision, armed with knowledge only time travelers could have. They staged it to look like a school shooting—likely to erase their tracks from history.

The other gunman paused just outside the closet door, his eyes scanning the hallway. Ethan held his breath, his body tensing with fear. Beside him, Oliver gripped Alex's good arm, keeping him steady.

The gunman reached for the closet door.

Ethan's mind screamed in panic—*they're going to find us*—but just as the door began to creak open, a distant sound—screams and shouting from another hallway—distracted them.

One of the gunmen muttered something under his breath and turned to his partner. "Come on, let's check the other rooms."

The footsteps retreated, fading down the hall.

Ethan let out a breath he hadn't realized he'd been holding, his entire body trembling from the narrow escape. Oliver wiped the sweat from his brow, and Alex let out a pained groan, clutching his arm as the blood continued to seep through his fingers.

"We need to stop the bleeding," Oliver whispered. "He's not going to make it far like this."

Ethan quickly grabbed some old rags from the shelves and handed them to Oliver. They fashioned a makeshift bandage, wrapping it tightly around Alex's arm to stem the flow of blood.

Alex winced, but he nodded in thanks. His face was pale, his eyes glassy, but he was still coherent.

"Thanks," Alex whispered, his voice shaky. "But...who are you guys? What's really going on?"

Ethan exchanged a glance with Oliver. There was no way to explain everything—not here, not now. But they couldn't keep Alex completely in the dark anymore.

"We're...friends, Alex," Ethan said, trying to keep his voice calm. "We know you're in danger, and we're trying to keep you safe. That's all you need to focus on right now. We'll explain more when it's safe."

Alex frowned but nodded, too exhausted and in too much pain to argue. "Okay...okay."

Oliver whispered urgently, "We need to get to the principal's office. It's the only place with a phone."

Alex shook his head. "Why don't we just stay here? Someone's probably already called the police."

Ethan nodded. "Yeah, let's just wait it out, Ollie."

Oliver glared at them. "Are you two idiots? This closet is too small and airtight. We'll run out of oxygen before they even shoot us."

Ethan blinked, suddenly alarmed. "Oh… I feel kind of dizzy already. Fine, we'll move—but not to the principal's office!"

Oliver huffed in frustration. "This isn't up for debate! We're going there. Rumor has it the principal keeps a gun in her desk— probably for emergencies like this."

Ethan's eyes widened. "A gun? Ollie, we're kids. We can't use a gun!"

Oliver flicked Ethan's forehead. "We are not kids!"

Alex groaned, clutching his arm. "Guys, can you stop whisper-arguing? My arm is killing me."

Without another word, they carefully slipped out of the janitor's closet.

The hallway exploded with gunfire as a gunman spotted them immediately. Bullets ricocheted off the walls, the sharp cracks echoing through the empty school corridors. Fear surged through Ethan's veins as he grabbed Oliver and Alex, pushing them forward.

"Run!" Ethan shouted, his voice hoarse with desperation.

The gunman's aim shifted, locking onto them, and the situation seemed hopeless—until Brett appeared out of nowhere, wielding a baseball bat. Without hesitation, Brett charged toward the gunman, swinging with all his might.

"Get away from them!" Brett yelled, his face a mixture of fury and fear.

The bat struck the gunman's arm with a sickening crack, causing him to stagger. The unexpected blow gave the boys a brief window of time, and they didn't waste it. Ethan, Oliver, and Alex took off, running as fast as their legs could carry them, their hearts pounding in their chests.

"Run!" Brett's voice echoed behind them, a desperate command that tore through the air.

Ethan glanced back just in time to see the gunman recover, his face contorted with rage. Without mercy, the man raised his gun and fired. Brett's scream was cut short, and he collapsed to the ground, his body falling limp.

"Brett!" Ethan cried out, his voice breaking with horror, but Oliver grabbed his arm, pulling him forward.

"There's nothing we can do! We have to keep going!" Oliver shouted, forcing himself not to look back. Brett had given them a chance—sacrificing himself so they could escape—and they couldn't let that be in vain.

Finally, they reached the principal's office. Ethan slammed into the door, his hands trembling as he fumbled for the knob. For a brief, heart-stopping moment, it felt like the door wouldn't open, but then it gave way, and they stumbled inside.

Oliver quickly locked the door behind them, his breath ragged. Alex collapsed into a chair, clutching his bleeding arm, his face pale and his expression distant, still in shock from everything that had happened.

"We made it," Oliver gasped, trying to catch his breath.

Alex winced, clutching his arm tighter. Blood continued to seep through his makeshift bandage, and his breathing was shallow, labored from both the pain and the panic. "I don't understand any of this."

Ethan looked around the principal's office, scanning for anything that could help. The phone sat on the desk, and he rushed over to it, dialing 911 with shaking hands.

The line crackled, and an operator's voice came through. "911, what's your emergency?"

"We're at North Ridge Middle School," Ethan said quickly, his voice low. "There's been a shooting. Two gunmen. We're hiding in the principal's office with an injured student."

"Stay calm," the operator said. "Police are on their way. Stay where you are and keep quiet. Help is coming."

Ethan hung up the phone, his heart still racing. Help was coming—but would it arrive in time? They had no idea how many others had been injured, or if the gunmen were still hunting them.

Meanwhile, Oliver frantically searched through every cabinet and drawer but found nothing. Frustrated, he muttered, "Hak-Kun swore the principal had a gun."

A few minutes passed in tense silence, broken only by the occasional pained groan from Alex as he tried to keep his breathing steady.

They had to survive this. They had to save Alex.

The future depended on it.

The door rattled under the weight of the chairs, a faint clicking sound echoing in the room as the handle turned. Ethan and Oliver's hearts pounded in unison, adrenaline coursing through their veins. They had done everything they could—locked the door, barricaded it—but the gunman had found them.

Oliver's eyes darted to Ethan, panic surging through him as they heard the gunman's footsteps drawing closer. He gripped Ethan's arm tightly. "Ethan...he's going to break in."

The gunman's shadow darkened the frosted window on the door, and a low, threatening voice muttered, "Come out, kids..."

Alex groaned softly from his corner, clutching his injured arm, fear etched across his face. Ethan squeezed Oliver's hand, trying to remain calm, but deep down, dread gnawed at him. They were trapped. And this time, there would be no escape.

The gunman kicked the door hard, forcing the barricaded entrance open. He quickly stepped in, aiming his gun at Alex, who was huddled in a corner, trying to shield himself.

Suddenly, the sound of gunfire exploded through the room. The gunman jerked violently, his body convulsing as multiple bullets hit him. He collapsed to the ground with a heavy thud, the gun slipping from his hand.

Ethan and Oliver barely had time to process what had happened when Officer Thomas burst into the room, his gun still smoking. Behind him, fellow officers stormed in, clearing the area. The boys stared at the lifeless gunman in shock, unable to believe what they'd just witnessed.

"Officer Thomas!" Ethan and Oliver cried in unison, running toward him.

They clung to him, trembling as the reality of their close call sank in. "Thank you... thank you!" they sobbed, burying their faces against his side. The terror they had felt moments earlier dissolved into overwhelming relief as they held tightly to the man who had just saved their lives.

Officer Thomas knelt down, wrapping his arms around the boys protectively. His voice, usually steady and authoritative, softened. "It's okay, boys. You're safe now."

The chaos outside still raged—sirens wailed, parents screamed as they searched for their children, teachers frantically gave statements to police, and medical teams rushed toward the injured. But inside the principal's office, the nightmare was finally over.

Moments later, the door swung open again, and Ben and Emily rushed in, their faces pale with fear. Ben's eyes immediately scanned the room, locking onto Ethan and Oliver, who were still clutching Officer Thomas.

"Ethan! Oliver!" Ben's voice cracked with emotion as he ran toward them, pulling them into a tight embrace. His heart raced with relief, his mind reeling from everything that had happened.

"You guys okay?" Ben asked, his voice shaking. He held them close, his usually composed demeanor crumbling as the weight of his fear lifted. He had almost lost them, and the thought of it left him breathless.

"We're okay," Ethan mumbled into Ben's chest, feeling a warmth and safety that had been absent during the harrowing ordeal. "We're okay, Dad."

Emily, her face pale with shock, knelt beside them, gently touching Oliver's arm. "Oh, my God... I'm so glad you're both safe." Her eyes filled with tears as she pulled them into her arms, kissing their foreheads.

They huddled together, a tangle of arms and whispered reassurances, while outside, the world still spun in chaos. But for that moment, nothing else mattered. The boys were safe.

Officer Thomas stood a few feet away, watching the emotional reunion with a small smile. He exchanged a knowing look with Ben, a silent acknowledgment of the danger they'd all just survived. Then, with a final nod, he turned to help the other officers manage the aftermath.

As the sounds of the world gradually faded back in—the sirens, the cries of relief, the chatter of police radios—Ben pulled back slightly, looking into Ethan's and Oliver's eyes. "I don't care what happens from now on," he said softly, his voice firm with conviction. "I'm just glad you're both alive."

Ethan and Oliver nodded, the weight of the day's events pressing heavily on their shoulders. They had stared death in the face and come out alive, but the relief was fleeting. Their minds drifted to Alex, who had been rushed to the hospital earlier by the medical team, his arm badly wounded. Though they had made it this far, a gnawing unease settled in—they knew this was far from over.

Chapter 53: In the Aftermath

The late afternoon sun filtered softly through the kitchen windows as Ben stirred a pot of sauce on the stove, the fragrant smell of a home-cooked meal slowly filling the house. His hands moved mechanically, but his mind was somewhere else. The events of the day weighed heavily on him—the shooting, the boys, and how close he had come to losing them. Every stir of the spoon was an attempt to push away the gnawing fear still lodged deep in his chest.

In the bathroom, things were quieter but equally heavy. Ethan and Oliver sat in the tub, their bodies submerged in warm water, the steam curling gently in the air. Their minds were racing, flashes of the day playing over and over—Alex being shot, the gunmen's cold, calculated eyes, Brett's desperate act of bravery.

The violence and fear clung to them, rooted deep in their bones, even as Emily gently scrubbed away the grime with a washcloth, her touch tender yet purposeful. Her eyes moved with care, inspecting their bare bodies for any wounds or lingering soreness from the ordeal, as if trying to wash away the trauma itself.

Ethan blinked, suddenly realizing his situation. His cheeks flushed slightly as he registered the fact that Emily had helped them undress and guided them into the bath without them really noticing. They were too lost in thought, and now, here they were—naked, vulnerable, and being bathed like children.

"Uh, Emily... I can... I can do it myself," Ethan started, his voice wavering as he tried to reclaim some sense of control. His mind flicked back to the gunmen, to the gunshots, and he found himself grasping for normalcy—anything to ground him.

Emily placed a gentle but firm hand on his shoulder, her gaze stopping Ethan in his tracks. It was a motherly look—soft yet resolute—the kind that could silence any protest. "Not today, Ethan," she said quietly, her voice calm and full of care. "You've been through enough. Let me take care of you."

Ethan hesitated, his heart thumping in his chest, but then he let it go. He sank back into the warm water, his body suddenly feeling heavy, drained. He had no fight left in him. He closed his eyes as Emily's hands moved over him, washing away the sweat, the blood, the fear.

Next to him, Oliver was silent. He hadn't said a word since they got home, his mind running in circles. His eyes were unfocused, staring at nothing in particular as Emily washed his back. He felt a strange sensation of being both present and not, his body here in the tub but his mind still locked in the chaos of the school. He could still hear the gunshots, still see Brett's body falling, the way the light had drained from his eyes.

"Oliver?" Emily's voice broke through his thoughts, and he blinked, suddenly aware of her hand on his shoulder. "Are you okay, sweetheart?"

He swallowed hard, not trusting his voice to answer. He wasn't sure how to describe what he was feeling—everything seemed jumbled and out of place. It was like he had been on autopilot since the shooting, just going through the motions without really processing any of it.

Emily's touch was soft, a gentle reminder of safety, of something good in a world that had suddenly felt so dark. "It's okay," she whispered, washing the last traces of soap from his hair. "You're safe now. You're home."

Oliver nodded slightly, but the words felt hollow. Safe. What did that even mean anymore? They had been in science class one moment, and the next, everything had descended into chaos. Could you ever really feel safe again after something like that?

Ethan, meanwhile, kept his eyes closed, trying to let the warmth of the bath and Emily's hands lull him into a sense of calm. But every time he tried to relax, he saw those gunmen again—he saw them walking through the halls, methodical, searching. His chest tightened. He knew, deep down, that it hadn't been a random attack. The way the gunmen moved, the way they targeted specific areas... They were after someone. After Alex.

"Today... it was..." Oliver finally spoke, his voice barely above a whisper. "It was too much."

Ethan opened his eyes and glanced at him. "Yeah," he agreed quietly, feeling a knot form in his throat. "It was."

Emily, sensing their tension, finished rinsing them off and wrapped a warm towel around each of them. "There you go," she said softly, her voice soothing, as if trying to mend their shattered world with the simple act of care. "Let's get you dried up and dressed. Dad is making dinner."

As she helped them out of the tub and into their towels, Ethan couldn't help but feel a strange comfort in her presence. She had stepped into the role of their caretaker so naturally, and at that moment, he didn't mind. He needed someone to lean on, someone to remind him that, despite everything, there was still good in the world. Emily was that reminder.

But even as she dried his hair and hummed softly under her breath, the weight of what had happened that day lingered in the back of his mind. The bath, the towels, the gentle care—it was all a temporary reprieve. The danger was far from over.

And as he caught Oliver's eye, he could tell his colleague and brother felt the same.

Chapter 54: Gone but Not Forgotten

The day of Brett's funeral arrived three days after the shooting, the sky heavy with gray clouds as if the weather itself had sensed the sorrow that blanketed the small community. The funeral was held at the local church, its humble stone walls now filled with people who had come to pay their respects. Among them were Brett's classmates, teachers, neighbors, and the families whose lives had been touched by the tragedy.

Ethan and Oliver stood with Ben, Emily, and Officer Thomas, their faces somber as they watched Brett's family, heartbroken and devastated, sitting near the front. Brett's parents, who had once been the proud parents of a vibrant, if sometimes misguided, son, now sat quietly, shattered by the weight of their grief. Brett had been their only child, and his loss left an unimaginable void.

The casket, a simple wooden one, was surrounded by flowers—white lilies, a symbol of purity, mingled with deep red roses, representing love and loss. There was something deeply painful about seeing the casket of a young boy, the finality of it too heavy for most to fully grasp. Ethan and Oliver found themselves staring at it, not quite believing that this was really happening.

Ethan nudged Oliver slightly. "I... I can't believe it," he whispered, his voice barely audible. "He saved us... and now he's gone."

Oliver nodded, his eyes fixed on the casket. "I know. We owe him everything, Ethan. We wouldn't be here if it wasn't for him." His voice was tight with guilt, knowing that the chain of events that had led to Brett's death had roots much deeper than anyone else could understand.

Ben stood nearby, his face shadowed with sorrow. He had heard countless stories from the boys about Brett's troublesome behaviours, but in the end, Brett had shown a side of himself no one expected. He wasn't just a bully—he had become a hero. Ben squeezed Ethan's shoulder. "It's hard to make sense of these things, but we need to honor what he did for you boys. He made the ultimate sacrifice."

As the funeral service began, the minister spoke in hushed, sorrowful tones, offering words of comfort that felt woefully insufficient against the enormity of the loss. The church was filled with quiet weeping, punctuated by the occasional loud sob from Brett's mother, whose heartache was palpable. She clutched a crumpled tissue in her hand, her body shaking as her husband held her close.

Emily wiped a tear from her eye, her heart breaking for the family. She had grown close to Ethan and Oliver, and now more than ever, she felt an overwhelming desire to protect them. She glanced at the boys, who stood solemnly, their young faces marked by far more than just the innocence of childhood.

Officer Thomas stood next to Ben, his police uniform immaculate but his face betraying the sadness he felt inside. He had been there that day—he had helped stop the shooters, but he hadn't been able to save Brett. That failure hung over him like a shadow. He took a deep breath and turned to Ben.

"I keep thinking, if we had been just a few minutes faster..." Officer Thomas said quietly, guilt lacing his words. "Maybe we could have saved him."

Ben shook his head. "You did everything you could, Vincent. We all know that. What happened wasn't your fault. Brett... Brett did something brave. He gave the boys a chance to escape."

Officer Thomas nodded, though the weight of the what-ifs still lingered in his mind. "I just wish I could've done more."

The church service ended, and as people began to file out to the burial site, Ethan noticed Alex standing quietly with his mother a few feet away. Alex looked different—haunted, almost—as if the weight of everything that had happened had finally caught up with him. His arm was still in a sling from where he'd been shot, but it wasn't the injury that had changed him. It was something deeper.

Ethan nudged Oliver again. "Look, there's Alex."

Oliver glanced over, his eyes narrowing slightly. "Do you think he knows? About... everything?"

Ethan shook his head. "No, I don't think so. But I think he's realizing something bigger is going on."

The two boys made their way over to Alex, who looked up as they approached. He offered them a weak smile, but his usual bravado was gone. He looked smaller, quieter, like a boy who had seen too much of the world too soon.

"Hey, guys," Alex said softly. "This... this is hard, huh?"

"Yeah," Ethan replied, unsure of what to say. "How's your arm?"

Alex glanced down at his sling. "It's okay. Hurts sometimes, but... I'll be fine."

There was a brief, uncomfortable silence before Oliver spoke up. "You were brave, Alex. That day. Running with us, even after you got shot... that took guts."

Alex looked away, his face darkening. "I didn't feel brave. Brett's the one who was brave. He tried to stop them. I should've done more..."

Ethan shook his head. "No, Alex. You did enough. You're alive. We're alive. That's what matters."

Alex's mother called for him from across the cemetery, and he nodded to the boys. "I've got to go. But... thanks, guys. For everything."

As Alex walked away, Ethan and Oliver exchanged a glance, their thoughts heavy. They knew they couldn't tell Alex the truth, not yet at least, but something told them that his role in all of this was far from over.

As they made their way back to Ben and Emily, the wind rustled the leaves of the trees above them, carrying with it a sense of quiet mourning. They reached the burial site, where Brett's casket was slowly lowered into the ground. His mother let out a cry of anguish, collapsing against her husband, and everyone around them stood in respectful, heartbroken silence.

Ben put a hand on Ethan and Oliver's shoulders, pulling them close as they watched the casket disappear into the earth. "Let's go home," he said softly.

Ethan and Oliver nodded, the weight of the day pressing down on them. Brett was gone, but the events set in motion by his death were only just beginning to unfold.

That night, after the emotional weight of Brett's funeral and the events of the past few days, Emily lay in bed next to Ben, staring at the ceiling. She couldn't shake the feeling that something was off, something about the boys, about their past, about the secrecy surrounding certain things. She had been a part of their lives for nearly a year now, and in her heart, she felt like their mother.

After a few restless minutes, she quietly slipped out of bed, making sure not to wake Ben, who was fast asleep. The house was silent, save for the occasional creak of the floorboards. Emily found herself drawn to the storage room—the one Ben had always told her not to enter. It was where, according to him, the boys' late mother's belongings were kept. But now, with everything that had happened, she felt a sense of duty to see what was inside. She wanted to understand more about the boys' past, to connect with them even further.

Her bare feet made no sound as she padded down the hall toward the room. She hesitated for a moment, her hand resting on the door handle. Her mind raced—was she betraying Ben's trust? But then, she thought of Ethan and Oliver, how much she loved them, how much she had come to care for them as if they were her own. She needed to.

Taking a deep breath, she turned the handle and gently pushed the door open.

The room was dimly lit, and at first, it appeared to be just like any other space of the house. A few boxes were stacked neatly in one corner, some old clothes draped over a chair, and a dusty dresser against the far wall. Nothing seemed out of place. Emily exhaled, feeling slightly foolish for her curiosity. She stepped inside and gave the room a quick look around. It was... ordinary. There was no sign of the personal belongings she had imagined—no pictures, no letters, no keepsakes. But then again, why would there be? The boys' "mother" hadn't actually been real.

As she turned to leave, a sudden, uneasy feeling washed over her. She couldn't place it, but something felt wrong. She lingered in the doorway, glancing around one last time. Everything seemed fine, perfectly normal. But the feeling persisted, gnawing at her. Shaking her head, she brushed it off and quietly closed the door behind her, returning to Ben's side in bed.

She slipped under the covers, her body finally beginning to relax. Ben shifted slightly but remained asleep, his breathing steady. Emily closed her eyes, trying to push away the nagging sense of unease. Maybe it was just the stress from the shooting and the funeral—it had been a heavy few days.

As she drifted off to sleep, she had no idea what had truly happened. The storage room had appeared ordinary, but the truth was far more unsettling.

The time machine was gone.

Unbeknownst to Emily, at some point during the night, the time machine—Lucas—had disappeared. It had been safely hidden away in that room for the past two years, and now, without warning, it was no longer there. The sleek, futuristic structure that had been the trio's only link to the 24th century had simply vanished.

Back in their shared room, Ethan and Oliver slept soundly, unaware of the disappearance. They had no idea that their connection to the future was severed. Ben, too, lay in peaceful slumber, oblivious to the monumental shift that had just occurred.

But the consequences of this sudden, inexplicable loss were bound to surface soon enough. When morning came, everything would change, and the questions would begin—how could the time machine just vanish? Who, or what, had taken it? And what did it mean for their already fragile existence in 1971?

For now, the night was quiet, but the storm was coming.

The next day was eerie. Ethan and Oliver were supposed to be in school, but after the tragedy of the shooting, classes had been suspended. The boys were still trying to process everything—the gunmen, Brett's death, the fear they had felt—but another dark shadow loomed over their lives now. Emily had gone off to work, leaving the house quiet except for the sound of the wind rustling the trees outside.

Ben, Ethan, and Oliver walked silently through the house, their footsteps echoing down the hallway as they approached the storage room. Just a few hours earlier, Emily had wandered into the room, finding nothing unusual. Now, the trio was heading there to consult Lucas, their time machine, about the recent events that had unfolded in their lives. Ethan reached for the door and pushed it open with a long, low creak. The three of them stepped inside.

But the sight before them froze them in place.

The room was empty.

Ethan's stomach twisted into a knot as he stepped forward hesitantly. "Lucas," he called out nervously, his voice shaky. "It's just us. You don't need to use stealth mode..."

Oliver didn't wait. He dashed forward, his arms flailing wildly as though trying to touch something invisible. "Lucas!" he shouted, his voice rising in desperation. "Come on, quit hiding! I know you're here!"

But his frantic search yielded nothing. He stopped suddenly, his arms falling limply to his sides. "It's gone," Oliver muttered, his voice barely above a whisper. His wide, tear-brimmed eyes darted to Ben. "Where's Lucas? Ben, where is it?"

Ben remained rooted in the doorway, his broad frame blocking the faint light from the hallway. His face was a mask of calm, but his sharp eyes betrayed the storm of thoughts swirling in his mind. Could the timeline have shifted? Had some critical event in the past—or the future—erased Lucas from existence? Or was there a more immediate and sinister explanation?

But Ethan's patience had already unraveled. "This isn't funny, Ben!" he snapped, his voice cracking with panic. "Where is Lucas?"

Ben sighed, finally stepping inside. He walked to the area where Lucas had once stood—a hulking presence that had become their lifeline. Now, there was nothing but empty space. He crouched down, pressing his palm to the cold, bare floor as if searching for a lingering trace of its presence.

"I don't know," Ben admitted grimly. "Without the gold conductor, Lucas can't boost its temporal core. It can't move on its own."

"Then someone took it!" Oliver cried, his voice tinged with panic. "That's the only explanation!"

Ethan shook his head vehemently, his chest tightening. "No, that's impossible. If anyone had come near, Lucas would've warned us. It wouldn't let someone just... take it!"

Ben's lips pressed into a thin line. He was trying to stay calm, but the cracks in his facade were beginning to show. "There's another possibility," he said quietly. "The timeline may have shifted so drastically that Lucas—and everything tied to it—was never invented."

"No!" Oliver shouted, tears streaming down his face. "That doesn't make sense! If Lucas was never invented, we wouldn't even be here! We'd be back in the 24th century because we never left!"

Ben sighed deeply, the weight of their situation pressing heavily on his shoulders. "I don't know, Ollie... I just don't know."

Ethan collapsed onto his knees, his small, 11-year-old frame shaking as sobs began to wrack his body. "No... no... this can't be happening," he cried. "We're stuck. We're really stuck."

Oliver's cries grew louder as he joined his brother on the floor. "We're never going back!" he wailed. "We screwed everything up. We're going to be stuck like this... forever."

Ben's heart clenched as he watched the two boys crumble before him. He had always prided himself on being the steady hand, the adult who could guide them through anything. But this? This was uncharted territory, even for him.

He crossed the room in a few long strides, kneeling beside them. His large hands gently pulled the boys closer, cradling their small, trembling bodies against his chest. "Shhh," Ben murmured, his voice calm and soothing despite the knot of fear twisting in his own gut. "It's okay. I'm here. I've got you."

Ethan pulled back slightly, his tear-streaked face scrunched in confusion. "What do you mean it's okay?" he snapped. "It's not okay! We can't stay here, Ben! We don't belong here!"

Oliver nodded through his tears. "What about our families? The future? Everything we left behind?"

Ben sighed, brushing a stray lock of hair from Oliver's forehead. His expression softened, though his resolve remained firm. "I know it feels like we've lost everything," he said gently, "but we haven't. Look around you. We have a life here. We have each other. You have me, and you have Emily. That's not nothing."

Ethan's frustration flared again. "But we're stuck as kids!" he yelled, his voice cracking. "How are we supposed to live like this? Forever?"

"You've been through worse," Ben said firmly, his hand resting on Ethan's shoulder. "Both of you have. We've faced death. We've faced time itself. You're stronger than you think."

Oliver wiped his nose on his sleeve, still trembling. "But we were supposed to fix things," he said, his voice breaking. "We were supposed to save the future... and now we can't."

Ben looked at them both, his gaze steady and unwavering. "Maybe it's not our job to save the future anymore," he said softly.

"Maybe... maybe this is where we're supposed to be. Sometimes things happen for a reason."

Ethan's face scrunched in frustration. "What if something happens to the people we left behind? What if something happens to us?"

Ben pulled them both closer, holding them as if his arms alone could shield them from the weight of their fears. "We'll figure it out," he promised. "One step at a time. But for now, we need to live in the present. Here. In 1971. We don't need Lucas to survive. We have each other, and that's enough. I promise you—I will protect you, no matter what."

Their sobs gradually quieted as Ben's words began to sink in. The truth was bitter and painful, but they had no choice but to accept it. Lucas was gone. The future was out of reach.

But deep down, they all knew this wasn't the end of their story. Whatever—or whoever—had taken Lucas wasn't finished with them. And sooner or later, they would have to face the unseen force pulling the strings.

End of Book 1

Please find Book 2 at

Book 2: https://www.amazon.com/dp/B0DY9GNML1

If you enjoyed this book, please consider leaving a positive review

https://www.amazon.com/gp/product-review/B0DVCCXZM9

Visit chrono-verse.com or scan the QR code below to explore over 20 captivating artworks featuring characters and scenes from the books. Enjoy original soundtrack songs and learn more about the rich universe and its unforgettable cast.